Let It
Be Me

Let It Be Me

A Misty River Romance

BECKY WADE

BETHANYHOUSE
a division of Baker Publishing Group
Minneapolis, Minnesota

Published by Bethany House Publishers
11400 Hampshire Avenue South
Bloomington, Minnesota 55438
www.bethanyhouse.com

Bethany House Publishers is a division of
Baker Publishing Group, Grand Rapids, Michigan

Printed in the United States of America

Library of Congress Cataloging-in-Publication Data

Names: Wade, Becky, author.
Title: Let it be me / Becky Wade.
Description: Minneapolis, Minnesota : Bethany House, a division of Baker
  Publishing Group, [2021] | Series: A misty river romance
Identifiers: LCCN 2020052232 | ISBN 9780764235610 (trade paperback) | ISBN
  9780764239175 (casebound) | ISBN 9781493425228 (ebook)
Subjects: GSAFD: Love stories. | Christian fiction.
Classification: LCC PS3623.A33 L48 2021 | DDC 813/.6--dc23
LC record available at https://lccn.loc.gov/2020052232

Scripture quotations are from The Holy Bible, English Standard Version® (ESV®), copyright © 2001 by Crossway, a publishing ministry of Good News Publishers. Used by permission. All rights reserved. ESV Text Edition: 2016

This is a work of fiction. Names, characters, incidents, and dialogues are products of the author's imagination and are not to be construed as real. Any resemblance to actual events or persons, living or dead, is entirely coincidental.

Cover design by Jennifer Parker
Cover photography by Aimee Christenson

Author represented by Linda Kruger

21 22 23 24 25 26 27   7 6 5 4 3 2 1

For the Lord God Almighty.

You have faithfully called and equipped me
to write year after year. Thank you for allowing me,
with each novel, a fresh chance to "fix my eyes
on the author and perfecter of my faith."
Partnering with you in this work
has been one of the greatest joys
and privileges of my life.

CHAPTER ONE

Mom and Dad are not my biological parents.

Leah Joanna Montgomery blinked slowly, then squinted at the DNA test results displayed on her computer screen, straining to digest the information displayed there. But no. She couldn't digest it. The very fast brain she'd relied on all her life was currently sitting in the corner, immobilized by shock, sucking its thumb.

Mom and Dad are not my parents? A metaphorical ghost reached past her skin and squeezed her organs in a cold, tight fist.

How could Mom and Dad not be her parents? She was twenty-eight years old, and this was the first time that any entity, human or computer, had given her a reason to think that they weren't—

"Do we have any snacks?"

Leah startled at the question and jerked her head up. Her seventeen-year-old brother, Dylan, had made an unusual excursion from his room and was standing very near the dining room table where she sat.

"Earth to Leah." It was what he said every time he discovered that she'd gotten lost in her own mind.

Subtly, she angled her laptop's screen away from him. She typically got lost in her own mind while navigating labyrinths of pure math. This was the first time she'd become lost in the rubble of a genealogical bomb. "Snacks?" She was finding it hard to switch from a life-altering revelation to the mundanity of food.

"Do we have any?" He'd dressed his six-foot-tall, thin, slouch-shouldered body in a Misty River High Football T-shirt and narrow joggers that hugged his calves. He had a mop of artful brown curls, expressive eyebrows, big and dark Bambi eyes, and a pale complexion. He resembled a poet who specialized in morose verse.

"We have whatever snacks are in the pantry," she said.

"Oh," he responded, as if this had not occurred to him. "Do we have Cheez-Its?"

"I think so."

Scintillating conversation concluded, he slunk toward the kitchen.

Almost cautiously, Leah looked around herself. If Mom and Dad weren't her parents, then could she trust these walls not to melt? The roof not to vanish? Another dimension not to suck her away?

"Father God," she whispered, those simple words asking for things she couldn't even name.

She gazed out the expanse of windows on the front side of her rectangular box of a home. The large panes of glass overlooked a steep, wooded valley with a creek at its base. On this seventh day of May, the crisp, vivid green of the trees blanketing the north Georgia Blue Ridge Mountains contrasted with the cheerful orange azaleas blooming in her front planting bed. She'd painted the interior walls of the house a calming off-white and stained the wood floor ashy beige. No clutter marred her simple mid-century modern furniture.

Her Friday afternoon had been following an entirely predictable routine. She worked as a math teacher at Misty River High, where Dylan was finishing up his junior year. They'd both returned home from school less than thirty minutes ago. She'd cracked open her computer and spotted an email from YourHeritage.com with a subject line proclaiming *Your DNA results are in! Discover your heritage!*

A balloon of interest inflating within her, she'd logged onto the YourHeritage site and clicked the button to reveal the results of the saliva sample she'd mailed in six weeks before.

Then she'd been walloped with the information that she was not biologically related to her mom or her dad. And her ordinary Friday had jumped its track and careened into a gorge.

"Where are the Cheez-Its?" Dylan called.

Leah joined him in front of the pantry. "I never fail to marvel over your assumption that my two X chromosomes function as GPS locational devices for household items." She plucked out the Cheez-Its and handed them to him.

"But they do." He held up the box. "See?" Popping the top, he made for his room.

"Nope," she said. "That box can't migrate to your room."

His sigh was so melodramatic that it would have been comedic had an adult attempted it. He leaned against their small square breakfast table and rattled Cheez-Its into his mouth.

Leah didn't let him eat in his room because she didn't want mess. But much more than that, if she let him eat in his room, he'd never come out. She'd have no one to socialize with except Han Solo . . . in her daydreams.

"What's for dinner?" Dylan asked.

She pulled several items from the freezer. Lasagna. Chicken pot pie. Burritos. "Any of these intriguing choices. Help yourself when you feel so inclined."

He looked unimpressed.

She returned the items to the freezer. "Are you doing okay?"

"Yeah."

"Sure?"

"Yeah."

"Have any plans tonight?"

"Nah."

"Want to watch *Star Wars* with me?"

"Which one?"

"Any one. Your choice." Dylan was the primary love of her life, and *Star Wars* had been their shared passion since he was little. Sadly, it had been months—maybe a year?—since he'd deigned to watch one with her. When he wasn't at school or football practice, he spent his time with his friends, creating ink on paper drawings, or staring at YouTube in a concerted effort to avoid homework.

"Please, O brother of mine?" she wheedled. "Humor me."

He gave a bored shrug and shook his head. "I think I'm done with *Star Wars*."

She covered her heart with her hands. "That's blasphemy, you realize."

"Uh-huh."

"What are you going to do with yourself all evening if not watch a movie?"

"I thought I'd look up the recipe for heroin."

This was their running not-so-funny joke. He knew very well that despite all the parental controls she'd instituted over the electronics in their house and her own careful oversight, she really was afraid that he'd find a way to do things like make heroin.

An amused grunt issued from him; then he set the Cheez-Its on the table and walked away.

"Contrary to what you might think, you will not perish if you spend a few hours outside the force field of your room," she said.

He didn't answer.

"Dearest boy of my heart!" she called with gusto.

His door shut behind him.

Leah pondered the view of the empty space where he'd been.

If Mom and Dad are not my parents, then Dylan might not be my brother.

As if she'd just pressed on a broken tooth, pain flared, warning her away from that line of thought. Dad had vanished from her life fifteen years ago. Mom had been an infrequent presence since she'd left to serve overseas in the Peace Corps ten years ago. As jarring as it would be to part with her biological connection to her parents, it would be a thousand times worse to part with her biological connection to Dylan—

That line of inquiry is premature, Leah. No need to ponder that until you must.

For the past several months, Mom had been on a genealogy

kick. In February she'd gifted Leah a DNA test kit for her birthday, though Leah would have preferred the book on category theory she'd requested. That said, she was someone who loved to accumulate knowledge, and since she knew next to nothing about her ethnic heritage or her ancestors, she'd sent in her sample with a sense of pleasant anticipation.

She slid back into the dining room chair and retraced the steps she'd taken after logging on to YourHeritage. The first screen full of results informed her that she was 72% Scandinavian, 20% Irish/Scottish, and 8% German. Noteworthy, but no great surprise, since she was fair, with blond hair and grayish-blue eyes.

She moved to the next screen of results. Right beneath the first heading, *Closest DNA Matches*, her mother's name should have appeared.

It did not. Instead, the site designated Leah's closest DNA matches to be people with faces and names that didn't ring a bell in her memory.

Riley Haskins. David Brookside. Margie Brookside Schloss. Emilie Donnell. Doug May. Ryan Brookside.

Who?

No Everly relatives from her mother's side in this list. No Montgomery relatives from her father's side.

Weeks ago her mom had granted Leah permission to view her YourHeritage data so that Leah could access the family tree Mom had been compiling. She visited her mom's page of DNA matches. Leah ought to appear here as her mom's closest match . . . but didn't. Mom's list included several relatives Leah knew—relatives who were conspicuously absent from her own list.

She checked her profile settings. Not wanting any of the strangers connected to her by DNA to see her pop up as a surprise cousin, she switched her settings to private, then knotted her hands in her lap.

She'd spent a lifetime trusting in the answers math provided. The world was not always logical. But math was. And she loved math for that.

Her saliva sample + laboratory analysis = the results she'd just received. Her inclination was to believe this sum because it was highly unlikely that there'd been a flaw in the equation.

The ghostly fist that had a hold of her insides squeezed harder.

She logged off and cleared her browser history. Grabbing her phone, she stepped onto her back patio and closed the sliding glass door behind her to ensure she was safely out of earshot of Dylan.

She dialed her mom, bracing herself the way she did for doctor's appointments and other such duties, which were occasionally necessary but never enjoyable. Mom rarely picked up when Leah called. Even so, Leah murmured, "Answer."

Mom did not pick up.

"Hello," Leah said, when invited to leave a message. "I just received the results of my DNA test at YourHeritage.com, and the findings are perplexing. Please call me back as soon as you receive this. Thank you."

Back when Leah had set up her account at YourHeritage in preparation to submit her sample, the site had given her a solemn warning about how upsetting the conclusions of DNA testing could be. She'd checked the box to acknowledge that, yes, she understood and was willing to accept the results.

At the time, she hadn't had an iota of concern.

Her fingers trembled slightly as she placed a call to the customer service phone number provided in her email from YourHeritage.

An agent named Heather politely and patiently assured her that the site stood by the outcome of her test.

Leah could only imagine the calls Heather must receive: "You got my mother right, but that man isn't my father!" "She's my half sister? I always thought she was my cousin!"

If Leah had concerns about the test's validity, Heather suggested that Leah take a retest, which Leah was most certainly willing to do once she'd discussed this with her mom.

After disconnecting, she stood immobile, her ballet flats planted on a flagstone paver. Stalwart trees encircled her.

The story of her conception was well-known to her and somewhat south of disappointing. Her mom and dad had fallen in love while attending Georgia State. Mom had become pregnant the summer before her senior year. Even though Mom had dreamed since childhood of traveling around the globe, she'd instead settled down, married Dad, and had Leah.

Why would a young woman who longed for independence and adventure adopt a child at the age of twenty-two? After nine months of pregnancy? Leah had seen the photos that documented her mother's pregnancy.

Had Mom been pregnant and lost the baby tragically?

Then gone on to adopt her? And kept her adoption a secret?

If something bizarre like that had occurred, why would Mom have given her a DNA kit as a gift, knowing what Leah would discover?

Was the DNA kit Mom's warped way of revealing to Leah that she'd been adopted?

That sort of subterfuge sounded nothing like Erica Everly Montgomery, her mother. Mom said things outright—unafraid of what people thought, uncowed by confrontation.

Leah hadn't been adopted, surely.

And yet . . . It was true that she'd never had a great deal in common with the rest of her immediate family. Her father, mother, and brother had brown hair and brown eyes. All three were more athletic than she was, messier than she was, grumpier than she was. None of them were interested in academics, the joy of Leah's life.

Even so, she hadn't imagined that her otherness had anything to do with genetics. A lot of people felt as though they didn't fit within their families. She'd simply concluded herself to be the odd one out.

Until now.

I received the results from the YourHeritage DNA test kit you gave me for my birthday," Leah told her mom on Sunday evening. "You're not listed as my mother and no Everly or Montgomery relatives are listed as matches."

Silence multiplied between them.

Leah had been gnawing over this for two days—two days!—while she'd waited for Mom to return her call. She'd practically given herself arthiritis in the knees thanks to the time she'd spent kneeling and praying.

"That's ridiculous," Mom stated emphatically. "I'm your mother."

"Not according to my DNA."

As soon as Leah had answered her phone, she'd shut herself into her car inside her one-car garage so Dylan couldn't overhear. In sharp contrast to Leah's surroundings, her mother was currently in Guinea, working on an agroforestry project. On the other end of the call, Leah pictured orange earth, palm trees, and huts. Mom had likely clothed her sinewy body in safari khaki. Her curls, which matched Dylan's, would be zigzagging from her head, and her close-set eyes and long face would be pinched with consternation.

As usual, contact with her mom submerged Leah in a complex mix of resentment, love, and resignation.

"Two weeks before your due date, I started bleeding," Mom said. "My back hurt. My belly hurt. We rushed to the hospital, and they diagnosed me with placental abruption."

This information was not revelatory. Leah had gone through a phase in elementary school when she'd been obsessed with her origin story and had peppered her parents with questions about her birth and herself as a baby. "The placenta had pulled away from your uterus," Leah said.

"Right, which is dangerous. They worried that you might not be getting enough oxygen, so they put me under and performed an emergency C-section. I have the scar to prove it!"

"I've seen the scar."

"Of course you have."

"I'm trying to reconcile all of that with the only logical explanation for my DNA results, which is that you adopted me."

"You can't always trust logic."

"On the contrary, the wonderful thing about logic is that you *can* always trust it. So I began to wonder . . . What if your baby

14

didn't survive the placental abruption? And, in your grief, you adopted me?"

"I most certainly did not adopt you, Leah. The emergency C-section saved you. They placed you in my arms shortly after I regained consciousness."

Leah remained quiet.

"Why in the world would I have adopted a baby?" Mom demanded, gathering steam. "I was trying to finish college at the time that I had you. I wanted to see the world! I wanted to travel. I was not ready for children. You know this about me."

"I do."

"I did not adopt you."

"And yet we're not related by blood. How do you propose to explain this?"

"Clearly the lab made a mistake."

"My DNA matches include people with surnames like Brookside and Donnell and May. Do you recognize any of those?"

"I don't. Listen, humans are involved in the process of DNA testing. If humans are involved, there's the possibility of human error. I'm guessing that your test tube was mistaken for someone else's test tube. Will YourHeritage let you retest?"

"They will."

"Good. Make sure they expedite your retest since this was their mistake."

Leah swallowed a sigh. Her intuition did not think this was the lab's mistake. "A new test kit is already en route to me. Once I send it in, I should hear back in less than two weeks."

"Tell them to give us our money back for both tests. They owe us that after the trouble they've caused." She didn't wait for Leah to reply before saying, "I'm off!"

Mom's words hung in Leah's ear as the line went dead.

If Mom had not adopted her, then only one theory remained that honored both her mom's version of events and the DNA test.

That theory: her mother's biological child had been switched at birth with someone else's baby.

CHAPTER TWO

Farmers markets were not his thing.

And yet, there he was. Sebastian Xavier Grant slipped on sunglasses as he walked from his parking space toward Misty River High School's athletic fields and rows of vendors shaded by pop-up canopies.

He'd come to this particular farmers market for one reason only: to support his best friend, Ben. An eleventh-grade science teacher, Ben was responsible for staffing every volunteer position at today's market, which was one of the high school's most lucrative fundraisers of the year.

Sebastian had offered to volunteer wherever he was needed. Apparently, he was needed in the booster club's spaghetti lunch line, located on the far side of the market stalls, near the base of the wooded hillside.

He checked his watch. 11:45. His shift started at twelve.

Sunshine fell over beige brick buildings that had been new back when Sebastian had gone to school there. Happy shrieks rose from the area where they'd set up inflatables, a game that involved kids wearing blown-up rings around their waists, and one of those plastic balls big enough for a person to climb inside and then roll down a lane. Today, the clean mountain air held no humidity, and only a few thin strips of cloud marked the blue of the sky. The forecast for this mid-May Saturday: seventy-eight degrees.

Sebastian strode past stalls selling beef jerky, jam, soap. Organic vegetables. Candles. Canned southern staples, like black-eyed peas. Locally crafted beer. Folk pottery. A fruit stand with peaches, plums, and blueberries.

He was just making his way out of the row when he heard a voice. A female voice.

It tripped his memory, and he came to an immediate stop. Listening hard, he weeded through the noise—conversations, the whir of a generator, laughter—until he caught a snatch of that voice again.

"Sure," he thought he heard her say. He had to strain to make it out. "You're welcome."

Recognition and certainty flooded him. *It was her.*

He spun and scanned the people in his field of vision.

He didn't see her.

Where was she?

Last November, not far from here, he'd swerved to avoid a car that had veered into his lane. His SUV had ended up nose-down in a roadside ditch, and the impact had knocked him out. When he'd regained consciousness, a woman had been inside his car with him. The voice he'd just overheard belonged to her.

His mind tugged him back in time to the morning of the crash.

"Sir?" she'd said to him.

Sebastian heard the feminine voice as if he were at the bottom of a hole. Chuck Berry's "Downbound Train" played on his SUV's radio.

"Can you hear me?" she asked, sounding worried and faintly out of breath. "Are you all right?"

Her voice was smooth and sweet like honey. He didn't want the woman with the voice like honey to be worried. Also, he didn't want to wake up because his head ached with dull, fierce pain.

"Sir," she said. "Can you hear me?"

"Yes," he said hoarsely.

"He fell on his knees," Chuck Berry sang, "on the bar room floor and prayed a prayer like never before."

Sebastian slit his eyes open. Pinpricks punctured his vision. He was inside his car, his seat belt cutting against his chest diagonally. What had happened?

Wincing, he lifted his chin. Cracks scarred his windshield. Beyond the hood, he could see nothing but dirt and torn grass. A pair of sapling trees wedged against his driver's side door.

He'd been in a car crash.

How long ago? Why?

He didn't know. He'd flown to the airstrip. He . . . He remembered getting into his car and pulling out onto the road in the fog. That's all.

He'd lost time.

Experimentally, he moved his fingers and toes. Everything was working fine except for the splitting pain in his head.

The one with the beautiful voice clicked off the radio. "Downbound Train" disappeared, leaving only a faint ringing in his ears.

"I'm relieved that you came to," she said.

The tone of her words softened the agony inside his skull.

Slowly, he turned his chin in her direction. He'd lost his tolerance for light and the pinpricks wouldn't go away. He squeezed his eyes shut against the disorienting sensation, then opened them and concentrated hard so that he could focus on her.

She . . . had the face of an angel.

An unforgettable face. A heartbreaking face, both hopeful and world-weary. He guessed her to be a year or two younger than he was, but she didn't look sheltered or naïve.

Long eyelashes framed almond-shaped gray-blue eyes as deep as they were soft. A defined groove marked the center of her upper lip. Blond hair, parted on the side. Neither curly nor straight, it had a natural, faintly messy look to it. She'd cut it so that it ended halfway between her small, determined chin and her shoulders.

Had he died? Was she an angel? She was there, which made him think he'd died. But his head hurt, which made him think he hadn't.

"Are you injured?" she asked.

"I'm fine. Except for my head."

Concern flickered in her expression. At least, he thought it did. He struggled to see her more clearly, furious that he couldn't look at her with his usual powers of observation.

She knelt on the passenger seat, the door behind her gaping open. "I've already called 9-1-1. Hopefully they'll be here soon."

"I hope not."

"Hmm?"

"I don't want them to take me away from you."

Her brows lifted. "I . . ." She gestured. "I was behind you on the road. I came around the bend just in time to see your car go off the edge. I pulled over and dialed 9-1-1."

"How long was I out?"

"Just a few minutes. Is there anything I can do for you?"

He extended his right hand to her. "Hold my hand?"

"Of course." She wrapped both of her hands around his. The heat of her touch had the same effect on him as her voice and appearance.

He suspected he'd cracked his head on his side window, which had knocked him out and likely given him a severe concussion.

"Would it help if I unfastened your seat belt?" she asked.

"Yeah." He was capable of freeing it using his left hand. But if she was offering to do it for him, he wasn't about to say no.

She let go of his hand to accomplish the task, and he cursed himself for making a tactical error. But then she braced one hand against the center console and reached across him, bringing her hair within a few inches of his nose. He drew air in and registered the scent of lavender.

Dark satisfaction curved his lips. He hadn't made a tactical error. His brainpower remained intact, and he was going to be just fine. The constriction of his seat belt released.

She arched back and resumed her earlier position.

He extended his hand.

She took it. "Better?"

"Much."

The sound of sirens reached him. In response, resistance sharpened inside him. He didn't want to be parted from her.

Twice before in his life, he hadn't wanted to be parted from people. When he was eight. When he was thirteen. Both times, his desires hadn't mattered.

"Is there anything else I can do for you?" she asked. "I'd be happy to call someone."

"No. I'm not the type . . . to alarm people . . . before I have solid facts." He paused for a moment to gather his strength. The pinpricks still wouldn't go away.

The sirens drew nearer. Louder.

He rested the back of his skull against his headrest but kept his face turned fully to the right, his concentration trained on her. "After I speak with the doctors . . . I'll make calls. To tell people what's happened."

"Okay."

The sirens grew so loud that they made conversation impossible.

She craned her neck to look toward the road.

Idiot sirens. Violently, he wished he could take back her 9-1-1 call.

He had to remember that he was a stranger to her. He couldn't expect her to feel about him the way he felt about her. She hadn't been in a crash. Her head was clear.

The noise of the ambulance cut away. Its lights continued to revolve, sending rays of red and blue against her face. She gave him a small, encouraging smile. "They'll be here in just a second."

He gripped her hand more tightly, holding her with him. He memorized the curves and lines of her forehead, cheeks, hair, neck, arms.

Men's voices neared.

She moved to exit his car.

He didn't release her hand. "Don't go," he said.

She leveled a bemused look on him. "I need to get out of their way. It's all right. They're going to take great care of you." Gently, she slipped her hand from his and scooted away.

All he could think was, *No. Don't go.* But he'd already said that, and it hadn't worked. He couldn't force her to remain with him.

"You're going to be just fine," she said.

He was not going to be just fine without her.

Two men in EMT uniforms filled the passenger-side doorway. They were leaning in, talking to him.

Sebastian had twisted, trying to keep sight of her, but in an instant, the fog had stolen her from view.

The book and movie character Jason Bourne had been hit on the head, woken up with amnesia, realized he was extremely talented at killing people, and gone on a series of high-adrenaline adventures.

Sebastian had been hit on the head, experienced short-term amnesia, and been so out of it when he'd come to that it hadn't occurred to him to ask for the woman's name.

He'd gotten only one thing right on the morning of his accident. He'd correctly understood that he was not going to be fine without her.

Instead of high-adrenaline adventures, his world had been muted and dull since his concussion. It was like he'd been walking through time in a space suit that kept out joy. Which he didn't understand, because he'd finally achieved the goal he'd been chasing for years. He'd become a pediatric heart surgeon, and his job was supposed to have righted the wrong that had happened to him when he was a kid. It was supposed to have brought him security, fulfillment, happiness.

To be fair, his job did bring him some of that. But not enough to free him from the space suit. Which made him mad.

Also, Jason Bourne sucked.

Sebastian jerked off his sunglasses and pushed them into the chest pocket of his lightweight gray-and-white-checked button-down. He wore the shirt untucked over jeans, the sleeves rolled up.

He saw all ages and shapes of people. But not her.

For weeks after his encounter with her, he'd racked his brain, trying to think how he could learn her identity. He'd never seen her car. She'd been wearing nothing distinctive that would have allowed him to track her down. She'd left no trace behind.

He'd contacted Misty River's 9-1-1 dispatcher and the EMTs to ask who she was. Neither had been willing to share her name. Privacy, they'd said. He'd hunted the social media feeds of his Misty River friends for a photo that included her. No success. He'd looked through old high school yearbooks, trying to find her picture in one of Misty River High's graduating classes. No success.

After a month of making himself crazy with frustration, he'd forced himself to quit searching. He'd told himself she could not be as appealing in real life as he'd made her in his imagination.

Unfortunately, his brain hadn't listened. His body might have stopped the search, but he'd continued to brood over her for the past six months.

To his left, he registered movement at one of the stalls. He glanced toward it in time to see a blond head rise from behind buckets of flowers on risers. The woman extended a hand and poured change into a customer's palm.

He could only see her profile, but that was enough.

It was the woman from the day of the crash.

His breath left him.

Finally. Amazingly, there she was.

His awareness centered on her, he moved forward. She turned to chat with the two acne-prone teenagers helping her sell flowers. A piece of butcher paper reading *Support the Misty River High Math Club!* hung in front of their folding table.

He'd been wrong when he'd decided she could not be as appealing in real life as he'd made her in his imagination. She was ridiculously appealing. More so than he'd remembered.

She had on a bright pink short-sleeved sweater. The rounded collar of the snowy white shirt underneath folded over the neckline. Her jeans were beige. No wedding ring. Very little makeup. Hardly any jewelry at all, just tiny earrings and a classic metal watch.

He stopped at her booth. She looked in his direction, and their eyes met.

22

Finally. Her.

"I don't know if you remember me," he said. "I was in a car accident last November. You were behind me on the road, and when you saw what happened, you came to help."

Realization lit her expression. "That's right." She smiled and crossed to him. "I'm pleased to see you again. I've thought about you often and wondered how you were."

"I've thought about you often, too."

"Did you sustain any injuries in the crash?"

"A concussion."

"And how are you now?"

"Fully recovered." He couldn't believe he'd found her, was talking to her.

"Excellent. You look impressively healthy."

"I am."

"And exceedingly handsome."

"You think I'm handsome?"

She tilted her head a few millimeters. "Most females must find you handsome," she said matter of factly, with zero flirtatiousness. "Do they not?"

A grin tugged at his mouth.

An elderly couple arrived, capturing her attention.

Hers wasn't the lean, hard beauty of a model. She had a more interesting, more subtle, more layered beauty. Her face projected many things at the same time: intelligence, kindness, confidence, and perceptiveness.

She stood at a height of maybe five foot six. Delicate, but not skinny.

Those eyes of hers made him want to protect her, which was ridiculous. She was clearly volunteering her time, just like he was. She didn't need his protection or the rush of emotions she was making made him feel. After existing in a gray haze for months, everything was suddenly sharper than it should be—his determination not to let her go again, sounds, the color of her sweater.

What was it about her that drew him? Her calm? The strength

he sensed in her? He wasn't sure, but there was definitely some-thing powerful about her presence. He'd never reacted to a woman this way before.

"I've been waiting for the chance to thank you," he told her once the elderly couple moved away. "For stopping that day."

"You're welcome. Glad to have been of assistance."

He grabbed the nearest bouquet from its bucket and passed it to her. "I'll take this one, please." At the least, he needed enough time with her to learn who she was. At the most, to convince her to go out with him.

"Outstanding choice." She considered the dripping arrange-ment. "Hmm. Two metaphors, right here."

"How so?"

"Well, flowers are already a metaphor for life in and of them-selves. But your bouquet is also gently spherical on top. It starts here, at birth, so to speak." She coasted her pointer finger from the lower edge of one side toward the center rise of the flowers. "Then expands to the fullest days of life. Then ends very much where it began on the other side, with death." Her finger continued its arc to the bottom edge on the opposite side. Her hands were pale and graceful, her short nails unpainted.

He was about as interested in metaphors as he was in farmers markets. But she could talk to him about metaphors for days, and he'd drink every word.

She turned toward the table to wrap the flowers in wax paper.

He could be too straightforward, he knew. He'd had to work on that when interacting with the parents of his patients. If he told her *"I need for you to go on a date with me,"* she'd think he was crazy.

Maybe he was crazy.

She tied an orange bow around the bouquet—

"Hey!" Ben's familiar voice cut through Sebastian's thoughts.

"Hey." He and Ben exchanged their usual side arm hug.

He was always glad to see Ben. Only, Ben's arrival at this par-ticular moment wasn't ideal.

A smile moved across Ben's mouth, his teeth gleaming white

24

against his dark brown skin. "I saw you guys talking and came over to introduce you."

She stepped toward them with the flowers. "Do you two know each other?"

"This is my best friend, Dr. Sebastian Grant," Ben told her.

"Ah!" she said. "You're one of the Miracle Five, like Ben."

"Yes."

"Ben's told me all about you."

"And this," Ben said to Sebastian, "is my friend Leah Montgomery."

For a terrible, disorienting second, Sebastian's mind blanked. Then denial filled it—red and loud.

No.

"I've told *him* all about *you*," Ben said to Leah.

"I hope you've been emphasizing my most sterling qualities."

"I have," Ben assured her with a dopey, infatuated look.

No!

Ever since Leah came to Misty River High to teach math more than a year and a half ago, Ben had had a crush on her. Ben was taking his time, content to build a wide base of friendship with Leah, in hopes that it would one day lead to more.

Last fall, Ben had told Sebastian that he loved Leah. Sebastian had given him a hard time for claiming to love a woman he wasn't even dating. But Ben had stood behind his statement.

Ben believed himself to be in love with her.

Which meant that Sebastian could never ask her out. Ben had found her first, and in the code of brothers, that meant that she was off-limits to Sebastian.

No.

"Small world," Leah said lightly to Ben. "Last fall I was driving behind Sebastian here when his car went off the side of the road. I kept him company until the ambulance got there."

"Oh?" Ben said. Then, "*Oh.*" Understanding was no doubt filling his brain.

Just as Ben had told Sebastian about Leah, Sebastian had told

Ben about the woman who'd been in his car with him when he'd regained consciousness. Ben knew about Sebastian's search for her and just how consumed by her Sebastian had been.

"Sebastian called me the day of the accident." The usual optimism was draining from Ben's expression. "He told me about the woman who stopped to help, but I had no idea that woman was you."

A high schooler approached the stall. "I'm heading out," he said to Leah. The newcomer was a few inches shorter than Sebastian with a soft, smooth face.

"Hello to you, too," Leah said to the teen. "I'm in the middle of a conversation." She indicated him and Ben.

"Cool," the kid said. "So . . . I'm leaving."

Leah regarded the boy with scolding affection. "I'm fine with you leaving, my darlingest of darlings, but before you go, I insist you make a stab at politeness by greeting these adults and then introducing yourself."

"Hello," the kid said in a monotone. "I'm Dylan."

"Sebastian."

"Good to see you, Dylan," Ben said warmly.

"Yup." Dylan loped off, flicking the fingers of one hand upward in a parting gesture.

Leah watched him leave, then handed the bouquet to Sebastian.

"How much do I owe you?" His voice sounded rusty. He was cool under pressure. Always. It was one of the things he was known for. At the moment, though, he didn't feel cool. He felt crushed and angry. The only positive part of this situation was that Ben had joined them before Sebastian had hit on Leah.

Unfortunately, it didn't make things better to acknowledge that things could've been worse.

"Twenty dollars," she told Sebastian.

Sebastian handed over cash. He also passed the bouquet he'd purchased back to her.

She gave him a questioning look.

"For you," he told her. "I appreciate what you did for me last fall."

"That's kind of you, but you don't need to give me flowers." She extended them back in his direction.

"They're yours," he insisted. "Thank you again." After nodding at her politely, he stalked toward the spaghetti line.

Behind him, he could hear Ben and Leah exchanging good-byes.

Ben caught up and fell in step next to him. They walked in silence for several strides until Ben said, "Hold up a minute."

They both came to a stop.

Ben stuck his hands into his jeans. "*Leah* was the woman who was with you in your car after your accident?"

"Yeah."

"I can't believe it."

"Me neither. I passed her table just now and recognized her."

Ben shifted uncomfortably, looking toward one of the gigantic human-filled balls. It revolved slowly down its course.

Sebastian held himself motionless, still struggling to absorb the fact that he'd found Leah and lost Leah in the space of less than ten minutes.

"I really care about her, man," Ben said. "We . . . we don't typically have the same taste in women. But this time we do."

"Obviously I'm not going to get in your way."

"Look, I'm sorry about this. I know how much you liked her."

"I don't even know her. I talked with her six months ago for a short period of time. That's it." Sebastian set his body in motion again, finding it too hard to stand still.

The situation made him feel guilty, which it had no right to do. Until now, he hadn't known the woman in his SUV was the Leah Ben had a crush on. The situation also made him feel resentful toward Ben. It had no right to do that either. "Who's Dylan?" he asked.

"He's Leah's younger brother. She has custody of him."

"Why does she have custody?"

"Their parents divorced when Dylan was young. After the divorce, Leah's mom forced Leah's dad out of the kids' lives, little by little."

"And her dad accepted that?"

"Yeah. Over time he let the kids go. So then Leah and Dylan were left with just Leah's mom. Ten years ago, she accepted a job overseas and voluntarily relinquished Dylan's custody to Leah."

"How old was Leah ten years ago?"

"Eighteen. Dylan was seven."

Sebastian's eyebrows shot up.

"Until I met Leah," Ben said, "I didn't even realize that eighteen-year-olds could be granted custody of younger siblings."

Sebastian was no stranger to issues pertaining to orphans. "In most states, including Georgia, eighteen-year-olds can gain custody of a younger sibling so long as they're able to show that they have the means to support them both, somewhere safe to live, and so on. How did Leah have the means to support herself and her brother at that age?"

Ben tapped him on the arm, stilling him again because they'd almost reached the food line. "So, I've told you, right, that Leah was a math prodigy?"

Sebastian gave a short nod.

"By the age of four she could do algebraic and quadratic equations. One of her elementary school teachers took her under her wing and made sure she was challenged, gave her all kinds of resources and opportunities. By ten, she was into complex numbers and math theories."

At ten, Sebastian had been into skipping school and hating the world.

"She stayed in public school through eighth grade," Ben continued, "then was offered a scholarship to the Program for the Exceptionally Gifted at the Clemmons School."

"I'm not familiar with it."

"It's basically a boarding school for girls who are off-the-charts smart in math. She graduated from there at eighteen with both a high school diploma and her bachelor's degree in math. Can you relate to any of that?"

Ben knew he could. Sebastian, too, had graduated from college at eighteen.

Ben scratched the hair behind his ear that he kept shaved close to his skull. "She didn't tell me this part, but I've read articles about her, so I know that she was then offered a chance to pursue her PhD free of charge at several of the best mathematics programs in the country. She chose Princeton and was all set to go when her mom took off. Leah ended up turning down Princeton's offer and looking for jobs as a math teacher."

"She wouldn't have had the certifications to teach, though. Would she?"

"No. But she immediately enrolled in an online master's program. If you have a BA in a subject and can show that you're pursuing a master's degree that will lead to certification, you can teach . . . assuming you can convince a principal and a school board to hire you."

"Which is the route she took?"

"Exactly. She was hired as a middle school math teacher in Gainesville while she was getting her master's. I've never heard of anyone else becoming a teacher so young. It's rare. But then, she's rare. Her math mind is one in a million. She should be working as a professor at a university, but instead she's here, teaching our most advanced math students. It's a shame for her, but it's been awesome for the kids. She's an excellent teacher."

Sebastian's mouth tightened. He'd never considered his lack of siblings to be fortunate. But because he hadn't been saddled with family responsibilities, he'd been free to accept the medical school offers that had come his way. "Why did she move to Misty River?"

"Dylan. He was struggling in Gainesville. His grades were terrible, and his friends were rough. She decided it would be best to give him a fresh start."

"How's that worked out?"

"Well, for the most part. I think he still gives her plenty of reasons to worry, but he's doing much better than he was."

A frazzled-looking gray-haired woman whistled and flagged Ben down by waving both arms.

"Got to go," Ben said. "I'll catch up with you later."

As Sebastian approached the man who appeared to be in charge of the spaghetti line, he allowed himself one last look in Leah's direction. He could only make out her bright sweater.

Disappointment snarled inside him, prowling for an outlet.

Math prodigy Leah Montgomery could not be his.

Your DNA results are in! Discover your heritage! popped up in Leah's email inbox two weeks after submitting her second sample.

Immediately upon seeing that subject line, her blood pressure escalated in a rush.

This time the message found her while she was sitting on the bleachers at a track and field meet, cheering for her students. During a long break between events, she'd checked her phone.

She clicked the link in the email, then asked God for His peace and strength as she typed in her username and password.

The screen populated, and Leah stared at the same ethnicity pie chart YourHeritage had served her the first time. She brought up the screen showing her genetic matches. The same unfamiliar pictures and names appeared in a long line. Haskins, Brookside, Schloss.

Sorrow crept over her.

Her mother believed Leah to be the child she'd given birth to.

This second test proved, unequivocally, that she was not.

She wasn't related by blood to her brother, her mom, or her dad. By blood, she was related to these people she did not know.

The starting gun signaled another race had begun. She raised her face and watched the runners dart off the blocks, pumping their arms and legs. Inside, her emotions were as chaotic as those churning, straining limbs.

Dylan.

For the past two weeks, her thoughts had been drawn to her DNA over and over again. It wasn't as if she'd had no warning about the potential loss of her biological connection to her brother. Yet this confirmation sliced her with a grief so new and painful, it felt like a personal insult.

For many, many years prior to Dylan's birth, she'd wanted a little sister of her own. Leah had been lonely, shy, uncoordinated, self-conscious—a solitary girl with a reservoir of love to give. She'd imagined that her little sister would look just like she did, love to graph parabolas like she did, appreciate tea parties with stuffed animals like she did.

Around the time she'd turned ten, she'd resigned herself to the truth. She was never going to get a sibling. Just like she was never going to get the Apple computer she asked for every Christmas.

A fifth grader going on the age of fifty, she'd put her longing for a sister on the shelf. There hadn't been time to mourn. She'd had her hands full with the miserable social aspects of her latter elementary years and an academic workload that would have challenged Einstein. Her parents had moved from town to town every few years, forever chasing and never catching new dreams, better jobs, greener grass.

And then, out of the blue, her mom and dad—never the masters of birth control—had experienced their second unplanned pregnancy. At first when they told her they were expecting a baby, she'd responded like any self-respecting preteen: with mortification. But after she'd had time to get used to the idea, the old yearning for a blond little sister had stirred back to life.

Her parents had waited to find out the sex of their baby. And so, when Leah had finally entered her mom's hospital room to meet her new sibling, excitement had bounced around inside her body like a pinball. Dad informed her that if the baby was wearing pink, it was a girl. If the baby was wearing blue, it was a boy.

Leah approached the little plastic box on wheels where the baby was sleeping. Long before she was close enough to determine the color of the baby's clothing beneath the blankets, she read the sign stuck to the inside of the baby's bed. *It's a boy!*

Mom and Dad's gender reveal plan had been spoiled by an obvious sign they'd failed to notice.

Benevolently, she acted surprised when she pulled the baby's blanket down and revealed blue.

Leah sat in the room's window seat, and Dad rested her tiny brother in her lap.

He was beautiful. A mini nose, a perfect doll mouth, slightly bulgy closed eyes. She peeked under his cap and found lots of dark, silky hair.

Overtaken with wonder, she'd hugged him against herself. In that moment, it hadn't mattered that he wasn't a girl or that he wasn't blond.

He was hers.

She was no longer alone with her erratic parents.

She'd found her person.

Love had vibrated through every cell of her adolescent self. And over the seventeen years since, that love had proven deep and staunch, the most unchanging aspect of her life.

Her relationship with Dylan was forged of much stronger stuff than blood. She'd been there for every important moment of his life. For the last decade, she'd been his caregiver.

Shared history. Love in action. Those are the things that family relationships are made of. She would, forever and always, continue to be Dylan's sister. But until this DNA test, she'd trusted in the fact that she was Dylan's biological sister. She'd wanted, very much, to continue to be Dylan's biological sister.

Now it felt as though Dylan, Mom, and Dad were on one side of a river, a party of three. And she was on the other side by herself.

A sheen of tears misted her eyes.

She was not who she'd always thought she was. Which begged the question . . . who was she?

Your identity has not changed, she told herself firmly. She was the very same person she'd been before the DNA results. Her truest identity, the only one that would last, was anchored in Christ and no one could take that from her. She'd spent hours preaching that truth to herself these past weeks. . . .

She only wished it had sunk in better.

She inclined her head, closed her eyes, and determinedly prayed the words she clung to every time bad news confronted her. *I'm going to trust in you with all my heart and lean not on my understanding. In all my ways, I'll acknowledge you. Please make my paths straight.*

Lifting her head, she consciously relaxed the muscles tension had seized.

Who were the parents she should have been given to on the day of her birth? What had happened to the baby who should have been given to Leah's mom and dad? And what chain of events had sent two babies home with the wrong parents?

CHAPTER THREE

Surgery days were Sebastian's best days.

He entered the operating suite at Beckett Memorial Hospital in Atlanta, an undercurrent of adrenaline sharpening his concentration more effectively than coffee. Markie, registered nurse and physician's assistant, came forward to help him slip on his sterile surgical gown and gloves. He'd already scrubbed in and put on his surgical cap, mask, and the loupes that magnified and enhanced his view of the field.

"Good afternoon," he said to the team.

"Good afternoon," they replied as a group.

Sebastian assessed the monitors, then the progress already made. Today's patient was three-week-old Mateo Peralta, who'd been flown in from Argentina for a ventricular repair on a heart approximately the size of a walnut. Mateo lay on the table with his eyes taped closed, head to the side, a ventilation tube in his trachea, tiny hands relaxed.

Sebastian prepared his surgical plans the way generals strategized complex battles. Even so, he sometimes altered his plans when he saw his patient's anatomy with his own eyes. Echocardiograms had grown more and more sophisticated, but there was still no substitute for looking into a chest.

Now that he was viewing the boy's heart, he was indeed going to adjust his plan of attack. He asked for his instruments. "Let's get to work, people." It was his customary phrase.

Markie shot back her customary response. "Some of us are already working."

Smiling a little, he bent forward and began.

Sebastian and his mentors had several things in common. They were all persistent perfectionists, determined to execute their role flawlessly. They were also confident. Thick-skinned. Tough-minded. Ambitious.

Sebastian was unlike the rest of them in one key way, however. He'd been a foster kid, and because of that, his street smarts were wickedly sharp. In elementary school, if he took a toy from another kid and that kid cried, he hadn't cared. Why should he care? He'd ended up with the toy. In middle school, he'd learned to defend himself with his fists. In high school and college, he'd used people to get ahead, he'd put his own interests first, and he'd bent every rule that didn't suit him.

Plenty of people had called him ruthless, but no one had ever called him humble.

Then he'd graduated and begun his internship, followed by his residency, followed by his fellowships. Working on children's hearts had a way of maturing a person. The job had taught him that no human or technological advance of the last century had the ability to improve on God's ingenious design of the human heart.

Sebastian was not the architect of the heart. He was simply a very well-trained plumber. His goal today, and every day, was to restore defective hearts as close as possible to God's blueprint. The more effectively he could do that, the better and faster his patient would recover.

The phone rang. Dave, the anesthesiologist, answered, then murmured to the caller.

Sebastian continued without pause, his attention fixed on closing the hole between the left and right ventricles. The heart-lung bypass machine hummed, doing the work of both the heart and the lungs during surgery by pumping the infant's blood through his body. The less time Mateo was on bypass, the better, so Sebastian had to make the right decisions, and he had to make them fast.

He also had to think two, six, eight steps ahead. The best surgeons possessed more than knowledge and skillful hands. They possessed feel. In this line of work, disaster was usually the result of several minor mistakes instead of a major one. He was learning to recognize subtle patterns and anticipate every way in which things could go wrong.

"A baby with transposition of the great arteries has been delivered in Macon," Dave said to him, holding the phone against his chest. "His name's Josiah Douglas. Fourteen hours old, eight pounds. They're transporting him here by ambulance."

Sebastian paused his stitching and looked up over his surgeon's loupes. "Have they started him on prostaglandins?"

"Yes."

"When will he arrive?"

"About an hour."

He bent his head back to his task. His current repair was progressing like poetry.

Josiah would need a septostomy procedure today. Then, after giving him a week or so to recover and grow, an arterial switch operation.

The Clinic for Pediatric and Congenital Heart Diseases here at Beckett Memorial was one of the most prestigious in the country, alongside Boston Children's, the Cleveland Clinic, Children's Hospital of Philadelphia, and the University of California San Francisco.

The surgical team and the pediatric intensive care team here ran an extremely successful defense against death. They'd do whatever they could to ensure that they did not lose Mateo. Or Josiah.

Not today, God.

Not on my watch.

When Sebastian entered Josiah's room that evening, a distinctive, now-familiar energy closed around him. None of the energy originated with the boy, who lay unconscious on his warming bed. All of it came from the bright, hard-working machines sustaining his life.

Josiah's light brown hair lay against his round head at strange angles. He had big cheeks and a small mouth.

As Sebastian stood at his bedside, feeling his tiredness, an image of Leah slipped into his mind. He saw again exactly how she'd looked at the farmers market, surrounded by flowers. He replayed the moment when her eyes met his—

Stop it.

Weeks had passed since that day, and he wanted her out of his head.

He was no longer a child who took toys from other people and felt nothing when they cried. But that didn't mean that it was in his nature to sit on the sidelines while other people pursued the things he wanted.

It wasn't.

It was in his nature to go after the things he wanted single-mindedly. Which is exactly what he would have done had the obstacle between himself and Leah been anything and anyone other than Ben. As it was, he could do nothing, which sent frustration scratching down his limbs.

She's off limits, he kept telling himself.

She's off limits.

Three days later, Ben stopped in the open doorway of Leah's classroom. "Want anything from the break room?" he asked.

She paused the motion of the sponge she was using to clean her whiteboard. Ben's easygoing, open personality never failed to brighten her day. "Watermelon-flavored sparkling water?"

"You bet."

He vanished. The space he'd vacated framed a view of the hallway, lockers, and passing students.

Ben occupied the classroom across the hall and four doors down from hers. They shared a free period, so at the same time almost every day, he stopped by to ask if she wanted anything from the teacher break room.

She finished cleaning her board and turned to observe her happy, tidy classroom. Semicircles of chairs radiated away from where she was standing toward the opposing wall, which contained a bank of windows. She'd stocked her bookshelves with textbooks, binders, and notebooks from her years at Clemmons, her large personal collection of books about math, and a few potted succulents and inspirational quotes.

Primary-colored portraits of the world's most renowned math minds filled every remaining patch of wall space. Thus Hypatia, Euler, Gauss, Cantor, and more looked down on her daily.

"Here's hoping I'm doing the lot of you proud," she said. "Please do intervene and speak up if I'm not."

She scooped a crumpled piece of paper and a pencil stub off the floor, depositing them in the trash before taking a seat at her desk. Outside, a breeze stirred the trees draping the hills.

Since receiving her second round of test results from Your-Heritage, she'd been working to metabolize her genetic truth. It had shifted the earth she walked on. It was confusing and painful. But the best course forward was to accept what could not be changed. And so, gradually, she was learning to coexist with the revelations about her DNA the way she might coexist with a mutt who appeared one day and insisted on following her everywhere.

She had no plans to reach out to her mom. Mom had been apprised of the situation and could call her for additional information whenever she chose. Nor did Leah have plans, at this point, anyway, to tell Dylan what she'd discovered. It would upset him, and what purpose would that serve?

So far, she'd settled on just one course of action. She wanted to find answers to the questions her DNA tests had raised.

She'd been born at Magnolia Avenue Hospital in Atlanta. If she could examine Magnolia Avenue's records on the babies born on the same day that she'd been born, she might be able to work out which biological parents were hers.

But first, she'd need to convince the hospital to show her their records. She knew just enough about the privacy regulations pertaining to hospital data to know that in order to gain access to those records, she'd need an expert on her side.

Ben sailed into her classroom and handed her the can of sparkling water. Today he'd paired a dark purple short-sleeved polo with gray pants and spotless black leather sneakers with thick white soles.

"Thank you," she said. "Do you realize that if we walk somewhere side-by-side today, we'll look like a study in color wheel opposites?"

"We will?"

"Yes. Yellow." She pointed to her blouse, then to him. "And purple."

"Ah."

"Sir Isaac Newton would be pleased."

"Because?"

"Because he was the first to split sunlight into beams of color and invented the color wheel."

"You know what I said to myself when I woke up this morning?"

"I do not."

"I said, 'Dress to please Sir Isaac Newton today, Ben.'"

She smiled. "Mission accomplished."

As usual, Ben settled into the student chair nearest her desk. A soft *pop* sounded as he opened his package of baby carrots.

She took a swallow of the chilled sparkling water, savoring it. The first sip was always the best. "The day of the farmers market you introduced me to your friend Sebastian."

Ben chewed, nodded.

"He's a doctor in Atlanta, right?" Leah asked.

"Yes. He lives there during the week but stays at his house here in Misty River most weekends."

"Do you think he'd be willing to speak to me? I have a few medical questions I'd like to ask."

Lines of concern indented his forehead. "Are you sick?"

"No. My questions have to do with old records."

"I'd be happy to relay your questions to Sebastian and get back to you with his answers."

"I appreciate the offer, but the records I'm after are a bit on the . . . personal side. I don't mind giving him a call." Leah opened the *New Contact* screen on her phone and passed it to Ben.

Because he was a doctor, Sebastian would know how to go about obtaining records. Additionally, doctors were good at keeping information confidential. Lastly, he'd be predisposed to help her because she'd helped him when he'd crashed his car.

Ben frowned slightly as he typed in Sebastian's details.

It had been unsettling in the extreme to watch Sebastian's car lunge off the road last fall. Terrified of what she might find, she'd parked and hurried down the embankment. The front of his SUV had crumpled, wisps of steam rising from it. Since the driver's side door was wedged against small trees, she'd jerked open the passenger door. She'd discovered a good-looking, dark-haired man slumped against his seat belt, unconcious. She'd climbed onto the seat and tried to wake him. At first there'd been no response. She'd been hugely relieved when he'd woken.

He hadn't been scared, just in pain and disoriented.

The lucid, virile Sebastian of the farmers market had been very different from the Sebastian of the car crash.

He was taller than she would have guessed. At least six foot two, with a forthright, masculine, chiseled face. His hair was inkier than she'd recalled—almost black. The day of his accident, he'd been dazed. The day of the market, his gray eyes had regarded her with extraordinary intensity. He'd spoken with assurance. There'd been no weakness in him at all.

Ben gave her phone back.

"Did you know Sebastian before the five of you were trapped by the earthquake?" she asked.

"No. He was a foster kid, and the church offered him a place on the mission trip, all expenses paid. He didn't want to go, but his foster parents insisted. That was the first time Sebastian had done anything with our youth group. He hated being there, and he was determined to hate all of us, too."

Leah had been young when the world's interest had converged on the five American children who'd been trapped underground by an earthquake while in El Salvador. So when a fellow teacher informed her that Ben was one of the Miracle Five shortly after her arrival in Misty River, she'd done what she always did after pinpointing a gap in her knowledge: she'd studied up. The next time she'd seen Ben, she'd been prepared to talk intelligently on the subject of the earthquake and their subsequent miraculous rescue.

Over time, she'd learned that the entire town harbored a great deal of respect for their five most famous sons and daughters. Ben, Sebastian, Natasha, Genevieve, and Luke had been in middle school when they'd been buried alive for eight days beneath rubble. It didn't matter to Misty River residents that the event had occurred nineteen years ago. They still regarded the kids, now adults, with a healthy dose of awe.

"So your first impression of Sebastian wasn't a positive one," she said.

"Not at all. He was blunt and argumentative. Mean." Fondness softened his expression. "But he grew on me."

"And you grew on him."

"It took time. After we came home, he said no the first ten or twenty times I asked him to do stuff with my family and me. But then my mom got involved. . . . You've met my mom."

"Yes."

"So you know that it's impossible to say no to her. Sebastian had met his match. She forced him to hang out with us. He started spending more and more time at our house, taking trips with us, coming to church with us."

"The way you talk, I was under the impression that your family had practically adopted him."

"Practically, yes. Technically, no. My parents didn't formally adopt him, but we did pull him into our circle."

"The famous Coleman charm softened fearsome Sebastian Grant."

Ben's good-natured grin caused his brown eyes to sparkle. "It overcomes everyone's defenses in time."

"Given that, how is it possible that you've made it to the age of thirty-two without marrying anyone, sir?"

His brows rose. "This topic again?"

"You know how I am when things don't make sense to me! And your unmarried state makes no sense to me."

"You're unmarried."

"I'm unmarriageable—"

"No you're not."

"But I am. You, however, are astonishingly marriageable."

He chuckled. "You're almost as bad as my mom."

"As stated, your charm can overcome anyone's defenses. Which means that the reason for your singleness must stem from womankind's inability to overcome *your* defenses."

He spread his hands. "That is not the reason. I'm open to a relationship!"

"Then allow me to set you up with Hallie." Leah could name several women who'd love to date him.

"No." He took his baby carrots and hightailed it toward the door.

"Malia?"

"No." He darted out of sight.

"Coward!" she called after him.

L ater that night, Sebastian paused the voice mail he'd begun playing while walking toward the hospital parking lot after work.

He propped a shoulder against the hallway wall, restarted the voicemail, and listened carefully.

"Sebastian, this is Leah Montgomery. We spoke briefly at Misty

River High School's farmers market. Thank you for the bouquet, by the way. I've enjoyed it." A brief hesitation.

Her voice was like moonlight. Clear, tranquil.

"Ben gave me your number," she continued. "I have a few questions about medical records, and I'm hoping you might be able to offer some insight. Feel free to give me a call back at your convenience. Sincere thanks."

Hospital staffers drifted past.

He replayed the message again. Then again.

Finally, he continued toward his car. Ben had given Leah his number? Ben hadn't told him he had.

Once inside his Mercedes C Class, he started the engine but made no move to put the car in gear. He collected his thoughts, then dialed Leah's number.

She picked up on the second ring. "Hello?"

Longing fisted around his chest. "It's Sebastian Grant. How are you?"

"I'm doing well. Thanks for returning my call. Can—can you hold on for one moment, please?"

"Sure."

He heard a door opening and closing, followed by the sound of birds and breeze. "I reached out to you," she said, "because I could use the advice of someone who's knowledgeable about hospitals and the policies surrounding medical records."

"I'm glad you reached out." It was an understatement.

"What I'm about to say is sensitive," she told him, "and I'm wondering if you'd consider keeping it confidential. I do realize that's an outlandish thing to ask, seeing as how I'm a stranger."

"I don't consider you to be a stranger, and I'll keep whatever you tell me confidential."

"Thank you."

He waited, trying to predict the situation she'd gotten herself into.

"I have reason to suspect that, immediately after my birth twenty-eight years ago, I went home from the hospital with the wrong set of parents."

Silence exploded inside Sebastian's car. He'd in no way predicted that. "You think you were switched at birth?" He kept his voice level. His career, his life, had taught him to absorb surprise while remaining outwardly calm.

She explained her DNA test, retest, and her mother's insistence that she hadn't been adopted. "I'd very much like to study the records concerning my birth," she said, "as well as the records of all the other baby girls who were born the same day."

"In order to learn the identity of your biological parents?"

"Yes. Also to determine what became of the baby my parents were supposed to have raised and what caused this outcome."

"Where were you born?"

"Magnolia Avenue Hospital."

His brain flipped through the information she'd provided. "In the state of Georgia, hospitals are only required to retain records for ten years."

A few seconds of quiet followed. "You're saying that the records of my birth have been destroyed."

"I'm saying that it's possible. Some hospitals, including my own, never destroy anything."

"I see." She sounded disappointed, and he didn't want to disappoint her.

"How about I make an appointment for the two of us with the hospital administrator at Magnolia Avenue? If your records still exist, we'll need the cooperation of those at the top of the hospital food chain in order to access them. We'll also need a court order."

"A meeting with the administrator would be excellent."

"When will you be available to drive to Atlanta for a meeting?"

"There are only six days of school left. Summer vacation starts June tenth, so anytime after that should work."

"I'll set up an appointment as soon as possible after that date. In the meantime, I recommend you gather all the documents you have. Your birth certificate. Printouts of your DNA test results. Information on your mother's pregnancy, and anything else you can think of."

"Will do."

"I'll call you when I have a meeting arranged."

She'd given him a chance to advocate for her, which pleased him more than anything had in a long time. He wanted to repay her for what she'd done for him the day of his accident.

And so he would, while keeping things simple and platonic between them.

While Leah had been talking to Sebastian, she'd descended her front walkway, crossed the street, and continued along the dirt trail that wound downhill.

Now she spent a few moments admiring the view of her very own Blue Ridge Mountain valley. She adored it at this time of day, painted in the thoughtful golden tones of the coming sunset.

Sticking her phone in the pocket of her white jeans, she started back up the path. Her house came into view. Small, yet also an architectural work of art.

After she'd accepted her position at Misty River High, she'd spent a Saturday touring available houses with her Realtor. They'd viewed a string of conventional, uninspiring homes. Then her Realtor had said something along the lines of "This next one is a little unorthodox, but it's in a great location and the price is right." The older woman hadn't sounded hopeful, so Leah hadn't felt hopeful, either. Then her Realtor had come to a stop here, at the base of the steep driveway. Leah had peered out the car's front window and promptly fallen in love.

The majority of Misty River homebuyers sought out rustic cabins, traditional brick homes, or the spindly Victorians in the oldest section of town. Not Leah. This mid-century modern gem suited her taste perfectly.

The kitchen occupied one end, the dining room and living room sat in the middle, and the two bedrooms and one bathroom occupied the other end. Glass trimmed in dark khaki paint comprised almost the entire front of the flat-roofed structure. The effect of the whole was very much that of a building striving to live in harmony with nature.

She'd hired workers to refinish the floors and install white stone countertops in the kitchen and bath. Together, she and Dylan had replaced the kitchen's knobs and pulls. They'd repainted the walls that had been painted originally and left natural the surfaces that had been natural from the start.

When they'd filled the space with her collection of simple, 1950s-inspired furniture, everything had fit as if the house had been made specifically for them.

She let herself inside. "How's the homework coming?" she called in the direction of Dylan's lair.

Ominous silence. Four years ago, one of her former students had committed suicide at the age of seventeen, the age that Dylan was now. That event had scarred her, and she'd been irrationally anxious about suicide, and every other danger teenagers could embroil themselves in, ever since.

"Dylan?"

No answer.

"Dylan?"

Her steps turned in the direction of his bedroom. She knocked softly on his door. "Dylan?"

Still no answer.

She'd made sure his bedroom door had no lock for moments such as these. Letting herself inside, she spotted her brother seated at his desk, one arm folded on top of an open textbook, his head resting on his arm.

He'd fallen asleep.

She crept across his messy room, as she'd done countless times since she'd become his caregiver, to make sure his chest was rising and falling.

It was.

From this closer vantage point she could see that while he might be sleeping on his textbook, the thing he'd actually been working on was a drawing. Beneath his lax fingers, a detailed drawing of a Spartan warrior scowled up at her.

Difference number two hundred between herself and Dylan: He was talented at art.

With tenderness, she considered the contour of his cheek and the way his curly hair flopped toward the desktop. Then she tiptoed from the room, struck a match, and lit the three-wick Hawaiian beach candle resting on her coffee table. She changed out her four favorite candle fragrances with the seasons. This one smelled like ocean, pineapple, coconut, and sunshine.

The trio of flames danced.

On the phone a few minutes ago, Sebastian hadn't told her that he'd *attempt* to set up a meeting with the administrator of Magnolia Avenue Hospital. He'd informed her that he would set up a meeting.

Leah had come across plenty of students and adults during the past ten years of her career who'd talked big and made confident claims, then utterly failed at following through. But Sebastian's focused demeanor the day of the farmers market and his unhesitating manner over the phone just now gave her reason to believe that he'd find a way to do what he said he'd do.

CHAPTER FOUR

Sebastian did indeed follow through.

He'd texted Leah to ask if the day and time of the appointment he'd scheduled with the hospital administrator would work for her. When she'd said that it would, he'd suggested they meet immediately beforehand at Magnolia Perk, the hospital's first-floor coffee shop.

Leah had concurred.

Her phone had predicted that it would take her one hour and thirty-eight minutes to drive from her house to Magnolia Avenue Hospital. Doused in mistrust in response to that estimate, she'd left herself a huge cushion of time and arrived twenty-seven minutes ahead of their eleven o'clock meeting. The sun had wrestled with grumbling gray clouds during her drive, but as she gazed out through the hospital's foyer windows, she noted that it was now, strangely, both bright and drizzly.

She sat at one of the coffee shop's square two-seater tables, absently drinking the chai tea latte she'd ordered. End of semester finals had concluded the day before last. Yesterday had been a teacher workday. And today was the momentous first day of her summer break. However, vacation ease had yet to arrive because she'd been too busy girding herself mentally for today's potentially confrontational interaction with the hospital.

Sebastian Grant strode into view, walking purposefully from the parking lot toward the entrance doors, looking for all the world like a man unfettered by anyone else's opinion of him.

She checked her watch. He was twenty minutes early.

He wore his dark hair cut short and stylishly. His white dress shirt was tucked into an exquisite pair of charcoal suit pants. Black wingtips and a simple black belt completed the look.

Based on his attire, he'd obviously made time in his workday to meet her here. Hopefully no babies with congenital heart defects were having to wait on him while he assisted her with this non-life-threatening pursuit.

He entered, his chin swinging in the direction of Magnolia Perk. She lifted a hand in greeting. He closed the distance, his charisma imposing.

She'd made the right choice when she'd opted to dress up for their appointment in a collared white blouse marked with rows of tiny purple and blue dots, a pencil skirt, and her best pair of heels.

He took the seat opposite hers, instantly dwarfing the table. "Hi."

"Hello."

His gaze was intent but not cold. In fact, it warmed her because it communicated resolution. Sturdiness.

"Would you like something from the coffee shop?" she asked. "My treat."

"Thank you, but no. I'm fine." He continued to study her. "How are you?"

"I'm well. I'll be better and better over the coming days, now that the school year's ended. That takes a lot off my plate."

"Ben tells me you're a math genius."

She laughed at the unexpectedness of his statement.

"I was mediocre at math," he said.

"I strongly doubt that you were mediocre at anything. Ben tells me that you're a medical genius."

"That's debatable."

"Harvard Medical School," she said. "A fellowship at Duke University. Another fellowship at Boston Children's Hospital. Then a job at Beckett Memorial here in Atlanta."

"You've studied me?" he asked.

"I didn't become a math genius by shirking homework."

He chuckled. "So you admit that you're a math genius."

"That's debatable."

"You graduated from the Program for the Exceptionally Gifted at Clemmons. Received a PhD offer to Princeton. Achieved a master's degree."

"I assume you know that I declined the offer to Princeton?"

"I do, but I'm not sure I understand why. Didn't they offer you a stipend?"

Her lips curved with amusement. "Some people might find that question to be nosy."

"Do you find it to be nosy?"

"As it happens, no. The elaborate dance of social niceties is confusing to me. Not to mention, a waste of time. I appreciate it when people speak to me very directly."

"So do I."

"To answer your question, I was offered a stipend. But even if I could have supported my brother and myself on that amount and figured out a way to squeeze my studies around the priority of raising Dylan, I couldn't have ripped him away from his home, his therapist, his school, and his friends in order to drag him halfway across the country. He was traumatized enough as it was after my mom left."

"Do you still plan to get your PhD?"

"Yes. I've dreamed of becoming a university professor since I was seven years old."

"Have you started coursework?"

"Not yet. Years ago, I decided to postpone additional graduate work until after Dylan goes to college." She inclined her head toward Sebastian. "You certainly didn't postpone any of your graduate work. You became a full-fledged surgeon a year ago at the age of thirty-one."

"Yes."

"Even though most doctors don't become pediatric heart surgeons until thirty-five or thirty-six."

"Yes."

"How many surgeries have you performed in the past year?"

"Three hundred and thirteen. I don't receive as many referrals as the others, but I'm on call more than they are. I take all the patients that come in during my on-call hours."

"How many of those three hundred and thirteen survived?"

"All but five."

She couldn't fathom carrying five deceased children around on her conscience. Yet he'd saved three hundred and eight. "That equals a mortality rate of approximately one and a half percent." She made a mental note to research the topic further, but she guessed that a one and a half percent mortality rate for a first-year congenital heart surgeon who operated on very sick, very young patients was excellent. "How many of those didn't make it because of a physiological problem beyond your control?"

"Three. The other two had postoperative issues, potentially related to how long they were on the pump. Still, I take responsibility for those two because there may have been a technical issue with my work."

Somehow, she doubted it. She sipped her chai tea and tasted cinnamon, cloves, nutmeg. "The homework you did on me makes me sound very dull. I feel compelled to mention that I'm more interesting and well-rounded than I sound on paper."

"Oh?" Humor flavored the sound. "How so?"

"I love hiking and planning road trips on a shoestring budget. I occasionally compete in chess tournaments for fun. I'm rebellious because my teachers used to warn me that I needed to learn to do math in my head because I wouldn't be able to carry a calculator around with me once I became an adult." She reached into her purse and lifted her graphing calculator just high enough for him to see before dropping it back into the confines and straightening. "Joke's on them. Now you go."

"I watch soccer and movies. I'm a fan of anything related to aviation. I spend a lot of my free time with the Coleman family. I'm excellent at killing houseplants. I like to mow my lawn, and I listen to Sinatra because, obviously, he produced the best music ever."

The entire conversation was taking place at a very fast pace, akin to a ball being walloped back and forth across a tennis court. "Interesting assertion," she said. "I contend that the 1980s produced the best music ever."

"Wrong."

"Musical preferences are a matter of taste, Sebastian. One genre's superiority over another cannot be proved."

He shifted in his chair, setting a forearm on the table. His surgeon's hands were large with short, clean nails and blunt fingertips. Even though relaxed, his fingers communicated proficiency.

After a long moment, he spoke. "You asked me over the phone if I'd keep your information confidential. I told you I would. Now I'm wondering if you'll keep what I'm about to say confidential."

"Of course."

"Because this will get me in trouble with Ben if he finds out." She angled her head. "Oh?"

"He'd like to go out with you."

Her eyebrows steepled.

"I want to put in a good word for him," he continued. "He's like a brother to me . . . one of the best people I know."

She held herself still even though she was flailing around like a drowning swimmer on the inside. "Ben wants to go out with me?"

"Yes."

"Ben is romantically interested in me?"

"Yes. You didn't know?"

"No. I . . . don't always pick up on undercurrents that other people understand intuitively."

"Ah."

"I happen to agree with your assessment of Ben. He's an outstanding person. Stellar."

"He really is. Will you consider giving him a chance?"

She looked him straight in the eyes. "No."

"No?"

"Nothing against Ben, but I have no interest in dating anyone. I don't do romance."

"You don't do romance?" he repeated.

"No. I've never aspired to a dating relationship and certainly not to marriage."

"Can we back this train up?" He pondered her the way he might ponder a complex X-ray. "Why don't you do romance?"

"In order to explain, I'll have to back this train *way* up. All the way to my childhood."

"I'm listening."

"You're really interested in this?"

"I promise you that I am. You told me you prefer for people to speak directly. You can trust me to do just that."

"Well . . ." She sniffed, then rested her hands in her lap. "When all the other little girls were drawing pictures of families, with mothers and fathers and children, I was drawing pictures of myself surrounded by math equations. I know that most people envision romantic relationships as part of their future, but I never did."

"Why is that?"

"Several reasons. The first was environmental."

"Explain."

"My parents' marriage was . . . deplorable. It in no way sweetened me toward the institution."

"Understandable."

On top of that, during her middle school years, no boy had displayed a shred of romantic interest in her. Back then, not only had she been socially awkward, she'd also worn glasses and possessed a nose that was too large for her face. "I attended an all-girls school, which was glorious because, for the first time, I was surrounded by friends with whom I had much in common. There were no boys present, however, so I certainly wasn't tempted to try dating during my teenage years."

The peaceful environment at Clemmons had poured Miracle-Gro on her confidence. There, her roommate had invited Leah to church and Leah had, for the first time, met God. She'd placed her faith in

Him. In response, the unconditional love she'd spent her life craving had poured through her. God's grace had revolutionized her soul.

"And after you graduated from Clemmons?" he asked.

"Almost all the men I met were coworkers, and I was too young for them." It had come as a great surprise to her when a few of her colleagues had asked her out. By then, she'd traded her glasses for contacts. Her other features had grown so that her nose had come into proportion. She'd entrusted herself to a skilled hair stylist and learned how to shop for clothing that complemented her. While it had been pleasant to discover that she no longer repelled men, that revelation had not converted to real-world application. "Besides, Dylan consumed my time. Whatever was left went to my master's program." She shrugged. "I seem to be missing the attraction gene."

"What do you mean?"

"All the women I know swoon with attraction over men. I do not."

Except . . . just as the words *I do not* left her mouth, she did experience a bout of physical attraction. A very real, warm tug of longing in response to Sebastian Grant.

Chills of delight—or maybe horror—slid along her arms.

Confound it!

What in the world was happening?

This felt like a pleasurable menstrual cramp even though the relationship between *cramp* and *pleasurable* was a non sequitur.

"I see," he said.

A blush glided up her cheeks. She neutralized it by drawing in air and common sense. Romance and marriage were not for her. The sentimentality of it all! The bad choices, the weakness, the flawed thinking that women in love displayed!

She had God, and years ago she'd resolved that He was quite enough, thank you very much. Ever since, she'd worn her counter-cultural disinterest in a spouse like a badge of honor. "Number theory thrills me, but romance does not. I've found contentment in my long-standing relationship with Han Solo."

"You're a Han Solo fan?"

"Very much so." She woke her phone to show him the Han Solo photo she'd set as her background image.

"Your name is Leah, so how could you not like him?"

"Naturally. Princess Leia and I don't spell or pronounce our name the same way, but we both have a weakness for scoundrels." She angled the phone back toward herself and saw that just five minutes remained before their meeting. "Shall we?" She gestured toward the bank of elevators.

He nodded.

She tossed her cup in the trash as they crossed the lobby.

Once inside the elevator with an old man and young woman in scrubs, Sebastian punched eight and up they went.

"Han Solo is clearly the best character in the Star Wars galaxy," Sebastian commented.

"Clearly."

"Luke was too wholesome."

"Too wholesome," she agreed.

They exited on their floor and entered a suite of offices. The receptionist invited them to sit and informed them that Donna McKelvey, hospital administrator, would be with them shortly.

They sat.

Despite the high stakes of the coming meeting, Leah found it difficult to focus her thoughts on anything other than Sebastian's nearness. Muscle laced his frame. She caught an intriguing whiff of cedar and citrus-scented soap. "Will you communicate my position on romance to Ben?" she asked, her voice pitched low.

"I don't know how I can without revealing that I've talked to you about your dating life."

"An excellent point. However, I would hate for him to put his dating life on hold on my account, seeing as how I'm not a viable option."

"I think you should explain your position to him."

"Without provocation? He's never asked me out. It would read as presumptuous, would it not, if I suddenly announced my dating policy to him, absent of cause?"

"Have you considered the possibility, Leah, that you simply haven't dated the right man yet?"

"Ms. Montgomery and Dr. Grant?" the receptionist said.

They rose, and the woman led them to Donna McKelvey's corner office, which was no doubt the envy of her co-workers. The sky backlit her tall leather desk chair like a sunrise behind a throne.

Donna greeted them with firm handshakes. She wore a suit jacket, a red silk top, and a scarf patterned with red, white, yellow, and orange. Likely in her mid- to late-fifties, Donna had a stocky build, a pleasantly angular face, and a dark blond power bob. Had she been auditioning for the role of First Lady, Leah would have cast her at once.

They started with small talk, during which Donna interacted with Sebastian in a way that indicated that she'd like, very much, to poach him from Beckett Memorial.

Sebastian cut to the heart of the matter once they took their seats. "We scheduled this meeting today," he told Donna, "because Leah was born here."

The older woman turned an expectant look on Leah.

"I recently submitted my DNA for testing in order to gain insight into my genealogy," Leah explained. "I learned that I'm not the biological daughter of either of my parents. I think that I was switched at birth here twenty-eight years ago."

Donna's smile slipped.

"Here's the data I collected." Leah removed a large envelope from her purse. Inside, she'd placed copies of all the relevant documents and DNA tests. She set the envelope on Donna's desk.

"Occasionally, adoptive parents don't inform their children that they're adopted," Donna said.

"That may be, but that's not what happened in my situation," Leah replied. "I called my mother after receiving the DNA test results. She's always believed me to be her biological daughter. She was so certain the test was faulty that she encouraged me to take it again. Which I did. And now I'm here."

Donna probably hadn't been affiliated with this hospital at the time of Leah's birth, so the fact that Leah had been given to the Montgomery family couldn't reflect poorly on Donna personally. Yet it could reflect very poorly on the hospital as a whole—of which Donna was now the head.

"As you'll see, my birth certificate shows that I was born to Erica and Todd Montgomery, the two people who raised me." She relayed the events surrounding her mom's labor and delivery.

Donna extracted the documents from the envelope and examined them. "Nowadays we take extreme precautions to make sure that this doesn't happen."

Donna's statement implied that at the time of Leah's birth, precautions may not have been quite so extreme.

Sebastian remained silent, intensity flowing from him.

As soon as Donna set down the papers, Leah spoke. "I'd like access to the hospital records concerning my birth. Are those records still in existence?"

"They are."

Relief relaxed Leah's spine.

"We keep old records off-site with a data management company," Donna said. "We'll simply need for you to fill out a records request form and for your mother to sign a waiver. A few days later we can have them here for you. You're welcome to look at the original documents. Or we can provide print copies or copies in an electronic format."

"I'd also like to examine the records of the other baby girls born on my birthday so that I can figure out who my biological parents are."

Donna mounded her hands on top of her desk—a relaxed posture. However, white rimmed the edges of her fingertips, which informed Leah that her hands were exerting pressure. "That, I cannot do. You'll understand that our patients' records are kept in strictest privacy."

"Of course," Sebastian replied smoothly. "And you'll understand that in sending two children home with the wrong parents, a negligent act was committed. If we return with a court order granting us access to the records, will you allow us to view them?"

"Should you return with a court order, I'll be more than glad to cooperate with you as fully as the law permits." Her attention settled on Leah. "However, it's extremely unlikely that a judge will release the records of every baby girl born on your birthday. HIPAA laws are stringent. Almost certainly, you'll have to show the judge why you believe yourself to be the biological daughter of, for example, John and Jane Doe. If you make a compelling case, the judge may release to you the records of only Baby Girl Doe, born here on your birth date."

"I see." Leah possessed a single clue regarding the identity of her birth parents: the list of DNA matches YourHeritage had provided. If she did some detective work on the site using the family trees her biological relations had made public, adding logic and a process of elimination . . . she might be able to deduce her parents' surname.

"I'm very sorry that this happened to you," Donna said. "I can only imagine how upsetting this has been."

"Thank you." She pegged Donna as smart, principled, decent. Whether those qualities would prove true remained to be seen.

What didn't remain to be seen? Sebastian's status as a powerful ally. He was more than a match for Donna, or, she'd guess, just about anyone. His hands were laced together in his lap. But no telltale white pressure marks marred his fingertips.

It was dark by the time Sebastian returned home that night. Starving, he stuck the premade dinner his meal service had left for him into the microwave, then stared at the light behind the appliance's see-through door.

Like a tugboat, his mind pulled him to Leah.

He'd been starstruck, sitting across the table from her this morning. He wasn't someone who got starstruck. But he couldn't think of a better word to describe the effect she had on him.

He suspected that she was the smartest person he'd ever met in his life, and he wasn't exactly an academic slouch. Nor were his medical school classmates and teachers.

He'd found himself wishing he could get a glimpse of what was going on inside her head. In *The Matrix*, the characters had been able to download knowledge directly into their brains. That's what he'd like to do with Leah . . . hook a cable from her head to his so he could import even a portion of what she knew.

He sensed she had more intelligence, more integrity, more optimism, and more compassion than he did. However, she was also crazier than he was if she believed that dating and romance weren't for her.

He'd bet a million dollars that, with the right person, she could experience physical attraction as powerfully as any other woman. Maybe with him, she could—

That is, with Ben. Maybe *with Ben* she could.

The microwave dinged, and he opened the door to find that it contained nothing. No dinner.

What had he done with his food? It wasn't sitting on any of the counters. He opened the refrigerator. Not there. Not in the freezer, either. He pulled back the pantry door and spotted it.

Instead of warming his meal as he'd intended, he'd been so distracted by Leah that he'd put it in the pantry.

Great, Sebastian. Really sharp. He sighed irritably and placed it in the microwave.

He'd guess Leah's nerdiness had been obvious when she was younger. These days, only a shadow of it remained. He'd seen it in the candid, old-fashioned way she spoke. The way she tipped her chin up, just a little, when thinking. The way she moved her hands.

She might be a professor at heart, but she resembled a pin-up girl on the outside.

He'd been frozen in place by her striking eyes. Her hair looked like she'd ridden in a convertible with the top down, then combed her fingers through it—a style so casual that it contrasted with her very tidy clothing. There hadn't been a single wrinkle in her shirt or skirt, and both had been modest . . . so much so they were almost fussy. Yet, strangely, he found her clothes just as sexy as her hair.

After they'd left Donna McKelvey's office, they'd stopped at a different area of the hospital so that Leah could fill out record request forms and receive a waiver to forward to her mother.

When she'd informed him that she planned to contact an attorney in Misty River about pursuing a court order, his body had bristled. No way could he stand to the side and watch an attorney gouge Leah's bank account. Especially because he didn't feel he'd repaid his debt to her in full.

He'd said that his attorney friend Jenna owed him a favor. The technically true part of that was that he had an attorney named Jenna. He'd told Leah that Jenna would reach out to her soon and asked Leah to include him when she returned to the hospital. As good as Jenna was, he was the only one of the three of them who had experience with hospital administrators.

The microwave finished, and he peeled back the container's packaging. Italian meatballs and marinara sauce over zucchini noodles. He carried the steaming food to his living room and filled his big screen with a replay of the Manchester United versus Liverpool soccer match from last season. Leaning back, he crossed his feet on the coffee table.

His apartment looked and felt like the sort of place that would go for top dollar on Airbnb. He'd hired a friend of a friend of a friend to design it for him, and she'd done a good job. The modern pieces of furniture worked fine. The building was new. He had a sixth-floor view of downtown and could walk to the hospital from here.

Even so, he didn't like the apartment much. Nothing about it was personal.

He only felt at home in two places. Ben's family's house and his own house in Misty River.

Ben.

He frowned while chewing, the light of the TV screen glowing on his face. He'd texted Ben days ago to let him know he was helping Leah with issues of hospital bureaucracy. He'd texted Ben again today to say that the hospital meeting had gone well and that at least one follow-up meeting would be needed to secure the information she wanted.

Ben had answered with a brief thanks both times. Since the farmers market, Sebastian had seen Ben once, when they'd gone to a Braves game. There'd been a slight unspoken strain between them. Ben, who usually talked about Leah a lot, hadn't mentioned her that day. Neither had Sebastian. They'd both had to work a little too hard to make things between them seem normal.

Sebastian would travel to Misty River a week from today for Ben's parents' fortieth anniversary dinner. He'd get their friendship back on track then. If he wasn't going to date Leah, and he wasn't, then the trade-off had to be a good relationship with Ben.

Watch soccer, idiot.

Sebastian liked things done a certain way. He didn't get embarrassed, and he wasn't afraid to anger people when necessary. He was persistent. Stubborn.

Ben liked to ask him dryly if there was anything on earth Sebastian didn't have an opinion about. The answer was no. He had strong feelings toward everything.

Ice cream flavor? Cookies and cream.

Sport? Soccer.

Indoor temperature? Seventy-two in the summer, sixty-eight in the winter.

Practicing medicine? Nothing but excellence would do.

Problem was, he could feel all his persistence and stubbornness and strong feelings funneling in one direction.

Toward Leah Montgomery.

His ability to focus, usually an asset, was becoming a flaw.

His phone's pager system went off. Squinting, he checked his secure messages.

A baby with blockage in all four pulmonary veins had just been delivered, and he was needed immediately.

CHAPTER FIVE

Excuse me?" Mom squawked over the phone four days later. She'd finally called Leah from Guinea to inquire after the second DNA test.

"I'm not your biological daughter," Leah repeated calmly. It was late on a Tuesday night. Dylan was sleeping over at a friend's house, and Leah had paused *Return of the Jedi* to answer her phone. Beyond the walls of her house, the heavy darkness of the mountains reigned.

"Yes you are, Leah. You're my biological daughter."

"No, it turns out that I'm not. Which doesn't have to change anything between us."

Mom continued as if she hadn't spoken. "They placed you in my arms in the hospital."

"Yes, but you were unconscious for my delivery, so you didn't see the face of your baby. There's no telling what happened between the time you delivered your daughter and the moment they brought me to you. The only thing that's certain, at this point, is that I'm not the baby girl you gave birth to."

She'd been researching switched-at-birth cases. It was both mind-boggling and fascinating to read about people who'd been stowaways in families not their own. In every case, the children who were switched were of the same gender. They were born at the same place on the same day, often within minutes of each other. Sometimes their mothers shared the same first name.

When a person went public with their switched-at-birth story, attention covered them like a rain shower. Because of that, it seemed to Leah that those who discovered they'd been switched at birth later in life—well after they'd made their way in the world and established families of their own—weathered the storm best.

Which confirmed her initial decision not to tell Dylan, or anyone other than her mother and Sebastian, what she'd uncovered. Leah didn't aspire to be a whistle-blower. Didn't want money from the hospital via a court settlement. Didn't plan to crusade for hospital reforms. She simply wanted to know who her biological parents were and—if possible—to understand how this had occurred.

As she'd read article after article, she'd wondered just how many people who'd discovered they'd been switched at birth had chosen the path she'd chosen and decided to remain silent. A fair number, possibly.

"That's crazy," Mom stated. "Those results are wrong."

"Choosing denial?" Leah asked mildly.

"YourHeritage probably didn't even bother to run the second sample you sent. I bet they just gave you the same answers as last time."

Hopefully, Mom would remain in a state of denial. If so, she wouldn't mount a search for her missing child. Which would make things easier for Leah.

"You haven't told Dylan, have you?" Mom asked.

"No."

"Good! Don't tell him. It will just rile him up."

"I agree." Leah was momentarily disoriented. Were she and Mom actually in agreement?

"And there's no sense getting him riled up over something that's not even legitimate. You are my daughter."

"I'm not going to tell Dylan. Will you please sign the waiver that I faxed to you?"

"Why would I?"

"Because it means a lot to me and because I'm asking nicely."

After a taut moment, Mom said, "Fine."

"Thank you."

"Have you been feeding Dylan enough kale, Leah? And also chia seeds? Chia seeds provide fiber, and you both need lots of fiber in your diet."

Leah bit her tongue, as she always did, in response to Mom's random parenting suggestions. When Mom had chased her ambitions overseas, she'd both forfeited her right to parent and removed much of Leah's ability to control her own life.

Leah had responded by dedicating herself to controlling what little remained—her well-being and Dylan's well-being. Leah was the one who supported Dylan, who stocked the pantry, bought his clothes, paid for his phone and car insurance. Leah was the one who made sure he went to the doctor and did his homework and cleaned his room and avoided parties with kegs.

Because of her ingrained responsibility for her brother, every dream she'd had since taking over his care had been an anxiety dream. Her struggling to get Dylan out in time while their house burned. Her failing to watch him carefully as he stumbled into the street in front of a speeding car. Her losing Dylan in a crowd. Her remembering suddenly that Dylan lived in the bedroom next to hers and realizing that he must have starved because she hadn't fed him anything in weeks.

Thus, if anyone had the final say on kale and chia seeds . . . it wasn't Mom.

It was her.

The Coleman family barbecue sauce recipe was an old and closely protected secret. Very dark in color, it tasted like Georgia: southern and spicy with sweetness underneath. The smell of that sauce swamped Sebastian when he stepped out of his car into evening sunshine the night of the anniversary party for Ben's parents.

Ben was the third of four kids. His siblings were married and had already given him four nephews and two nieces. The Colemans also had a large extended family and a huge circle of friends. All of whom had big appetites.

Since Ben's dad, Herschel, owned only one barbecue, he'd no doubt gained the cooperation of several neighbors, and was cooking ribs and chicken on multiple grills at once.

Sebastian started toward the party, past all the cars that had forced him to park a block away. He carried a gift under one arm like a football, even though the invitation had specified no gifts. He'd never had an easy time following rules he didn't personally agree with.

Atlanta weather was humid in the summer. But not here, thanks to Misty River's altitude. Cool mountain breezes tugged away some of the stress of his workweek.

The Colemans' house had been built in the late sixties in a style that reminded him of the *Brady Bunch* house. Roomy, with a retro rock fireplace, it had a stairway made of wooden slats that led upstairs from the front door. Because the house was located at the end of a cul-de-sac, the backyard widened from the porch like a pie slice, expanding out into undeveloped land.

Based on previous cookout experiences, he knew it would be loud and crowded inside, so he let himself through the side gate into the backyard. The sound of conversations increased as he neared.

CeCe, Ben's mom, would kill him if he showed up in scrubs, so he'd brought a change of clothes with him to work that morning. His jeans were in good shape, but the car ride had creased the light blue dress shirt he wore untucked.

People he didn't know were playing cornhole beneath the big sweetgum tree at the far edge of the lawn that had once supported a tree house. When he'd first started coming here, he and Ben had been thirteen. They'd been too old to play in tree houses, but Sebastian had still used it as an escape whenever he'd needed a break from all the talking, eating, and cleaning inside the house.

He'd grab his homework or one of the books he'd checked out from the library, and climb the wooden rectangles hammered into the trunk. Through an opening in the floor, he'd enter the simple square box with no roof.

He remembered sitting on the tree house floor in hot weather and in cold, when the space had seemed large for his frame and after it had become small. The branches provided privacy. Spider webs stretched across the corners, and twigs and leaves littered the floor. The wood had been old and rough, quick to give splinters.

The final time he'd visited the tree house, he'd been seventeen and had almost reached his full height. When he'd pulled himself up into it, the entire thing had creaked and threatened to collapse.

He'd sat very still, his weight evenly distributed, reading a textbook. He'd been in a relatively good place in his life. He'd been on his way to achieving his goals. He had the Colemans. Yet on that day, his eyes had stung with sorrow, because he'd known that trip to the tree house would be his last.

He wasn't a crier. During his childhood there were many times when crying would've been the healthiest response. But on those occasions, his eyes had remained dry and his heart had been cold as stone.

On his next visit to the Colemans, every piece of the tree house had been gone. The only sign that it had been there was the damaged bark where the steps had been. The loss had hit him like a blow.

He threaded his way through the guests, nodding to people he knew, making his way onto the deck.

He found Ben's dad exactly where he'd known he'd be, in front of the barbecue, surrounded by friends.

"Sebastian," Hersh said with deep affection. The older man hugged him and bumped a fist against his back. "Love you, man."

Love you, man and *yeah* made up about half of Hersh's vocabulary. For decades he'd worked for a company that sold trucks to corporations. A big man with a bald oval head and a goatee, Hersh was so good-natured that smile lines permanently indented his face.

Hersh extended his tasting plate to Sebastian, who pulled off a crispy piece of rib meat. Sebastian chewed slowly. "Delicious."

"Good, right?"

"Better than good." Sebastian licked his fingers.

Hersh made a merry sound and snuck another taste for himself. "What's that you got there?" He indicated the present Sebastian carried.

"A gift for your wife that she'll probably like better than whatever you bought for her."

"Man, I booked a trip for the two of us to Mexico. There's no way your gift is better than that."

"You're right. It's not better than— "

"I believe I get to be the judge of that." CeCe had arrived. Short, plump, and opinionated, she made up in feistiness what she lacked in inches.

She'd combed her graying black hair tightly away from her face into a twist at the back of her neck. In the mid-2000s, she'd decided she had "springtime coloring" and since then had worn only pale purple clothing. Her features were plain. But when you spoke with her, nothing about her read as plain because of the force of her personality.

After the earthquake, Ben was the one who'd invited Sebastian over numerous times. CeCe was the one who'd insisted he become a part of their family. She'd been very firm on that, especially the times when they'd butted heads and he'd tried to pull away. Her own kids had never found a way to disobey her, and neither had Sebastian.

CeCe gave him a hug filled with the scent of a flower garden and the press of long, fancy fingernails. Then she clasped her hands on either side of his face, eyes narrowing as she studied him. "You're late," she said.

"Hi."

"You're late," she repeated, setting her hands on her round hips.

"I can't be late until the barbecue is served. Also, the invitation said this was a come-and-go thing from five until ten."

"Not for you! You're family, so you should've been here at 4:45 to help deal with me when I was having my pre-party hissy fit."

"As sorry as I am to have missed your pre-party hissy fit—"

She sucked air through her teeth.

"—I had to work. I got in the car and drove here as soon as I could. Also, I brought you a gift." He handed over the package. He'd convinced Markie to wrap it for him in gold paper with a big white bow.

After pulling free the wrapping paper, CeCe opened the box. Within lay a crystal wine glass.

"What!" she crowed. Her eyes rounded, and her lips formed a blazing smile. "It's my holy grail!" She lifted it from the box and held it up like a trophy.

Before their wedding, CeCe had registered for twelve Alana crystal goblets by Waterford. Several years ago, when washing goblets after a baby shower, one had slipped and shattered. The Alana style was discontinued, and CeCe had been unable to purchase a replacement. She'd never gotten over it. Several times she'd complained loudly to Sebastian about having only eleven goblets. *An odd number! What on earth am I supposed to do with eleven goblets?*

"My holy grail!" she screeched again.

Sebastian grinned.

She whooped and danced in place while Hersh egged her on by clapping. "Where did you find this?" she asked.

"A website that brokers hard-to-find pieces of glassware. The Alana is a hot commodity. I set up an alert and asked to be notified whenever one became available. Even so, other buyers beat me to it the first five times."

"You were at a disadvantage because you're nowhere near your phone when you're in surgery," she said.

"Yeah," Hersh murmured.

"This goblet became available at two a.m. a few weeks back, and it was immediately mine."

"Immediately *mine*, you mean." She held it against her heart. "Thank you, sweetie."

"Love you, man." Hersh patted him on the shoulder.

"You do know that this goblet isn't going to get you out of the post-party cleanup chores, right?" CeCe asked.

"Right."

"Hersh and I are going to be dog tired after all this, so we'll be putting our feet up. We had kids and grandkids so we wouldn't have to handle cleanup." She bobbed her head toward the far side of the deck. "Did you see Ben? He invited that blond teacher he likes."

Within Sebastian, something fundamental went completely still.

"When she showed up a few minutes ago," Hersh commented, "he about wet his pants."

Sebastian steeled himself and looked. Leah was talking with Ben. She wore a green cardigan over a blue-and-white sundress, which had a wide skirt that ended at her knees. The sight impacted him like a defensive tackle. He couldn't think of anything to say.

He wished he'd had some warning. Ben hadn't told him he'd invited Leah.

"Go see if you can help him out with her," CeCe suggested.

"Okay."

"Well." She made a shooing motion. "Go on, then."

"Happy anniversary."

"Sure. Now go on."

He moved in Ben's direction as CeCe turned toward the interior of the house. He heard her yell, "My holy grail!" to her sister.

Ben's older brother stopped Sebastian with a question about health insurance deductibles.

An aunt asked him who he was dating these days.

Finally, he approached Ben and Leah. Ben was smiling like it was winter and Leah was sunshine.

She stopped speaking mid-sentence as he drew near. "Sebastian," she said warmly.

"Hey."

Ben hugged him.

"I'm glad you came tonight," Sebastian said to Leah. "Ben's parents are great."

"Don't let them catch you calling them my parents," Ben said. "Mom will hit the roof since she wants you to view them as your parents, too."

"I'm fresh out of parents," Leah said. "Can they be my parents?"

Ben's face brightened. The comment could be taken to mean that she'd like Herschel and CeCe as her mother- and father-in-law. "Done!"

Leah looked pleased and so pretty that Sebastian forced down a swallow.

"We were discussing our summer plans when you walked over," Leah told him.

"I know about Ben's family trip to Florida," Sebastian said, "because I'm joining them for part of that one."

"We're the unmarried uncles." Ben swung his thumb back and forth between them. "Which means we're the two adults who spend the most time playing with the kids."

"Playing how?" she asked.

"They like to throw wet sand," Ben answered, "and build sandcastles on the beach and go boogie boarding. For some reason, they also like us to get down on all fours so they can ride around on our backs and have sword fights with pool noodles."

"They call that fighting horses." Sebastian felt obligated to talk Ben up in front of Leah. "Ben's better at all of it than I am." He considered himself to be a decent uncle, but objectively, Ben *was* better. Ben would play those games with the kids for hours. Sebastian's patience was limited, and he'd rather read a book with a kid than carry one around on all fours. . . .

As if thinking about the kids had called one to him, Hadley Jane, Ben's three-year-old niece, ran in Sebastian's direction with her arms lifted up.

He scooped her into the air and positioned her on his hip.

"Sebastian!" she sang, wrapping the hair at the back of his neck around one of her small fingers.

Until he'd had kids in his life to love, until he'd watched a child grow from an infant to a toddler to an elementary schooler, he hadn't fully grasped what a child's life was worth. Now he did, because of the Coleman grandkids. Which had made him a better doctor.

Hadley Jane shot Leah a look that said she believed Leah had come to the party as either a kidnapper or a burglar.

"Have you met Hadley Jane?" Sebastian asked Leah.

"I haven't."

"This is Miss Montgomery," Sebastian said to the little girl.

"How do you do," Hadley Jane said.

Ben chuckled with a fist in front of his mouth. "Who taught you that?"

She shrugged slyly.

"Your brother did," Sebastian told Ben. Then, to Hadley Jane, "Miss Montgomery was about to tell us about her summer plans."

"I'm taking my brother on a road trip to New England," Leah told him. "We'll be gone three weeks."

"Where are you staying?" Sebastian asked.

"RV parks. I'm renting a twenty-three-foot Airstream trailer. It has a bedroom for me, and a dinette that converts into a bed for Dylan."

"You're going to haul an Airstream to New England and back?" Sebastian asked. That didn't sound safe.

Hadley Jane pushed her lips to the side skeptically.

"I am. It'll be a first," Leah admitted. "We go on trips every summer, but in the past we've stayed in a tent."

"You've pulled an RV before," Sebastian said to Ben.

"Yep."

"You could give her some pointers."

"Definitely."

"If you decide you enjoy the trailer," Sebastian said to Leah, "you two should organize a group camping weekend this fall."

"I'd like that. Who could we invite to join us?" Leah asked Ben. "Definitely Connor."

"Did I hear my name?" Connor asked. He'd been standing a few groups away and now made his way toward them.

Sebastian had met Connor, the art teacher at Misty River High, a couple of times before. He was the type of handsome that women liked. Tall. In his late twenties. Red hair and beard. He had a relaxed, reasonable personality that made him easy to talk to.

"You remember Sebastian?" Ben asked Connor.

"I do. Good to see you again."

"Good to see you, too." They shook hands.

"Ben and I were discussing the possibility of a camping weekend this fall," Leah said to Connor.

"I'm down for a camping trip anytime," Connor replied.

Talk of camping led them to talk of the adventure races Connor participated in. Ben asked him about the wilderness navigation involved, and Connor explained the basics.

Hadley Jane squirmed, so Sebastian set her on her feet. She ran off.

He was left alone with the three teachers, who seemed very happy together. Sebastian stood there, stiff, jealous, and unnecessary.

During a break in the conversation, Leah and Connor stepped to the outdoor table for appetizers.

Ben leaned toward Sebastian. "Stop it," he said under his breath.

"I'm trying to help you out with her."

"I got this. I don't need you to help me out."

Shame needled Sebastian. Ben didn't know it, but he'd already tried to help him out when he'd told Leah about Ben's feelings for her. Ben wouldn't approve of his actions, which had made Sebastian wonder, after the fact, if it had been a mistake to take matters into his own hands and try to set Leah up with Ben. Part of him felt badly about telling Leah Ben's secret. But most of him believed he'd done the right thing. Ben had liked her for almost two years, and Leah had had *no* idea. How was she supposed to warm up to the idea of dating Ben if she didn't even know he wanted to date her? "This courtship is coming around more slowly than the World Cup," Sebastian grumbled.

"Some things are worth the wait."

"Like puberty? When do you think that's finally going to come around for you?"

As Sebastian had known he would, Ben broke into laughter.

Leah returned carrying a paper plate of food. She and Ben discussed the new superintendent.

Since Ben knew him better than anyone, Sebastian was having to work to pretend he had no more than a casual interest in Leah. Inside, though, he felt something far, far stronger. He was arrested by her.

Though he was doing and saying the right things to help Ben's cause with Leah, he hated the thought of them as a couple. His brain was shouting *No!* to the possibility of a romance between them—even though the correct answer was *yes*. Leah could not do better than Ben. Ben was the best uncle, and Ben would also be the best boyfriend.

And yet, *no*.

Yes.

Everything in him was demanding that he tear down heaven and earth to make Leah his.

What am I going to do? he wondered with the urgency of someone trying to escape a claustrophobic room.

He wasn't going to do anything. Except treat her in the polite way he'd treated the women Ben had dated in the past.

Ben's clueless uncle Eugene hooked an arm around Ben's neck. The Colemans urged Eugene to play his saxophone at almost every gathering—funerals, weddings, birthday parties—despite the fact that he lacked talent. No doubt he'd perform an anniversary number later. "We're arguing over which restaurant in Misty River makes the best biscuits," Eugene said to Ben, dragging him away. "I need you to come over here and talk sense into these people." He glanced at Sebastian and Leah. "Sorry, y'all. I'm going to borrow him for a bit."

Then Ben and Eugene were gone, and Leah's observant eyes flicked up to meet his.

He shuttered his expression, not wanting her to see too much.

"I spoke with your attorney a few days ago about obtaining a court order," she said. "She's excellent."

"Good. Will you keep me updated?"

"I will." She lifted a homemade potato chip from her plate. "Did you undertake any heart surgeries today, Dr. Grant?"

"Only one."

"I've been reading up on pediatric cardiac surgery since we talked last week."

"Have you?"

"I have."

Surgery disgusted most people. The rest were bored by technical details. Acquaintances usually asked him a few surface questions about his career and left it at that.

"What type of surgery did you perform today?" she asked.

"A biventricular repair."

"To address which condition?"

"A double-outlet right ventricle."

"Does that mean that both the aorta and the pulmonary artery were rising out of the right ventricle?"

He schooled his face so Ben wouldn't catch him smiling at her like he was impressed. "Yes."

"So the right ventricle was pumping blood through both outlets?"

"Correct. The left ventricle had no outlets, so it was shooting blood through a hole into the right ventricle."

"And you fixed it by . . . ?"

"Creating two functioning ventricles."

"Did your patient come through it well?"

"She came through it very well."

"So far today, I've slept late, hiked, cleaned my house, and forced my brother to go to summer school. So . . . your day wins."

He quirked an eyebrow. "That depends on how challenging it was to force your brother to go to summer school."

Her bluish-gray eyes glittered, which gave him a sharp stab of satisfaction. Her nearness was ripping away the space suit he

74

was trapped in, the one that dulled everything. She enabled him to feel things.

"What motivated you to become a doctor?" she asked.

"The white jackets, terrible hours, and the pay." He spoke the lie smoothly. "In that order."

The tips of her hair slipped against the sides of her delicate neck. Her bottom lip was fuller than her upper lip. Light caught in her little gold hoop earrings.

Pushing his hands into the pockets of his jeans, he made himself take a step back and dropped his attention to her appetizers. Raw vegetables, chips, and melon wrapped in prosciutto, pierced by a toothpick.

"I feel self-conscious eating in front of you," she announced. "Aren't you hungry?"

I am. For so many things. He shook his head.

"My melon's cut in such a way that it forms an almost perfect rhomboid. You have the self-control to pass up rhomboid melon?"

"I do."

"I do not." She took a bite and he groaned inwardly. "Did you grow up in Misty River?"

"I was born in Chicago. My mom brought me to Georgia when I was five."

"Was your dad in the picture?"

"No."

"Not ever?"

"No."

"What was your mom's name?"

"Denise."

"Why did Denise move you from Chicago to Georgia?"

He hated talking about his pre-Coleman childhood years, and yet he didn't want to say no to her. About anything. "The spring before I started kindergarten, my mom felt pressured to make a decision about our future. She didn't want to stay in Chicago, but she also didn't want to move me around a lot after I was in school.

She started looking for a new place to settle, where we could both be happy for a long period of time."

"Why did she choose Georgia?"

"She loved nature and wanted a warmer climate. She applied for work up and down the southern section of the Blue Ridge range and got a job here."

A bee buzzed close to Leah. Sebastian brushed it away.

"What did you think of Georgia when you arrived?"

He shrugged a shoulder. "I liked it. On her days off, we'd go to the lake or a river or a waterfall."

"What happened to her?"

A memory split into his head, and he saw his mother lying in front of him, with just days to live. When she'd gotten too sick to work, the two of them had moved into the apartment of the old lady next door, who'd been grumpy and, at the same time, soft-hearted enough to take them in. At first they'd shared her guest bedroom. But then, when Mom had worsened, hospice had placed a hospital-type bed in the old lady's living room for her to lie in.

For her to die in.

Every day he'd taken the bus home from school, then stood next to that bed. The apartment smelled faintly of cigarettes, even though the old lady had quit years before. A dark brown recliner and a sagging corduroy sofa were lit by two ugly matching lamps on end tables. The white porcelain lamps had been painted with orange and brown flowers, and Sebastian *hated* them and every single other thing about the lady's apartment and his mom's health and his life.

"Were you nice to your teacher today?" Mom had asked, looking right at him with sunken eyes.

"Yes."

She smiled affectionately. "No you weren't. Did you try your best?"

"Yes."

"No you didn't." Mom was still trying to tease him the way she always had. "I can tell that backpack you just set down is empty. You didn't bring any books or your homework home."

This ain't my home, he thought.

"How do you expect to pass second grade?" she asked. "By learning through osmosis?"

He didn't know what osmosis was. And he didn't care about passing second grade. His mother was skinny and pale and getting weaker every day. Gut-wrenching fear had consumed every inch of mental space he had.

Sebastian refocused on the present, on Leah. "Ben's told you my story, right?"

As personal as it felt to Sebastian, and as much as he wished he could protect it, his story was part of the public domain. Anyone who read the book or watched the movie about the Miracle Five could learn much more about him than he was comfortable with their knowing.

"I know that your mom died," she said. "But I don't know how."

"A terminal illness she'd had since childhood."

"I'm sorry. How old were you at the time?"

"Eight." He could lose himself in Leah. He *wanted* to lose himself in her. "I went into the foster care system."

"How many years after your mom died did you meet Ben?"

"Five."

"And the Colemans became your family."

"Yes." That was the simplest way to communicate a complex answer. As a rule, Sebastian didn't form attachments. One, he didn't like to rely on people. Two, he didn't want the fear and potential loss that came with loving people.

The Colemans were the only people he'd let in over the past twenty-four years. For them, his feelings ran deep, and his loyalty was unshakable. They were the closest thing to a family he had, but calling them his family made him feel like he was cheating his mom, his *actual* family member, of her due. Also, as much as he cared about the Colemans, he was always aware that he didn't fully belong with them.

He was the one Caucasian guy in a big African-American family. The one member who'd entered their group as a teenager, instead of being raised in their ranks. As successful as he'd become, he'd always be their charity case.

"I owe them a lot," he said.

Thoughtfully, she bit into a carrot.

He'd never forget the unselfish things the Colemans had done for him. Too many times to count, he'd entered Ben's room to find the family's army cot already made up for him. Camo sleeping bag. Down pillow covered in a clean white pillowcase.

They'd taken him with them in their van on trips. CeCe would bring a small cooler and pass back Capri-Suns and bags of pretzels during the long hours of driving.

They'd held parties for him when he'd graduated from high school, college, and med school. Each time, they'd stretched the same black-and-gold *Congratulations!* banner above a dining room table covered with his favorite dishes.

"How often do you come back to Misty River to see the Colemans?"

"As often as possible. I have an apartment in Atlanta, and I spend the nights there during the week, but my house is here. In fact, I was driving from the airport to my house the day of the car crash."

"Airport?"

"The regional one, outside Clayton."

"You have your pilot's license?"

"I do. I like to fly back and forth when I can."

"It seems I'm going to need to study aviation next, in order to keep up with you."

"You don't have to keep up with me."

"I think that I do." She beamed.

CeCe rang a metal triangle, as if calling ranch hands to the chuck wagon.

Sebastian hid his disappointment at the interruption. He wanted, but wasn't going to get, more time with Leah.

The noise outside immediately lessened. "Supper is served," CeCe announced. "I don't want any of you to dawdle because dawdling when the food is hot is one of my biggest pet peeves. If I see you doing it, I'll take this to your backside." She held up the metal rod she'd clanged against the triangle. "Make your way indoors, where we have two long tables set up with food. You can go down both sides of both tables. Understood?"

"Understood," the guests answered.

CeCe pulled Herschel forward, and he blessed the food.

Ben returned for Leah, and the two of them were separated from Sebastian by the crowd.

Once he'd filled his plate, Sebastian purposely avoided Ben and Leah's table and sat with Natasha and Genevieve. The sisters who'd been trapped belowground with him and Ben after the earthquake had become good friends. The two of them—plus Natasha's husband, Wyatt, and Genevieve's boyfriend, Sam—kept the conversation going so that Sebastian didn't have to contribute much.

He was facing away from where Leah was seated, but he kept catching snatches of her voice and, if he was very lucky, her laugh.

After dinner the guests mingled and ate cake. Whenever he looked toward Leah, he kept his line of sight moving past her so that no one could catch him staring. Even so, she distracted him so much that he kept losing track of what people were saying to him.

It was brutal to be with her in a crowd of Colemans because her presence reminded him that, while he might be successful and busy . . .

Essentially, he was also alone.

CHAPTER SIX

Conversing with Dylan was somewhat akin to lugging a big, heavy tree branch to a dumpster.

Two nights after the Colemans' anniversary party, Leah sat at her dining room table with her brother and Tess and Rudy Coventry, the couple who'd become their unofficial grandparents.

"How's your math class going?" Tess asked Dylan. He was taking precalculus this summer because he hadn't passed it last semester, despite having a built-in math tutor at home.

"Okay." Dylan's hair fell around his head more rakishly than usual. She suspected he'd donned his gray T-shirt after picking it up off the floor. Its neckline revealed his thin, pale clavicles.

Leah knew from his summer session teacher that he was doing a little less than okay. "When's your next quiz or test?"

"Thursday."

"You might want to start studying tonight."

He shrugged. The window behind Dylan framed him with color. On this warm, bright evening in June, wisps of cloud had snagged their hems on the peaks of her valley.

"Do you want to sit down and work on it with me after dinner, before you go to Jace's house?" she asked. His usual technique of procrastinating until the night before a test gave her hives.

"Maybe." Which meant no. He chewed a mouthful of pizza, well on his way to consuming his customary enormous quantity.

"Do elaborate, dear brother," Leah said grandly, "and tell us how we can become patrons of your math success." She'd learned that a teasing response to Dylan's sullenness drew him out more effectively than a serious one.

"Yes, Dylan," Tess said. "Please do tell how we can help." The older woman cut her bangs ruler-straight and allowed the rest of her pale gray hair to hang flat to her shoulders. The hazel eyes that tipped downward at the outer corners bracketed an imposing nose. She always wore a shade of lipstick called Frisky Peony and a pair of earrings that looked like miniature modern art sculptures—gold circles mounted inside larger silver circles. Her face radiated pragmatism.

In contrast, Rudy's face radiated sweetness. His ears were long, his glasses slightly askew. A rosy, healthy glow underlit his lined, age-spotted skin. Tess ensured that his white hair remained neatly trimmed. Nonetheless, it managed to look disordered, as did his clothing.

"This subject is boring," Dylan said.

"No, indeed," Leah countered. "We're all waiting with bated breath for you to tell us about your summer school math class, utilizing more than five words at a time."

"There's not a lot to talk about. I mean . . . I'm bad at math."

He'd said that to annoy her because he knew it rubbed her the wrong way. *No one* was bad at math. Many people didn't respond well to the way math was taught in school. But that did not mean they were bad at it. She hadn't responded well to the way basketball was taught in PE when she was growing up. But she didn't go around declaring herself bad at basketball.

"I understood math fine until it started using the alphabet," Dylan added.

Rudy chuckled. "Yes! What are A and B and X and Y doing in math problems?"

"Rudy," Tess said sternly. "Letters have earned their rightful place in math problems."

Leah sent her an appreciative glance.

Rudy straightened in his seat repentantly.

Dylan started to explain his current math unit and why he disliked it. The rest of them listened, their meal of store-bought pizza and salad (that Leah had provided) and homemade bread rolls (that Tess had provided) garnishing the table.

Leah had met Tess almost ten years before. At the time, Leah had been navigating her first year of teaching, and Tess had been volunteering for the PTA at Leah's school. When Tess realized that Leah was a teenager tasked with the job of raising her younger brother, she'd taken Leah under her wing.

A few times a week, Tess had stopped by Leah's classroom to help out and to deliver batches of homemade oatmeal chocolate chip cookies. Eventually, Tess started inviting Leah and Dylan to her home for Sunday lunch after church. In return, Leah invited them to Dylan's Pee Wee football games and school events. When the couple had shown up at those events, she'd been overwhelmed with gratitude, knowing that when her brother looked into the audience, he'd see more than one person there to support him.

Once, when Leah mentioned to Tess that she planned to spend the weekend painting a bedroom, Tess and Rudy had appeared on her doorstep with roller brushes and paint pans.

They played dominoes with Dylan and Scrabble with Leah. Tess gave Dylan practical gifts like coats. Rudy gave Dylan impractical gifts like Nerf guns.

Over time, Leah had come to trust Tess and Rudy enough to let them babysit Dylan, which had opened up Leah's world a little. She'd been able to go out in the evenings with friends, take part in occasional chess competitions, or go hiking alone. To this day, they were the ones who stayed with Dylan on the rare occasions when she went out of town.

God had known she and Dylan needed grandparents, and He'd provided Tess and Rudy. They were the ones who had shown her— more than anyone else ever had—what it looked like to love through action.

"I suggest you take your sister up on her offer of tutoring," Tess said to Dylan.

Dylan made a noncommittal sound and helped himself to another slice of pepperoni with veggies.

"What's going on with football?" Rudy asked, clearly eager to talk about sports, something that interested him a mile more than math.

"Nothing much."

"Do elaborate, dear brother, and tell us how we can become patrons of your football success!"

"Right now, we're lifting weights and getting ready for a seven-on-seven scrimmage."

It was as if Dylan's every word were a pearl dropping into midair that she, Tess, and Rudy were doing their best to catch.

"We're looking forward to your games this fall." Tess speared a bite of salad. "We'll be there to cheer you on."

"You bet we will," Rudy added happily. "Let me know if you need a ride to practice or summer school." For years, Rudy and Tess had served as Dylan's faithful cab drivers.

"Thanks," Dylan replied.

"He drives his own car now," Tess reminded her husband, then expelled an impatient sigh. Tess communicated most of her feelings through sighs.

A year and a half ago, when Dylan had turned sixteen, Mom had sent two thousand dollars to him for a car. They'd bought a small blue pickup truck.

"Oh, sure!" Rudy pretended he hadn't forgotten. As was typical, he responded to Tess's scolding like an amiable golden retriever. "But if it breaks down or something, I want him to know he can call me."

This was a second marriage for both Tess and Rudy. Tess and her first husband had divorced. Rudy's first wife had died. They'd married each other twenty-five years ago, when Tess was fifty-six and Rudy fifty-eight. Shortly after, they'd bought a vacation cabin in Misty River.

When Leah decided that she needed to move Dylan out of Gainesville, Tess and Rudy had encouraged them to move here. Leah had done so, and now the older couple spent the bulk of their year in Misty River, too. Tess had one son, and Rudy had two daughters. Combined, they had several granddaughters, but all their children and grandchildren lived out of state.

"Is the truck running well?" Rudy asked Dylan.

"Yeah."

"How's everything with your friends?" Leah asked.

"Good."

"Really? No drama?"

"No."

"Are you being cyberbullied?" Leah asked, only half kidding.

He snorted. His liquid chocolate eyes blazed disbelief. "No."

"Busy trying to order prescription painkillers through the mail?"

"You can order prescription painkillers though the mail?" Rudy asked excitedly.

"Rudy," Tess chided. "Eat your meal."

"But—" Rudy said.

"And put your napkin in your lap."

"Are you interested in dating any of the girls in your grade?" Leah persisted. Dylan was polishing off his food and would bolt in seconds.

"No."

Should she believe him? Or should she add "teenage love" to her list of fears, right before guns and right after bomb-making?

He picked an olive off his slice and took his final bite. He'd picked the olives off since he was small.

"I wonder if he's being cyberbullied," Leah said companionably to Tess.

"I don't believe so," Tess said back. "No."

Moving as if wearing a body that wasn't quite the right size for him, Dylan rose and carried his dishes toward the kitchen. "I'm not being cyberbullied."

"Are you sure, O love of my life?" Leah called after him. "No one's heckling you?"

"I don't even know what that word means," Dylan said.

"Heckling means tickling," Rudy announced.

"No," Tess instantly corrected. "Heckling is abusive speech."

"No one's heckling *or* tickling me," Dylan said loudly from the kitchen.

"Truly?" Leah asked. "No girls are tickling you?"

"I'm leaving to go hang out at Jace's," Dylan said.

Leah had vetted Dylan's evening plans with Jace's mom earlier. "Leave us here if you must, pining for your presence."

He appeared in the doorway between the kitchen and dining area. "Thanks for the dessert," he said to Tess, lifting one of the cookies she'd brought. "These are awesome."

"You're welcome," Tess told him indulgently, followed by a loving sigh.

Dylan skulked out of sight, and Leah could hear him gathering his keys and wallet. Their kitchen ended in a door that led to a small mudroom containing their washer and dryer. Leah had cajoled him into using the mudroom as a dumping ground for his backpack, athletic bag, water bottles, spare change, wallet, and keys. Thus, he always came and went through the back door.

"Be safe!" Leah yelled. "Love you!"

Muffled grunt. The door closed behind him.

When Dylan was younger, he'd been challenging because he'd been wounded by Mom's abandonment, hungry for attention, in need of constant supervision, full of energy, and not in the least independent. But he'd been good company.

Now he didn't want attention, didn't require much supervision, had low energy, and was very independent. And Leah really, really missed his company.

Why was it so easy to focus on the difficulties that came with a specific phase of a relationship? As soon as that phase ended, you mourned the benefits.

"And you?" A roll in one hand, Rudy stretched his knife toward the butter dish. Tess moved the butter dish out of his reach. His attention swung to Leah. "Are you interested in dating any of the young men you know?"

"I'm not. No."

"None of them has been tickling you?"

"Not a one." Rudy wanted her to fall in love. Unsuccessfully, she'd explained to him that she was already married to her goal of achieving her PhD. *That* was the only thing she needed to keep her warm in bed on a cold night.

Tess and Rudy stayed for coffee, cookies (of which Tess allowed Rudy two), and a speed round of Scrabble (since Rudy's bedtime was ten).

When they left, Leah waved them off from her dark front lawn, Rudy's question echoing in her ears. *"Are you interested in dating any of the young men you know?"*

She'd thought about Sebastian Grant often over the past few days, because thinking about him caused delight to rumble within her like kernels of corn about to pop. At the Colemans' party, he'd been very composed and controlled. Yet she'd felt the energy in him, pulsing under his skin. Behind his bland expressions, she sensed a tremendously sharp, alert mind. He was focused, but remote. Intelligent, but not open. Determined, but difficult for her to read.

There'd been a moment when he'd looked at her so directly that sensitivity had bloomed across her skin. When he'd told her about his mom's death, she'd had a wayward, but powerful, urge to comfort him.

She'd been telling herself that the physical attraction she'd experienced for him when they'd met at the hospital coffee shop a week and a half ago was an outlier, a data point differing significantly from the rest of her responses to the opposite sex. But now that it had occurred again, she couldn't classify it as such.

She returned to the house, picked up her laptop, and walked straight through to her miniature back patio. Exterior and interior light spilled illumination onto the pavers that formed a curving shape just large enough for an outdoor chair, footrest, and side table.

After lowering onto the chair, she hooked a toe beneath the footrest, pulled it into position, then settled her computer so that it formed a bridge between her thighs and abdomen.

Due to the waiver that Mom had finally submitted, Magnolia

Avenue Hospital had gathered the files about her birth. She'd been born at a time when records were kept only on paper. However, she'd requested them in an electronic format, so the hospital had scanned the pages. Earlier today she'd begun reading them via an online portal.

She'd seen at once that doctors' reputation for illegible handwriting wasn't unfounded. For several hours she'd combed through the documents, slowly deciphering words, taking notes. Now she could revisit them and finish researching the oddities she'd found the first time through.

Immediately after birth in the delivery room, her weight had been listed as eight pounds, one ounce. Two days later, when she and her mom left the hospital, the log noted her weight as seven pounds, one ounce.

She surfed the web and discovered that it wasn't unusual for a formula-fed newborn to lose five percent of her body weight after birth. But according to her chart, she'd lost twelve percent of her body weight.

Her mother's biological daughter was the one who'd weighed eight pounds, one ounce. Leah had likely weighed close to seven pounds at birth.

Mom's blood type was recorded here as type O. A Google search informed her that O was common. So was Leah's blood type, A. Her dad had type B, which was more unusual. A few of the times he'd given blood when she was a kid, he'd taken her along. Those occasions had imprinted on her memory because . . . needles. Blood. *"I've got to help out my fellow Bs,"* he'd told her. Afterward, he'd winked and cajoled the staff into giving Leah a carton of juice and a package of saltines.

She located a chart listing how blood types descended from parents to children. Ah. It wasn't possible for a type O mother and type B father to have a type A daughter.

She'd already known she wasn't Erica and Todd Montgomery's child. The DNA said so. Her improbable weight loss as an infant said so.

So why did this fresh confirmation lower onto her shoulders like a lead blanket?

She read back over every item—the doctor's scrawl regarding the caesarean section, her mom's blood pressure stats, the notes on the baby's feeding times, the results of the pediatrician's exam.

Her mother's baby had been whisked from the delivery room to the nursery because of concerns over a rapid heartbeat. As far as Leah could tell, the baby's heartbeat had stabilized quickly. The remainder of Mom's stay at the hospital appeared ordinary.

Not a single detail pointed to the question of *how*. How had two babies been switched?

Leah tilted her head up. Trees conspired to crowd out most of the starry sky. It might not be possible to answer the question of how. But it should be possible to answer the question of *who*. Who were her mother and father?

She logged in at YourHeritage. Starting with the DNA matches that the site designated as her closest relatives, she'd been studying each person one by one. Many had opted to keep their information private. Some who'd made their family trees public had only used the site for genealogical purposes and therefore hadn't included living relatives. Others had only traced one branch of their tree.

Borrowing and building on the research they'd made available, she'd been striving to assemble a master family tree for herself. It was laborious.

The site says this woman's my second cousin. But how? Through whom? Who are her parents, siblings, and kids?

Given more time, however, she had faith that she'd be able to crack the code.

Two days later, she did.
    Maybe.
    She'd taken her computer on a breakfast date to The Grind Cof-

fee Shop and was just finishing up a chai latte when she suddenly located a jackpot of a family tree.

It had not come from one of her closest DNA matches. It had come from a distant relation named Cheryl Brookside Patterson. An obvious overachiever and a woman after Leah's own heart, Cheryl had made public the most thrillingly thorough family tree Leah had ever seen.

Section by section, Leah compared her fledgling tree with Cheryl's enormous tree until—finally—she found the place where her tree overlaid with Cheryl's tree exactly. If she slotted a man named Jonathan Brookside into her tree as her father, then the few matches she'd been able to determine fell into place.

Many of the people on Cheryl's tree had been born in Connecticut. However, Jonathan had been born in Atlanta. He had no siblings. At the age of fifty-seven, he was certainly of the right generation to be her father.

It seemed she was . . . a Brookside.

No information beyond his birthdate and place of birth had been given. She ran a search for him at YourHeritage, then on Google, then on social media sites.

No hits, which frustrated her curiosity but did not detract from the fact that she now, very likely, had enough DNA data to justify a court order for Baby Girl Brookside's records.

Leah wouldn't presume to call her knowledge of music well rounded. When she was young, her parents had introduced her to the 1980s soundtrack of their high school years, and she'd never found songs she liked better.

However, she was familiar enough with TLC's hit "Don't Go Chasing Waterfalls" to know the lyrics suggested that you shouldn't go chasing waterfalls, but instead stick to the rivers and lakes you were used to.

Which was preposterous.

Case in point: She'd spent a glorious Friday morning chasing a waterfall at Tallulah Gorge State Park. She'd hiked from the rim down to the floor. From her current spot on a shaded rock, the river tumbled past, crystal blue and frothing white. A hundred or so yards away, Hurricane Falls cascaded over ancient rock and filled the air with an underlying drone of nature's power.

She'd have missed all this if she'd stuck to the rivers and the lakes she was used to.

After unpacking the lunch she'd brought in her backpack, she checked her phone and found a new email from Sebastian's attorney, Jenna Miles. Leah had called Jenna immediately after deducing that Jonathan Brookside was her father, and Jenna had wasted no time.

Leah opened the email, a smile growing as she read the contents.

Then she spent far too long formulating and proofreading a text message to Sebastian. She was determined that no person would ever, ever, receive an email or text from her riddled with typos.

> Jenna just informed me that she was granted a court order. She'll deliver it to Donna McKelvey at Magnolia Avenue Hospital within the hour and request that Baby Girl Brookside's documents be made ready for my perusal on Tuesday. You'd asked me to keep you informed about upcoming meetings, and I'm upholding my end of the bargain. Thank you very much for securing Jenna's services on my behalf.

She could only hope that the detective work she'd done to pinpoint the identity of her father had been sound. If it hadn't been, the effort to secure a court order pertaining to a baby girl with the surname Brookside would be wasted when Magnolia Avenue Hospital informed them that said records did not exist.

She completed her hike and was backing out of the parking lot when her phone dinged. She pressed the brake as if on the verge of flattening a pedestrian, even though no one was nearby. Bobbled her phone. Then plucked it up and checked her texts.

Sure enough. From Sebastian.

Let me know when to meet you at the hospital
on Tuesday. I'll do my best to be there.

> Please don't feel duty-bound to attend.

I want to be there.

> I'm sure your schedule is full, and I'm sure Jenna
> and I can handle it.

I'll see you Tuesday.

Sebastian sent his text and swiveled his office chair so that his vision landed on the pictures that his patients' parents had sent him. Smiling babies.

He understood hospital politics and procedures better than Leah and Jenna. It was justified, generous even, for him to attend the meeting in order to provide backup.

So why did he feel guilty?

He pressed from his office chair and headed toward the stairs that led to the PICU, one floor below.

He felt guilty because he didn't know how much his desire to see her again was influencing his certainty that she needed him at the meeting. Did his desire to see her again account for twenty percent of his motivation to be present at the meeting? Fifty? Eighty?

At exactly what point did helping Leah cross the line into betraying Ben? Had he already crossed that line?

No.

During his meeting with Leah at the hospital coffee shop, he'd encouraged her to date Ben. At the Colemans', he'd talked Ben up. When he saw Leah this next time, he'd advocate for Ben again.

If Leah found the information she needed on Tuesday, that meeting would likely be their last. She'd no longer need his help with her search into her past, and so he'd see her again only through Ben. If he went out with Ben's friend group in Misty River. Or if Leah became Ben's girlfriend.

His stomach churned.

He strode toward Josiah Douglas's room. Sebastian had performed a successful arterial switch operation on him a few weeks ago. Since then, they'd been monitoring him around the clock and administering medicine to improve his blood flow.

When Sebastian entered, Josiah's mom and dad pushed to their feet to greet him. Josiah, awake and relaxed, still hooked up to his IV, was cradled in his mom's arms.

"Good news," Sebastian told them. "After morning rounds, we discussed Josiah's case, and we all agreed he's ready to go home. I'm discharging him."

Instantly, Josiah's mom's eyes filled with tears.

"Thank you," her husband said, looking more grateful than if he'd won the lottery.

It strained families to have their child admitted here for weeks or sometimes months at a time. The opportunity to go home was always celebrated, and Sebastian was always glad for them. This was the outcome he worked toward—hearts with congenital defects, repaired as much as medicine allowed.

However, he understood better than Josiah's parents did the difficulty of the road before them. The surgeons here could not cure patients. They could only exchange a life-ending condition for a serious chronic condition. Josiah's needs—medicine, check-ups, vigilance—would demand a lot from his parents. He was at risk for leaky valves, arrhythmias, and more.

"I know the staff here has been teaching you how to take care of him," Sebastian said. "I just want to remind you to keep an eye on his weight gain, his growth, and his oxygen levels. Call us if he has any feeding or breathing problems. All right?"

They both nodded.

Sebastian stepped forward and swept a few fingers across the top of Josiah's springy hair.

The baby peered up at him with a trusting expression.

"Good-bye," Sebastian said. "Stay healthy."

Leah was about to be granted a peek into the hospital records of Baby Girl Brookside.

Who was her. Or . . . had been her for a short time. Before she'd been given to Erica and Todd Montgomery.

Over the past few days, after Jenna had delivered the court order to the hospital, she'd been half expecting a call informing her that Magnolia Avenue did not possess records for an infant girl named Brookside, born on her birthday.

But that call never came.

Leah waited for Sebastian and Jenna at the same table at Magnolia Perk where she'd waited prior to the last meeting with Donna McKelvey. Unlike last time, it was late afternoon. Like last time, she'd arrived early—

And there was Sebastian. Also early. The electronic doors *whoosh*ed open dramatically as he swept in alongside a sleek woman in her forties.

He had on a pale gray dress shirt and navy suit pants. All the vitality in the place seemed to pull toward him like ocean water whizzing back out to sea. Was Leah the only one who noticed? She glanced around. Everyone else seemed to be carrying on as usual.

When the pair reached Leah, Sebastian introduced the woman as Jenna Miles, attorney. Jenna promptly excused herself, making a beeline for the coffee counter.

He didn't take the chair opposite Leah, so she looped her purse over her shoulder and stood. Together, they moved out of earshot of the other tables.

"Thanks for coming, Dr. Grant."

"I wouldn't have missed it, Professor Montgomery."

"I'm not a professor."

"You will be. Besides, the title suits. You're more of a professor than most of the professors I had in school." He was only thirty-two, but his life, his career, and the pressures he lived under made him look a few years older than that. There was nothing soft or young about Sebastian Grant. "So. We talked about Ben's interest in you the last time we were here together."

"We did, yes."

"And you said you weren't interested in him in return. I heard you, but—"

She arched a brow at him.

"What?" he asked.

"When a woman expresses her stance and a man responds with 'I heard you, but,' that doesn't bode well for the quality of the exchange." It was the honest truth, delivered teasingly.

To his credit, he laughed. "May I have permission to finish my thought?"

She nodded.

"I want to encourage you to keep an open mind where Ben's concerned. I mean, it couldn't hurt to go out to dinner with him, could it? What's the worst that could happen?"

"A, I could end up ruining my relationship with my closest friend at work. B, and far more chilling, I could fall for him."

"That would be great."

"That would be a catastrophe."

"You're smart enough to keep it from becoming a catastrophe."

"I'm book smart, not romance smart." She looked toward Jenna, who'd moved to the side to wait for her drink. The attorney wore her auburn hair in a short pixie cut that flattered approximately one percent of women. Jenna was in that one percent.

Leah straightened her short-sleeved crewneck sweater—raspberry in color with dark pink flowers stitched across it in horizontal rows. She'd paired it with narrow gray pants and heels.

"You can learn to be romance smart," Sebastian said.

She sighed. Ever since Sebastian had told her Ben liked her, that knowledge hadn't been sitting well. "I've actually been considering going out to dinner with Ben," she admitted.

"Hmm?"

"I've been considering it," she repeated. When Leah glanced at Sebastian, she found him watching her. Dinner with Ben would give her a private, unhurried setting in which she could ask about his feelings and ensure that he wasn't holding out false hope where she was concerned.

"You'll go out with him?" he asked.

"Yes."

He swallowed, and his jaw appeared to harden.

"Which is what you've been lobbying for. So I'm confused as to why you don't look pleased."

He shook himself slightly. "Sorry. I got distracted for a second." A wide smile overtook his mouth. "I'm pleased."

"Then that's settled. Dylan and I are leaving in a few days on our trip. When I get back, I'll have dinner with Ben."

"Is it time for your doomed road trip to New England?"

"It is, but I take exception to your choice of the word *doomed*."

"Right, because you'll be taking a teenager and an Airstream trailer on a three-week-long road trip across the country. What could go wrong?"

"Many things. But the laws of probability suggest that none of those things will come to fruition."

"Your trip's as doomed as Han Solo's trip in *A New Hope*, when he was supposed to transport Luke, Leia, and Obi-Wan to Alderaan."

She grinned. "I admire the blunt way you just shoved that Han Solo reference into the discussion."

"I used force instead of skill."

"I'll have to think of skillful ways to reference aviation in conversation. Because of you, I read a book on the basics. Thrust, lift, drag. I was instantly enamored. I love physics."

"What's not to love about physics?"

"Nothing," she said earnestly.

His soap smelled so wonderful that she'd like to stockpile candles in that fragrance. All of a sudden, she could hear her pulse in her ears—

The click of high heels intruded. Jenna broke the bubble that had enclosed Leah and Sebastian by commenting on her preference for coffee beans from Tanzania.

The three of them made their way to the administrative offices. This time, they were shown into a boardroom. Leah's group arranged themselves on one side of the table. Donna McKelvey and the director of medical records sat on the opposite side.

After a brief conversation, the director produced an army green file folder containing Baby Girl Brookside's original records. At Jenna's request, he'd also made photocopies of the file and scanned images of it onto a flash drive—both of which Leah could take home with her.

"On behalf of the hospital," Donna said to Leah, "I'd like to apologize once again for what happened to you. I sincerely wish you the best."

"Thank you."

"You're welcome to stay here for as long as you'd like in order to look through the original paperwork."

The hospital employees and Jenna excused themselves, leaving Leah alone with Sebastian in a room that smelled of new carpeting. The only sound: air whirring through vents.

"And you?" Leah asked Sebastian. "Do you have other commitments? If so, I don't want you to feel obligated to stay."

His eyes flashed a gray as lustrous as moonstones. "I'm sticking around. I only have one commitment this afternoon. And it's to you."

CHAPTER SEVEN

Leah pulled the original file toward her. Chest tightening with expectation, she opened it.

The papers within had turned beige and brittle with age. A smattering of mold splayed across the top right edge. She positioned the first two sheets side by side.

Her biological mother's name: Trina Brookside.

Eagerly, she read the remaining information. As far as Leah could tell, things had gone well with Trina's labor, but after the baby had been delivered . . . She narrowed her eyes, trying to understand. "I'm following the doctor's notes right up until the baby was born."

"The staff in the delivery room knew that Trina was diabetic, and they were prepared for the complications that can cause," Sebastian explained. "As soon as the baby was delivered, they noted that she had cyanosis, which means she was bluish in color. She was taken to the nursery and given oxygen. Her condition improved quickly, and the pediatrician on staff concluded that she was healthy. Essentially, she just needed a little time to get acclimated to life outside the womb."

Leah's brain constructed a chain of events. "Erica Montgomery suffered placental abruption, so they put her under and performed an emergency C-section. Her baby girl was born at 10:10 a.m. with a rapid heartbeat. They took her directly to the nursery for treatment." Leah pointed to the paper. "It says here that Trina

Brookside gave birth to her baby eighteen minutes later, at 10:28. Trina's baby girl was also taken to the nursery. Is it likely that either a rapid heartbeat or cyanosis could have caused problems down the road for the babies?"

"No. Both babies had issues that, once stabilized, were no longer of concern."

"I'm guessing it was during the interval when the babies were being treated in the nursery that they were switched."

"That would make sense."

"As soon as the babies were well, they must have been sent to the wrong mothers. Erica's baby was taken to Trina. And I, Trina's baby, was taken to Erica. Who do you think might have been responsible for the switch? A doctor? Nurses?"

"Most likely nurses. They're the ones responsible for transporting babies between rooms."

Leah moved the pages to the side, revealing two new pages. Her eyes scanned the lines of text. Trina and Erica had stayed in the same wing of the same hospital for *two days*, both of them bonding with each other's baby, before Trina had gone home.

Trina had been twenty-seven years old at the time. Married. This pregnancy was her first. Her address: 11482 Riverchase Road, Atlanta, Georgia. Ten numbers had been written clearly and decisively onto the line beside *Phone Number*. Those numbers practically blinked like a neon sign. What if she dialed that number and *her biological mother answered*?

Surely, her mother would not answer. This number was a landline from The Time Before Everyone Had a Cell Phone, which meant that Trina probably wasn't using the same number now that she'd used then. It was also a stretch, but perhaps not as large of a stretch, to think Trina might still live at the house on Riverchase Road. As soon as Leah left here, she'd drive there. Just to look.

She uncovered the next two pages. One was a birth certificate. Katrina Elizabeth Wallace Brookside and her husband, Jonathan Delaney Brookside, had named their daughter Sophie Grace.

Trina and Sophie. Leah rolled the unfamiliar names around

in her brain. She tried on Leah Brookside for size—except, she'd never have been Leah Brookside. Had things gone differently, she'd have lived her life as Sophie Grace Brookside.

The next page divulged information about Trina's pregnancy, including the fact that her blood type was B, which meant her husband's blood type must be A, like Leah. It also meant that Sophie's possible blood types—B and O—would not raise any red flags with her or her parents because those types could naturally occur from Trina and Jonathan.

Unless Sophie did DNA testing like Leah had done, she'd have no reason to discover that she was not related to her mother and father.

The next page showed a photo of baby Sophie. The child in this photo was Erica Montgomery's baby. Yet Leah was looking at a face that Erica and Todd had never had the opportunity to look upon.

The infant had slit her eyes open as if she found the light of the world to be an unwelcome assault. Her lips formed a pink rosebud. Her eyes were dark, as was her dusting of hair.

She looked just like Dylan had when he'd been a newborn.

Sebastian had never felt such an overwhelming pull toward a woman in his life. He knew why he felt the pull. Leah was brainy, kind, at peace with herself, challenging, funny. He loved that she said random things about flowers serving as a metaphor for life and melons shaped like rhomboids.

What he didn't know: Why, of all people, did the woman he felt this way about have to be the woman Ben loved?

After leaving the hospital, they came to a stop at Leah's car, parked in an outdoor lot.

She dashed a piece of hair away from her face. "My head is spinning with everything I just learned."

"I can imagine." He wished he had something more comforting to offer. "Are you going to contact Trina and Jonathan Brookside?"

"I don't know. At this point, I'm simply planning to stalk the Brooksides on the Internet . . . in a very friendly, non-creepy way—"

"Very non-creepy."

"—to see what I can learn about their lives and about their daughter's life."

When Sebastian was young and had asked his mom about his father, she'd told him plainly that she'd met him at a party and that they'd had a one-night stand. Later, when his mom discovered she was pregnant, she'd contacted his father as a courtesy. Sebastian suspected they'd both been relieved when they'd learned the other was happy to continue leading separate lives. His father didn't have to be a father. His mother could be a mother without a stranger's influence.

Sebastian knew his father's name, but felt nothing toward him except vague resentment. No connection. No affection. No desire to communicate with him.

Leah held her purse strap with both hands, stacked one atop the other. "I can't thank you enough for stepping in and helping me with all of this."

"Not a problem."

"No, really." She regarded him steadily. "Thank you."

His body roared in response, and he had to lock his teeth together to keep from saying *Don't fall in love with Ben. Please don't.* "You're welcome."

His awareness of the rest of the world—the noise, the cars, the colors —sucked away.

"There's something special about you, Sebastian. Something appealing. You should feel very proud of the man you've become."

Her words came as such a shock that it took him a second to compute them. She found him appealing? Pleasure collided with guilt, freezing him.

She slid into the driver's seat of her gray Honda Pilot, which was old but in good condition. "Good-bye." Holding the door ajar, she waited for him to respond.

Say something, you idiot.

She started her car. "Good-bye," she repeated, maybe thinking he hadn't heard the first time.

"Good-bye," he said.

She shut her door and drove away.

As soon as she was out of sight, he swung on his heel and tunneled his hands into his hair.

The day of the farmers market, Ben had said that Leah was rare. He'd been right. She was rare.

And she wasn't coming back.

H ad that been awkward? What she'd just said to him?

"There's something special about you, Sebastian. Something appealing. You should feel very proud of the man you've become." Her words had seemed appropriate to her while she was speaking them, but then his face had gone strangely blank in response.

She replayed it. Huh. The statement still seemed acceptable to her. Friendly and complimentary. Of course, it was possible that that *had* been an awkward thing to say and had only seemed normal to her.

If so, it wasn't as if she hadn't warned him about her lackluster social skills.

And, of course, it could have been worse. She could have confessed her fascination with his lips or, unforgivably, failed to solve a quadratic equation in his presence.

Where was she driving?

She'd been so preoccupied with Sebastian that she'd failed to type Trina and Jonathan's address into her GPS before leaving the hospital. Smoothly, she pulled into a strip mall and parked. She peeked at her reflection. Even now, after the gale force winds of her parents' identity and Sebastian's nearness, it mollified her to see that she looked calm.

She typed *11482 Riverchase Road* into her phone.

"Turn right at Beverly Road," her phone's Irish male voice instructed her. She had a closer relationship with that voice than she'd ever had with a boyfriend.

She followed the Irishman's directions.

A twenty-minute drive brought her to the well-established Morningside Lenox Park neighborhood. Hilly tree-lined streets harbored homes that had been built in the first half of the twentieth century. This neighborhood would have been pricey for a young family three decades ago, just as it was now.

Leah parked a little ways down and across the street from 11482.

Feeling conspicuous, like a cop on a stakeout, she scoured the length of the street, then eyed Trina and Jonathan's house. What if one of her family members walked out that door? Or spotted her from inside and came out to question her?

Stillness encased the entire block. Nothing moved, except for gently swaying branches. Most likely, she could stay here for a short period of time without anyone noticing.

The Dutch blue trim of the home emphasized its muted brick exterior and charming black front door. Planting beds tucked tidy shrubs against the base of the structure. The flowerpots on the front step burst with geraniums.

When she was brought home from the hospital as a newborn, she ought to have been brought here, to this stately Americana home. It was easy to picture a baby nursery in that front right room. It would have a big window, wood floors, crown molding.

In her earliest memories, she'd lived in an uninspiring two-bedroom apartment. Dad had had the design aesthetic of a frat boy; Mom had accessorized their hodgepodge furniture with international treasures from places she'd never had the opportunity to visit. A wall hanging from India. Art from Venezuela. A tablecloth from Thailand. Those items had been colorful, but they'd also reinforced the message Mom had communicated in a million subtle and not-so-subtle ways. Namely, *I'd rather be anywhere other than here.*

How different would her childhood have been, had Leah grown up in this place?

Very different.

Memory-laden minutes slid past.

She had enough familiarity with Zillow.com from when she'd been shopping for a house in Misty River to know that the site provided data on a property's prior sales. She accessed the site on her phone and ran a search. After some scrolling and clicking, she discovered that this house had been purchased by new owners five times since the year of her birth.

In fact, it had been sold just four years after she'd been born, ostensibly by Trina and Jonathan, if they'd been owners and not renters when they'd lived here. Either way, Trina and Jonathan hadn't resided here in a long, long time.

She was glad she'd come, nonetheless. This detour had provided insight into her biological mother and father and what her upbringing might have been like had they been the ones to raise her.

Her family life hadn't been wretched. Her needs had been met. That said, her family life hadn't been as pretty as the picture this house presented, either.

Just because the house looks ideal on the outside doesn't mean that the Brooksides' life was ideal, Leah.

Yes, but what if the family life on the inside *did* match the ideal on the outside? If so, how was she supposed to reconcile herself to that?

When Leah arrived home from Atlanta that evening, her house welcomed her with silence and a lingering whiff of pineapple from her unlit candle. Dylan was gone, hanging out with his friend Braxton.

She hurried to her computer the way she'd hurried to Math Olympiad contests in fifth grade and opened Facebook. She hoped the Brooksides were the type of people who, unlike her, shared their lives often and freely on social media without regard for privacy settings.

She entered *Trina Wallace Brookside* into the search bar. Only one of the results looked like she could be the right fit. However, Leah opted to rule out the more unlikely candidates first. A few of them were too young. One had been born in England and lived there still.

Finally, anticipation mounting, she brought up the most likely Trina. The woman had created a close-up profile picture from her larger cover photo. The photo captured her solo, standing on a balcony overlooking a beautiful Italian-looking town. She was half turned to the camera with a relaxed smile.

Leah went still. Trina's face was lined with years, but her facial structure, height, and body type were very similar to Leah's. She'd styled her blond hair in a long bob that was slightly shorter in back than in the front. She wore a navy-and-white-striped boatneck shirt with roomy sleeves.

Unfortunately for Leah's purposes, Trina was indeed someone who had regard for privacy settings. She'd made zero information about herself available to people she hadn't approved as Facebook friends.

Leah typed *Sophie Brookside* into the search bar. Again, she knew at once, from the picture alone, who her Sophie was. Again, she eliminated the others first before visiting her Sophie's page.

The circular profile picture of Sophie (Brookside) Robbins revealed a lovely brunette. For her cover photo, she'd chosen an outdoor wedding shot. In it, she was beaming at the camera while holding the hand of her good-looking groom. She'd chosen a strapless wedding dress and knotted her hair into a sophisticated style at the nape of her neck. The veil attached to the top of her bun extended into the breeze in a whimsical line. Her groom regarded her with a besotted grin.

Sophie was slender, stylish, and, judging by this photo, terrifically happy.

Leah had never wanted to marry! Even so, a slither of jealousy snaked around her ribs and squeezed.

Was Sophie (Brookside) Robbins living the life Leah was supposed to have lived?

Was Leah the one who'd been intended for the gown, the veil, the groom? But instead had become, because of all the "nurture" factors in the "nature vs. nurture" equation, the one supporting her brother on a teacher's salary?

Like her mother, Sophie shared no personal details with those outside her circle of friends.

Leah opened Instagram and hunted for Trina and Sophie there. She only found Sophie, who'd used the same wedding photo on Instagram as on Facebook. Here again, she maintained a private account. Leah tried the remaining social media platforms but wasn't able to find them.

She surfed back to Trina and Sophie's Facebook pages and spent more time absorbing the images.

Upon further reflection, she did not feel that she'd been intended for a gown, veil, and groom. But she did feel—very strongly—that she was intended for a PhD. It had been her dream since Ms. Santiago, her second-grade teacher, had told her about the career paths open to academics.

If she'd gone home from the hospital with Trina and Jonathan, she might have been free to follow through on Princeton's PhD offer. She might be teaching at a university right now. Writing papers, giving lectures, meeting with students.

Grief sent her bolting into the kitchen. She opened a can of mixed nuts and munched while her mind churned. With one hand, she scooped up more nuts, with the other, she slid her phone from her pocket and indulged in her guilty pleasure—browsing the digital album where she kept the dozens of pictures of Princeton she'd collected over the years.

She had so many pictures of the school, and had studied them all so carefully, that she probably knew the campus and the college's history better than most of their incoming students.

She never could decide if these pictures were a healthy way to process her loss or an unhealthy fixation on her loss.

Both?

She could bear without too much difficulty the idea that she may have missed out on a wedding because she'd been switched at birth. But it was much harder to bear the idea that she could have missed out on the chance to further her education because she'd been switched at birth.

She still had every intention of furthering her education when Dylan left for college. She'd take as many courses as she could handle time-wise, while continuing to work, and money-wise, while contributing to Dylan's tuition. Eventually, she'd achieve her PhD. She would. It's just that, to get there, she'd have to climb a challenging uphill path. The prestigious, fully funded route of years ago was gone.

She shoveled more nuts into her mouth.

It was too soon to think about her doctoral work. Nearly a year remained until Dylan's graduation. For now, her primary focus was to ensure that he made it to his freshman dorm room in one piece and well prepared for independence.

With God's help, she and Dylan had come a long way together. With God's help, they'd cross the remaining distance.

A snide voice within her sneered, *He's not even your brother.*

"Yes he is," she whispered to the empty room. The mighty ties of love and loyalty that bound her to him had not changed. The truest truth of her life was that she'd love Dylan always. Unconditionally.

The things she'd learned today didn't have to mean that Sophie had been the beneficiary of the switch and Leah the loser . . . because Leah had gotten Dylan, and she wouldn't relinquish him for anything. She'd chosen his well-being above Princeton, and she'd chosen rightly. She didn't regret it. Given the same set of circumstances, she'd make the same decision.

It would serve her well to remember that none of the ramifications of the switch were Sophie's fault. She and Sophie had been minutes old when the mistake had occurred. Both of them helpless newborns. Victims. Sophie had been robbed of the opportunity to grow up with her biological family just like Leah had.

She should feel kinship with Sophie. And she did. . . .

It's just that she felt a bit of hostility toward her, too.

How many nuts had she just eaten? Hopefully not half the can. She set them back on the shelf and returned to the dining room to Google Jonathan Brookside.

She hadn't been able to find anything on him last week, but she'd given up after the first three or four pages of hits. This time, she'd dig deeper.

Sure enough, on the eleventh page of hits, she came upon two future-casting articles attributed to Jonathan Brookside, Founder, Gridwork Communications Corporation. The pieces were both well written. One article had appeared six years ago, the other eight. She had no way of confirming if this was her Jonathan, because no information was given about his age or family status.

She went to Gridwork Communications Corporation's website and learned that they were a computer services company located in Atlanta. It made sense that a man who'd lived in Atlanta in young adulthood might have founded a business in the same city.

Carefully, she deleted her browser history in case Dylan attempted to snoop.

She and her brother were about to leave on their epic road trip. Her goal for their time away: to rest and to fill her days with new places and experiences. She refused to let this thing with her past distract her so much that she couldn't enjoy the vacation she'd spent six months planning.

Fate, destiny, paternity were weighty issues. Twenty-eight years had gone by without her knowing anything about the Brooksides. It wouldn't hurt to give herself time to strategize her next move.

One afternoon in mid-July, Sebastian assessed the couple who'd just taken the seats across from him in his office at Beckett Memorial.

Timothy and Megan Ackerman, both around his age, were sitting in the two chairs no parent wanted to sit in. All the parents who sat in those chairs were forced to face one of the worst things that can happen to a person—the life-threatening sickness of their child.

A sonogram in the middle of Megan's second trimester had shown that their daughter, Isabella, had a combination of heart problems, including a faulty ventricle. Less than a week ago, at thirty-six weeks of gestation, the doctors in their hometown recognized that Isabella's heart was starting to fail, so they delivered her by emergency C-section. Once testing confirmed that her heart was dangerously malformed, Isabella had been transported here. For the past several days, the PICU staff had worked to stabilize her. She'd been on a ventilator, sedated, with tubes carrying medicine into her bloodstream. Tomorrow Sebastian and his team would operate.

"The environment in utero is very supportive of babies with congenital heart defects," Sebastian said. This situation was so upsetting and foreign to parents that they didn't always grasp the information they were receiving. Prior to surgery, he met with parents for as long as was needed to make sure he had their informed consent and that they understood the options and risks. "The environment outside the uterus is much less kind. We've been giving Isabella prostaglandins, which have helped us replicate the benefits she was receiving before birth. However, the benefits they provide won't fix anything, and they only last so long. Which is why we're moving forward with surgery."

Megan's skin was pale, her eyes grim.

"I wish that we could repair Isabella's heart through surgery, but we can't," Sebastian continued. "The best we can do tomorrow is put temporary fixes in place that will hopefully keep her heart functioning until a donor heart can be found, and we can perform a heart transplant."

"Okay," Timothy said.

"I'll seat a band around her pulmonary artery, ligate her duct, and install a pacemaker." Sebastian slid a diagram from his desk drawer and explained the procedures.

They listened, their posture tight with desperation. Sebastian knew that whatever part of their focus was here with him, the larger part was with their baby in the PICU.

Timothy looked like he could've played on the defensive line of his high school football team. He had a sandy brown beard and kind eyes.

Megan wore a maternity shirt that reminded Sebastian that she'd given birth just a few days before. As terrible as she must be feeling emotionally, she couldn't be feeling great physically, either. Her blond hair was short in back, but her bangs were long and swept to the side around an earnest face.

Markie had already informed him that Timothy and Megan had been waiting and praying through infertility for four years. They'd gone through two in vitro fertilization treatments and been ecstatic when they'd conceived Isabella, their first baby.

The baby they'd waited and prayed for would soon be wheeled into the operating room to have her chest opened.

"If you were us, would you opt for your child to have this surgery?" Megan asked. She searched his face for guarantees.

Sometimes, this question wasn't easy to answer. Sometimes parents faced two choices with evenly matched advantages and disadvantages. This was not one of those times. This surgery was Isabella's only hope. "Absolutely."

"Do you think she'll make it through?" Megan asked.

"I think she will make it through, yes."

"We're Christians," she said. "And we believe that God is still in the business of doing miracles."

Sebastian nodded.

"He did a miracle for you once," she said. "Right?"

"Right." Clearly, they'd researched him and learned about the earthquake.

"Are you a believer?"

"Yes." Sebastian didn't elaborate, though he wanted to remind them that God didn't often provide miracles on cue. In fact, only occasionally did He answer prayers for critically ill humans by healing them here on earth.

"It's clear to us that God chose you to be Isabella's doctor." Megan glanced at Timothy, then back at Sebastian.

"We'd like to move forward with the surgery," Timothy said.

"The two of us, our family, and our church will all be praying for Isabella and for you, Dr. Grant. We're trusting the Lord to bring her through the surgery and, eventually, to give her a whole new heart."

CHAPTER EIGHT

In the northeast corner of the United States of America, Leah was engaged in a game of smashball with Dylan. The two of them played barefoot on a wide strip of grass situated between their trailer's spot in the RV park and the dusky blue of Moosehead Lake, Maine.

Had they been keeping score, Dylan would have been beating her one hundred to zero. Happily, they were working as a team, their objective to keep the ball going back and forth between them.

She'd been unable to afford some of the more expensive items and activities Dylan had wanted on this trip. But at $10.95, the price of smashball had been right, so she'd purchased the two wooden paddles and rubber ball in Bar Harbor a week ago.

They'd hiked in Vermont. Gone canoeing in New Hampshire. Followed a walking tour map of Boston.

Without the pressure of schoolwork, friend dynamics, and football, Dylan had been more communicative. Another bonus—Leah hadn't had as many reasons to worry about him because he was usually within her line of sight.

The Airstream had turned out to be more difficult to tow than anticipated. Twice she'd needed the help of a passerby to navigate her way through gas stations. Once—horror of horrors—she'd been forced to back the trailer up. Also, she now knew more about emptying the trailer's sewage tank than she'd ever wanted to know.

Overall, though, the trip had been everything she'd hoped.

She hit the ball back to Dylan too softly. He made a comical dive forward and popped the ball into the air. Hampered by amusement and poor athletic reflexes, she couldn't get her paddle under it in time. The ball plunked to the earth.

She set her hands on her knees and laughed.

"You're tragic at this," he pointed out helpfully.

"I know. I'm tragic at every sport I've ever attempted. Take pity."

"No pity."

She fed the ball to him. He hit it straight back to her. Her return shot sprang up, and he had to do an acrobatic leap to knock it back. Her next shot went wide right.

He lunged and got his paddle on it. "Aim toward me!"

"I'm trying!" She hit another sky ball. He leapt into the air again but this time missed. He gave her a mock glare.

"You're breathing hard," she observed. "Is it taxing to play a team game with me?"

"The best athlete in the world isn't in good enough shape to play a team game with you, Leah." He served the ball to her again. *Thwap, thwap, thwap.*

"Do trips like this make you miss Mom and Dad?" she asked over the sound of the ball. Leah brought their parents up from time to time so he'd know he could talk to her about either of them whenever he wanted to.

"No. I don't even remember Dad."

"Mom, then? It's been a long time since we've seen her. It's okay, you know. To miss her. That won't hurt my feelings."

"It'll be fine when she comes for her next visit. But I don't miss her."

"She told me she's planning to come for Christmas again this year."

"'Kay." He shrugged as if he truly didn't care one way or another. The heart of a teenage boy was a difficult thing to understand.

"Have you thought any more about our dinner conversation last night?" she asked.

"What? About quesadillas?"

"About colleges." They'd already visited four that fell within the overlapping parameters of her budget and his GPA and test scores. They had a few more to visit. So far he didn't seem enthusiastic about any of them, and she couldn't tell if that was because of his glum-colored glasses or because he didn't want to expend energy writing essays and answering application questions.

"It's too early to think about college," he said.

"It's the middle of July, and many colleges open applications in August."

"Yeah, but applications stay open until December or something."

"When do you intend to submit your applications?"

"December or something."

She let the ball fall to the ground and put her hands on her hips. "If you apply early, I suspect that you'll give yourself an advantage."

"I don't want an advantage. I'll just wait."

She gave him a look of outrage.

"It's too early to think about college," he repeated.

"It's exactly the right time—"

"Too early," he said stubbornly.

"In that case, let's at least talk more about fields of study and possible career paths."

"Yawn. C'mon. Feed me the ball one last time, then I'm gonna go."

"And do what?"

His face said, *duh*. "Check my phone."

"Yes, because why would you want to experience this lake in Maine when you can stare at your phone?"

"I've experienced this lake in Maine enough. C'mon."

They volleyed the ball.

They'd stay here another two nights, then point the Airstream south and begin the three-day journey home. She was simultaneously sorry that their trip was drawing to a close and ready to return to a space larger than twenty-three by eight feet, her shower, her home's valley views, the cinnamon rolls at Sugar Maple Kitchen. And, of course, in Misty River, she'd be closer to Sebastian—

Confound it.

Look where she was! New England! With the person who was closest to her in the world. Who cared about proximity to Sebastian Grant?

Oddly . . . she did.

"I'm done," Dylan declared when she once again failed to control the trajectory of her strike. He handed her his paddle and headed to their trailer.

Leah drifted to the lake's edge and sat. Placing the paddles and ball to the side, she leaned against her wrists. Large rocks the color of pewter descended to the mirror-like surface of the lake, which reflected the clouds. Trees crowded the shoreline. Someone rowed a distant boat in her direction.

She imagined that it was Sebastian rowing. He'd moor the boat, then stride toward her. . . .

She'd have been more successful at avoiding daydreams of Sebastian while on this trip had she not had so many night dreams of him.

Sleeping in the bedroom of the Airstream that smelled of barbecue smoke and orange-scented Pledge, her customary anxiety dreams about Dylan had given way to dreams about Sebastian. Burnished, marvelous dreams, rippling with sensations. In them, Sebastian had slow danced with her. He'd sat next to her and looked across his shoulder into her eyes, laughing. He'd run a fingertip down the inside of her arm.

She'd entirely forgotten how wonderful dreams could be. So wonderful that the instant her conscious mind interrupted one of her dreams of him—even before she was fully awake—she started regretting the dream's end.

Physical attraction was, it turned out, quite a delightful thing to undergo. Like eating an oatmeal chocolate chip cookie. Or calculating partitions of a number.

Physical attraction was also a perplexing thing to undergo, see-ing as how she had informed Sebastian that she was missing the attraction gene.

It wasn't that she'd *never* experienced tugs of interest toward men. She'd experienced tugs of interest in the past and even gone on a few dates in her early twenties. However, it had been clear to her that none of those flickers of chemistry had the potential to convert into an actual relationship, because the flickers had been so extraordinarily temporary in nature.

She'd certainly never felt a fraction as strongly about any man as her friends felt for their boyfriends and husbands. She'd con-cluded that she was wired differently than other women . . . much less prone to the type of deep and long-lasting attraction and love that led to marriage.

Leah was already unusual in several ways. Her brain was unusual. The fact that she'd begun raising a child at the age of eighteen—unusual. The fact that she'd been working as a teacher and pursuing a master's degree when her peers had been graduat-ing from high school—unusual. It hadn't been a stretch to accept that she was unusual when it came to romance, too.

She'd decided to place the idea of a boyfriend on the shelf and simply go without. She was proud of that choice in the same way that she was proud of herself for going without the type of luxuries that had the power to destroy her monthly budget.

She wasn't fated to fall in love. She'd made peace with that.

And yet, here she was: sitting on this lakeshore during her va-cation, envisioning Sebastian Grant rowing a boat toward her.

She'd been very aware of her powerful responses to him the times they'd met at Magnolia Avenue Hospital and at the Colemans' bar-becue. Her reactions to him had been different than anything she'd experienced before. Even so, she'd expected them to prove fleeting.

Instead, a peculiar thing had occurred. An unprecedented thing. It had been more than two weeks since she'd seen him, yet her con-scious and unconscious mind returned to him often. If anything, her draw toward him was intensifying.

Had she reached a hasty conclusion when she'd determined that she wasn't capable of feeling the way other women felt?

No self-respecting mathematician ever trusted a hasty conclusion. So, if that's what had happened here, she'd made an error.

Admittedly, her data set of romantic interactions was small. In order to test her conclusion about her wiring, she'd need to enlarge that data set. To do that, she'd need to see Sebastian again.

She had no expectation of acquiring Sebastian as a boyfriend. For one thing, he'd given her no reason to think he liked her in that way. For another, Ben was romantically interested in her, and Sebastian was his best friend. So even if Sebastian did like her in *that way*, nothing could come of it.

Which was actually . . . freeing.

She could talk with Sebastian, measure her responses, and indulge her curiosity without worrying that he might get the wrong idea.

The following night before leaving the hospital, Sebastian drew to a halt at Isabella Ackerman's bedside.

He'd told Isabella's parents that he expected their daughter to make it through surgery, and she had.

Isabella occupied the same room Josiah Douglas had occupied weeks ago. Before and after Josiah, numerous other babies had been treated in this room. As soon as they discharged one, others always arrived.

Josiah had been a full-term newborn. Tiny Isabella weighed less than six pounds. A cap covered her bald head. Long eyelashes rested against the ivory skin of her face.

Outwardly, she looked like a perfectly formed preemie. Her exterior didn't reveal her life-threatening interior flaw.

Megan, Isabella's mother, had told him they were trusting God to give their daughter a new heart. But Sebastian knew that one in four babies in need of a transplant would die before a donor organ could be found.

He pushed the thought from his head.

When Megan had asked him if he was a believer, he'd said that he was. Which was true. Yet his history with God was not clear-cut.

He'd had zero familiarity with God during his early years. Then the worst thing that could have happened to him—his only parent's death—had happened. He'd landed with Christian foster parents who'd taken him to church. There, people had occasionally said things to him like "God's ways are mysterious." Or "God is with you in your grief."

He hadn't believed in God's existence, so Christianity had seemed like an idiotic waste of time. But even if he had believed God existed, he wouldn't have wanted anything to do with a supposedly all-powerful God who could have kept his mother alive and hadn't. Mostly, the idea of God made him angry.

Then he'd been forced to take a scholarship slot on a junior high mission trip to El Salvador, which had only made him angrier. Their group had just finished running a kids' sports camp for the day when a counselor had asked him and a few others to return equipment to a nearby building. He'd been carrying stacks of orange cones through a basement hallway when the earthquake hit and everything had gone black.

The floor and walls jerked and jerked. Terror subsumed him. *Escape. Get out!*

A girl was panting and gasping behind him.

Dropping the cones, he stumbled toward the dim light ahead. His shoulder rammed into the wall. Dust rattled over him, clogging his nose and mouth. *Why won't it stop?*

A hand wrapped around Sebastian's forearm and yanked him forward, then forward again. He staggered into a small central room where two hallways met. Rectangular windows at sidewalk level above revealed the scene. A kid named Luke had pulled him out. Ben and Natasha stared at him with terrified eyes, their arms spread for balance as they fought to stay upright.

The building groaned and metal screamed. Pieces of the ceiling crashed down. Two of the room's concrete walls collapsed inward, crashing into each other and forming a tent shape above their heads.

His heart roared. *We're going to die.*

He'd continued to believe that for every one of the eight days he'd spent underground. Ben, Natasha, Genevieve, and Luke had families who loved them and were desperate for their safe return. Next to them, he was the broken toy nobody wanted.

We're going to die.

When the search and rescue team took the building apart in an effort to reach them, he'd been sure the structure would cave in and they'd be crushed. Instead, God had protected them in the clearest way possible.

Sebastian had come face to face with the God he'd denied.

God *did* exist. He'd been wrong about that. But what was he supposed to do with a God who hadn't saved his mother but had saved him?

After returning from El Salvador, he, Ben, Natasha, and Genevieve spent months traveling around and telling their story to reporters, churches, authors, screenwriters. The Colemans brought him to church with them on Sundays, sent him to church camp in the summers, took him on another mission trip, talked with him again and again about faith.

When he was a teenager, he'd prayed for salvation. His motives had been partly good. He'd honestly wanted God to fill the hungry hole within him that longed for security. But his motives had also been partly selfish. He'd been a practical, street-smart kid who'd seen the wisdom in hedging his bets for eternity.

To this day, he attended church semi-regularly. However, he'd never gotten over all of his resentment toward God. Nor could he bring himself to trust God fully.

In high school, he'd worked for a college scholarship. In college, he'd worked for a med school scholarship. In med school, he'd worked to become a surgeon. Himself, his degrees, his job, his bank account. Those things he could trust in.

Yet even though he'd gotten everything he'd ever wanted, his life had been flat for months. Now that he could finally stop clawing and scraping for the next achievement, he was realizing that . . .

It still wasn't enough. Which infuriated him and left him feeling betrayed. Deceived.

No one would look at him these days and think of him as a broken toy nobody wanted.

No one, that is, except him.

He'd worked incredibly hard to prove everything he'd had to prove. By rights, his accomplishments should have made him feel secure and given him vengeance over his mother's death and repaid the loss he'd suffered when he was young.

But that's not how things had gone down. He might look healthy on the outside, just like Isabella Ackerman did. But, like her, he was flawed on the inside.

As flawed as he'd always been.

He smoothed the tubes draping over the side of Isabella's bed.

The team at the Clinic for Pediatric and Congenital Heart Diseases had helped Isabella as much as she could be helped at this point. Their task now? Keep her alive until she reached the top of the transplant list.

The intensivists and the experienced group of nurses here made it their business to know every detail about every child. The best nurses came to care for each patient and, often even more so, their parents, because the parents were the ones who talked with them, who shared their stories and their fears.

Sebastian couldn't afford to invest too much of himself in any one patient. Or, after the things that had happened to him, in any one person.

Leah included.

So how come he still couldn't let her go?

"There's something special about you, Sebastian. Something appealing." Her words to him were nothing, really. Yet, he'd replayed them over and over. When stressed. When he couldn't sleep.

When he retreated to his office after receiving bad news on one of his patients.

The memory of her saying that to him loosened the hard knot at the center of his chest.

But as soon as the knot loosened, he'd remember how Ben felt about Leah, and shame would twist his stomach.

He had more than enough to keep him busy here at the hospital. His life should be complete. But it was as if Leah's reentrance into his world had shined light on the emptiness that had been inside of him for a long time.

He'd been pretending the emptiness didn't exist and doing a semi-decent job of that.

Until her.

The morning after Leah and Dylan returned to Misty River in late July, Dylan rushed off to see his friends as purposefully as a baby animal seeking its mother.

Once Leah had clothes tumbling around inside the dryer, the fridge stocked, and her suitcase stored in the garage, she turned her attention to her search for her birth parents.

So far, the only thing she'd decided concerning Trina and Jonathan was that she wanted to see them. Live and in person. In order to accomplish that, she needed a current address.

She placed a call to her Misty River real estate agent. After what felt like more than enough time exchanging empty pleasantries, but may not have been enough time (Leah never knew), Leah informed the older woman that she had a question.

"All right. How can I help?"

"Is there a way, using home ownership records, for me to type in the name of a person who lives in a certain town, and discover which house is theirs?" She winced. The question sounded ripe with unpleasant, potentially illegal motivations. Perhaps the opening pleasantries had been wasted on this conversation.

"Are you thinking about investing in real estate?" the agent asked. "Oftentimes investors will want to access to the names so they can send notes to owners, letting them know they're interested in buying their home."

"No, I'm not interested in investing in real estate at this time. Maybe someday."

A few confused seconds of silence passed.

"You can access a seller's name on MLS," the older woman said, "which is used by real estate agents."

"And if the property is not for sale?"

"Some appraisal districts have websites. In that case, you'd go to the appraisal district's site and search for a property by owner name."

"Excellent! Thanks so much."

Within seconds, they disconnected.

Leah hunted the web until she found appraisal district sites for the counties nearest the house where Trina and Jonathan had lived at the time of her birth. Fulton County. Gwinnett. Forsyth. DeKalb. Cobb. And finally, Cherokee. Each time, she ran a property search by owner's name.

Each time, she found no properties.

Chewing on her bottom lip, she peered through the windows at the comfortingly familiar curves and dips of the Blue Ridge Mountains.

On a fresh wave of inspiration, she swiveled back to the screen. She found an appraisal district database for her own county, Rabun, and input the name Sebastian Grant.

This time fortune smiled upon her.

He owned property at 1248 Black Cherry Lane.

What an excellent house number. 1, 2, 4, 8. Each subsequent number doubled the one that came before. Very promising.

Tomorrow was Saturday, and he often spent his weekends in Misty River. She'd already been planning to go walking tomorrow for exercise. So instead of a hiking trail, why not amend her plans?

She'd walk past his house instead.

The next day she parked a mile away from Sebastian's address and set out on the three-mile loop she'd charted. Striding at her fastest clip, she started in a neighborhood of half-acre lots. Gradually, the lots grew bigger. Then bigger, until nature surrounded her on both sides. The road plateaued before climbing steeply.

Whenever she had her backpack with her, she kept her phone inside. For quicker, less remote walks like this one, she carried her phone and car key in a band strapped to her upper arm. After a time, her phone's male Irish voice spoke from that arm band, notifying her that 1248 was coming up on the right.

Male Irish voice was rarely wrong. Which was one of the things she valued about him. She reached over and turned off the GPS.

At first, Sebastian's house played hide-and-seek between the trees. Leah continued forward until a luxurious modern-day cabin slid into view. Dark wood siding. Stone chimneys. A short central hallway connected the two main wings, the narrow front sides of which faced forward. The wings were of equal width and both had identical obtuse rooflines. However, the one on the left was one story. The one on the right, two stories. Porches spread forward from the bases of the wings, and a balcony jutted from the second-story sliding glass doors.

Manicured grass and planting beds curved between stands of pines. No driveway to be seen, so that must wrap around from a different point to the rear of the building.

It was a fantastic house.

Unfortunately, though, for her purposes, it sat dark and empty.

However, when she walked by his house again, one week later . . .

He was home.

CHAPTER NINE

Even before Leah arrived at Sebastian's house for the second time, she could see through the foliage that some of his interior lights were illuminated.

Anticipation floated upward within her.

Glass covered much of the front of his house, so chances were good that she'd be able to see him inside as she passed. If so, she planned to knock, explain that she'd been walking by, noticed him, and wanted to say hello.

And he likely wouldn't mind the intrusion because they were friends. . . . Or friendly, at least.

When she reached the edge of his property, she saw him standing on his lawn, attempting to start a push lawnmower.

"Sometimes I amaze . . . even . . . myself." The Han Solo quote stumbled like a drunk person through her head.

Sebastian was just yards away. Wearing basketball shorts. And no shirt.

Leah resettled her attention respectfully forward. She hadn't prepared a plan for this particular scenario! She wasn't experienced at carrying on conversations with shirtless men.

He didn't have the self-indulgent, puffed-up body of someone who lifted heavy weights at the gym. Nonetheless, he clearly did spend time exercising. His frame was imposing. His chest and abdomen, firm and smooth.

"Leah?"

At the sound of his voice, she turned, her motion halting.

He'd straightened to his full height, his face a portrait of surprise.

"Oh! Hello." She approached him.

The dark stubble on his cheeks informed her that he hadn't shaved this morning. Hurriedly, she worked to absorb the remaining details of his appearance.... The piercing pale gray of his eyes. The blunt nose and determined lips. The weathered plane of his forehead. The vertical furrow between his brows. He looked like a man who'd been to war and lived to tell the tale.

"Dr. Grant."

"Professor Montgomery."

"Nice to see you again."

"Nice to see you again, too."

"You told me once that you like to mow your lawn."

"And you told me once that you like hiking."

"I guess neither of us was lying."

He smiled. "What brings you to this part of town?"

"I get bored walking my neighborhood, so I frequently drive to areas of town I haven't yet explored and walk other people's neighborhoods," she lied.

"You're not carrying a purse." His attention flicked down to her tennis shoes and back up. "So where's your graphing calculator?"

She laughed. "I'm heartened to inform you that I actually can accomplish quite a bit of math in my head, so I keep my calculator near me most of the time but am not obliged to keep it with me *all* of the time."

"You're not afraid you might encounter a math problem you can't solve in your head while out walking?"

"If I do encounter that type of problem while out walking, I'm confident that I'll be able to remember it well enough to input it into my calculator at the first available opportunity."

"Very brave."

And there it was, that living, crackling, thrilling allure. And not because of his shirtlessness. Because of *him*. His quickness and understated humor. And also *them*. Their alchemy.

Very, very intriguing.

It was glorious to banter with him again. In fact, talking to him gave her the same feeling she'd experienced when she'd returned to Misty River from New England—the delight of coming home.

"Ah," she whispered.

Wait. Had she said that out loud?

A h what?" Sebastian asked. He could not believe that Leah Montgomery was standing in front of him. He felt like he had the first time he'd seen her inside his wrecked car—dazzled and stupid. His responses to her were much too big. Ridiculous. His heart was pounding, and his senses were rushing.

She'd dressed in a light blue workout top, yoga pants, socks that had pom poms at the back of her ankles above her tennis shoes. She'd pulled the front of her hair to one side and fastened it with a barrette. Exertion had turned her cheeks pink, and she was the most beautiful thing he'd ever seen.

"*Ah*, isn't this summer heat wonderful?" she finished in answer to his question.

"*Ah*, isn't this mountain air perfect?" he countered.

"It is."

"Go on any doomed road trips recently, Professor?"

"No." She sniffed. "I did, however, go on a *lovely* road trip. Have you repaired any damaged baby hearts lately?"

"A few. Competed in any chess tournaments?"

"Sadly, no. Listened to Sinatra?"

"Happily, yes."

"Driven off the side of any roads?"

He made a sound of amusement. "Nope. Gone out to dinner with my friend Ben?"

"Not yet, but we've scheduled it for Wednesday."

That information sent a slash of pain through him. After a few moments, he realized he'd been staring at her too long without saying anything. He motioned toward his house. "Would you like to come in?"

"Certainly, though I don't want to interrupt your mowing."

"The mowing can wait."

They walked across overgrown grass he wished he'd had the chance to cut before she'd seen it.

Mowing his lawn was a throwback to the set of foster parents he'd lived with the longest. Jim had taught Sebastian to mow. Once he'd learned how, Sebastian had run the lawnmower over their front and back lawns every two weeks.

Jim's motto had been *"If something's worth doing, it's worth doing well."* By that point in Sebastian's life, after El Salvador, Sebastian had agreed. He'd found that he liked mowing and mowing well. It relaxed him to do something outdoors with his hands. Back then, many things in his life—mostly the fact that he had no parents—had been a mess. But he'd had the ability to cut the grass perfectly.

Things could and did go wrong with his patients' health, but to this day, he had this. He could still control his lawn.

"Ben and some of our other friends are coming by any minute," he said. "They're going to help me trim the hedges and plant flowers."

"Sounds like you've compiled a whole landscaping team." She paused in front of the entry to look up at the structure. "Your house is gorgeous."

Her compliment pleased him more than anything had in weeks. "Thank you."

"Did you hire an architect to draw up plans?"

"Yes. I was not an easy client. I'm sure she was glad to get rid of me." He held the front door open for her.

Inside the foyer, he grabbed his T-shirt off the small table next to the door. In one fluid movement, he pulled it over his head.

"May I have a tour?" she asked, then added, "Is that a presumptuous thing to request?" before he could respond to her first question.

"I'd be glad to give you a tour."

He wanted to take her face in his hands and make out with her. Instead, he led her to the one-story side of his house. While she was distracted, looking at the surroundings, he studied her gentle profile. Her opinion of his place meant something to him. It felt as if he was watching her open a gift he'd given her.

"It's fabulous the way the ceiling's vaulted and supported with all those beams," she said. "And I like how this whole area is just one open space. Kitchen, dining room, sitting area."

"This is the part of the house I use the least."

"Oh?"

"If I were married or had a family, it would probably be the part of the house I'd use the most. As it is, I'm usually here alone. I don't have much use for a dining room table or a sitting area."

"What about the kitchen? Do you cook?"

"Not really. You?"

"Not really." They made their way to the two-story wing.

Downstairs, he showed her the half bath and the den where he watched TV. Upstairs, they walked through the guest bedroom, connecting bathroom, and the room that served as his office. Then they stepped into his master bedroom, which thankfully, he kept clean.

He wouldn't have thought twice about showing anyone else his bedroom. But this was *Leah*. The fact that he was showing *her* his bedroom made this seem intimate. Irrational things he'd never say out loud crammed into his head. *Marry me. Sleep here with me. Live here with me.*

They reached the landing at the top of the stairs. "I love your house," she told him. "You and the architect who was glad to get rid of you did an excellent job."

Their eyes held. For a split second his brain blanked, and he couldn't find words. "Have . . . have you learned anything new about Jonathan and Trina Brookside since I saw you last?"

"Not much. I visited the house where they lived twenty-eight years ago and found pictures of Trina and Sophie online."

He wanted to say, *"Please let me know how I can help."* But he only let himself nod.

He heard the back door open.

Ben, no doubt. He needed to give his friend warning. "Look who was walking down my street," Sebastian called as he and Leah made their way downstairs.

Right when they reached the foyer, Ben came into view. He hesitated for only a moment before a grin broke across his face. "Leah! Great to see you."

"You too," she answered, hugging him.

They stepped apart. "I didn't think I'd get to see you until Wednesday," Ben said.

"Same."

Sebastian's gut knotted. Ben filled Sebastian in on a lot of aspects of his life, but he no longer spoke about Leah. Until Leah had mentioned her date with Ben earlier, he hadn't known about it.

"How was your trip?" Ben asked.

While she described a few of the highlights, she pulled out her phone to find some photos to share.

Ben took the opportunity to send Sebastian a look that said, *What are you doing with my girl?*

When Leah returned her phone to her arm band, Ben's friendly expression snapped back into place.

"Would you like something to drink?" Sebastian asked.

"Water would be great."

In his kitchen, he surveyed his pantry. "What about something to eat? I've got crackers, sunflower seeds, protein powder, collagen." He considered the contents of his fridge. "Greek yogurt, leftover chicken and rice, olive tapenade." He motioned to the bowl on the counter. "Clementines, bananas, sweet potato."

"Collagen and sweet potato, please." Leah spoke from her position across the island next to Ben.

Ben bent at the waist, chuckling.

Sebastian arched a brow. He wasn't above a challenge. "I can make you a collagen shake—"

"No, no, no," she said. "Just water and a few crackers, please."

"Ben?" Sebastian asked.

"I'll have a banana."

He passed out water and food, glad for the chance to give her something, even something small.

They stood around the island, snacking, talking. The whole time, Sebastian could sense Ben's suspicion.

Leah looked between them with interest. "How long have you two been friends?"

"Nineteen years," Sebastian answered.

"I'm envious. I wish I'd had a friendship like yours."

"How come you didn't?" Sebastian asked.

"I made some good friends back when I was around the same age that you were when you became friends. But then we all went separate directions when we were eighteen. One of them lives in California. One in Florida. One in New York. I've kept in touch with most of them, but less and less as the years passed." She adjusted her barrette. "I'm convinced that you two are the gold standard in male friendships."

It didn't feel like that at the moment, since he was certain Ben wanted to punch him and he'd like to punch Ben back.

"Nah," Ben said good-naturedly. "We're not the gold standard. We're just two normal guys."

"Who were rescued from earthquake rubble by a supernatural act of God?" she asked dryly.

Ben released an amused whistle.

"What do you like best about each other?" she asked.

"I like that Ben's loyal," Sebastian said.

"Sebastian's determined. More than any other person I know, he gets things done."

"Okay. So what drives you crazy about the other?"

Ben lifted his eyebrows. "You really want to stir that pot?"

"I do. What drives you crazy about Sebastian?"

"He's opinionated, and he'll fight for his side, even when he's wrong."

"That's true," Sebastian told her.

"What drives you crazy about Ben?" She broke a cracker in half and popped a piece into her mouth.

"Instead of confronting me, he'll sometimes stay quiet about the things I do that bother him."

"Also true," Ben said.

She ate the rest of the cracker.

"Have you demoted us from the gold standard?" Sebastian asked.

"Not in the least."

"I realize that I haven't known you as long as I've known Sebastian," Ben said to her. "But you do have a friend in me, Leah."

"I know," she said. "I'm thankful."

If these two became a couple, he'd have to see them together often. If they married, he'd attend their wedding. Then he'd visit them at their first house. Then he'd hold their baby in his arms.

The thought filled his body with a wash of dismay.

A knock sounded, immediately followed by the *whoosh* of the front door. "We're here!" a feminine voice called.

"In the kitchen," Ben called back.

Natasha and her younger sister, Genevieve, pulled up short when they saw a stranger in their midst.

Ben performed the introductions, finishing with, "This is Leah Montgomery, the most outstanding advanced math teacher in Georgia."

Understanding swept across both sisters' faces as they realized that this was *the* Leah Ben had been talking about for months.

"I'm delighted to meet you," Genevieve said.

"Ben's great, isn't he?" Natasha asked.

"We adore Ben," Genevieve explained.

"Can you confirm my suspicion that Ben's the best science teacher in Georgia?" Natasha asked.

"Since I'm not acquainted with all the science teachers in Georgia," Leah answered, "I'm afraid that I can't say that definitively. But my best guess is yes."

"I knew it," Natasha said to Ben.

"*We* knew it," Genevieve corrected.

"Are you here to help us with yard work?" Natasha asked Leah.

"If not, you're still allowed to stay." Genevieve lifted the stack of cookies she'd brought from Tart Bakery. "I came under the guise of planting flowers, but I'm mostly planning to eat cookies, talk, and maybe drink iced tea."

"I don't have iced tea," Sebastian said.

"Dream killer," Genevieve murmured.

"Actually," Leah said, "I was out walking when Sebastian saw me, and I stopped to chat. I have a few more miles to go, so I'll head out."

"We'll be trimming hedges," Ben said to Leah. "I know you can't resist trimming hedges."

"Amazingly, I can." Her lips curved. "Thanks for the house tour and the food, Sebastian."

"You're welcome."

Her gaze remained on him. "I'll be driving to Atlanta next month so that Dylan can tour colleges. I've been trying to introduce him to various career tracks in a desperate attempt to motivate him and was wondering if it might be possible to bring him by your hospital while we're there."

"Of course," Sebastian answered. "Just text me and let me know when you'd like to come by."

"Will do."

"We'll walk you out." Genevieve and Natasha ushered her away before Sebastian could say good-bye. "Here, let me give you my number!" Genevieve said, then the sound of feminine voices faded to quiet.

Ben frowned at him. "Dude."

"Everything happened the way she said. I was trying to get my lawnmower to start. I looked up, and I saw her walking by."

"What was she doing, walking in this part of town? She doesn't live anywhere near here."

"She told me she gets bored walking her neighborhood, so she likes to branch out and walk other people's neighborhoods."

"Seems like a weird coincidence that she walked right by your house."

"I agree."

"What were you guys doing upstairs?"

"She asked for a tour of the house."

Ben's mouth tensed. "Is anything going on between you two?"

"No."

Long pause. "Okay," Ben said.

"Really?"

"Yeah." Ben had always been slow to anger and quick to let anger go.

Natasha and Genevieve returned. "Ben!" Genevieve took hold of his shoulders. "She's beautiful."

"She really is," Natasha echoed.

"I'm glad you two finally got to meet her," Ben said.

The sisters went on and on about Leah.

Natasha, a mother of two, was currently on leave from practicing law. She was fit, blond, practical, and, in his opinion, slightly eccentric. She'd completed what she'd called "A Year of Living Austenly," and this year had kicked off "A Year of Living C. S. Lewisly." A few weeks back, she'd told him about the theology she'd been reading, the letters she'd been writing, and her determination to smoke a pipe before the year was out.

Natasha's younger sister, Genevieve, had long hair, browner at the top and blonder at the bottom. He'd never caught her without makeup, nail polish, earrings, and a coordinated outfit. Outgoing and self-deprecating, she'd surprised him by building an extremely successful career as a Bible study author and Christian speaker.

"So, what's the latest with you and Leah?" Natasha asked Ben. She and Genevieve settled on the island's stools. "Any change?"

"Today's the first time I've seen her in about a month. She was traveling, so we've been keeping in touch through texts. Here, look." He pulled out his phone and passed it to the sisters. After they'd each taken a look, Genevieve turned Ben's phone in Sebastian's direction. The photo Leah had texted Ben showed Leah and Dylan sitting in a canoe, smiling.

"A few days ago, she suggested we go out for Korean food this week," Ben said.

"Wait." Natasha faced Ben. "What?"

"Why didn't you say something sooner?" Genevieve asked.

"Because I don't want to get my hopes up. I think it might just be a friend thing. Not a date."

"Wear something semi-nice, in case it is a date in her mind," Genevieve suggested. "Women don't like to feel overdressed."

They continued to talk in painful detail about what Ben should wear, what he should order, how he should handle trying to pay.

Miserable, Sebastian drained the last of his water, then peeled another clementine, even though he hadn't been hungry for the first one he'd eaten.

CHAPTER TEN

An elevator carried Sebastian down through the center of the hospital on Wednesday night.

What was he feeling?

Jealousy. Why? Because Ben was on a date with Leah tonight.

Fear. Why? Because he was afraid that Leah would fall in love with his best friend. Which was self-centered. No one could make her happier than Ben could. Ben was the better man. Ben didn't have the baggage Sebastian carried.

He needed to be honest enough with himself to admit that he had serious issues with trust. The walls he'd built didn't make him a good bet as a boyfriend.

If his feelings for Ben and Leah were true, he'd want them to end up together.

That's what was in their best interest.

Many miles to the north, Leah's eyes sank closed reverently as she sampled the first bite of her meal: bibimbap, Korean comfort food.

Ben, unsure of what to order, had followed her lead. Thus, matching stone bowls of food sat before them. Rice formed the base of the dish, crowned with a fried egg surrounded by colorful mounds of spiced beef, bean sprouts, carrot, zucchini, spinach.

"So good," Ben said.

"So good," she confirmed, adding an additional squirt of chili paste to the dish, then mixing all the ingredients together. "You know, when you and Natasha and Genevieve showed up at Sebastian's house the other day, I couldn't believe that I was surrounded by four of the Miracle Five."

"Impressive, aren't we?" he joked.

"It was a rare honor." The only one who'd been absent was the one who'd never joined the rest, even when they were young, in their public appearances and interviews. Luke Dempsey. "Is Luke still in prison?" He'd spent the last seven years in prison for felony theft.

"Yeah, but he's supposed to come up for parole soon. We're hoping he finally gets out."

She asked Ben to tell her more about Natasha and Genevieve, and he filled her in.

On this midweek night in early August, most of the restaurant's seats were occupied by tourists enjoying summer vacations. The establishment had a crisp, modern atmosphere. Dark gray tiled floor, pops of lime green fabric, a white and silver lighting scheme.

Ben had offered to pick her up this evening, but she'd told him she'd meet him here. If he'd driven them, it would have given the evening a datelike feel. Also, she didn't enjoy relying on others for rides. Doing so made her feel helpless, and she loathed feeling helpless.

For tonight's outing, she'd chosen a full skirt and a sleeveless shirt printed with little yellow birds. He'd arrived looking slightly more formal in a green dress shirt, flat front pants, leather shoes.

They were situated at a cozy table for two. Eating out. Away from their usual environment of the school. Away from the rest of their teacher friends. Dressed in fancier clothing than normal.

She might be wrong, because she could never trust her conclusions about such things, but this *did* feel datelike to her, despite that she'd driven herself here.

As she met Ben's beautiful eyes from across the table, her nerves stretched. The intimacy of this dinner was confirming for her that she still wanted the same thing she'd always wanted from Ben. Friendship.

The relationship they already had was not a small thing to her. It wasn't as if she had a large and close-knit circle of adult friends. She had Tess and Rudy. Ben. And a few more casual friendships at school and church. That was it. She was more than grateful for their current relationship.

But the hopeful look on his face was substantiating what Sebastian had told her—that Ben wanted more. Which made her feel like an appalling human being because she truly, *truly* did not want to hurt him. He was one of the kindest people she'd ever met. Encouraging, thoughtful, supportive. Dozens of times he'd paved the way for her at Misty River High. He was a fantastic listener and, like Sebastian had pointed out, he was loyal.

She'd been eating with a fork, but now fiddled with the unused chopsticks lying next to her napkin.

"Is something wrong?" Ben asked.

"I . . . have an awkward question to ask you. Do you think our friendship can handle an awkward question or two?"

"Absolutely. What's your question?"

She stilled the chopsticks, mounded her hands in her lap. "I'm interested in knowing if you like me as more than a friend."

His head pulled back a few inches with surprise.

She waited.

"Come again?" he said.

"I'm interested in knowing if you like me as more than a friend."

"Uh. Well." He fidgeted. "What motivated you to ask that?"

"Curiosity. I'd like to be sensitive to where you're coming from, but I can't tell where you're coming from. In order to find out, I have to ask."

He gave her his thoughtful look, the one that he gave students when he wasn't sure how to respond. "Do you like me as more than a friend?"

In her life, she'd often been *too* much of something for other people. Too much of a brainiac. Too nerdy. Too interested in things no one else was interested in.

Much of the journey God had taken her on so far was a journey toward accepting and then embracing who she was. In this case, being true to herself meant being honest with Ben. "I wish I could say yes. In fact, if I could create a software program that would calibrate a woman's heart to want to date the most ideal man, then I'd calibrate my heart to want to date you. Of course, if I could create that program, I'd also revolutionize dating and make a mint. But that's just an aside."

His expression dimmed. The reaction was subtle, but telling.

"Do you like me as more than a friend?" she asked. "You haven't answered my initial question."

"I was kind of hoping you'd forgotten your initial question."

"I don't tend to forget things that are important."

"If—if you're asking if I'd like to see if this could lead to more, then the answer's sure I would."

He'd replied to that skillfully. He'd kept his admission relaxed and, in doing so, made this discussion easier for them both. He often did that—made things easier for her.

"But it sounds like you're not into the idea of dating me," he continued. "Which is cool."

"I'm content with our friendship. In fact, I feel fortunate to have you as a friend."

"Same here."

"I'd hate for you to waste your time . . . waiting for me."

"I won't." He gathered food onto his fork. "Should you ever come to your senses and want to go out with me, though, let me know."

"Okay."

"But I won't hold my breath."

"Best not to."

"Because there are a lot of fish in the sea."

"So many!"

"And a math genius for a girlfriend might come with a whole set of issues."

"Now you're thinking. When they handed me the menu earlier, I had a hard time concentrating on the food because I was busy rounding the dollar amounts of the items and adding them in my head."

"Right. That would be super annoying to deal with."

"I'm doing you a favor by taking my name off the list of contenders."

He shot her a smile tinged with sadness.

I really am doing you a favor, she wanted to insist. He deserved someone who would love him wildly. Her intuition was telling her that God had someone picked out specifically for Ben.

However, that person was not her.

The next day, Sebastian sat alone in the staff break room at the hospital, his lunch on the table in front of him. He picked up his phone after it began to ring. Ben. "Hello?"

"Hey."

Something was wrong. He could tell by the sound of his friend's voice. "What's the matter?" he asked, a tendril of fear sprouting in his stomach. Were the Colemans all okay?

"I talked with Leah about my feelings for her last night."

Sebastian put on the armor of control he wore whenever things went wrong in the operating room and the air started to smell like panic. "And?"

"She told me that she likes me as a friend and nothing more."

The air squeezed from his chest.

Leah wasn't falling in love with Ben. And yet . . . what came as a tremendous relief to Sebastian was devastating his friend. "I'm sorry."

"She just suddenly brought up the subject. Out of the blue. Which makes me think that you must have told her that I like her."

Crap.

"Did you tell her that?" Ben prodded.

138

"Yes."

"And did you also tell her to go out to dinner with me?"

"Yes. I was trying to help."

"I didn't need your help," Ben said tightly, clearly struggling with his temper. "I didn't want your interference."

"She had no idea that you liked her, Ben. She was never going to figure it out unless someone told her."

"I disagree. She would have figured it out for herself. I wanted it to happen naturally."

"You've known her for two years. When? When was she going to figure it out for herself?"

"I don't know, but I was content waiting."

"I wasn't content watching you wait."

"My relationship with Leah isn't about you or your preferences," Ben snapped.

Sebastian bit his lip to force himself to shut up. Tension filled the silence. He'd thought recently about how quickly Ben usually got over his anger. It didn't look like that was going to happen this time. "You're right. I apologize."

More jagged quiet.

"You told Leah," Ben said, "that one of your frustrations with me is that I don't confront you when you do things that bother me. So let me tell you something outright."

Sebastian braced himself. "Go ahead."

"I've shared a lot with you over the years. My room. Vacations. Family gatherings."

"Yes."

"I know you like Leah, but I draw the line at sharing her with you."

He didn't answer.

"Sebastian?" Ben demanded.

"Okay."

The line went dead. Sebastian cursed.

Ben had shared a lot more with him than the things he'd mentioned. During Sebastian's two years of high school, Ben had shared some of his paycheck with Sebastian, so that Sebastian could join him at the movies, so that Sebastian didn't have to wear an uncool brand of socks, so that Sebastian could split the pizzas Ben ordered. Ben had shared his parents' attention with Sebastian. He'd shared his time and sweat moving Sebastian from one dorm room to another. These days, Ben even shared his nieces and nephews with Sebastian.

It had taken nineteen years, but he'd finally found the limit to what Ben was willing to share.

Y*ou're braver than you believe, stronger than you seem, and smarter than you think.* Those inspirational words by A. A. Milne scrolled across a decorative sign displayed on the bookcase in Leah's classroom.

Alas, though. The start of a new school year in August always tempted her to deduce that she was less brave than she believed, weaker than she seemed, and dumber than she thought.

By week two, things had started to settle. By week three, the kids gave her reason to hope. And now, on week four, they'd found their rhythm.

When Dylan was at football practice or out with his friends, she kept an eye on him via the phone app that tracked his position. When he was at home in his room, she spot-checked to make sure he wasn't dead. During their nightly dinners, she forced him to have a conversation with her and to eat healthy meals that contained vegetables.

Blessedly, the dynamic between herself and Ben hadn't been as uncomfortable as she'd feared after she'd divulged her position on dating him. His laidback, cheerful manner remained intact.

She continued to threaten to set him up because, earnestly, she *wanted* to set him up. If she found someone for him, she wouldn't have to feel guilty about her failure to be to him what he'd hoped she might be. So far, he'd evaded her attempts at matchmaking.

Her search for a current address for Jonathan and Trina Brookside had proved equally unsuccessful. They were annoyingly savvy about protecting their privacy online. She couldn't shake the notion, though, that the Brooksides' current address must be ripe for the finding *somewhere*. She simply needed to peek under the correct rock.

She'd revisited the two online articles attributed to Jonathan Brookside at Gridwork Communications Corporation. It very well might be, of course, that another man with the same name had written those articles. But the location of Gridwork, just miles from the hospital where she'd been born, made plausible the possibility that the man who'd penned the articles was, indeed, her biological father.

During quiet moments, she mulled over how best to confirm whether the Jonathan of Gridwork was *her* Jonathan. And, if so, how to obtain his address from the company without arousing his suspicion. She'd yet to settle on the optimal strategy.

Sebastian continued to visit her in her dreams. Sebastian, lying beside her in the grass, propped up on an elbow, looking down at her. Sebastian, kissing her knuckles.

Occasionally, she indulged herself by driving by his house. Once, she spotted an empty plastic water bottle snagged in a cluster of bushes out front. Since his house was dim and obviously empty—and because she now comprehended that he valued a tidy lawn—she'd darted from her car and confiscated the bottle.

However, she had not had an opportunity to see him or talk to him for more than a month.

Until, that is, she traveled to Atlanta with Dylan to tour two colleges and visit one particular hospital.

CHAPTER ELEVEN

It required an act of God and a generous portion of histrionics, but Leah managed to pry Dylan from his bedroom at their Airbnb and convey the two of them to Beckett Memorial Hospital ahead of their prearranged meeting with Sebastian. An assistant ushered them to Sebastian's office and informed them that he would join them shortly.

Thus, on the first Monday of September, a day she had off work for Labor Day, Leah was given an unexpected chance to scrutinize Sebastian's office without him present. The space boasted one large window. Two high-quality leather chairs. An office chair. And a desk, on which four items rested: a lamp, thick white notepad, Montblanc pen, computer.

A yard-wide strip of corkboard ran vertically from the floor to the ceiling of the wall next to his desk. Photos and cards had been pinned to it. Leah stood before the collage, enthralled, reading fast because she was afraid he'd arrive before she had a chance to ingest it all.

The pictures highlighted smiling infant faces. The parents who'd written the cards clearly believed that Sebastian's efforts had saved the lives of their babies.

As much as she loved math, ultimately, math was theory. Sebastian's job impacted living, breathing children and families.

Ever since she'd reached out to Sebastian a week and a half ago to schedule this appointment, she'd been looking forward to this the way she looked forward to her beloved budget road trips. So far, it did not disappoint. And Sebastian hadn't even appeared.

Dylan was far less enthused. He'd wanted to spend this holiday sleeping late, shirking homework, working on his drawings, and hanging out with his friends. He was currently slumped in one of the chairs, scrolling sullenly through his apps. His interest in pursuing a career in the field of healthcare hovered at a negative ten.

She'd spent the weekend putting Dylan first. Touring potential schools. Allowing him to choose where they ate. Helping him with his college applications. She'd pitched this hospital visit as something she'd sought out for his sake, but that was an outright lie.

This was the one thing on their itinerary that she'd arranged purely for herself. She wanted another chance to see Sebastian.

It felt divine to be here simply because she wanted to be—

The door swept open. She hadn't seen Sebastian in weeks, and now, suddenly, here he was. Tall and broad. He wore a white T-shirt with green scrubs and retro-looking black-on-black Adidas. She met his eyes, then watched his vision flick down to her chin before tracing its way back up. As usual, his demeanor communicated observant intensity.

The awareness that existed between them rushed to life.

Distantly she thought, *I haven't finished reading everything on the corkboard. Which means I'll have to come back one day. That's the only tenable solution. Also, am I imagining the electricity between us? I can't be so out of touch with reality that I'm the only one feeling this, can I?*

"Hello," she said.

"Hi."

"Thanks for making time in your schedule for us."

"Of course. I'm sorry that I kept you waiting. One of my colleagues asked for a consult on a case."

"No problem. We're not in a hurry."

His attention slanted toward Dylan.

"Do you remember my brother, Dylan?" she asked.

"I do."

She shot her sibling a don't-forget-my-warning smile. She'd deemed it necessary to threaten him with a fate worse than death (the removal of his phone) if he didn't exhibit politeness on this tour.

Dylan rose, his stoop-shouldered posture appalling, and shook Sebastian's hand.

"Your sister tells me that she's been introducing you to several different career fields."

"Um, yeah."

"Anything catch your interest so far?"

Dylan scratched his temple. "Just art."

Behind Sebastian's back Leah tilted her head in a way that said, *Ask Sebastian questions.*

"So." Dylan pushed his hands into the pockets of his artfully ripped jeans. "You went to Misty River High School, too?"

"I did."

"And what job do you have now?"

"I'm a pediatric cardiac surgeon."

"And what . . . uh . . . what did you have to do after you graduated high school to get this job?"

Sebastian explained his schooling and training.

A wince pinched Dylan's face more and more as Sebastian spoke. "So. Uh. I guess you're not grossed out by the sight of blood?"

After all that Sebastian had said, *that* was the best question Dylan could muster?

Amusement creased Sebastian's face. "Nope, I'm not grossed out by it. Are you?"

"Yeah. For sure."

"In that case, we'll avoid the sight of blood on this tour."

"'Kay."

They exited his office. Leah fell in step beside Sebastian, Dylan behind them.

"How've you been?" he asked.

"I've been well, thank you. Busy, adjusting to my new classes."

"Have your students been treating you with the awe and respect you deserve?"

"Awe and respect are in short supply with teenagers."

"They're in short supply with non-verbal infants as well."

"Kids these days."

He was spending more time looking across at her than he was looking forward. His almost-black hair was in mild disarray. Tiredness edged his features, causing her to wonder what might have cost him sleep last night. An emergency here? A date with a new girlfriend?

He asked her questions about her students. She asked him questions about his surgeries.

They sailed through a set of automatic doors.

He showed them the areas of the surgical floor they were allowed to see and explained several different jobs to Dylan. Dylan feigned interest but his body language communicated that he cared about as much as he would about the hospital's bylaws. Conversely, Leah—always hungry for deeper understanding of a topic—soaked in every word.

When Sebastian finished, Dylan responded with the sparkling verbal parry of "Huh."

They visited the room where the doctors met each morning to view X-rays before rounds. Then they moved on to the Pediatric Intensive Care Unit.

"Do Dylan and I need a pass in order to enter?" she asked.

"Not if you're with me. I gave one of the administrators a heads-up that you were coming."

The PICU felt like a high-tech spaceship on red alert. A central desk served as the command center.

Again, Sebastian paused and talked through the many roles the PICU employees filled. "Do any of these jobs sound like something you'd want to do?" he asked Dylan.

"I mean . . . maybe."

"Really?" Sebastian asked skeptically.

"No, to be honest. No offense. I mean, it seems like you're doing okay, but . . ."

Leah's mouth formed a horizontal line.

"But I'm not into this. At all." Dylan yawned gloomily.

"Well," Sebastian said to Leah, "I guess we can cross health professions off Dylan's list."

"I guess so. Narrowing things down is helpful."

Dylan wandered toward the nearest bathroom.

"Would it be possible to look in on a few of your patients?" Leah asked Sebastian.

"If you'd like to, yes."

"I'd like to."

She followed him into a room filled with machines and monitors. On the miniature bed lay a dark-skinned, black-haired infant.

"This is Levi. He's beating the odds. Right after his birth he survived an emergency procedure with a mortality rate of ninety-five percent."

"What was his diagnosis?"

"Hypoplastic left heart syndrome, but without an atrial septal defect. Usually, we close up holes in hearts. But in his case, his lack of a hole was causing blood to back up into his lungs. So my colleague ran a catheter to his heart and punched a hole in exactly the right spot."

Her eyebrows rose. "Have you operated on him since?"

"Yes. The Norwood procedure, six days ago."

"You had to build a new aorta."

"You're right. I also had to make his right ventricle pump blood to the body through the aorta and to the lungs through a new path to the pulmonary artery."

"What are his prospects?"

"Good."

It was one thing to read about congenital heart defects and the surgeries employed to repair them, quite another to observe one of the children who'd been impacted.

Levi seemed impossibly small and frail. And, of course, all kids radiated sweetness when they were sleeping. She knew this to be true because she'd been peeking in on Dylan while he was sleeping since he'd been this size.

146

From the start, Mom had delegated a sizable share of Dylan's care to her. She'd done a great deal of babysitting, feeding, rocking to sleep, and bathing. Dylan had rewarded her efforts by turning into an adorable curly-haired toddler who'd hugged her, snuggled with her, held her hand, and climbed onto her lap.

He'd been just two years old when she'd left home for high school. Right away, she'd discovered that she missed him far more than any other person. If not for him, she wouldn't have made the effort to return home on the weekends. By that point, Dad was gone. She and Mom weren't close. She'd enjoyed a far greater sense of belonging at Clemmons than at the apartment Mom had moved them into for Leah's final year of middle school.

She'd come home because she'd needed to see Dylan. More often than not, she'd arrive at their apartment complex to find Mom's car packed and waiting to pull away from the curb. The second after Leah arrived, Mom would depart. She wouldn't return until two days later—when Leah had to head back to campus.

Leah had been fourteen years old, yet for weekends at a time, she'd been in charge of Dylan. It had been scary. It had also been oddly wonderful, because she'd been free to do whatever she deemed best. They watched *Go, Diego, Go!* and visited the playground. She read him *The Very Hungry Caterpillar* a million times. She made them ice cream sundaes topped with whipped cream and caramel sauce and chocolate sprinkles. They roved through the two parks and the one library within walking distance of their building.

She'd thought she'd understood what it meant to be responsible for Dylan. But then, when he was seven, she'd received full custody. As soon as Mom had left for the airport to catch her flight overseas, Leah had realized that no, she hadn't truly known what it was to be responsible for Dylan. The weight of becoming his 24/7 caregiver had crashed down on her.

The first several days, fear had stalked her. She'd been so overwhelmed that she'd spent hours on her knees after tucking Dylan into bed each night, begging God for strength and mercy.

God had shown up in those dark hours.

Patiently, He'd siphoned His courage into her.

She'd laid every decision before Him that she'd felt incapable of making on her own. Should she move them to Princeton? If not, how should she support Dylan?

Every time, He'd guided her. Sometimes through a sense of rightness that tugged her in a specific direction or a sense of unease that warned her away from another direction. Sometimes through Scripture. Sometimes through a pastor's message. Sometimes through a conversation with a friend.

Obediently, gratefully, she'd followed where He led. Her rock-solid belief that she could rely on Him to make her paths straight turned the impossible job of parenting Dylan while she herself was still a teenager into something she *could* do—with the Lord's equipping.

Dylan had paid her back by continuing to adore her through his elementary school years. He was rambunctious but also kind. Truly kind.

Then his middle school years had crept in. The little boy who'd built his life around her became a gangly adolescent. He'd started to pull away. Give her attitude. Establish his independence. Indulge in moods.

As the years marched on, he'd become more reclusive, and now Dylan was a boy-man with long arms and hairy legs and the beginnings of facial hair and a voracious appetite.

She grieved their former closeness. And, in moments like this one, she ached for the affectionate baby, the trusting preschooler, and the pure-hearted elementary schooler he'd been.

On good days, she told herself that he'd likely become a contributing member of society one day. On bad days, it seemed frighteningly possible that he'd end up wearing an orange jumpsuit in a penitentiary.

It was humbling to observe baby Levi because she was certain his parents were praying fervently that he'd simply have the chance to grow into a boy-man with long arms and hairy legs. She hoped Levi received the opportunity God had given Dylan—the opportunity to experience all the passions, trials, and victories that life offered.

Next, they entered the room of a baby girl. A pink blanket had been folded over and smoothly tucked around her sides. Tape held a ventilator tube to her mouth. IVs snaked into her veins.

A blond woman set aside the book she'd been reading and rose. Sebastian introduced her as Megan.

"This is my daughter," Megan said to Leah. "Isabella."

"She's beautiful."

Isabella shifted slightly. She moved her mouth as if to make noise, but remained soundless.

Sebastian appered to be reading Isabella's monitors.

"Do you . . . live in Atlanta?" Leah asked Megan.

"We live two hours away, in Augusta. At first I drove in every morning and drove home every evening, but that was just too hard. So now I'm staying at the Ronald McDonald House. My husband works during the week in Augusta and joins me here on weekends."

"I'll stop by later," Sebastian said to Megan.

"Sounds good."

He headed out.

"Nice to meet you," Leah said before following Sebastian. They walked back toward the central desk. "How common is it for one parent to live here and the other in their hometown while their child is being treated?"

"Very common. Spending time with Isabella has become Megan's full-time job. She's here most of the day, every day."

"What's Isabella's diagnosis?"

"She has a rudimentary ventricle that isn't composed of myocardium. It's not functional. She's seven weeks old, and she's never breathed on her own, never been fully conscious."

Leah recalled how, when Dylan was nine, a bad case of pneumonia had hospitalized him for two nights. Her anxiety had been so all-consuming that she'd barely slept.

"Isabella's been here seven weeks?"

"Yes."

"What's her treatment plan?"

"A heart transplant is her only option."

A stone of dismay dropped through Leah. "No."

He regarded her steadily. "I'm afraid so."

She spotted Dylan standing in front of a series of framed ink-on-paper drawings. Sebastian started toward him and Leah was on the verge of doing the same when a female voice spoke near her shoulder.

"You're the only personal friends he's had here, other than the Colemans."

Leah turned to find a sixty-something woman with matte brown hair and false eyelashes.

"Is that right?" Leah asked pleasantly.

"That's right." Wearing scrubs patterned with llamas, the woman was wearing a badge that proclaimed her to be a PA named Markie. She moved her chin in Sebastian's direction. "What's your relationship with him?" She asked the question with unconcealed interest, as well as a trace of protectiveness.

"We're friends."

"Hmm." Markie sized her up. "Well. Dr. Grant is bossy." She made a *tut* sound. "Bossy's not really the best word. . . . Hard-charging? Certainly high maintenance. A perfectionist. But here's the deal: In my opinion, a few of the kids he's treated have lived mostly because he was so determined that they wouldn't die."

Her words gave Leah chills.

"Unfortunately," Markie confided, "that also means that he takes the losses harder than is healthy. We all take them hard, don't get me wrong. But Dr. Grant takes them too hard. And I want him to have longevity at this because unless I miss my guess, and I don't think I do, he's destined to become one of the world's best."

"I see."

"It sure would be nice for him to have someone to come home to. Someone he could talk to about things other than medicine and heart defects. Someone who could remind him about the best things in life."

Like geometry? "I'm sure that would be very nice, but that someone won't be me. I don't do romance."

A beat passed. Markie released a cackling laugh. When Leah didn't laugh in return, Markie sobered and said, "Piffle," with feeling. "He's very alone."

"I'm also very alone. For many of us that isn't a detriment."

"Dr. Grant's alone to the point that it's not good for him. Between you and me, the youngest nurse here, Ellie, is crazy about him. She's been doing her best to catch his interest—and she's a pretty little thing—but she's not having any luck. But you . . ." She eyed Leah speculatively.

"I'm not girlfriend material."

"*Piffle!*"

Sebastian approached. "Markie," he greeted the older woman.

"Dr. Grant."

"Have you been pumping Leah for information?"

"Not at all!" she said with pretend outrage.

"Blasting her with a fire hose full of information, then."

Markie tossed another cackle over her shoulder as she went about her duties.

"Sorry about that," Sebastian said. "She's always got her head so buried in everybody else's business that she doesn't realize when she's making people uncomfortable. Did she throw me under the bus or praise me?"

"A little of both?"

"I—" A shrill sound interrupted him. He pulled his phone from his pocket. "My pager," he explained. Clicking off the noise, he read the alert on the screen with a serious expression.

"I presume you're needed elsewhere," Leah said.

He lifted his head. "I am. I'm sorry."

"Don't be," she said merrily to cover her sharp sense of regret. Their time together was at an end. There was no way to know when and if she'd see him again . . . when and if she'd encounter these delightful and highly unusual sparks and pangs. "Thanks for meeting with us." She poked Dylan's calf with her toe.

"Yeah, man," Dylan said. "Thanks."

Sebastian's forehead wrinkled. "I wish we had more time."

"Dylan and I have already taken too much of your time."

"Will you be able to find your way out?"

"I was a math prodigy, remember? I'm more than equal to this hospital's floor plan," she said laughingly, waving him off. He was making her nervous about whatever situation awaited him at the other end of that page. She didn't want to burn precious seconds.

"Good-bye."

"Go save babies!"

Sebastian vanished around a corner.

"You have a crush on him, don't you?" Dylan asked.

"I have no idea what you're talking about, beloved brother of mine."

He did an embarrassing impression of her. Big, adoring eyes. Dazed smile.

"That is *not* how I acted just now."

"You have a crush on him."

"I most assuredly do not." *What I have are some dreams of him and melting sensations when he looks at me.* Why had two people in the span of five minutes determined that she and Sebastian should be romantically linked?

"How come you never go on any dates?"

"I've been on some dates."

"When was the last one?"

"Six years ago."

"That's forever."

"No. Six years ago is six years ago. Forever is another mathematical concept entirely."

"How come you haven't dated anyone since then?"

"Because I haven't been interested in anyone."

"That's weird."

"No it's not. It's countercultural, but countercultural is not synonymous with weird."

"What are you, thirty?"

"Twenty-eight."

"Probably time to get a move on. Tick tock."

She sighed. "That's the most asinine comment you've made all weekend. It accepts as logic several illogical conclusions. That women need a man. That women expire at a certain age. That—"

"Yeah, yeah."

"I haven't dated because I haven't met a man I wanted to date."

"Well." Dylan angled his chin toward where Sebastian had disappeared from sight. "Now you have."

You have a crush on her, don't you?" Markie asked Sebastian an hour later. "The woman who visited you today?"

He accepted the coffee he'd ordered from the barista at the coffee shop a half block down from the hospital. Slowly, he faced Markie. It might be coincidence that she'd made a coffee run at the same time he did. It was far more likely that she'd followed him here like a bloodhound trailing the scent of new gossip.

"That's none of your business," he answered.

"So you *do* have a crush on her. How'd you two meet?"

"No comment."

"How long have you known her?"

"*I draw the line at sharing her with you,*" Ben had told him. "No comment." He pushed through the door onto the sunny, busy city sidewalk.

Leah. Impossibly beautiful. Completely off-limits. He hadn't had enough time to talk with her, look at her, memorize her presence before he'd been called away. And now she was gone.

He'd have liked to spend the rest of the day hitting a punching bag, but he had work to do. Which meant no vent for the grief and anger and desire twisting within.

Markie caught up to him, moving quickly to keep pace. "She told me that she doesn't do romance. What in the world does that mean?"

"She's not interested in falling in love."

"Everyone's interested in falling in love!"

"Not her."

"But—but I could read her like a book. She *does* like you, Dr. Grant."

"She's never said so."

"Maybe she hasn't admitted it to herself. In time, she will. Don't give up."

"I wish I could give up."

"Why?"

"Because even if she is interested in me, I can't be with her. Ben loves her."

Markie gaped at him, fell back, then rushed up to him again. "Does she love Ben?"

"No."

"Well. Has anyone had the sense to ask her how she feels about you?"

"No."

"I see. You're determined to be a martyr."

He grimaced. "I'm determined to do right by my best friend."

"So you're not going to do *anything* where this woman's concerned?"

"No comment."

He was going to do something.

He was going to fix things with Ben. They hadn't talked since their phone call because he'd been giving Ben time to cool off. Soon, though, he'd contact him.

Ben was a brother to him. If Sebastian couldn't keep his relationship with Ben strong, then something was even more seriously wrong with him than he'd feared.

It was never a ringing endorsement of Leah's teaching style when one of her students fell asleep in class.

It wasn't terribly unusual to catch a student snoozing. She often dimmed the lights in order to illustrate examples on her white-board. And teenagers weren't exactly known for their disciplined sleeping habits.

Her policy upon noticing a sleeping student: Do nothing while the other students were present to avoid humiliating the napper in front of their peers.

Two days after Labor Day, she activated her policy when she spotted Claire Dobney asleep in the back row. After the dismissal bell rang and the rest of the class filed out, Leah approached Claire. The girl had rested her head atop her folded arms. She dressed her round body and soft limbs in enormous shirts, as if hoping the shirts would provide her with a mobile tent to hide inside.

"Claire," Leah said.

Claire's torso snapped upright. She held her eyes unnaturally wide, in a bid to show how awake she was.

Lunch period had just begun, which meant they both had a brief pocket of time. Leah made herself comfortable on the chair next to Claire's. "You fell asleep in class."

"I did? Oh. Gosh. I'm sorry, Ms. Montgomery."

"Apology accepted. Is everything all right?"

"Mm-hmm." Perfectly groomed eyebrows capped small eyes ac-cented with unflattering green eye shadow. Her cinnamon-colored curls formed an oval around a circular face.

"You've looked tired to me for a while now," Leah said. "I'm just wondering if there might be something in your life that's bothering you."

"Not really."

"I'm a good listener."

Though Claire existed in a perpetual state of uncertainty, she was bright enough to have made it into Leah's class—the highest level of math available at Misty River High—last year and this year. Last year, Claire's sophomore year, she'd earned Bs. So far this year, she was struggling to maintain a C.

Leah waited, saying nothing.

"I guess I haven't been sleeping that well," Claire confessed.

"Any particular reason?"

"There's been a lot of—" she rolled her wrists in the air— "fighting at my house."

"Who's fighting?"

"My parents."

Leah knew what it was to live on the turf of that battlefield. "Is anyone hurting you physically?"

"No."

"Verbally?"

"No. . . . I mean, not much."

"My parents used to argue, too. I understand how hard that is." She also understood why Claire would fall asleep here. Here, it was safe.

"It's not too bad," Claire said.

Claire had confided in Leah, her teacher. Which probably meant that it was really, really bad. "Do you want to talk to me about it?"

She gave a worried shake of her head.

"Do you know Ms. Williams, the counselor?"

"Not really."

"She's great. I'm going to contact her and have her reach out to you and set up a meeting."

"If I talk to her, will my parents get in trouble?"

"At this point, you're simply going to have a conversation with a counselor. That's all."

A package arrived for you," Leah told Dylan the following evening when he returned home from football practice.

"Huh?" He made his way from the mudroom into the kitchen, where Leah was eating one of Tess's cookies as an appetizer before dinner.

"A package. Arrived for you."

He followed her into the living room, where she'd propped the large rectangular box near the inside of the front door.

"Who's it from?" Dylan asked.

"An art supply company in Atlanta. Did you order art supplies?"

"I can't afford more art supplies." Sweaty and smelling strongly of teenage boy, he carried the package to the dining table and ripped it open. The box contained a huge assortment of products. Paper. Pencils. Erasers. Pens. A T-square, ruler, triangle. A card sat on top. He read it and grinned. "The doctor you don't have a crush on sent this to me."

"What?" she exclaimed.

He passed her the card.

This is my way of supporting your graphic novel. Reserve a copy for me when it's published.

—Sebastian Grant

"You're working on a graphic novel?"

"Yeah."

"Since when?"

He shrugged. "A few weeks."

"Why didn't you tell me?"

Another shrug.

"That's wonderful, Dylan! Seb . . . Sebastian knows?"

"Uh-huh. I told him when we were looking at the artwork one of his patients did." Starstruck, he examined each item. "Wig!"

"Wig?"

"So cool my wig flew off," he explained.

He hadn't shown this much joy over anything in a long time. The sight of it caused a lump to form in her throat. "I have his number. You'll have to call him and thank him."

"I already have his number. He gave it to me."

"When you were looking at artwork together, I presume?"

"Yeah. I'll call him."

Sebastian had sent a teenage boy he hardly knew a wonderfully thoughtful gift.

After Dylan had taken his treasure into his cave, Leah texted Sebastian.

> Thank you for the art supplies you sent to Dylan. In case his teenager-speak makes it impossible to interpret his gratitude, I want you to know that the gift meant a lot to him.

Sebastian's reply arrived forty-five minutes later.

> I'm glad.

She'd been hoping for something that invited further conversation and waited for him to send a follow-up text. But he didn't. Just *I'm glad*—a cordial, to-the-point conversation-ender—and nothing more.

A week later Leah finally hit upon a plan of action pertaining to Jonathan Brookside and Gridwork Communications Corporation that might enable her to access the Brooksides' address.

Problematically, she did not possess the disposition of a double agent. The idea of placing a deceptive phone call made her feel the way she'd felt when she'd developed hives after a bee sting at the age of ten. Itchy and anxious.

She tapped Gridwork's number into her phone. Hesitated.

Restless, she paced to the windows of her classroom. Her final class of the day had concluded thirty minutes prior. Outside, a smattering of kids still dotted the campus, hurrying through the drizzle toward cars, talking with friends beneath overhangs. Inside, quiet reigned, thanks to her classroom's closed door.

She caught herself scratching her forearm and ceased the motion. *You don't actually have hives, Leah.*

She wanted more details about Jonathan and Trina and Sophie.

Her choices were simple: Make this phone call. Or wait and see if she could unearth any other sources of information. Or give up her quest for answers.

She hit the button to connect the call.

"Gridwork Communications Corporation," a male voice answered.

"Hello, I was hoping to reach Jonathan Brookside's personal assistant." Surely, someone with the title of *Founder* would have an assistant.

"One moment, please."

Classical music came on the line. Leah rubbed her thumb against the windowsill. She'd been forwarded, which indicated that Jonathan Brookside was still affiliated with Gridwork and *did* have an assistant. Had the receptionist offered to connect her to Jonathan directly, she'd been prepared to hang up. She couldn't allow her first communication with her biological father to come in the form of a deceptive phone call.

"Meredith Tibbs," a woman said. She sounded both grandmotherly and efficient, like a retirement-age Mary Poppins.

"Hello! I'm hoping you can help me."

"I'll certainly try."

"I'm a friend of Trina's. We volunteered together years ago."

"Ah! At Hands of Grace?"

"Yes. We hadn't seen each other in a log time, but I ran into her the other day, and she was so kind and encouraging. I sent her a note afterward but it was returned to sender. I don't think she lives at the address I have for her anymore."

"What address do you have?"

"11482 Riverchase Road."

"My, that is an old one. Very old."

"Time flies!"

"It really does. Do you have a pen and paper handy?"

"I do." Leah rushed to her desk, her heart whacking against her ribs as she jotted down a current address for Jonathan and Trina Brookside.

CHAPTER TWELVE

Sebastian leaned against the side of the main house at Sugar Maple Farm and talked with Natasha and Genevieve's dad while dusk fell over Misty River.

A year ago Genevieve had moved into the guest house here at the farm and fallen in love with her landlord, Sam Turner. Since then, she'd invited Sebastian to several social events here. Genevieve loved people, loved talking with people, and loved hosting people, especially now that she had access to a great setting (Sugar Maple Farm) and a boyfriend who could do all the cooking (Sam).

On this last Saturday in September, the heat had topped out in the eighties, then slipped into the seventies. To take advantage of the weather, Genevieve had convinced Sam to move his dining room table and chairs outside to the grassy area on the side of the house. She'd sunk tall wooden stakes into the earth, then draped string lights back and forth from the house to the stakes, so that the lights formed a canopy over the table.

Genevieve had told Sebastian they were having a "small group" over for dinner tonight. He knew her well enough to know that "small group" could mean thirty. Because of that, he'd thought it possible that Leah might attend. He'd gotten his hopes up. Showered and shaved, chosen his clothes carefully, spent time on his hair.

Which was stupid. Embarrassing.

He found out after he'd arrived that tonight's "small group" meant twelve. He'd shown up early along with Genevieve's parents, Sam's dad and stepmom, Natasha and her husband, Wyatt. Ben, Eli, and Penelope would be here soon.

Sebastian kept wondering why he was feeling let down. Then remembering . . . it was because Leah wasn't coming.

Almost three weeks had passsed since he'd given her and Dylan a tour of the hospital.

His life and hers overlapped too little. So little, it was making him crazy. Weeks would go by without his seeing her. Then, when he was finally near her again, he experienced the kind of high that made him crave more. Then more weeks would go by without her.

It reminded him of the conditioning he'd learned about in Psychology 101 in college. The occasional reward of seeing her motivated him to wait and watch and wait and watch for more.

He spotted Ben making his way toward the gathering, and excused himself. He and Ben had talked a couple of times since Ben's date with Leah, and things were getting back on decent footing between them. However, this was the first weekend Sebastian had spent at his Misty River house this month, so this was the first time they were seeing each other in person.

"Hey," Sebastian said.

"Hey." Ben offered his hand for a fist bump.

They executed the elaborate fist bump motions they'd made up when they were fourteen. They tapped elbows. Ben jumped and spun so that his back was facing Sebastian. Sebastian pretended to lower a crown on Ben's head and Ben pretended to pull a royal cape up over his shoulders. They'd gone through this routine before all of Ben's baseball games.

Ben took his measure. "Don't look so serious. We're cool."

"Are we?"

"If we do our fist bump, you know we are. Besides, there's a lot to be happy about tonight. Sam's cooking, right?"

"Right. Unfortunately, there's also a lot to be sad about tonight."

"Like?"

"Your shirt."

"My shirt?"

"Did you steal that from a Hawaiian retiree?"

"Men wear pink!"

"Some men shouldn't. Especially pink with palm trees and flamingos on it."

"Man!" Ben laughed. "I look sweet in this shirt."

"If by sweet you mean precious, then I agree."

"Now, now, boys." Genevieve met them, carrying a tray. "Play nice with each other. Appetizer? The toothpicks are for the meatballs and the dip is for the zucchini sticks."

Both men helped themselves to the food.

"I can't get over this piece of property," Ben said.

Sam's historic farm was owned and leased to him by the National Park Service. The tract of land included an orchard, a farm-to-table garden, and large bands of untouched nature.

"I love it here," Genevieve said.

"I can't get over this food," Sebastian said.

"Is all of this paleo?" Ben asked.

"Every single thing you'll be eating tonight is paleo."

"I don't understand how Sam makes healthy stuff taste so good," Ben said.

"Me neither." Natasha drifted over and speared a meatball.

"It's his spiritual gift. It can't be understood." Genevieve leaned in. "People might suspect that I fell for Sam because of this place or his food. And I get it because, honestly, both are spectacular. But the truth is that I'd have fallen for him if he lived in a shack and could only cook frozen waffles. Don't tell him, though. I want to keep him on his toes."

"How can anyone say with confidence that they'd have fallen for someone under different circumstances?" Natasha asked. "The circumstances are what they are, and they *do* play a role in falling in love."

"I'm telling you, Natasha, I'd have fallen for Sam under any circumstances. He's just . . . my person. I don't think there would have been any mistaking that."

"Except that you *did* mistake that for the first few months after you met him." Mischief danced in Natasha's eyes.

"A commonsense observation like that has no place in a conversation like this one about love." Genevieve's big earrings swung against her thick hair. "I know what I know."

"Speaking of love." Natasha zeroed in on Ben. "What's the latest with Leah?"

Sebastian stiffened.

The humor in Ben's face leaked away. "She told me a few weeks ago that she just wants to be friends."

Sadness pulled both sisters' mouths into frowns.

"Why?" Genevieve asked.

"She doesn't feel romantically toward me."

Sebastian remained statue-still, listening as Natasha and Genevieve expressed their sympathy.

"I don't get it," Genevieve said to Ben. "If Leah can't see how amazing you are, she's nuts."

Ben glanced at Sebastian, gauging his reaction.

Sebastian met his friend's eyes levelly.

"It's not that Leah can't see how amazing I am." Ben focused on the sisters. "She can. I mean, my amazingness is pretty hard to miss." In this group, Ben was the one who lightened everyone's mood. He was trying to fulfill his role, but none of them was buying it tonight. "She told me she wishes she could feel that way about me. But she just doesn't."

"That might still change," Natasha said.

Sebastian clamped down on the edge of his tongue.

"I can't expect that, though," Ben said reasonably. "She's made herself clear, and I have to respect where she's at."

"Of course," Genevieve replied. "I'm just *so* bummed. For you and for her, too. You'd have been good for her."

"So, what's your plan?" Natasha asked. "Are you going to start going out with other people?"

"In theory, yes." Ben took a bite of his zucchini stick. "But I'm still hung up on Leah, and I don't know how to change that."

"Aww." Natasha linked her arm with Ben's.

"And you?" Genevieve asked Sebastian. "Dating anyone new?"

"No." *I'm also hung up on Leah.*

"How many promotions have you earned since we saw you last?" Natasha asked. They liked to rib him about his professional success. "Five?"

"No promotions since I saw you last."

"Slacker," Natasha said affectionately.

"Good evening."

The four of them turned toward the voice, which belonged to Eli, a friend of Sam's. Eli, a fighter pilot, had married Penelope, a Misty River local, last December, shortly before the Air Force sent them to Germany. As far as Sebastian knew, this was their first visit back to Georgia.

Genevieve thrust the tray into Sebastian's arms in order to give the newcomers hugs, tell them how great they looked, and how glad she was that they'd come.

"How's life in Germany?" Natasha asked.

"It's excellent for me, because Penelope's there," Eli said. "So long as she's with me, I'm good."

Penelope slanted a look of appreciation toward her husband. "Overall, I'm really enjoying living overseas," she told the group. "Until I had the chance to travel, I didn't realize how much I enjoyed experiencing new places."

"'You are never too old to set another goal . . .'" Natasha tapped her sister's forearm.

"'. . . or to dream a new dream,'" Genevieve finished. "That's a—"

"C. S. Lewis quote," Sebastian said.

"Well done, Sebastian!"

How long was he going to be stuck holding the appetizer tray like a waiter?

"I'm just glad that you kept Polka Dot Apron Pies open here in Misty River," Ben said. Penelope had converted a 1950s camper trailer into a food truck. For years she'd sold pie from her spot near Misty River's downtown square. "I'm a huge fan of your apple pie."

"Thank you! Does it taste the same as it always did now that Kevin's managing the pie truck for me?"

"It does."

Penelope looked pleased. "Kevin's fastidious about following my recipes."

"Are you still baking pies in Germany?" Natasha asked.

"I don't have a storefront. But people on the base place orders with me, and I bake out of our kitchen. I've also been working on a cookbook."

"I'll buy the cookbook the moment it comes out," Natasha vowed.

"She's an incredible baker," said Eli, who apparently couldn't compliment his wife enough in public.

"Here's to those of us who have significant others who know their way around food." Genevieve lifted a meatball as if it were a champagne glass.

Sebastian couldn't have cared less whether Leah knew her way around food. He could pay to have food delivered.

Sam called them over. Genevieve lifted the tray from him, and they found their place cards and took their seats.

Light gray clouds drifted lazily through a dark purple sky. Candles, pumpkins, and berries decorated the center of the table. The conversation flowed. Laughter expanded into the night.

Genevieve sat next to Sam, her hand draped over his elbow, her eyes sparkling at something he'd said. Sebastian had been concerned when Genevieve had turned her life upside-down like a bucket of golf balls and moved from her home in Nashville to Sam's farm. In an effort to win back her mental and physical health, she'd stepped away from writing contracts, speaking engagements, and social media for the last ten months. She'd slowed the pace of her life.

It turned out that his concern had been misplaced. Genevieve had never looked better, never seemed more at peace than she did now.

As glad as he was for her, this dinner was giving Sebastian the same unsettling sense he'd experienced many times before when surrounded by cheerful people . . . the sense that he was an island, and the rest of them were an ocean, flowing around him. He was close to them, but he was separate, not a part of them in the same way that they were a part of one another.

After the main course wound down, Sam rose to his feet. He clinked his butter knife against his glass until the voices quieted. In the semi-darkness, his pale eyes looked even paler than usual next to his olive skin and brown hair. "Before we serve dessert, I'd like to say a few words." His Australian accent carried on the air.

"Ooh." Genevieve's overly emotional mom rested a hand on her chest. "That would be lovely."

"Before I met Gen, I'd been living alone on this farm for four years," Sam said. "I told myself that's how I wanted it, but to be honest, I was miserable. And then thirteen months ago, Gen showed up. Even as I was giving her permission to move into the guesthouse, I was regretting my words."

Genevieve laughed. "And then, after I moved in, I gave you a lot more reasons to regret them."

"A lot more." Sam regarded Genevieve with softness.

"I bring drama," Genevieve stated.

"And worry."

"And chaos."

"You added difficulty to my days at first," he acknowledged. "But then you began to add other things. Color and laughter and hope."

Sebastian shifted uncomfortably. This conversation felt like it should be private, between Genevieve and Sam. But it looked like his opinion fell in the minority. Everyone else sat forward in their chairs, fascinated.

"With you," Sam continued, "God gave me a second chance that I still don't feel like I deserve. But I value it more than anything, because I know how much it's worth. You've become my favorite person. My best friend. I want to pull your long hairs off my sweaters and make you coffee and tease you about your terrible taste in music—"

"My excellent taste in music, you mean."

Sam sobered. "I want an opportunity—a million opportunities—to make you smile. The best I can hope for the days I have left is to spend them all with you. I don't want to be apart from you for a single one of them."

Genevieve's face communicated amazement. Moisture gathered on her lashes.

"I've got this farmhouse, this property, a restaurant, some savings, a tractor, and a beat-up truck," Sam said. "Everything I have is yours. My loyalty, my support, my commitment, my heart. Me. Always."

"*Sam.*"

"I love you," he said.

"I love you, too."

Sam reached into his pocket. Excited murmurs raced between the guests as Sam lowered to one knee beside Genevieve. He pulled out a small jewelry box and opened it to reveal a diamond ring.

Genevieve appeared to have been struck by lockjaw.

Sam hesitated. "You okay?"

"No. Sam! Yes . . . I'm okay." She gestured for him to go on. "Please continue with whatever you were about to say." Tears slipped down her face toward her grin.

"Sure?" he asked.

"Please continue!"

"Because if another time would be better—"

"Another time would not be better!"

"All right, then." Sam looked into her face. "Genevieve Mae Woodward?"

"Present."

"Will you marry me?"

"*Yes,*" she answered.

Sam slipped the ring onto her finger. They stood. Kissed. Then Sam wrapped her in his arms.

The rest of them pushed to their feet in a mass, everyone clapping, some whistling or whooping. The guys exchanged high fives.

The women hugged. Genevieve's mother wept with joy, and Genevieve's dad tried to find a pack of tissues for his wife. Natasha snapped pictures.

Sam whispered something to Genevieve. She whispered something back, admiring her ring. He pressed a kiss against the crown of her head and pulled her against him.

The guests crowded around the newly engaged couple to congratulate them.

From the first time that Sebastian had met Sam, Sebastian had seen how perfect he was for Genevieve. She was outgoing and passionate. He was honorable and even-keeled. In fact, as far as Sebastian knew, Sam was so even-keeled that he'd only ever lost his head over one thing.

Genevieve.

Eight days later, Leah traveled to Atlanta.

This time, she did not make the trip in order to see a whip-smart doctor. This time, she made the trip to see a house. Jonathan and Trina Brookside's house, to be precise.

She drove past their address slowly. Then she parked her Honda—far enough away to be safe, close enough to observe.

Jonathan and Trina now lived in the Tuxedo Park neighborhood of Atlanta, surrounded by some of the region's wealthiest families. Their sprawling Tudor sat on its lot like a queen on her throne. The oak trees, dogwoods, and lush landscaping surrounding her pledged fealty.

In an alternate version of her life, Leah would not be parking on the street, a stranger. She'd be intimately familiar with this house and its occupants. She'd come here often for holidays, meals, family gatherings. When Jonathan and Trina traveled, she'd stop by to feed the cats or water the flowers or collect the mail.

Then again . . . maybe not. Had these people raised her, she'd likely have attended Princeton. In which case, she might have opted to teach at one of the East Coast universities. In which case, she wouldn't be living in Georgia.

Her actual life and her possible life had diverged from each other the day of her birth. The more years that passed, the farther apart the two paths grew.

She tapped her fingertips on the lower curve of the steering wheel. The past few weekends, work responsibilities or Dylan-related responsibilities had prevented her from making this pilgrimage. However, she'd spent plenty of time planning her sleuthing tactics and staring at this house on Google maps—which had in no way prepared her for the appeal of the real thing.

Ultimately, she'd decided to make the trip to Atlanta early on this Sunday morning because, under the section of her mother's obstetrical records marked *Religious Affiliation*, Trina had checked the box next to Christian. Not all Christians attended church regularly on Sunday mornings. But a large number did. Should Jonathan and Trina drive to church this morning, she'd be poised to follow. Churches were public, unthreatening places that welcomed visitors. No one would give her presence a second thought, and she'd be able to get close enough to the Brooksides to get a good look at them.

She'd arrived here at 7:45, right on schedule.

As her watch ticked off one hour, then another, the plan that had seemed solid to her back in Misty River began to tarnish. Both she and her car appeared harmless. However, a woman sitting alone on a residential street for hours at a time could not expect to go unnoticed. Eventually her presence *would* raise suspicion.

She had a multitude of papers to grade back home. She and Dylan needed groceries, and it would be excellent if she could find time to go walking today, because she hadn't found time Friday or Saturday. Most important, she didn't want to leave Dylan to his own devices for the entire day. He'd promised to go to Tess and Rudy's for lunch, and Tess could be counted upon to call Leah if he didn't show. Still. Dylan might be vaping marijuana at this very moment, while she was chasing her phantom history.

Checking his location on her phone, she saw that he was at his friend Isaac's house, just like he'd said he'd be. Isaac's mom was trustworthy.

Everything was fine. Dylan wasn't vaping marijuana . . . probably.

The Brooksides' home remained motionless, concealing its secrets.

She killed time browsing wistfully through her Princeton album. Nassau Hall, once George Washington's capitol of the fledgling United States, with its bell tower and stoic façade. Blair Hall, with its castlelike turrets. Alexander Hall, with its Tiffany stained-glass windows.

When she'd looked through all her photos and scoured the Internet for a few more to add to her collection, she checked Beckett Memorial's website to see if she could find a picture of Sebastian there.

She couldn't.

Since she'd seen him at his hospital almost a month ago, she'd often mulled over his appearance—giving her memories of him color and three-dimensional depth. Again and again, she'd envisioned him in his T-shirt, scrubs, Adidas.

She'd thought of Levi and Isabella, too. For those babies and their families, the specter of death wasn't some abstract, distant thing. She'd felt just how close it was when she'd visited them. Levi and Isabella were small and helpless. Death, big and dangerous.

Sighing, she returned her focus to the house just as a shiny black BMW sedan finished backing out of the driveway. The car turned in her direction, and she dropped low in her seat with a gasp.

What! A car? Who was inside it?

Despite the glaze of sun and shadow against their windshield, she glimpsed two passengers in the front seat before the vehicle slipped past.

She executed a three-point turn as quickly as possible.

The BMW turned left at the end of the street.

Adrenaline jerked through her system. She was tailing a car like in the movies!

They wound through the neighborhood onto increasingly larger streets, until ten minutes later, the BMW pulled into a church parking lot.

She'd hypothesized that they'd leave their house for church this morning, and they had. Little pleased her more than forming a hypothesis based on logic, then watching that hypothesis proven true.

She parked two rows away from them in the lot, which gave her a clear view of the woman and man who exited the car. Based on the Facebook cover photo Leah had so carefully studied, the woman was definitely Trina Brookside. The man, very likely Jonathan Brookside, was of medium height and distinguished. Trina wore a pink cardigan over a classy blouse and skirt. Jonathan wore a black suit.

Leah watched them walk inside.

Rapidly, she finger-combed her hair and applied lipstick, then merged into the stream of people heading toward the service. Anticipating that this morning might include a church service, she'd chosen a tailored white shirt, bright blue blazer, cigarette pants.

A greeter handed her a bulletin, and she eased into a formal sanctuary. An orchestra lined the front. White-painted square columns rose to the soaring ceiling on either side of the stage.

She searched the congregants for a pink sweater in combination with a black suit. Where had they gone? She panned back and forth across the milling people, searching—

There. She made her way toward them and slid into the pew directly behind theirs. She sat slightly to the side of their position, so that when she looked toward the pulpit, a direction that would seem natural to those around her, the two of them fell within her line of sight.

The building buzzed with the sound of musicians tuning their instruments, talking, background worship music.

Leah was *thrillingly close* to Trina and Jonathan.

Trina had styled her blond hair the way she had in her Facebook photo, into a long, flattering bob.

For a man of fifty-seven, Jonathan had a full head of blond-gray hair, expertly trimmed. His suit oozed quality. She caught a hint of his luxurious aftershave.

Jonathan and Trina alternated between periods of quiet and periods of chatting in undertones. They'd been married a long time, and while she didn't see evidence of fawning adoration, she did see evidence of rapport, companionship, respect. Her parents' relationship had been tempestuous and transitory. The couple before her seemed to represent the opposite.

The service opened with worship music, and the congregation stood to sing. Near the end of the first song, Trina looked to the side, smiled, and lifted her hand in a gesture of greeting.

Leah followed the direction of her gaze—

A pang vibrated through her, because she recognized Sophie approaching. Closely behind Sophie, Sophie's groom. And then a third person. . . . A young woman with long blond hair who resembled Trina strongly.

Father God, does Sophie have a sister?

Do I have a full-blooded sister?

Her lungs reminded her that she'd forgotten to breathe, and she pulled air into a tight chest.

Clearly, Trina and Jonathan had saved seats because the three newcomers easily made themselves at home in the pew.

Leah moved her lips as if singing, but for the remainder of the worship time, no sound emerged. The family before her commanded her full attention.

The blonde had to be a sister. By the looks of her, she was a few years younger than Sophie.

Leah thought of her lonely childhood . . . of all the times she'd wished for a sibling and imagined a blond-haired sister. It was almost as if she'd been implanted with knowledge of the sister biology had intended for her.

Did Jonathan and Trina have more children? For all she knew, they might have five kids. Seven kids. And every one of those children, other than Sophie, would be a full-blooded biological

172

sibling of hers. They might look like her and think like her. Talk like her. Love math like her. Fail at sports like her. She couldn't imagine the security of growing up in that type of homogenous family, because her own experience had been so different.

A minister prayed and made announcements. "Before we continue with worship, please stand and take a few moments to greet one another."

The minister's invitation provided her with a golden opportunity that felt like the culmination of five months of research, waiting, and soul-searching.

Sophie turned in her direction first, and Leah was taken aback by how much she looked like Dylan, with her fair skin and big brunette curls. She could see both her mother, Erica, and her father, Todd, in this woman who'd been born at Magnolia Avenue Hospital just minutes before Leah.

"Hi, I'm Sophie Robbins." She offered a manicured hand.

Leah shook it. "Leah Montgomery. This is my first time to visit this church."

"Oh? I'm so glad. Welcome! Here, let me introduce my family. This is my husband, Logan." He was handsome in a money-buffed sort of way. "Abigail," Sophie said, to gain the blonde's attention.

The blonde smiled at Leah. Her eyes were hazel, not misty blue like Leah's own eyes. But her face shape, height, and body type were all very similar to Leah's.

"This is my sister," Sophie told Leah.

"Nice to meet you," Abigail said.

"You too."

"And these," Sophie continued, "are our parents, Jonathan and Trina."

Her pulse darted into a sprint. Was there an alarm buried within parents that enabled them to recognize their child even if they didn't know the child existed?

Jonathan and Trina shared parting words with the couple they'd been greeting, then faced Leah.

"This is Leah, a first-time visitor," Sophie said to them.

"Thanks for joining us," Trina said warmly.

"I just met your daughters." Leah motioned toward Sophie and Abigail. "Do you have other children?"

"No, these two keep us on our toes." Trina made a wry sound of amusement. "Do you live nearby, Leah?"

"A few hours away, actually. I'm just in town for the day."

The opening notes of another worship song began. Jonathan gave Leah a polite nod before facing the stage.

No! She'd had so little time.

"Whenever you're back in town, please stop by again," Trina said.

"I'd like that."

Trina swiveled to the front.

Trina exuded an elegant yet friendly vibe. Jonathan's demeanor struck Leah as reserved, proper.

They had not recognized her.

Was she relieved or sorry?

More relieved than sorry. Her highest hope for today had simply been to see Jonathan and Trina. Meeting them had been a boon. The disappointment sifting through her was due only to the fact that their exchange had been so brief.

Be grateful, she told herself, resuming her fake singing. Jonathan and Trina had led her to Sophie, Logan, and Abigail. She'd learned things she hadn't been able to learn in weeks of investigation. She'd learned that the Brooksides had two children, both daughters. She'd learned what her father and sister looked like. What their voices sounded like. Their manner.

Sitting side by side on the pew before her, they formed a clear family unit. She could sense the long history, ease, and affection between them. They probably had no idea that Sophie was not their biological child.

Should Leah tell them at some point that she and Sophie had been switched at birth?

A case could be made that she had that right. If she divulged the truth, she might gain a family, and they might gain a daughter.

But wouldn't inserting herself into their lives be like thrusting herself, uninvited, between them on that pew? If she did so, she'd probably fracture their close-knit, familiar status quo.

She might also fracture the close-knit, familiar status quo she shared with Dylan, because if she came clean to the Brooksides about her identity, then Sophie would no doubt want a place in Dylan's life.

Yet Dylan was so very much *Leah's*. She didn't know if she could share him with Sophie or stand for him to know she wasn't who he'd always believed her to be.

Was it selfish of her to deprive Dylan of his blood sister? Or would that be somewhat acceptable in this case, because Dylan already had a sister? He couldn't mourn the lack of Sophie, because he had no inkling that anyone was missing from his life.

It made her head hurt to wrestle with the ramifications of the choices before her. Which course was moral, right, compassionate?

She didn't know.

As the service progressed, Leah noted every whisper, glance, and shift of position the Brooksides made.

Why had she and Sophie gone home in the arms of the wrong mothers all those years ago?

Nothing she'd uncovered so far had shed light on that issue.

Essentially, mathematics was the art of solving problems. While she pondered whether to reveal herself to Trina and Jonathan, she'd begin solving the problem at the heart of her switched-at-birth story.

What had gone wrong on the day of her birth?

CHAPTER THIRTEEN

When Ben found out that Sebastian planned to spend the second weekend in October in Misty River, he'd asked Sebastian to help him chaperone his club's fundraising table at the football game. Sebastian had said he would.

But his motives had not been pure.

The fundraising tables were positioned past the ticket booth. Spectators walked toward those tables before forking in two directions to take their seats. Dylan played football. Leah would probably come to the game to cheer for her brother. Based on the location of the tables, his chances of seeing her were excellent.

He was not a saint. Nor was he as good a friend as he wanted to be.

If Leah showed, he'd pay the price for his sins because talking with her tortured him as much as it pleased him. A smarter man, a man with more self-control, would have stayed away.

Ben had left the table to get the kids drinks, so Sebastian finished unloading T-shirts from a cardboard box. Straightening, his attention pulled toward the ticket booth—

Leah.

She'd hadn't seen him yet.

A Misty River High pennant poked out of her purse, and she carried a padded bleacher seat over one arm. She'd dressed in a blue-and-gold football jersey, jeans, and slip-on sneakers. Once again, her hair looked like she'd ridden in a convertible. It curved close to the corner of her eye on one side and was tucked behind her ear on the other side. Her face was soft in the most appealing way. Quiet contours. No harsh angles. The pale pink of her lips complemented the pale pink of her cheeks.

Her vision dashed past him, then back.

He gave her a slow smile as emotion ignited within him for the first time in what felt like weeks. Everything about the setting dimmed, except for her. Guilt remained.

Approaching, she glanced at the club's sign. "Are you volunteering for the Equity for All student club this evening, Dr. Grant?"

"I am. I'm a big fan of the Equity for All movement and their catchy slogan."

"Which is?"

"A woman's place is in the House and in the Senate."

"Very catchy. And do I miss my guess, or is that a Susan B. Anthony quote on your T-shirt?"

"I don't think you often miss your guesses, Professor."

"Let me see." She nodded toward the T-shirt one of the girls had given him to wear when he'd shown up for duty. The T-shirts they were selling came in four terrible colors—pink, lavender, peach, and aqua. He'd told himself he'd been lucky to score an aqua shirt. But he didn't feel lucky. They'd only ordered women's sizes, and even the XXL was too tight. He pulled the shirt down in front so that she had a better view.

"'It was we, the people; not we, the white male citizens,'" she read. "Ah, in reference to the Constitution. Susan B. Anthony indeed."

"Yes."

"Well, obviously, I'm going to have to purchase one of those shirts."

"Was it my effective modeling that sold you on it?"

"That, and the opportunity to support gender equality. But mostly your modeling."

She leaned forward to select a shirt, and he caught the scent of lavender. Not too sweet, but distinctive. She handed cash to one of the girls. "It's nice of you to assist Ben this way," she said to him.

"To be honest, I showed up for the free T-shirt."

She laughed. "And yet you're the one who's present, and Ben, the faculty advisor for this club, is absent."

"He'll be right back."

She studied him like he was a chess game she was winning.

"Are you a football fan?" he asked. The round pin attached to her jersey showed a picture of Dylan, kneeling in his football uniform.

"Growing up, I went to exactly one football game. When I was in middle school."

"To receive an academic achievement award at halftime?"

"How'd you know?"

"Wild guess."

"The crowd was much more interested in securing halftime snacks than they were in my award."

He wanted to drag a trail of kisses down the side of her throat, then continue along the line of her collarbone—

"I've been making up for the deprivation of football in my early years," she went on, "since Dylan started playing. I haven't missed a single one of his home games."

The girls handed Leah her change and a bag containing her new shirt. She put the change away and looped the bag over her wrist, then met his eyes. He felt the reverberation of it deep in his chest.

"Can you give me an update on Levi and Isabella?" she asked. "I've thought and prayed about them often."

Have you thought about me, Leah? Because I've never stopped thinking about you. "Levi went home."

"Wonderful."

"Isabella struggled with fluid around her lungs, but now she's on the mend."

"I gather no heart's become available?"

"Still no heart."

"I'm sorry."

178

He didn't want to make her sorry. About anything. He wanted to make her life lighter, not heavier. "How's Dylan?"

"Content to drag his feet with his college applications and to procrastinate conversations about potential career tracks. In other words, he's fine, but I'm dying inside because of the feet dragging and procrastination."

"I see."

"Thank you again for the art supplies you gave him. He loves them. So much so that I regret not giving him a set like that for his last birthday."

"Not all of us can be superior gift givers."

"The next time you realize what gift my brother requires, will you kindly text me to let me know?"

He dipped his chin.

The announcer's voice came over the sound system. "Welcome! Please find your seats. Sophomore Daisy Harris will sing the national anthem in five minutes."

Don't leave, he thought.

Her hair dipped over her eye. She pushed it back.

Stay.

"I always sit with my friends Tess and Rudy," she said. "You and Ben are welcome to join us when you finish your shift here."

"Thank you, but . . . " *Ben won't want to sit with you if I'm there, too.* "The Colemans saved us seats."

"Okay. I'm glad we ran into each other."

"So am I. . . ." His sentence faded as he caught sight of Ben. His friend stood several yards away. People drifted between their two positions, yet Ben was looking right at him and Leah.

How long had he been watching?

Sebastian refocused on Leah. "I'm glad, too."

Leah left and Sebastian's world turned dull and flat. Ben handed drinks to the girls. He said nothing about Leah, but Sebastian could almost hear the wheels of his friend's mind turning.

As in many small southern towns, Misty River's high school football team was the whole town's team. It didn't matter whether

a resident had a child in high school or whether they'd graduated from Misty River High. For many, including the Colemans,
cheering for the Mountaineers at Friday night home games was
a family tradition.

Sebastian sat in the stands with a niece on one side of his lap
and a nephew on the other. He remained mostly silent during
sporting events. The Colemans didn't share his approach. From
every side of him, they shouted a running stream of encouragement and criticism at the players and referees.

After the Mountaineers kicked a field goal to win the game,
the spectators filed from the stadium in a satisfied tide of blue
and gold.

In the past, Sebastian had kept one car in Atlanta and one car
in Misty River so that whenever he flew here, a car was waiting
for him at the field. But he'd wrecked his Misty River car the day
he'd met Leah and hadn't replaced it. Because of that, he'd been
driving here lately instead of flying since it was a headache to get
around town without a car. This weekend was the exception. He'd
missed flying enough to pilot the twin-engine here earlier today.

Ben had given him a lift to the game, so they walked together
toward the faculty lot. The farther they went, the more the crowd
thinned. Only the light from the outdoor fixtures punctuated the
darkness.

"Everything okay?" Sebastian asked. Ben had been subdued
during the game.

For several seconds, Ben didn't respond. Then he said, "I'd like
to know how you feel about Leah." He kept his head fixed straight
ahead.

"Nothing's going to happen there—"

"Sebastian," Ben said calmly. "Please just tell me honestly how
you feel about her."

Sebastian pursed his mouth. If their friendship was going to
continue to be as strong as it had been, it wouldn't be because of
lies. "I feel the same way I felt about her the day I met her. My
feelings haven't changed."

They walked without words.

"I could tell that by the way you were looking at her tonight," Ben said. "And I could tell, by the way she was looking at you, that she's attracted to you."

"Ben—"

"I regret what I said when I called you at work the day after she and I went out to dinner. I was disappointed. And jealous. And selfish."

"And honest. I understood why you said what you said. You've shared everything in your life with me."

"Here's the thing, though. That doesn't give me the right to decide whom you're allowed to date. I was kidding myself to think that it did." He looked across at Sebastian briefly. "You and I both like Leah, but she only likes one of us back as more than a friend. And it's you."

"No."

"Yes."

"If so, she's made a mistake. You're the right person for her."

"I'll be the right person for someone someday, God willing. But I'm beginning to think that you're the right person for Leah Montgomery."

Because such powerful hope was rising in him, Sebastian *had* to make sure he reacted not in the way he wanted but in the way that was right. "Let's say she is interested in me. And let's say we get together. It would be painful for you to have to see us together, to have to hear about our relationship. I can't be with her if I know it's going to make you unhappy."

They'd reached the fender of Ben's Jeep. They faced each other.

Ben knew him better than anyone, and Sebastian couldn't help but feel as though his skin was being pulled back so that Ben could see inside.

"Remember that time," Ben said, "when we were in middle school and those two kids hissed racial slurs at me when they passed us on the field? You ran after them and started punching them in the face. All three of you got suspended."

"Yeah."

"I could name at least five other times when you've stuck up for me. I think you felt like you had to defend me because I was Black and because I've never been the kind of person who strikes back when someone insults me. But you might not know that I've also always felt the need to defend *you*. Because of your history, I can't help but want the best for you."

Sebastian bristled, his brow knitting.

"Don't give me that look. I don't pity you, Sebastian. I just want what's best for you."

Except that Sebastian suspected that Ben *did* pity him, regardless of the things he'd accomplished.

"Go ahead and ask Leah out," Ben said. "I won't stand in the way."

Sebastian stared at him with disbelief. "Like I said, even if she does want to be with me, I can't be with her if it's going to make you unhap—"

"Good grief. Can you stop being so bullheaded for one minute?"

Sebastian supposed the question was rhetorical.

Exasperated, Ben shook his head. "I really do deserve a medal for putting up with you all this time."

This statement, too, seemed rhetorical.

"You might not have noticed, but I'm no longer someone you have to defend," Ben said. "I'm a grown man, and I can deal with pain."

"But—"

"Men fall for women all the time who don't end up feeling the same way about them. The fact that Leah doesn't want to date me isn't going to ruin me."

Sebastian set his jaw.

"I'm trying to give you my blessing," Ben said. "The only thing I'm worried about is whether or not you're ready to open yourself up to a real relationship. Are you?"

"I don't think she's going to want to date me, let alone get into a serious relationship with me."

"That's a non-answer."

"It's all I've got. I honestly don't know what I'm ready for."

"She's my friend. So I don't want you to insult her or me by keeping her at arm's length like you've done with your past girlfriends."

"I don't think she's going to want to date me," Sebastian repeated.

"I think she will want to date you. But she's not like the others." Ben considered him. "I have to believe that you're not going to be able to hold back your feelings with her, even if you try." Ben pulled out his keys. "In fact, between you and Leah, you're probably the one in need of prayer."

A text arrived from Ben's mom, CeCe, the following morning while Sebastian was running.

I'm going to be working in the garden for the next two hours. Come see me.

Sebastian read her message on the smart watch he wore while exercising. Sweat ran down his face. His shirt stuck to his skin in wide patches.

He'd intended to mow his lawn after this. But now he'd shower and Uber to the Colemans. A message like this from CeCe was equivalent to a command from the president.

You did not—could not—say no.

CeCe got right to the point when he arrived at her side. She was harvesting broccoli from her vegetable garden, located in a raised planting bed that ran along one side of her home. "Ben tells me that you're interested in Leah and that Leah's interested in you."

183

Surprise made him unsure what to say. In telling his mom about the situation with Leah, Ben had made a strategic move. Ben would have known that CeCe would get involved immediately. He'd wanted that either as a way of showing Sebastian that he'd meant what he'd said last night or as a way of shutting the door for good on his own hopes for a romance with Leah. Or both.

"If Ben thinks she's interested, then she almost certainly is," CeCe stated. "But of course you're concerned about dating her because Ben has liked her for so long."

"Yes."

"That's kind of you, Sebastian."

"Thank you—"

"But *stupid*." She straightened. Gardening gloves covered the hands she set on her round waist. "If you like that woman, go after her with everything you've got. Marriage and family— that's the hardest stuff of life. But it's also the very best stuff. So you're a fool if you pussyfoot around Ben's feelings and miss your chance."

"He's your son."

She shoved his shoulder. "You're my son, too." Her glare dared him to contradict her. "Ben will be just fine."

He said nothing.

"Go after her," CeCe demanded.

"I want to."

"Then do."

"It's not that simple."

"No, it's not simple. Neither is medical school. But you did that, didn't you?"

A smile cracked across his face.

She knelt and yanked several carrots from the soil. She brushed one off and handed it to him. "Eat that."

"Ma'am?"

"Eat it. You look skinny."

He wasn't skinny. Dirt stuck to the carrot, but he knew that CeCe believed the dirt was good for them. He'd offend her if he cleaned off his carrot more than she'd cleaned off the one she was eating. The bite he took crunched between his teeth.

"I hope you don't think you owe Ben or any of the rest of us anything, Sebastian."

"You're kidding, right? I owe you guys everything."

She shot him a slit-eyed stare. "Like what, exactly?"

He hesitated. "I wouldn't have any success or any family if it weren't for you."

"*Bull.* You earned your success yourself, every day, with every paper and assignment and test and patient. Now, we did pull you into our family—and hardly gave you much choice in the matter, that's true enough. But the love we have for you was, is, and always will be free. Totally free. There are no debts between us. Do you understand me?"

He'd lost count of the times CeCe had belligerently asked him, *"Do you understand me?"* over the course of his life.

"Do you understand me, Sebastian?" she repeated, when he didn't answer quickly enough.

"Yes."

"Then, c'mere." She tugged him down so she could kiss his cheek. "Go on now and steal the heart of that girl," she whispered.

Sauntering toward the back door, she pulled off her gloves. Then turned. "What're you waiting for? Chop chop. I've got about ten chores for you to do inside."

Since May, Sebastian had been in an almost constant bad mood over the way things stood between him, Leah, and Ben. Yet at least the way things stood had made sense to him. He couldn't make sense of the encouragement that Ben and CeCe had given him regarding Leah.

He'd felt rotten every time he'd thought about the possibility of Ben and Leah as a couple. It had to be the same for Ben when

Ben thought about him and Leah together—yet Ben had taken the noble course. Ben always took the noble course. Ben had been raised in an environment that nurtured nobility. Sebastian had been raised in an environment that nurtured survival.

Five days after his conversation with CeCe, his phone alerted him to an incoming text message. He should have gone home for the day a few hours ago, but he was still in his office, trying to catch up on work.

He focused on the screen through eyes gritty with weariness. It was Ben.

Have you asked Leah out yet?

No.

If you won't at least try to win her over, I'm going to be mad.

Sebastian scowled.

His phone chimed again. A text from CeCe.

We're having a family dinner at our house on Sunday, and I'm making your favorite. Shrimp in butter sauce with mashed potatoes, green beans, and homemade rolls. You're not allowed to come, though, unless you've asked out that woman by that time. I really hope you can come, because I'd hate to give your shrimp to Eugene.

Groaning, Sebastian bent forward and set his forehead on top of his forearm on the desk. He didn't deserve the things they did for him. He'd never felt that he did. Which was one of many differences between him and them. The things they did had nothing to do with whether or not he was deserving. The things they did were motivated by simple love.

For him, love was not simple.

Another text from Ben.

The PE teacher and the vice principal at Misty
River High both have a crush on her. You're
burning valuable time.

And then, from CeCe:

Call her. Or I will.

In his whole life, he'd only formed two deep attachments—with
his mother and the Colemans. Loyalty to Ben ran in his blood.

It was difficult to think about acting contrary to that.

It was also difficult to think about how to protect his heart from
Leah if she agreed to go out with him.

It hadn't been difficult to avoid giving women the power to hurt
him in the past. But he already felt uncomfortably far gone over
Leah, and they weren't even a couple.

Warnings were stirring inside him. He heard them. Yet they
were pitted against his attraction to Leah, and Leah was winning.

She'd told him point-blank that she was not looking for romance.
If she did agree to go out with him, she'd want to keep things light.
Right? Yes. Which was reassuring. It meant she wouldn't demand
vulnerability from him.

What should he do?

Should he really move forward with this?

He wrote a text to both Ben and CeCe.

Are you sure you're okay with the idea of me
and Leah?

CeCe answered almost immediately.

As sure as God made little green apples.

Then from Ben:

As sure as death and taxes.

Sebastian picked up his phone and selected Leah's contact. Filling his lungs, he remembered how she'd looked at the football game

in her jersey. Her pale hair. Her long eyelashes and straightforward gaze. She was quirky, self-reliant, sacrificial. Her personality entertained him. Talking to her challenged him. He often dialed-in conversations with people. But he'd never be able to dial in a conversation with Leah Montgomery. Keeping up with her demanded his full attention.

He connected a call to her, then went to stand at his window in his wrinkled scrubs. Outside, the lights of Atlanta sparkled against a black backdrop of sky. He concentrated on a distant window glowing with yellow light as if, should he try hard enough, he'd be able to see her there.

Leah's brows glided upward when she saw the identity of the incoming caller. Sebastian was calling her? *Sebastian?* "Hello?" She sounded woefully breathless.

"Leah, it's Sebastian. How are you?"

"Very well, thanks. And you?"

"Doing well."

The deep voice she'd heard a few nights ago in a dream curled around her like a warm silk blanket. "Still wearing the Susan B. Anthony T-shirt?" she asked.

"No. It was so tight I had to use a vacuum attachment to suck it off me when I got home."

"The idea that 'we, the people doesn't mean we, the white male citizens' has never been a comfortable one for men to wear."

He laughed. "True."

"I happen to love my T-shirt. I'm wearing it while grading papers at this very moment, in fact. Eminently comfortable."

A pause of quiet. Why had he called?

"I wondered if you'd be interested in having dinner with me," he said.

Her shocked mind took a ride on a Tilt-A-Whirl. "For what purpose?"

"For the purpose of enjoyment."

What did that mean? She didn't want to misunderstand. "Are you asking me out on a date?"

"I am."

A thrill sizzled along her spine.

"Right after I met you," he said, "I wanted to contact you, but I didn't know your name. I couldn't believe my luck when I ran into you at the school's farmers market. Except, right after we started talking I learned that you were the Leah who Ben's been interested in for so long."

"Oh."

"He's talked about you since you started teaching at the school. When I discovered who you were to him, my hands were tied."

"So you encouraged me to date him."

"It seemed like the right thing to do. For everyone concerned."

She tried and failed to wrap her mind around the idea that Ben and Sebastian could both be attracted to her.

"Ben saw us talking at the football game," Sebastian said. "Afterward, he told me it would be fine with him if I called you and asked you out. Are you interested in going out with me?"

"No—that is . . . Yes." She cleared her throat. "On one hand, I *am* interested because I'm attracted to you even though, as I told you weeks ago, I truly thought I was missing the attraction gene. On the other hand, no. I'm not interested because I refuse to come between you and Ben."

"Ben has told me that our friendship will be fine."

"Maybe, but I don't see the point in testing that. Or risking the good rapport that you and I share by going on a date. After all, based on my romantic past and your romantic past, the odds of a fulfilling relationship materializing from our date are abysmally low."

"I don't expect every date I go on to convert into a fulfilling relationship."

"No? Then why bother with dating? Isn't the point of it to find a life partner?" That's what was logical. To the best of her knowledge, that's why her friends subjected themselves to dating.

"For me, the point is to have fun."

"Fun?"

"Yes, Leah. Fun. Go out with me, and I'll show you what I mean."

From her spot in the dining room, she stared at the books about New England she'd brought back from her trip and stacked on a living room end table.

She knew Sebastian well enough to know that his friendship with Ben was the most important relationship he had. It wasn't worth jeopardizing in pursuit of "fun." "I appreciate the kind offer. But the answer's no. I'm chagrined because I realize that makes me sound ungrateful. When, in actuality, I'm very grateful for your assistance with my hospital records and the gift you sent Dylan. I owe you."

"You do?"

"Yes."

"If you think I'm too honorable to leverage that into convincing you to go out with me, you're wrong."

She snickered. See? This was the problem with him. She genuinely liked him. She had a weakness for scoundrels.

"Good night, Doctor."

"Good night, Professor."

Click.

S ebastian grinned.

Leah had just said no to him, but instead of disappointment, he experienced a stab of determination. She was unsure of him. But their conversation had only made him more sure of her.

He hadn't risen to his current position by luck. He'd gotten here through a whole lot of dogged, stubborn effort.

At this point, he needed to respond with patience and strategy. He needed to give her a reason to say yes.

CHAPTER FOURTEEN

The sunshine on this mid-October Saturday was behaving like a teacher's pet, making an unabashed bid for Leah's favor as it slid through the front window of Sugar Maple Kitchen to burnish Tess, Rudy, and their breakfast table.

Tess continued updating Leah on her son. "Trey and Carla have their bags packed and plan to start driving as soon as they hear that Sasha's in labor so they can arrive in time for their grandchild's birth."

"So exciting."

"I have a photo."

Leah chewed her waffle, and Rudy poured extra syrup on his pancakes while Tess fussed with her phone. After a moment, she showed Leah the picture of Trey's very pregnant daughter and her husband.

"Sasha looks both adorable and uncomfortable," Leah commented.

"She really does look very uncomfortable," Rudy seconded. "Poor thing!"

"This will be your third great-grand, right?" Leah asked.

"Our fourth," Rudy answered.

Tess jabbed him with an elbow. "Our third."

Rudy bobbled his fork. It clattered onto the floor. "Oops."

"Rudy," Tess scolded.

He scooped up the errant fork and held it out in front of him like a flower as he approached the coffee bar to ask for a replacement.

Tess gave a long-suffering sigh.

Leah told herself to eat her waffle and her two strips of crisp bacon more slowly. Breakfasts at Sugar Maple Kitchen were meant to be savored.

Tess took a ladylike sip of coffee. "Update me, please, on Dylan's college applications."

"He's decided to pursue a degree in art, but so far he's only submitted one college application. One!" She could bemoan Dylan to Tess and Rudy because she was certain of their adoration of her brother.

"Even I know that he ought to have a portfolio of applications, so to speak," Tess said. "Some schools that are aspirational, some practical, some you can be sure he'll get into."

"Precisely."

"Don't lose heart. Everything is going to turn out beautifully for him."

"It's hard to see how, with him so . . . recalcitrant."

"The main thing is to find a school that suits him, a place where he'll be appreciated and inspired to learn."

"I agree, of course. It's just . . ." She blew a tendril of hair out of her way. "He's maddening!"

"Leah," Tess said.

Leah met the older woman's eyes.

"It will work out. You're doing an excellent job." The force of Tess's will was not to be quibbled with. "It will work out."

Rudy sank into his chair. "I'm just going to keep this here from now on." He stuck the new fork behind his ear. He grinned at Leah, and she smiled back. He looked both ridiculous and cute.

"Rudy," Tess warned.

Cowed, Rudy held the fork properly, then regarded his plate with awe. "I'd love some chocolate sauce to top this off."

"Absolutely not," Tess replied. "You're borderline diabetic."

Leah spotted a familiar face leaving the to-go line. "Connor!"

His expression brightened when he saw her. He neared, carrying a drink holder with two coffees in one hand and a bag of pastries in the other.

"Bringing breakfast home to your mom?" Leah asked.

"You guessed it."

She introduced Connor to Tess and Rudy, who both sized him up with ill-concealed interest.

"Connor grew up here," she told the older couple, "then went to college in California and stayed on the West Coast for several years."

"I love Disneyland," Rudy announced. "So much fun!"

"He started teaching art at the high school," Leah explained, "the semester after I started there."

"What brought you back to Misty River?" Tess asked.

"I came back to help my mom after she was diagnosed with ALS."

"Ah." Rudy's demeanor radiated empathy.

"How's your mom doing?" Tess asked.

"She has some mobility issues, but overall, as well as I could hope." He asked Tess and Rudy questions about their history with the town. Tess provided answers before Rudy could.

Both Ben's and Connor's friendship had greatly enriched her work life. She was closer with Ben because she spent more time with him. But Connor was great, too. His mellow nature immediately put everyone at ease. He was the same age as Leah but more mature than most of the other men she knew in their late twenties. Simply put, he was *good*, through and through.

Connor's kind gaze settled on Leah. "I'm glad I ran into you today."

"Likewise."

"I'll see you Monday." Then, to Tess and Rudy, "Really nice to have met you." He threaded toward the exit.

"Leah," Rudy stage-whispered loudly. "Have you been on any dates with that young man?"

"Rudy!" Tess rushed to say. "Of all the inappropriate questions."

"Sorry." Impishness sparked behind his glasses. "Well? Have you?"

"No, nor will I. We're just friends."

"Friendship can lead to love," Rudy said.

"Connor's interested in someone else, a woman he's liked since middle school."

"Oh?" Rudy asked. "That's a long time to like someone."

"A very long time." So long that Leah had a hard time imagining it. She'd formed zero attachments to the boys at her middle school. "Connor's steadfast."

"Has the woman he likes given him a chance?"

"She's had a boyfriend for years. They recently broke up, so she's currently in mourning over that. I'm hopeful that once she comes out of mourning, she'll give Connor a chance."

"Have you been on any dates with *any* young men recently?" Rudy pressed.

"It's not nice to pry," Tess said.

"I went on one date back in August, and I was asked out on another date two days ago. However, nothing came of the date in August, and nothing will come of the offer from two days ago." An image of Sebastian arriving in his office the day of the hospital tour, with disordered dark hair and a tragic past, coalesced in her memory—

She shook herself. She'd always pitied man-crazy women. She had no intention of becoming one of them.

Rudy's shoulders slumped.

"Sorry to disappoint," Leah said.

"You've never disappointed us." Tess spoke staunchly. "Not in any way."

"That's very true," Rudy told her. "You're perfect."

"I'm not the slightest bit perfect!"

"So perfect," Rudy insisted, "that I want you to end up with a man who appreciates you."

"And I want to end up with a PhD that I can appreciate."

"Of course you do," Tess said. "Rightly so."

"May I have that?" Rudy reached for the mini muffin that sat next to fruit slices on Tess's plate.

Adroitly, she intercepted his hand with a defensive maneuver. "Borderline diabetes," she reminded him. Resigned sigh. She checked her watch. "Finish up because I need to take you to your water aerobics class at the Y."

"Do I have to go today?"

"Absolutely. You made a commitment when you signed up for the series of classes—"

"Really, it was you who made me sign up."

"—and now we have to follow through."

"I don't like water aerobics," Rudy confessed to Leah.

Ten minutes later, the older couple headed out the door.

Leah slipped her laptop from her messenger bag and settled it on the table. Here, away from Dylan's prying eyes, she could turn her attention to the pursuit of answers regarding the events that had occurred the day of her birth.

Since she'd followed the Brooksides to church almost two weeks ago, she'd been combing through more and more accounts of real life switched-at-birth cases.

The majority occurred because of an accident. Two sets of twins were inadvertently mixed up so that the pairs of brothers grew up thinking they were fraternal twins when they were identical. Hospital staffers lost ID bracelets. Girls born five minutes apart were confused with each other.

However, some switches derived from even more obvious negligence. A drunk nurse set two babies in the same incubator to treat them for jaundice, and then returned them to the wrong mothers. Twins placed in foster care were reunited with their parents, who later learned that only one of the boys returned to them was their biological child.

In at least one case—the most famous of them all—babies had been switched on purpose out of a misguided sense of compassion. A couple had been trying for years to conceive a child. When they finally gave birth to a baby, it was discovered that the girl had a grave heart condition. Allegedly, a doctor instructed employees to give the sick baby to a family that already had five children, and to give the healthy baby to the couple who'd struggled to conceive.

In carefully going back over the paperwork from her mother's delivery and hospital stay, Leah had taken extra notice of a detail she'd previously skimmed past.

The names of the nurses.

Sebastian had mentioned that he thought it more likely that a nurse had been responsible for the switch than a doctor. Between the labor and delivery room and the neonatal nursery, four nurses had handled her care in the first hour after her birth.

Lois Simpson

Bonnie O'Reilly

Tracy Segura

Joyce Caffarella

The nurses represented a potential source of new information. If she could locate where they were now, she could ask them questions.

She typed *Lois Simpson nurse Atlanta, Georgia* into Google.

The very first link that popped up read *Lois Simpson Obituary— Milledgeville, Georgia | Legacy.com*.

A sense of gravity settled over her as she followed the link and read the obituary. Lois had passed away two years before, at the age of eighty-six. Thus, she would have been sixty when Leah was born. The obituary mentioned that she'd worked as a nurse at Emory University Hospital and Magnolia Avenue Hospital for a combined total of thirty years. Lois, a mother, grandmother, and great-grandmother, had been famous for her homemade lemon pound cake and singing in her church's choir.

Leah would not be able to contact Lois.

She began again with the name Bonnie O'Reilly.

Several hits came up—websites, more obits, images. She scrolled through them, clicked on a few. It didn't take long to determine that none of these Bonnie O'Reillys were the one she sought. She visited the most prominent social media sites without luck. Returning to Google, she combed through four more pages of results.

She hadn't found an obituary for a Bonnie O'Reilly who'd been a nurse in Atlanta, which meant Bonnie might still be living. If so, Bonnie was not, apparently, posting about her life for the world to see. Nor could Leah find any articles that mentioned her.

When Leah ran a search for Tracy Segura, she instantly came upon a Facebook profile that listed Magnolia Avenue Hospital under the "Work and Education" heading. A thin woman with strawberry blond hair, Tracy must have been in her early twenties when Leah was born, because she looked no older than fifty now.

Leah shook out her fingers, then composed a Facebook DM to Tracy. She explained that she'd been born at Magnolia Avenue and asked if Tracy would be willing to answer a few questions.

Finally, she entered Joyce Caffarella into the search engine. The third result appeared promising.

Joyce Caffarella—RN—St. Joseph's | LinkedIn. Joyce's LinkedIn profile provided a treasure trove of information. Her picture revealed a stout woman with a broad smile. Mousse and hair spray pushed her short platinum hair high. According to her page, she'd started at a pediatrician's office, accomplished a brief stint as a surgical nurse, then moved to Magnolia Avenue for six years. Since then, she'd been working at a hospital in Peachtree City.

Leah sent her a private message identical to the one she'd sent Tracy.

Just how long, she wondered, should she expect it to take before she heard back?

S omebody gave you a gift," Dylan called out to her the next day when Leah returned home from a hike.

"Hmm?"

She found him at the dining room table, his attention on his phone, laying waste to a box of Cheez-Its. Near his elbow sat a small gift wrapped in ivory paper and tied with an orange satin bow.

"Where did this come from?"

"Dunno. I saw it sitting on the front door mat when I got home from Braxton's."

"No packaging? No address?"

"Just that little card."

She picked it up. The miniature card affixed to the bow simply read *Leah*.

Dylan slanted a mocking look at her. "You should probably be really careful with that. You don't know where it came from, and it might be filled with explosives. Or poison. Explosives and poison are dangerous."

"Quite right! I encourage you to be cautious of unidentified packages. Also, be wary of underage drinking and speeding and twerking. Never engage in any of that."

He snorted and returned to his phone and food.

Leah slipped off the bow and raised the lid. Within, a gold necklace glimmered against a backdrop of velvet. A smattering of tiny stars and dots engraved its oval charm.

Wonder moved through her like flour through a sifter. The necklace was delicate. Classy.

She pulled the velvet backing from the bottom of the box. Beneath, she found a single piece of stationery marked with the name of a jewelry store.

The necklace shows the brightest stars in the sky on the night you were born. Some things might have gone wrong on that day, but you weren't one of them.

—Sebastian

Since she'd received her DNA results, she'd sought to address her birthday mix-up in the way that had always served her best: with logic. Logically she knew *she* wasn't the mistake.

198

Emotionally, that was a little harder to internalize. Across her early childhood years, she'd always felt that she didn't fit. She'd come to accept and even own that fact. But now evidence proved that she was more than simply someone who didn't fit. She was, without a doubt, a tremendous oddity. She'd been switched at birth when no one else she'd met or was likely to meet in her lifetime had been switched at birth.

Some things might have gone wrong on that day, but you weren't one of them.

A heated ball glowed in the vicinity of her heart.

Glancing up, she discovered Dylan watching her smugly. "Is that from Dr. Grant?"

"Yes."

"The guy you don't have a crush on?"

"Correct." She shut herself into the bathroom and tried on the necklace. The chain fell to just the right length.

She dialed Sebastian's number.

Her call went to voice mail.

He was no doubt busy rescuing a sick child from the jaws of death.

Sebastian was going to have to take Isabella Ackerman off the heart transplant list.

Her parents, Megan and Timothy, waited nearby while he finished his examination. Megan looked like a thinner, harder version of the woman he'd first met. Timothy was as stocky and bearded as before. But his posture had started to stoop. Their expressions pleaded with Sebastian to say that he could make their daughter well.

He hated this part of his job. "Isabella has developed sepsis," he informed them. Last week, one of his colleague's patients had become septic and died within twenty-four hours.

Megan anxiously tucked her hair behind her ears. "How are you going to treat it?"

199

"Antibiotics. Additional medications for her blood pressure and cardiac function. Increased ventilation."

"How long do you think it will take until she's better?" Timothy asked.

"I don't know." There was no guarantee of "better" for Isabella. Her small body might have endured all it could take, in which case this would be the final blow. If she did recover, "better" for her would mean she'd still be so sick that she'd need this Pediatric Intensive Care Unit to keep her alive.

"Here's what I can tell you for sure," Sebastian said. "Those of us on staff are committed to doing everything we can to help her." It made him furious that the best care and the best science couldn't save them all.

"Can she remain on the transplant list?" Megan asked.

"I'm afraid that I'm going to have to remove her from the list. For now."

Their faces fell. They knew that removing Isabella from the list meant removing her shot at survival.

"I'm sorry," Sebastian said.

Weighted silence answered.

Isabella fidgeted.

Megan pressed a kiss to the baby's forehead, then took hold of her daughter's hand. "I'm worried she's uncomfortable."

"She's comfortable," Sebastian said. "We wouldn't allow her to be otherwise." Not many years ago, children like Isabella had simply been protected from pain with palliative care until they died, a few days after their birth, in their parents' arms.

Treatments had come a long way in a short time, and now parents almost always chose to intervene surgically. Even when the odds weren't in their favor, they were willing to try a Hail Mary pass to give their child a chance at life.

"Several of our family members are coming by to visit her later today," Megan said. "Do you hear that, sweetheart? A whole group of people who love you are on their way. They've met you, but they can't wait for you to meet them."

He saw it all the time—large interconnected families, hanging on every breath of their newest, youngest, sickest member. They crowded into waiting rooms during surgery. Filled sections of the cafeteria and lobby. They often brought balloons, stuffed animals, cookies.

Those big families always threw his own situation—the fact that he had no one but the Colemans—into perspective.

"Everyone at our church has been praying for Isabella," Timothy said to Sebastian. "Her story has spread to other churches in Augusta, and we've heard that they're all praying, too."

"We'll let them know about the sepsis," Megan said, her voice cracking. "And they'll double down on their conversations with God."

"You'll put her back on the transplant list as soon as the sepsis is gone, right?" Timothy asked.

"When the sepsis is gone, we'll reevaluate." Sebastian excused himself and turned toward the break room.

He never made promises to family members that he couldn't keep, because his mother had once assured him that she'd recover. He didn't know if she'd believed that when she'd said it or not. Either way, she'd lied.

She'd died on a Tuesday, while he was at school.

The hospice staff had believed that she had several days left, and his mom had wanted him to continue his routine. So he'd gone to school even though he'd hated school and been nauseous with worry every morning when the old lady neighbor they were staying with walked him to the bus stop wearing her house shoes.

On that Tuesday when he'd returned home from school, he'd knocked on the door of the old lady's apartment.

A young female voice had called, "Come in."

He entered and watched two women raise their faces toward him sadly. The old lady was there, but so was the young one with curly brown hair who'd been coming around. They called her his social worker, except he wasn't really sure what that meant.

His vision jerked to his mom, in her hospital bed. Smooth

blankets covered her to her shoulders. Her eyes were closed, and she was too still. Too white.

Terror tightened his stomach.

"Sebastian," the old lady said, "your mother passed away while napping a few hours ago."

He couldn't move or speak.

Your mother passed away.

No.

Your mother passed away.

No!

"I'm so sorry," the social worker said.

"It was peaceful," the old lady told him.

His lungs weren't working, and a terrible buzzing noise filled his head.

"We didn't know if you'd want to see her before she goes," the social worker said, "but we wanted to give you that option. It's totally up to you."

His mom had died? And he hadn't been there?

He was going to be sick all over his shoes.

"I want you to know that you'll be safe and cared for," the social worker said. "There's a plan in place. As soon as you're ready, I'll take you to a family who lives near here. They have a room ready for you, and they're very kind people."

He hated the social worker with the curly brown hair. He'd never be safe, and he'd never be cared for, and he'd never be ready to leave this apartment. This is where his mom was.

His mom. She was his family.

These ladies were strangers.

He'd remained silent the rest of that awful day. They'd let him sit at his mom's bedside for a long time. He'd stared at her because he'd been too scared to hold a dead person's hand.

Sebastian forced his thoughts back to the present. In the break room, he downed trail mix and poured himself a mug of coffee. Then he took the mug with him up to the second highest floor of the building.

Occasionally, he needed fresh air to clear his head. It didn't matter the season. The steamy heat of summer, the freezing wind of winter. He'd investigated every hospital he'd worked at until he'd found at least one space that could offer him quiet and privacy outdoors.

He passed through a rarely used conference room and exited onto a balcony. At the rail, he breathed the damp afternoon air. The coffee was bitter, but it also provided a needed shock to his senses. He took regular sips until he'd drunk half of it.

Checking his phone, he saw that he'd missed a call from Leah. The realization affected him like sunlight. It shoved aside the gray clouds.

He placed a call to her, anticipating the sound of her voice.

"I received a necklace from you today," she said as soon as she picked up. "Did you hand deliver it?"

"I did, this morning. Before I got called back to the hospital."

"The necklace is exquisite. Thank you."

"You're welcome."

"However, it's not my birthday."

"I hope not. I plan to do much better on your birthday."

"Sebastian!" she said, half laughing, half chiding. "I cannot possibly accept lavish presents given to me for no reason."

"That wasn't a lavish present."

"I have a sneaking suspicion that it was."

"And it was given for a reason."

"Which is?"

"I like you."

"That's not a *valid* reason."

"That's the most valid reason there is."

"This is too kind. . . ."

"Is there such a thing as too kind?"

"Too generous—"

"Is there such a thing as too generous?"

"I value my independence. If I need a necklace, I will buy a necklace."

His smile grew. "You're one of *those people*, I can tell. The sort who don't know how to accept a gift. I think you need more practice."

"And I think you need to return the necklace and invest the money."

"I view the necklace as an investment. Besides, I'm no fool. I bought you a custom-made necklace that can't be returned."

"In an effort to make me feel even more indebted to you so that I say yes to a date?"

"Exactly. But also to make you happy."

"Has anyone ever told you that you're difficult?"

"Everyone I've ever known. But you're a math prodigy because you've figured out how to solve difficult problems. Right?"

"I haven't the foggiest notion how to solve problems of the adult male variety."

"Will you go out on a date with me?" he asked.

"No."

"In that case, will you travel to Atlanta next weekend to see me?"

"No."

"Fine. Then I'll come back to Misty River next weekend to see you."

"I recommend that you spare yourself the effort."

I'll see you then, he thought.

On Monday, a top-of-the-line graphing calculator arrived at Leah's front door. She hadn't known calculators could be personalized. But apparently they could be if someone was persistent enough, because *Professor Montgomery* was etched into its back.

It could not be returned.

On Tuesday, Dylan received an Atlanta Falcons jersey with *Montgomery* stitched across the shoulder blades.

It could not be returned.

She began to pray, asking God to let her know if going on a date with Sebastian was a viable option or an absolute no.

She couldn't discern His answer.

On Wednesday, a copy of *The Theory of Numbers*, first edition, published in 1914, landed on Leah's doorstep. In an act that verged very near desecration, someone had written *Property of Leah Montgomery* in Sharpie on its first page.

It could not be returned.

On Thursday, two very large boxes addressed to Dylan were delivered. The instant he returned home from football practice, she handed him a pair of scissors so that he could open them. Inside each box lay two hubcaps for his truck. Upon closer inspection, she noticed they were each engraved, in small print, with *Dylan is chillin'*. Subtle.

What wasn't subtle? Sebastian's methods.

The hubcaps could not be returned.

This could not go on!

A date would be preferable to this—this *deluge* of presents. The prospect of continuing to accept charity from him carved ice into her soul.

God had not yet made His guidance clear regarding Sebastian. But if gifts were going to continue to arrive daily, she didn't feel she could postpone her decision until she'd received divine confirmation.

She dialed Sebastian and, for once, he answered.

"You rang?" he said.

"I'll go on a date with you this weekend on one condition."

"Which is?"

"You agree to cease sending Dylan and me presents."

"Done," he said immediately. "Can I pick you up at seven on Saturday?"

He was beyond exasperating! "Fine."

As skilled as she was at chess, she sensed that Sebastian was no amateur at his tactics.

CHAPTER FIFTEEN

On Saturday morning Leah regarded her reflection critically in the dressing room mirror of the Buttercup Boutique.

She did not have the funds to spend more than a meager amount of money on clothes. The ladies at the boutique understood this. They also knew Leah's taste for classic-yet-current clothing. Bright, clear colors. Collared shirts and fitted cardigans. Sweaters. Tailored pants. Items that affirmed her uniqueness. They called Leah when something they thought she might like went on sale. Over time, they'd helped her curate items into a small capsule wardrobe.

The sapphire blue dress she had on at the moment wasn't exactly a capsule piece. But at thirty-seven dollars, the price was right. Plus, it seemed just the thing for a date with Sebastian Grant.

The neckline folded over into a panel that traveled straight across her chest and around her upper arms, leaving her shoulders bare. It fit snugly to just below her waist then flared into folds that ended at her knees. Simple, yet sophisticated. Modest, yet flattering.

She angled her back toward the mirror and looked over her shoulder at her reflection.

What was she doing?

She should rebel against Sebastian's wooing techniques by dressing in her very worst clothing for tonight's date. Perhaps pajama bottoms and the stretched-out Jabba the Hutt T-shirt Dylan had given her when he was eleven?

She couldn't bring herself to give that plan serious consideration.

In part, because she was strangely . . . excited about tonight's date.

In part, because she had pride, after all.

She could pair this dress with the 1930s-inspired high-heeled Mary Janes she already owned.

One of the boutique's employees stopped outside the dressing room to check on her.

"I'll take it," Leah said.

Leah answered Sebastian's knock a few minutes before seven that night to find him on her threshold, wearing a suit and confidence.

The visual power of the scene before her—the lines of his charcoal jacket, his snowy white shirt, black hair gleaming in the light of her fixtures—was too overwhelming to absorb.

"Good evening," Leah said, acutely glad that she'd splurged on a new dress.

"Good evening."

She gestured for him to come inside and discovered more to adjust to. The sight of Sebastian Grant in *her* home. He was larger than she'd recalled, more debonair.

In the direction of her brother's room she called, "Dylan, come out and say hello."

No response.

Sebastian stared at her with admiration in his eyes.

What was she supposed to do with a large and debonair man? Dating was awful. The worst of all inventions. "I will not be kissing you at the conclusion of this evening," she announced.

Humor tugged at his lips. "That's fine. In fact, I'm glad you brought that up. In a way, I forced you to go out with me. But I'd never force you into a kiss."

"Excellent."

"When we kiss—"

"*If* we kiss."

"It will only be because you want to."

Ruefully, she already wanted to.

Dylan sidled out of his lair.

"Hey, Dylan," Sebastian said.

"Hi, Dr. Grant." They shook hands.

"Thank you for the gifts you sent me this week," Dylan told him. "They're awesome."

"You're welcome. How've you been?"

"Pretty busy with football and stuff."

"I was at your game a few weeks ago. I thought you played well."

If Sebastian had spotted Dylan on the field, he must have been watching for him with an eagle eye because her brother's playing time had amounted to approximately four minutes. Dylan was a far better athlete than she was, yet he wasn't cut out to be a starter on the team because he didn't have ferocious internal drive or a commanding physique. Frankly, she was thrilled he'd made the team again as a bench warmer.

"Football's cool," Dylan said. "It's just hard. You know?"

"I'm sure it is."

She often thought about how much Dylan had aged in comparison to the Dylan she'd known four years, six years, twelve years ago. But in comparison to Sebastian, Dylan seemed incredibly young. The two of them might as well belong to different species.

Dylan scratched the side of his face. "Have you been doing a lot of . . . surgeries?"

"Quite a few, yes."

"Anybody die?"

"Not since I saw you last."

"Sweet. If they're still alive they might . . . stay that way."

"That's the plan."

Dylan's vision landed on Leah. "A couple of my friends are gonna come over later."

"Who?"

He rattled off the names of four kids she knew well.

"What are you guys going to do?" she asked.

"Snort cocaine." Dylan gave her the first genuine grin she'd seen out of him all day.

"Absolutely no cocaine, any other kind of drug, alcohol, or girls."

He pretended astonishment.

"Movies are fine." She'd set parental controls. "So are the video games we already own."

"What about board games?" Sebastian asked her wryly.

"More like bored games," Dylan answered, taking a clunky stab at humor.

"Board games are allowed. As are puzzles. You can cook anything except meth. And, of course, arts and crafts are always a wholesome option."

"They could make jewelry," Sebastian suggested, deadpan.

"Or tie-dye shirts," Leah said.

"They could color."

"Or do macramé."

Dylan shook his head and took a few steps back. "Can I, uh . . ." He gestured to his room. "Go now?"

Delightful child. Such an open, winning, sunny personality. "Yes."

Dylan stopped just in front of his room and looked back. "I told my sister to go out with you a while ago, Dr. Grant."

"You did?"

"Yeah."

"And?"

"She shot down the idea." He rolled his eyes. "I wish I'd bet her money on it. I'd be richer." Then he was gone.

"I really like your brother," Sebastian said.

Did he know that the statement had just scored him a thousand points?

"And I really like your place," he continued. "What's your favorite thing about it?"

"I'm a fan of this architectural style, but my absolute favorite thing about it is the view." They stopped side by side in front of the enormous plate glass living room window. The sun had recently set. Clouds of pink, peach, and moody lavender capped the dimming hills. "I'm endlessly fascinated with this view. It's different every hour of the day and every season of the year." She peeked at him and found that he was already looking down at her.

"Beautiful," he said.

Fireflies took flight within her. She needed to remember that she'd agreed to this date in order to bring a halt to the flood of gifts.

They made their way to his Mercedes, and he drove them to a restaurant located inside a winery in neighboring White County. Smooth white stucco walls and a ceiling crisscrossed with timbers the size of tree trunks surrounded them as they took their time over appetizers at the bar.

Eventually, a hostess escorted them to a linen-covered table near a cavernous fireplace. A creamy mix of firelight, can lights, and flickering candlelight covered everyone in the dining room with a warm glow. Beyond the windows, tidy rows of grapevines snaked into the darkness. Her napkin was so heavy she could wear it as a shawl. The tiny ceramic pot adjacent the salt and pepper shakers held mums, ivy, and red berries.

Leah had enjoyed a few fancy dinners in her lifetime. But every one of those meals had been underlain with the wincing knowledge of the expense, which inevitably made her wonder whether the experience was worth the price.

Sebastian didn't seem to care about the costs involved. Since he'd lobbied for this date so relentlessly, it served him right to get stuck with the bill. Brazenly, she ordered salmon.

It arrived glistening beneath a buttery sauce. Braised red cabbage dotted with goat cheese and smashed fingerling potatoes crusted with big granules of salt completed the dish.

The deliciousness of the first bite liquefied her spine.

"What's the latest with your search into your birth family?" Sebastian asked, cutting into his steak.

"I met them."

His motion paused. "What?"

She brought him up to speed on how she'd found the Brooksides and the brief exchange they'd shared at church.

"That must have been strange," he said. "To introduce yourself to them as if you were a stranger."

"To them, I am a stranger."

"But to you, they're much more than that."

"True. At present, I'm trying to understand how Sophie and I were switched. In fact . . ." She considered him speculatively. "You might be able to help me."

"I'll do anything for you."

She drew her brows together. "Would you please refrain from making statements like that?"

"Statements like what?"

"Statements that can be construed as epically . . . romantic." She said *romantic* the way one would say *swamp*.

"I'll try."

"You might be able to help me by explaining the differentiation of responsibilities of the nurses who cared for me right after I was born."

"As I recall, you were immediately taken to the postpartum nursery."

"Yes."

"So it's very likely two distinct groups of nurses were involved. The nurses assigned to labor and delivery and the nurses assigned to the nursery."

"Would I have been taken to the nursery by the labor and delivery nures?"

"Yes."

"What would have occurred then?"

"The nurses assigned to the nursery and the staff pediatrician would have treated you."

"On my paperwork, I found the names of two labor and delivery nurses and two nursery nurses. I'm researching all four of them in hopes of gaining a more complete picture of the circumstances."

"Let me know if there's anything I can do."

Leah dabbed her lips evasively.

"Please let me know if there's anything I can do," he reiterated.

"If I do, I'll be more indebted to you."

"Good. That will benefit my evil master plan." He gave her a slightly wicked smile.

"Let's talk about you now," she said.

"Let's not."

"I might not be a dating expert—" she began.

"I think you are," he cut in. "This is the best date I've ever had."

"You are not allowed to make epically romantic statements!"

Sebastian laughed, then took an unrepentant sip of his drink.

"I might not be a dating expert," she said, trying again, "but common courtesy demands that we spend half our time talking about me and half talking about you, does it not?"

"I find you to be a million times more interesting than I find myself."

"If so, that would make you an extremely rare person. Everyone prefers to talk about themself."

"Not me."

"I'd like to hear, from the horse's mouth, so to speak, about the miracle part of the Miracle Five."

"What would you like to know?"

"Well, it seems as if the first eight days in the collapsed basement were a bit of a status quo."

"They were. It was dark and hot and dusty. The only thing that changed during that time was our access to water. We didn't have any. And then we did."

"Thanks to your ingenuity."

"Thanks to my stubbornness," he corrected. "The quake exposed a pipe. I was determined to break the pipe open even though it was just as likely to carry sewage as water."

"But it carried water, which allowed you to survive."

"Yes."

"I'd like to hear about your last few hours in the basement."

He pressed his shoulders into his chair's back. The open collar of his shirt formed a V around the indentation between his collarbones. She had an urge to trace that groove with a fingertip.

"For hours," he said, "we heard machines getting closer. They were dismantling the building from above to remove weight, and they were also trying to drill toward us from the side. Have you ever been inside an A-frame house?"

She nodded.

"It was like that down there because two concrete slabs had fallen against each other above us." He set his elbows on the table and tipped his fingers together, demonstrating. "We were sitting on the bottom of a triangle."

"Understood." She'd heard this story, but it was raising the hair on her arms to hear *him* tell it. This wasn't academic for Sebastian. He'd lived this.

He rested his hands on his thighs. "I suggested that we sit against one of the walls."

"Were you the leader of the group?"

"I guess. Luke's a year older than I am, and he was the most popular kid on the trip . . . the most popular kid at Misty River Middle School. But his younger brother, Ethan, had come with us to return the sports equipment to the basement. He'd been annoying Luke with questions, so Luke told Ethan to go to the back of the line. Luke wanted a break from him for a few minutes, which shouldn't have been any big deal. But then the earthquake hit. Luke pulled four of us out of the hallway. He was going back for Ethan when it caved in."

Leah regarded him solemnly.

"I think Ethan died instantly because we never heard him calling for us. He was only twelve years old."

Her memory conjured a picture of twelve-year-old Dylan, dressed in a tie for his middle school midwinter dance. "Heartbreaking."

"While we were trapped down there, Luke was immobilized

213

by shock and grief. Ben was optimistic. Genevieve was frightened and prayed a lot. Natasha reassured and took care of everyone."

"And you decided which wall to sit under as the rescuers approached."

"I had a few coins in my pocket. I took out a quarter and said, 'Heads, that wall. Tails, that wall.' I tossed it and it landed heads up. So the five of us went to sit against the winning wall. As the machines drew closer, the building began to shift. The wall across from us crashed down."

"And the other wall, the one above you, held in place."

"Right, but it shouldn't have. It had been resting against the wall that fell. The mathematicians like you, the structural engineers, the architects . . . they all agreed. It should not have stayed in place. Science can't explain why it remained there, protecting us from falling debris until we were loaded onto the chopper. Only then did it collapse. We all saw it and heard it."

"Christians concluded that God intervened. He held the wall there because of the prayers prayed for you around the world."

"Yes," Sebastian said simply.

"Do you believe He held the wall?"

"I do."

"You encountered a miracle." God had come through for Sebastian in ways his mother had been unable to. Leah chewed her potatoes. "How did that event change you?"

"It made me realize my life was worth something. I'd received a second chance, so I decided to make the most of it."

"After you were rescued, how long did it take you to realize that the five of you were famous?"

"Two minutes."

"It must have been bizarre to learn that everyone on earth was following your story."

"Yeah. I went into that building a forgotten, discarded kid. I came out a celebrity."

Throughout the remainder of their dinner, Sebastian watched her with the kind of concentration that seemed to miss nothing.

He asked their server for more water even before her glass was empty. When she looked around, wondering where the restroom was, he told her where it was located before she could ask.

In Leah's regular daily life, there were always so many thoughts and theories circulating in her head that she often found it challenging to focus fully on a conversation. This was extraordinarily true when she found the subject being discussed less interesting than the things going on in her head.

With Sebastian, conversation was more interesting than her thoughts or theories. He had a curious mind, and he liked to delve deeply into a topic. They discussed heart surgery. They discussed math.

He wasn't content with the vague information she usually dispensed when people asked about math. He wanted her to explain number theory and combinatorics and why she loved algebra.

He'd topped out with calculus in college, but he remembered it well, and that base gave him an educated vantage point from which to view the landscapes where math had taken her.

On their drive home, the dashboard lights glowed against his hard-cut profile. She caught whiffs of his aftershave. She noted the faint lines across the top of his wrists and the five o'clock shadow beginning to darken his cheeks and jaw.

Tonight's date had gratified the homely, unpopular nine-year-old inside her to a surprising degree. Until this evening, she hadn't understood how much that nine-year-old wanted to experience at least one successful, fairy-tale-esque night out.

Dylan's friends' cars lined the street outside her house, so Sebastian pulled onto her steep driveway and killed the engine. She stepped out of the car and waited for him on the wide steps that ran parallel to the driveway.

Cool weather wrapped her in a strange stillness. She could see light and vague movement inside her house. But outside, no wind at all. No animal sounds. Even the stars were few tonight, and distant. It was as if God had turned a giant glass bowl upside down and placed it over Misty River.

He stopped a few feet away from her, hands in his pockets, il-luminated by the exterior lights mounted on the garage.

She wanted to drown in a Jacuzzi of the feelings he produced in her. Why had she stipulated that they would not kiss tonight? That may have been rash.

"Tell me what I need to do to convince you to see me again tomorrow," he said.

Tilting her head, she considered how to reply. She'd agreed to go out with him to stop the flood of gifts, but this evening hadn't felt like a means to an end. It had felt like a luxurious little vacation dropped in the center of her day-to-day life.

She'd do well to recall that her day-to-day life was her *real* life. Luxurious little vacations were, by nature, short-lived. "As you know, I've never been interested in acquiring a boyfriend. So, in order for you to convince me to see you tomorrow, I simply need you to assure me that you won't be foisting any nonsensical ro-mantic notions upon me."

"I will not foist."

"We are not"—she used air quotes—"dating."

"Agreed. You're not commiting to anything except spending more time with me."

"Spending more time with you doesn't sound completely repul-sive," she said primly, interlacing her hands in front of her waist.

"Let's negotiate terms for tomorrow. Where should I take you?"

"Nowhere. Tonight was plenty extravagant enough, thank you."

"Dinner at my house, then?"

"That's acceptable."

"I'll have food delivered."

"No, we'll cook dinner together. It'll be less expensive, and it'll give us something to do."

He gave her a scorching look. "I can think of plenty of things for us to do."

"We'll cook together," she said firmly.

He stepped closer. Her abdomen contracted with longing.

"What kind of dinner should we make?" he asked.

"The easy kind."

"Baked lobster tails?"

"Goodness no. Stir-fry?"

"Shrimp curry?" he suggested.

"Hamburgers?"

"Enchiladas."

Her shoulders relaxed a few degrees. "I love enchiladas."

"With ground beef and red sauce?"

"With chicken and salsa verde, plus sour cream and white cheese."

"Additional terms?"

"I request 1980s background music."

"I'll agree to a playlist containing three-fourths eighties music and one-fourth Sinatra."

"Fine." She was warming to her subject. "I also request a mowed lawn, clusters of red grapes for snacking, flattering lighting—"

"A disco ball, perhaps?" he suggested dryly.

"Why not? And an indoor temperature of seventy degrees—"

"I'll compromise at sixty-nine degrees."

"Very well. Additionally, I'll require a cheesecake from Tart Bakery."

"Done."

"Oh, and no flowers or gifts."

"Spoilsport. Anything else?"

"No. The items aforementioned will be sufficient." She retreated backward toward her door. "Thank you for dinner."

"You're welcome."

"Good night."

"Good night, Professor."

Sebastian watched Leah walk inside, then returned to his Misty River house. He prowled the rooms, too preoccupied to sit or to concentrate on anything except her.

She'd told him she would not become his girlfriend, which, in light of his inability to commit, was amazingly convenient. A relief. So why was his brain taking him down wild tunnels of thought that all ended in things he wanted to do for her? Give her gifts. Take her places. Lift some of the weight of caring for her brother. Do whatever was necessary to ensure that she got her PhD.

He stopped in his foyer and shoved both hands through his hair with a sound of irritation. *Get ahold of yourself.*

As usual with her, his reaction was too much. He'd gone out with her one time.

Get ahold of yourself.

CHAPTER SIXTEEN

At two o'clock the following day, Sebastian approached the Colemans' house carrying a wrapped birthday present.

All year long, he received a steady stream of reminder texts from CeCe and Ben's sisters. *Don't forget to send flowers for Great-Aunt Clarice's funeral, poor dear. Just don't send roses. She hated roses, remember.* Or *Cousin Drew got a promotion at work so you might want to shoot him a congratulations text. We're trying to give him lots of positive reinforcement because we all feared he'd never amount to anything.*

Almost every week the Colemans gathered to celebrate someone's birthday, anniversary, or accomplishment. It was more than he could keep up with. He attended only when he was in town and when they were meeting for a reason he cared about even slightly.

He cared more than slightly about today's party, which was in honor of Hadley Jane's fourth birthday.

Ben's dad greeted Sebastian with a hug. "Love you, man. Glad you're here."

"Is that you, Sebastian?" CeCe yelled from the direction of the dining room.

"Yes, ma'am."

"Get in here right now. We're about to sing."

He set his present on a coffee table full of gifts, then he and Hersh jammed themselves into the dining room. The family welcomed him with an assortment of hugs, fist bumps, and smiles. Ben, seated across the table from him, gave Sebastian a friendly nod.

Guilt pulled at him.

Sebastian had been making an extra effort to communicate with Ben in their usual ways. Even so, their friendship wasn't normal right now. Again this morning, he'd asked Ben if it really was okay with him if Sebastian went out with Leah. Ben had said that it was, but then he'd said, "Can you do me a favor, man, and not talk to me about her for a while?"

CeCe walked in carrying a Barbie doll standing in the center of a dome of cake and frosting. The doll wore a silver top and crown. Pink candles stuck out of the cake, which was only big enough to feed about four of the forty-plus people who were present. Not that he really wanted to eat cake that had been pressed up against plastic doll legs, anyway.

Hadley Jane crouched on her knees on the chair at the head of the table. Her silver-and-white dress matched the Barbie's. She stilled, wide-eyed, as everyone sang "Happy Birthday."

She blew out her candles. Sebastian clapped along with everyone else, then took the long way around to the kitchen. He found CeCe there, cutting the cake skirt, surrounded by her sister, a daughter, and a son-in-law. Holding a knife covered in frosting, she paused long enough to give him one of her assessing looks before hauling him down into a one-armed hug. "I saw your face in there when I brought in the cake. You were thinking that it's too small for everyone." She clucked her tongue. "As if I'd feed this whole group a little itty-bitty cake! Those—" she waved the knife in the direction of two enormous sheet cakes—"are the cakes for the family."

"I deeply apologize for my doubt. I should have known better."

"You missed lunch, so it's not good enough at this point for you to stand there apologizing and looking pretty as a mess of fried catfish. Come over here and start delivering cake."

He'd missed lunch because he'd been buying supplies for tonight's dinner with Leah. He served cake until everyone had the size of slice they preferred.

"Sit down, Sebastian," CeCe ordered. "I saved you a plate."

He settled at the kitchen table, which overlooked the back deck. A meal of pot roast, carrots, and mashed potatoes landed in front of him.

"Thank you." His mouth watered, and he remembered how hungry he'd been the first time he'd come to this house and she'd fed him. Starving, really. For much more than food.

Ben and several others took the remaining chairs and made progress on their cake. After a time, CeCe demanded, "Eugene! Where are you hiding? Don't think you're going to get away from here without playing your saxophone for us!"

"Yeah," Hersh seconded.

For CeCe, no Coleman event would be complete without one of Eugene's mediocre sax solos. Everyone responded with enthusiasm larger than Eugene's talent. The older man retrieved his instrument and played something that sounded like it might be the soft jazz hit "Just the Two of Us."

Hadley Jane appeared at Sebastian's side. He pushed his chair back so she had room to climb onto his lap. "Thank you for the dollhouse," she said just loud enough for him to hear.

"You haven't even opened your gifts yet."

"But I know that's what you got me."

The last time he'd seen her, she'd asked him very seriously to buy her a bright pink L.O.L. Surprise! Cottage for her birthday. He had mad respect for her because she'd chosen her mark well. She'd known he was good for it.

She reached up and twisted the hair at the back of his neck around one of her fingers. How long did he have before she'd stop doing that? Another year? Two? It hurt to love children who kept insisting on growing all the time.

"Can we play fighting horses?" she asked him.

He didn't want to play fighting horses. For one thing, he didn't like fighting horses. For another, once they started that up, they wouldn't be able to stop until *all* the Coleman grandkids had a turn.

Unfortunately for him, he was more likely to quit his job than he was to say no to Hadley Jane.

"Anything for you," he told her.

A few more minutes of the concert droned past.

"Is it almost over?" she asked.

"One never knows."

As soon as Eugene finished and took his false-humble bows, Hadley Jane grasped Sebastian's hand and Ben's hand and pulled them toward the family room.

"Are we playing fighting horses?" Ben asked Sebastian, correctly reading the situation.

Before Sebastian could reply, Hadley Jane yelled, "Fighting horses!" loud enough to alert her cousins.

"Had I known to expect this, little girl," Sebastian commented, "I'd have brought my knee pads."

"Exactly." Ben lowered onto all fours. "Fractured kneecaps weren't really part of my weekend plans."

"If anyone's going to fracture their kneecaps, it's going to be me. You only weigh a buck fifty." Sebastian went to his hands and knees a few feet from Ben.

Ben laughed. "Unlike some people, I'm fit."

"Thin isn't the same thing as fit."

"Heavy isn't the same thing as fit, either."

"It's a good thing for me, then, that muscular is."

Hadley Jane climbed onto Sebastian's back and commanded her little cousin to run and go get two pool noodles out of the hall closet.

Two of the boys tried to climb onto him behind Hadley Jane, who protested loudly. Three or four other kids all rushed to beat the others onto Ben's back. They ended up getting there at the same time and entering into a king-of-the-mountain-type struggle, which turned into a wrestling match. Sebastian and Ben tickled the kids and, at the same time, attempted to prevent them from hurting one another.

He hadn't wanted to play fighting horses, but now that he was covered in laughing kids, belonging settled over him. He didn't fit in here perfectly. But this was as close as he ever came to fitting in. He'd eaten Coleman family pot roast a hundred times before. He knew that the lamp on that sofa table hadn't worked for a year and that the door to the hallway bathroom stuck. He knew when to humor CeCe and when to compliment her. He understood the rivalries and personalities of the nieces and nephews. And he knew that Ben Coleman was the best friend he'd ever have.

In time, with work, he had to believe their friendship would be all right.

Typically when they played fighting horses, Ben and Sebastian were an even bet. Ben was quicker. Sebastian was stronger.

Tonight though, Sebastian took his punishment, allowing Ben's riders to whack him in the head and shoulders with a pool noodle.

Since he was the one eating dinner with Leah tonight, taking it on the chin during fighting horses felt like the least he could do.

All day Leah had told herself not to concede too much time or mental energy to her upcoming visit to Sebastian's house. It was merely an engagement on her calendar that promised to be diverting. Nothing more.

However, the commonsense self-talk hadn't stopped her from going through the same time-consuming process she'd taken when preparing for dinner out with Sebastian. Long shower. Makeup. Time styling her hair into tousled waves. She dressed carefully in an orange V-neck sweater, gray capri pants, and silver flats.

All this made her feel, sheepishly, like an animal undertaking elaborate mating rituals when said animal had heretofore been too smart for elaborate mating rituals.

She parked in front of his house, then carried the miniature plastic disco ball she'd purchased up the walkway. The lawn, she noted, looked to have been expertly mowed.

If a stranger were to approach this house or study Sebastian's career, they might assume that he'd lived a charmed life, that he'd had every advantage handed to him. When, in fact, the opposite was true.

He opened his front door before she had a chance to knock and surveyed her with eyes both piercing and warm. His black hair was combed starkly into place. The severity of his slate-colored crewneck shirt and low-slung jeans emphasized the rugged planes of his body.

"You're wearing the necklace I gave you," he said.

"I am." Where was her brain? Why couldn't she think of anything to say? "I . . . realize that some of the demands I conveyed last night may have been challenging to meet." She lifted the disco ball. "I brought this in order to save my reputation as a low-maintenance dinner guest."

"Very clever."

She followed him into the kitchen, where he gestured to an identical disco ball already sitting on the island. She laughed. "Did you buy yours at Riverside Drugstore?"

"Yeah. You realize, right, that these matching disco balls represent our perfection for each other?"

"No." She set her ball next to his. "They simply represent that we both pay attention to detail—a conclusion anyone could reach based on our academic records."

He punched a command into his phone and the song "With or Without You" flowed from unseen speakers.

"1980s music," she noted.

He pointed out the rest of his preparations. "Grapes." Several small triangular bunches of grapes rested on a plate. "Cheesecake from Tart Bakery. Can you tell that the thermostat's set to sixty-nine?"

"Oh yes. I'd recognize this temperature anywhere."

"Anything else I can do to please you?" He gave a wolfish smile.

"No. These are exactly the conditions I require when cooking dinner."

He'd already set out some of the items needed for enchiladas.

Groceries. A baking pan. A mixing bowl. "I printed out a recipe," he said.

"An easy one?"

"I challenge you to find an easy recipe for chicken, white cheese enchiladas with a salsa verde sour cream sauce."

"'Let's keep a little optimism here.' That's a—"

"Han Solo quote." He held her gaze. "I memorized his twenty most famous lines in order to impress you."

I t was the best night he'd had . . . ever?

The only night that could compete with it was the previous night.

They'd cooked together and eaten at the table he never used when he was here alone. After the sun set, he'd lit a fire in the fireplace that anchored the sitting area on the far side of the kitchen. The windows surrounding the space let in views of his backyard.

They were currently sitting on the sofa, finishing slices of cheesecake.

The necklace he'd given her swung forward as she leaned toward the coffee table to collect another bite. When she sat upright, it settled back into a new position against her pale, creamy skin.

He was in serious trouble.

Be mine, he kept thinking every time he noticed her lips, her profile, her almond-shaped eyes surrounded by thick lashes. *Be mine.*

Just like the first time he'd met her, he had a powerful desire to keep her with him.

Experience had matured Leah Montgomery. She wasn't shallow or wrapped up in things that didn't matter. She made him feel sharply alive, and she also stilled the part of him that was usually grasping and discontent.

"Good?" he asked once she'd finished her cheesecake.

"Unbelievably good."

"Ready for the disco balls?"

"I am if you are."

He set the disco balls on the coffee table, turned them both on, then dimmed the overhead lights. Colored dots danced across the walls, across the front of her sweater, across her unforgettable features.

Leah stood, a look of wonder on her face.

It might be that she'd been so consumed with providing for herself and her brother that there hadn't been much room in her life for things as impractical as disco balls. There hadn't been much room in his life for them, either.

He opened his playlist, hit Air Supply's "All Out of Love," and quickly added four more slow songs to the queue before setting his phone to the side.

When he drew her body against his, satisfaction slid through him, fast and sure, like a knife through a strawberry. Their chemistry was strong enough to bulldoze trees and houses. Strong enough to bulldoze *him*.

They swayed together. When the final strains drifted away, their motion continued as they waited for the next song to begin.

"This is what I imagine the very best high school prom would be like," she said.

"I wouldn't know. I never went to any dances in middle school or high school."

"Neither did I." The next song started. "Last night and tonight . . . they almost feel like too much."

"What do you mean?"

"Embarrassingly self-indulgent."

He grunted. "I bought dinner ingredients at a grocery store, dessert at a bakery, and an inexpensive disco ball at a drugstore. Expect more indulgence than this in the future."

"What future? This is a non-date."

"Right. But I plan to take you on more of these."

"Non-dates, by nature, do not merit the assumption of more."

"It's not nice to joke about non-dates."

She looked into his eyes to show him that she was not joking.

226

"Leah," he growled. "Why don't you want to go on another non-date with me?"

"I'm genuinely concerned about Ben."

"That's valid," he said. "Will you talk to him? I think that might help."

She pushed her lips to the side, clearly thinking it through.

"What else is the matter?" he asked. He could see there was more.

"Honestly, my singleness is part of my identity. I like being unattached. My job and my brother are challenging, so it's wonderful to have one aspect of my life that's simple."

"I'm not asking you to become attached to me. I'm only asking for a few more non-dates. Simple."

The music continued, but he stopped their motion.

With the lightest pressure possible, he drifted the fingertips of one hand from her chin along her jaw. His touch circled her earlobe and skimmed down the side of her neck. His heart began to pound. "I have a confession," he said.

"Do tell."

"Running into you at the football game was not a coincidence. I volunteered that night because I knew you'd be there."

"We only talked for five minutes," she whispered breathlessly.

"It was worth it."

"Running into you outside your house the day I went walking wasn't a coincidence, either."

"Oh?"

"I found out where you lived, parked nearby, and walked your neighborhood."

"Why?"

"To test my magnetic response to you. And you know what?" She smiled a little. "It was worth it."

Pleasure poured into him. "You hammered out several terms for tonight's date. But there's one term you didn't insist on this time."

"I didn't specify that we would not kiss."

"Exactly."

"That was not an oversight on my part. I omitted that term because I no longer wanted to abide by that term."

His body howled with need, but he made himself move slowly. He supported her jaw with his hands. Shared her breath.

W ith effort, Leah stayed immobile while her body flushed. When he pressed his lips to hers, his mouth was warm, soft, confident . . . and her physical form turned to flame.

She tasted him. Smelled his spicy scent. Felt his hands sliding into her hair. *Confound it.* Kissing him was like standing, exhilarated, at the edge of Niagara Falls. Hearing the roar. Letting the emotions shake through you.

Opulent minutes spun, one into the next.

No wonder women behaved foolishly over men! This was splendid and humbling. She'd been so smug about her good, safe decisions when it came to the opposite sex. But that was before she'd experienced for herself the mighty temptation a man could present.

"Will you," he said when they pulled slightly apart, "meet me for another non-date?" His voice sounded gravelly.

Her lips tingled. She didn't want to talk. She wanted to kiss him more. And not so that she could enlarge her data set of interactions with men. Because of how he made her feel.

He kissed the inside of her wrist, then drew it up and behind his neck. "Please?"

"You're a hard man to say no to."

"So I've been told."

A sound of amusement escaped her. "Fine. I'll meet you for another non-date."

His lips met hers again. Demanding and raw. Intimate and tender.

Kissing Sebastian consumed her consciousness and forced her to live so fully in the present that every one of her concerns dropped away.

CHAPTER SEVENTEEN

A tentative knock sounded on Leah's classroom door the next morning.

Leah straightened from the stack of quizzes she'd been grading. "Come in."

Claire Dobney shuffled forward for their scheduled tutoring session wearing a voluminous sweater, this one in shades of beige. Black leggings and Converse that had seen better days completed the outfit.

Shortly after Leah learned about the stress the teenager was under at home, she'd suggested Claire meet her for math tutoring twice a week during Leah's planning period, which was also Claire's advisory period.

Leah waved her to the chair nearest her desk. "How are you?"

"Okay."

Leah had learned from Claire that she was the oldest of four. Her sister Becca was in middle school. Her brother Mason was in fourth grade. Her sister Annie was in first.

Leah's role as Dylan's older sister had sculpted her character. She'd never forget how protective she'd felt toward her brother when her parents were fighting, so she knew what it was to harbor anxiety not just for your own well-being but, much harder to bear, for the well-being of a sibling.

"Have things improved at home?" Leah asked.

"No."

Claire's answer supported Leah's own suspicions. She'd been keeping an eye on the girl, who seemed even jumpier and wearier lately. "Is your dad physically abusive toward your mom?"

Claire looked down at her knees, where she clasped her math binder and textbook with both hands.

"Please know," Leah said, "that you can tell me the truth. My shoulders are strong enough to carry it."

"No, he hasn't been physically abusive, but I'm worried he'll get that way soon."

"Because?"

"Well . . . he's always had a temper, but it's gotten worse the last few months. He's mad a lot, so then Mom gets mad, too. He's been throwing things, breaking things."

"Any idea what caused this change?"

"I think things have been bad for him at work."

"I'm really sorry, Claire."

"It's okay."

"Is there anything I can do?"

"I don't think there's anything anyone can do."

"I know you've continued to meet with Ms. Williams." Leah had been in communication with the school counselor about Claire. "Has that been helpful?"

Claire shrugged. "Sort of."

"Do you have reservations about talking with her?"

"She's nice . . . for sure. I just don't know her well, so it feels really weird to tell her stuff."

Worry circled within Leah because her intuition was telling her that Claire needed to be confiding in trustworthy adults. "How about you add my number to your contacts? If you ever need to call me—to come and get you or for any other reason—please do." Though she was sixteen, Claire didn't yet have her driver's license.

"Thank you, Ms. Montgomery."

Later that day, en route to her car after work, Leah checked her phone and saw that an unfamiliar number had left a voice mail for her. She retrieved it and listened as she walked to a loud and husky female voice say, "This is Joyce Caffarella calling. I just now saw that you sent me a message a while back on LinkedIn saying that you were born at Magnolia Avenue Hospital during the years when I worked there."

Leah's forward movement came to a swift stop.

"Here's hoping you weren't one of the babies that I dropped on their heads." Scratchy laughter burst from Joyce. "Just kidding. I didn't drop any on their heads. Well, not many anyway." She chuckled. "You left your phone number and invited me to call so I'm doing just that. Sorry I missed you. Feel free to call me back at this number."

One of the nurses who'd cared for her as a newborn had called her!

The other two nurses, Bonnie and Tracy, had remained elusive. Leah's continued attempts to locate Bonnie online had failed. Tracy hadn't responded to her Facebook message.

Joyce Caffarella. Joyce was the one with the solid frame and the spiky platinum hair. Had she been fresh out of nursing school the year she'd started the first job she'd listed on LinkedIn, her age would now be hovering just above sixty.

Leah slung the messenger bag filled with work that needed grading into her Honda, then headed home. Dylan was still at practice, which meant she could place a return call in private.

Once she'd dumped her things on the kitchen counter, she took a few moments to gather herself and whisper a prayer. Gazing out the sliding doors that led to her back patio, she connected a call to Joyce.

Joyce answered almost instantly. Leah introduced herself and spent a few moments exchanging pleasantries with the outgoing older woman. There was no easy way to segue from *thanks for taking the time to return my call* to *I was switched at birth on your watch*, but Leah managed to convey the basics of her story.

"What?" Joyce squawked. "No kidding?"

"No kidding."

"I've heard switched-at-birth stories, of course, but that type of a mistake is actually really, really uncommon. It's blowing my mind to think that this happened to you during one of my shifts."

"It's true that cases like mine are extremely rare, but maybe not quite as rare as we thought a few years ago. Then, no one could easily test their DNA, so an unknown number of cases likely went undiscovered. Now we can inexpensively submit our DNA to a lab. I've watched interviews of two other people who discovered they were switched at birth the same way that I did."

"Jiminy Cricket!" Joyce made a *whoeee* sound. "You said you were born twenty-eight years ago?"

"Yes, I turned twenty-eight this past February. By chance, do you remember anything about me? Or my parents, Erica and Todd Montgomery? Or my biological mother and father, Trina and Jonathan Brookside?"

"I'm sorry, hon. I don't. I've been working in labor and delivery now for almost forty years. I've cared for so many mothers and babies. So many."

"I understand." The chance that one of the nurses would remember her or her parents had been a long shot. "I was switched with a baby named Sophie." She explained the facts of her birth and Sophie's birth.

"How close together were you born?"

"Eighteen minutes."

Joyce gave another *whoeee*. "Sophie would have been brought to the nursery, too. And neither mother would have had a chance to get a good look at the face of her child."

"Do you think it's most likely that the switch occurred in the nursery?"

"Yep, I do."

"According to the hospital records, Lois Simpson, Bonnie O'Reilly, and Tracy Segura were working the same shift that you were. Do you remember those women?"

"Lois Simpson! Now, that's a name I haven't heard in a long time. A long, long time. She and Bonnie were of a different generation, my parents' generation. Lois was sweet and motherly. I remember that we celebrated her retirement with a cake decorated to look like an RV because she and her husband planned to travel around in one. Do you know what happened to her?"

"She passed away two years ago, at the age of eighty-six."

"I hope she and her husband burned up the highways in their RV."

"What about Bonnie O'Reilly?"

"Bonnie I knew better. Our shifts aligned often during my six years at Magnolia Avenue. Bonnie's like one of those stern RNs in movies. Strict, but with a heart of gold."

Outside, the trees of Leah's backyard preened with autumn color. "Approximately how old would she have been at the time of my birth?"

"Fifty-ish, I'd say."

"Do you remember anything else about her?"

"She was single. Oh, and she had at least one . . . maybe two children. That's about all I recall."

"And Tracy? Any memories of her?"

"Tracy was young. Always rubbed me the wrong way. She was uptight and pessimistic and since I'm the opposite of those things, I have a hard time with people like that. We worked together for a couple of years before she was let go."

"Why was she let go?"

"Bad attitude. With supervisors and patients alike."

"I'm hoping to chat with Bonnie and Tracy, too. Do you have contact details for either of them, by chance?"

"Hmm. When I moved south and started at a different hospital, I lost touch with both of them, but I'll dig around for you. Back in the day, I bent over backward to keep my address book and my Christmas card list up-to-date. I might have contact details for them somewhere."

"Thanks for checking for me. I appreciate it."

"Look, I don't think that I was the one who accidentally switched you with that other little girl," Joyce said. "But if I was, I'm really sorry. I never would have wanted that for any of my babies. Never on God's green earth."

They said their good-byes.

Leah wasn't the best at reading people, but Joyce seemed genuine. It could be, though, that Joyce's jovial personality was a costume constructed to put people at ease. For all Leah knew, Joyce's motives might truly be a dark river, and she'd switched the babies on purpose.

First thing the following morning, Leah found a text waiting for her from Joyce.

> Score! 1990s address book for the win!

She'd included phone numbers and addresses for Bonnie O'Reilly and Tracy Segura, then closed with

> Let me know if there's anything else I can do! I'm a pack rat, so I might be able to find more stuff from my years at Magnolia Avenue Hospital in one of my closets. LOL!

Since a phone call at such an early hour wouldn't be considered polite, Leah waited until her lunch break to dial the numbers Joyce had supplied for Tracy and Bonnie. Both calls ended in error messages announcing that the number was no longer in service. She tried them a second time, just to make sure she'd input the digits correctly. She had. Error messages again.

Inside her desk drawer, she located the cute package of notecards one of her students had given her. Bonnie and Tracy no longer used their old phone numbers, but they might still live at their old addresses. She'd write two notes introducing herself as a former patient, expressing her desire for a brief chat, and supplying her phone number.

She stilled, thinking. It might be best to address the letters to Bonnie and Tracy "or current resident." Otherwise, should new people live at the addresses and receive something addressed to an old tenant, they'd almost certainly trash her letters.

On her way home, she'd drop them by the post office in time to go out with today's mail.

Since Sebastian had returned to Atlanta early Monday morning, he'd gone through his days feeling each of the one hundred-plus miles separating him from Leah.

Talking to her on the phone wasn't nearly as good as being with her in person, but it helped. She'd informed him that non-couples shouldn't talk on the phone for more than thirty minutes per day. So he'd been using up all thirty of his daily minutes.

He'd also requested a week's vacation from work. When the woman in HR had asked him when he wanted time off, he'd answered, "As soon as possible." He *needed* uninterrupted days with Leah in Misty River.

On Wednesday evening, he was stretched out on the sofa in his apartment wearing track pants and an old Harvard T-shirt. He and Leah had been on the phone for twenty minutes so far. While they'd talked, he'd been imagining her in her stylish, uncluttered little house.

"Will you come see me this weekend?" He'd asked the same question for three nights in a row. They'd scheduled him to be on call Saturday and Sunday, which meant he couldn't leave Atlanta. He was trying to be patient and not bossy, but he didn't think it was working. He felt bossy about this subject, because he didn't want to go two weeks without seeing her.

"No, I will not come see you this weekend."

He palmed the soccer ball that lay on the carpet next to him and began tossing it over his head one-handed and catching it one-handed. "But you have four days off," he pointed out. The school district was giving their staff and students a vacation Friday and Monday for fall break.

"Yes, but you're not my boyfriend. And I'm not inclined to take weekend trips to visit male friends."

"Right, but until now you haven't had a male friend that you kiss. . . . Have you?"

She sniffed. "No."

"I want to see you. Come see me."

"You're going to be on call! You probably won't have time to spend with anyone."

"I'll have plenty of time to spend with you," he vowed. "Try me."

"Every time I contemplate leaving Dylan for the weekend, I envision a montage of party scenes from high school movies. Kids drinking beer out of red cups and making out on every piece of furniture."

"You can leave him with the older couple you told me about."

"Tess and Rudy?"

"Sure."

"Excellent idea!" He could tell from her voice she was pretending to be astonished by his brilliance. "The answer's no."

Ben's classroom was empty, except for him, when Leah stepped inside it the following day. "Hello."

He twisted from where he'd been writing on his board. "Hello." He regarded her pleasantly, but not as openly as usual. She might be mistaken, but she thought she saw guardedness in his eyes.

"I'm going to lunch and wanted to see if you were interested in joining me."

"I'm meeting a parent in the foyer in a few minutes, but I'll walk toward the break room with you."

It was a good sign that he'd offered to walk with her. Wasn't it? She waited while he capped his marker.

Usually, they chatted daily and shared lunch with Connor and their other teacher friends a few times a week. Since her dates with Sebastian last weekend, he hadn't stopped by her room or texted. She'd opted to give him space at first. But, at this point, she was beginning to worry that giving him space might have been the wrong approach. It was possible that he'd translated the distance she'd extended to him as indifference on her part.

She frequently found herself at a loss when it came to navigating relationship dynamics. What would someone with a high EI do in this predicament? It seemed that they'd reach out to Ben.

They walked down the mostly deserted hallway lined on both sides with lockers. "Sebastian told me that you encouraged him to ask me out," she said.

He slipped his hands into the pockets of the flat front beige pants he wore with a green-and-white-checked button-down. "Yeah. I did."

"That was nice of you."

"He's a good friend."

"Right, and the last thing I'd want to do is get in the middle of your friendship with him."

They turned a corner in silence. "You won't."

"Or ruin my friendship with you."

"You won't."

"Ben." She stopped several yards from the break room.

He stopped, too, meeting her eyes.

"Is it going to upset you if I go on more dates with him? Because, if so, I won't go."

"Do you want to go on more dates with him?"

"I'm conflicted about that," she admitted. "But I think I do."

She saw maturity in the lines beside his eyes, lines which usually held laughter. "Sebastian is too solitary for his own good. It would mean the world to him to date someone like you, Leah."

She metabolized that. "Okay, but what about you? I've known you much longer than I've known him. You're important to me, and I'm trying to be sensitive to your feelings."

"I appreciate that, but I'm fine."

"Will you still want to hang out with me if I'm . . . seeing him?"

"I'll still want to hang out with you. Definitely. It's just . . ." He looked to the side, then looked back at her. "Maybe give me a little more time?"

"Of course. Is there anything else I can do?"

"Let a week or two or fifty pass before talking to me about your relationship with Sebastian."

"Agreed. Anything else?"

"Blueberry muffins."

"Blueberry muffins?"

"The next time you bake blueberry muffins with crumb topping, bring me some, and we'll call it good."

Ben truly was one of the best guys she knew. "Deal," she said, relieved.

Connor walked toward them from the opposite direction. He and Ben exchanged a fist bump.

"Ben has a meeting with a parent," Leah told him, "so it'll just be the two of us and our swanky packed lunches today."

"Turkey sandwich for you?" Ben asked Leah.

"Indeed. Veggie, hummus, and ham wrap for you?" she asked Connor.

"You got it. It won't be the same without you, Ben."

"I know. I'm the fun one of this group." He made an amused sound and sauntered off. "I'm trusting you two to muddle through without me."

Connor opened the break room door for Leah with a flourish. "Shall we?"

Hello, this is Arthur Duncan. I'm calling about the letter you sent to my house. You said you were looking for the lady who used to live here. Tracy?"

"Yes," Leah answered, pausing midway through the process of unloading groceries from her shopping cart into her trunk. She cupped her free hand over the phone to hear him better. Friday evening dusk hovered over the parking lot. "I'm Leah Montgomery. Thanks so much for calling."

"You bet. Ah, well, we bought this house from Tracy fifteen years ago now." Arthur had a thick Georgia accent and a rasp in his tone that indicated age. "She gave me her phone number in case something came up and I needed to reach her. Sure enough, that happened a couple of times. Ah . . . after I read your letter, I checked my files to see if I still had her number. Turns out, I did. I can go ahead and give it to you if you have a pencil handy."

"Yes, sir. Thank you so much."

What she actually had handy: the twenty-first century equivalent of a pencil and paper. Leah opened the notes app on her phone and typed the numbers into it as he spoke.

Arthur demonstrated that there were still plenty of people left in the world willing to do favors for strangers. She thanked him profusely, disconnected, finished unloading her groceries, then settled behind the wheel of her Honda. The late October nights had begun to turn cool, so she ratcheted up her car's heater.

She compared the number Arthur had given her for Tracy to the number Joyce had given her for Tracy and saw that the numbers were different. Hope stirred as she placed a call to the number Arthur had provided.

"Hello?" a woman answered, with a tone both suspicious and slightly sour.

In the friendliest and most appreciative way possible, Leah explained her identity and connection to Tracy.

"Are you the one who sent me the Facebook message?"

Leah winced. "Yes."

"How did you get this number?"

Leah shared the process she'd followed.

Stony silence.

"I won't be able to set this aside and move on," Leah said, "until I've done everything I can to find answers. I'd really like to talk with you."

"I'm not a phone talker. The government listens to everything we say."

Leah didn't presume that the government would be interested in this phone call unless Tracy was involved in espionage. "If you'd rather speak in person, I'm willing to drive to meet you."

Another helping of silence that even Leah recognized as awkward.

"I'm having lunch with my mother tomorrow downtown, near the corner of Edgewood and Peachtree," Tracy said. "There's a park across from the restaurant. I can meet you there at 12:45."

Edgewood and Peachtree—an intersection in Atlanta. "I'll be there."

"I have red hair, and I'll wear a gray coat."

Three hours later, Sebastian entered his apartment, lowered heavily onto one of the kitchen table chairs, and called Leah. He was so tired he couldn't think about dinner or about changing out of his suit or even about standing up until he'd heard her voice.

"Good evening," she said.

Instantly, he started to smile. "Hey. Will you come see me this weekend?" He could drain Isabella's stomach, repair VSDs, study echocardiograms, and debate what to do about fixing a bad repair done by a hack. But in order to do all of those things, he had to know when he'd get to see her again.

"Actually," she said, "yes."

"What?" He sat up straight. "You will?"

She told him that one of the nurses who'd cared for her at Magnolia Avenue Hospital was willing to meet her tomorrow in Atlanta.

Thank God. "My apartment only has one bedroom," he told her, "but you're welcome to stay in it. I'll take the couch."

"I will not be staying in your apartment, I—"

"I'll book you a hotel room, then. There's a hotel across the street and a few doors down from my building."

"I'm delighted to inform you that I've already booked and paid for my hotel room. It's non-changeable and non-refundable."

"Leah," he groaned.

"I learned something from all those non-returnable gifts you sent us."

"Tell me you're going to get in the car right now and start driving."

"I am not. I have to get Dylan squared away with Tess and Rudy tomorrow morning. It will take some time to bring them up to speed because I want to ensure Dylan's prohibited from situations that involve red plastic cups and teens making out on furniture while I'm gone. I should be there by mid-morning tomorrow."

"And you'll stay in Atlanta until Monday?"

"Yes."

Thank God.

CHAPTER EIGHTEEN

Finally," Sebastian said when Leah arrived at his apartment. She had on a gray collared shirt opened at the throat and patterned with polka dots bigger than quarters in bright pastel colors. Jeans. He took one long drink of the details of her—soft blond hair, defined eyebrows, gently sloping cheeks—before wrapping her against him. The side of her face came to rest against his chest and he set his chin gently on the top of her head.

He was ridiculously glad that she was here. The weather had been depressing so far today—wet and dark. But now that she'd arrived, everything was right and bright. Nothing could be better than it was in this moment.

For years he'd understood in a detached sort of way that he was lonely. But it was only now, with Leah, that he understood how deep his loneliness had been.

"Hi," he whispered, drawing her closer to him.

"Happy Halloween."

"Happy Halloween. Thank you for coming."

"You're welcome. Though I didn't come for you, remember. I came to talk with Nurse Tracy."

He looked down at her. "I don't care why you came, only that you're here." Besides, no matter what she said to him or to herself, she *was* here, at least in part, for him. Otherwise, she wouldn't be staying until Monday. She'd be heading back to Misty River today after her meeting with Tracy.

"I will concede," she said, "that the opportunity to see you while in Atlanta is a nice perk."

Her misty blue eyes *killed* him. They communicated so many things—wisdom and disappointments and commitments fulfilled.

"I'm determined to become the best perk ever," he said.

"Impossible. I've already received the best perk ever—a bag of wookie cookies given to me by a student last May the Fourth Be With You."

"I can be better than wookie cookies."

"You're overly competitive." Her attention slid to his chest, then back up again. "Have you been at the hospital this morning?"

"Yeah."

"I like this look."

"A white T-shirt and scrubs?"

"You are aware, are you not, that several Hollywood actors have built careers on this look?"

"Those guys are fake doctors. Chumps."

He kissed her. He'd planned to keep it quick—didn't want to scare her off—but at the first taste, need overwhelmed him. After a few minutes, he had to use all his self-control to break the contact. "Thank you for coming."

"You already said that."

"It was worth repeating." He gave a lopsided grin. "How much time do we have before the meeting with Tracy?"

"Are you planning to join me for the meeting?"

"Is it okay with you if I do?"

"Yes."

"Then I'll join you."

"We have two hours."

"That gives us plenty of time to grab some lunch."

I think this might be her," Leah said two hours later.

She and Sebastian had arrived early at the park Tracy had specified. They'd been waiting and watching for a redhead in a gray

243

coat, and the woman who'd just entered the park fit the bill. Her body language radiated caution as she scanned her surroundings.

Leah caught the woman's eye, raised her hand in a wave, then approached. She could sense more than hear Sebastian walking beside and slightly behind her. Wind had swept the morning's gloomy weather to the east, leaving hesitant sunshine, high-sixties temperatures, and rain-scrubbed foliage.

"Tracy?" Leah asked.

"Yes."

"I'm Leah. Thank you very much for taking the time to speak with me. This is my friend Sebastian."

Tracy nodded tightly at Sebastian. She was of average height and almost painfully slender. Her lovely hair was parted on the side and tucked behind her ears before continuing in a smooth, shiny plane to her mid-chest. It was the only soft and inviting thing about her. Her pointy features looked as if they'd been chiseled from marble.

"Would you like to sit down?" Leah indicated a picnic table nearby.

Tracy gave another nod. Leah and Sebastian took one side of the table, Tracy the other.

"As I mentioned over the phone," Leah said, "Magnolia Avenue Hospital granted me access to my hospital records, which is how I knew that you were working there the day of my birth."

Tracy's lips formed a horizontal line. "I decided to get a degree in nursing when I was eighteen years old. Worst decision I ever made. Magnolia Avenue was my first employer, and as soon as I started my job there, I realized I'd made a mistake. Nursing was not for me."

Apparently, the hospital hadn't exactly been fond of Tracy either, since she'd been let go after just a few years on staff. Leah supplied her birthdate, full name, and the names of both sets of parents. "Does any of that ring a bell?"

"Not at all."

"Do you remember the nurses who were working the shift with you that day?" She rattled off the other women's names.

"I hardly remember Lois. Bonnie was much older and treated me like I was a child. Joyce was loud and obnoxious. She never stopped talking."

"Do you happen to have any contact information for Bonnie?"

"No. We never saw or talked to each other outside of work hours."

"Do you remember anything about Lois, Joyce, or Bonnie's personal lives?"

Her jaw tightened. "Are these the types of questions you're asking the other women about me?"

"I'm seeking to get a sense of the big picture." She sidestepped answering Tracy's question directly. "Any and all information could be helpful."

The skin between Tracy's eyes creased. "Are you trying to pin the fact that you were switched at birth on one of us?"

"Like she said. She's just trying to get a sense of the big picture." Sebastian's tone was polite but firm.

"Joyce was always running short on money," Tracy said. "She had three kids and a husband who was a big spender. I wouldn't be at all surprised if she was taking medicine from the hospital and selling it to pay bills. I don't remember anything about Lois's or Bonnie's personal lives. I left Magnolia Avenue as soon as I was offered a job working as an administrator for a plastic surgery practice."

"Which practice is that?" Sebastian asked.

"I'd rather not say." She frowned at Leah. "*I'm* here to help *you*. I don't want anyone calling my boss and making trouble for me."

"No one will call your boss," Leah said.

"I hated nursing, but that doesn't mean I wasn't good at it. I worked hard, and I did my job. I was certainly sharper mentally than Joyce, who had the attention span of a gnat, and Lois, who was retirement-age." Tracy rose to stand. "If one of the nurses made a mistake with you, it wasn't me." She turned and walked away.

Leah watched her cross the street toward the row of shops and restaurants on the other side.

"Sweet lady," Sebastian commented.

"Not the most trustworthy of individuals. She struck me as . . . shifty."

"Same."

"I can believe that Tracy's capable of switching two babies, but I can't imagine why she would have been motivated to do so. I think I might try to root around in her past a bit more to see if I can uncover anything. If I can't, I might be at a dead end. I've already exhausted every information source I can think of concerning my parents and the Brooksides. I've spoken with Joyce and now Tracy. I can't find Bonnie." Facing him, she took in the striking ratios of his face. "Do you have any ideas?"

"What about checking county court records? You could do that while you're here in Atlanta, since this is where everyone lived at the time of your birth."

"Court records?"

"For civil cases. Criminal cases." He lifted a muscular shoulder. "Because of my job and the amount I pay in malpractice insurance every month, my mind naturally goes there. You could check to see if your parents, the Brooksides, or the nurses had charges filed against them."

She was as far removed from the world of arrests and lawsuits as the sun from dwarf-planet Pluto. The prospect of court records hadn't crossed her mind. Yet, if one of the parents or nurses was sued or arrested, that could provide all kinds of valuable insights. "Where can I access court records?"

"The Fulton County Courthouse, I think." Sebastian jutted his chin toward the far side of the park. "Shall we?"

"We shall."

Before they'd left his apartment, they'd finalized their plans for the day. Meet with Tracy. Relax at the park. Eat Halloween dinner out. Tomorrow, they'd revisit the church the Brooksides attended so that Leah could hopefully get another glimpse of them.

He wedged the blanket he'd brought from home under his arm. They walked from the more crowded area of the park toward the quieter, less manicured section.

She checked her phone in case Dylan had called or texted her. He hadn't.

"How's your brother?" Sebastian asked, correctly guessing the reason she'd peeked at her phone.

"Hopefully not injecting amphetamines as we speak."

He shot her a grin, and attraction jolted through her.

"I'm pleased to report," she said, "that I received some good news about him yesterday. The dean of the fine arts program at Georgia Southern emailed me to say he was impressed by the drawings Dylan submitted with his application. Should Dylan be admitted there, the dean said he hopes he'll consider choosing them and listed half a dozen scholarships he should apply for."

"That's great."

"I was astonished. I've known for some time that Dylan's a talented artist, but I hadn't realized he was talented enough to receive personal interaction from a prospective college."

"Good for him."

Sebastian unfurled the waterproof side of the blanket across a patch of grass and they stretched out side by side. The sun's rays—and a wave of peace—seeped into Leah's skin.

She was not someone who experienced chemistry with men or days this splendid.

Except, now, somehow . . . she did?

Since she'd gained custody of Dylan, she'd only ever left him overnight with Tess and Rudy for chess tournaments or to travel as a chaperone on class trips. Perhaps she should have made an effort to get away a little bit more often. Why hadn't she?

Because until now, she hadn't known how freeing this would feel. Here, removed both geographically and psychologically from Dylan and her job, ropes of stress were unwinding from her.

For this one weekend, she could just be Leah. Not Leah the caretaker, teacher, grocery shopper, wage earner, or house cleaner.

She pondered the geometry of the autumn trees that formed a canopy above, then peered into the unending sky. "'The infinite! No other question has ever moved so profoundly the spirit of man.'"

"Who are you quoting?"

"Mathematician David Hilbert. Even though we don't know whether the universe is infinite or not, it's certainly larger than my ability to comprehend. Every time I pause and take a moment to look—*really look*—into the sky, it reminds me of infinity."

Sebastian propped up on his elbow, facing her.

Her mouth went dry because her view of him was much, much better than her prior (excellent) view of trees and sky.

His personality was both determined and good. When a determined man liked you, his affection was resolute. When a good man liked you, he tempted you to trust him. When she was with Sebastian, she felt as though she were the only thing in the world he saw or heard or cared about.

She needed to be very, *very* wary.

Even if she'd felt about men in the past the way she felt about Sebastian, she strongly suspected that her relationship with Sebastian would still have been a singular experience. There was nothing mundane or ordinary or predictable about him.

Her task this weekend: to enjoy his company without allowing herself to become serious about him in the detrimental way that her mom had become serious about her dad.

His position gave her an opportunity to study his masculine face, the lines of his shoulders and ribs, the way the strands of his hair fell.

She and Sebastian had both been cut off from their biological parents. Just how much of the tangible and intangible *stuff* that made them who they were had been passed to them by people who were not a part of their lives? "Did your mother have gray eyes?" she asked.

"She had blue."

"Is there anything about your appearance that resembles hers?"

"I have the same color hair that she did. Our mouths and chins have a similar shape."

So far, she knew only what he'd told her about his mother at the Coleman family's barbecue. Her name had been Denise, and she'd moved Sebastian from Chicago to Georgia. "Did your mom grow up in Chicago?"

"She was born and raised in Brooklyn, the youngest of five kids in a blue-collar family." He picked up a persimmon-hued maple leaf and spun it by its stem. "She never talked to me much about that part of her life."

"Why?"

"I'm guessing because those years were brutal for her. The summer after tenth grade, she took a job at a summer camp in upstate New York, and after that, she never returned to Brooklyn."

"She moved out after tenth grade?"

"Yeah. At the end of that summer, she went home with a friend she'd made named Cassie who lived in Chicago."

"Cassie's parents were okay with that?"

"I guess so. She moved in with their family for the rest of high school." He skimmed the leaf's tip along the hand that she'd rested on her abdomen. It left a trail of tingles, so she pushed her sleeve up past her elbow and turned her inner arm upward.

Taking his time, he trailed the leaf up and down.

"What did she do after graduating from high school?" she asked.

"She got a job in manufacturing and moved into an apartment with a few roommates."

"What was her personality like?"

"Stubborn, tough, willing to stand up for herself. Honest. Nothing about her personality was fake."

"You told me that she passed away when you were eight of a terminal illness."

"Yes."

"But you didn't mention which terminal illness."

His face went blank. She supposed that a long history of self-preservation had taught him how and when to mask his feelings.

"Heart disease," he said.

Comprehension rolled from the top of her head down to her toes. Sebastian had once been a child powerless to save his mother.

He was no longer powerless, and now he worked, every single day, to do for children what he'd been unable to do for her.

"Heart disease," Leah reiterated.

"Yes."

"Brought on by a congenital heart defect?" she guessed. He'd told her at the barbecue that his mom had had the condition all her life.

A small motion of his head told her she was correct.

"Which congenital heart defect?"

"Tetralogy of Fallot."

"But . . ."

"It's treatable," he finished, anticipating her confusion.

"Exactly."

"It's definitely treatable now, but it was even in those days." He watched the leaf track down her forearm. "Patients with her condition have to be followed closely long-term. Often, they develop a leaky valve, and they might need valve replacement surgery. My mother was a terrible patient. She smoked. She drank. She didn't take her meds. She never went to doctor's appointments."

"Why?"

"I think because she'd had her fill of hospitals and doctors. When she was a teenager, she basically gave the middle finger to her condition and decided to live her life as if she hadn't been born with a heart defect. Eventually . . . tetralogy of Fallot had the last word." A breeze whisked the maple leaf away.

Sebastian flopped onto his back and stuck a forearm behind his head. Leah rose onto her own arm and looked down at him. Grooves marked his forehead.

"How did you deal with her loss, emotionally?" she asked.

"I didn't. I've since learned that trauma splits an event from its emotion. My mom's death was the most terrible thing that could have happened to me. But when it happened, I felt cold and hard inside. That's all."

Sorry seemed far too trite and small a word. She picked up a waxy magnolia leaf, arranged his free arm just the way hers had been arranged moments before, and swept the leaf's tip delicately along the inside of his strong forearm. "Did CPS try to contact her family?"

"No. She refused to accept the fact that she was dying until just a few weeks before she did. At that point, she clearly specified that she wanted me to become a ward of the state of Georgia."

"Because?"

"Because she wasn't going to let me anywhere near her family, and she didn't have anybody else. She loved the mountains of northern Georgia and wanted me to grow up there." His lips firmed. "I think she believed the odds were best for me in foster care."

"Do you think you would have been happier with her family?"

"No. My foster parents were all good people who were fostering kids for the right reasons. They weren't the problem. By the time I went to them, I was the problem."

"How so?"

"My attitude."

"Elaborate."

"I was reclusive. Argumentative. Bitter. I hated the first family who took me in, even through they tried their best to help me."

"You were an eight-year-old child whose only family member died. Dylan was around that same age when my mother left. I saw how that affected him. He floundered, too, and I understood why. His grief was warranted. His anger was warranted. So was yours."

Sebastian didn't reply.

After what she'd been through with Dylan, she had a soft spot for the kid Sebastian had been and the heartbreak he'd endured. Dr. Grant, a man who appeared to have everything, did not have everything.

"Did your foster parents ensure that you received counseling?"

"For years. I hated that, too. I mostly just sat there with my mouth shut and waited for it to be over."

"You were a tough nut to crack."

"Still am."

Regret flashed within her because *she* wanted to be the person who cracked his hard shell.

Of all the disastrous, ill-conceived urges!

He lived like a bear in a cave, keeping those who did not have the last name of Coleman at arm's length. He was a heart surgeon who did not understand the inner workings of his own heart. He'd determined that he didn't want to love or be loved, and who was she to quibble with that?

She didn't want romantic love, either. But even if she did want that from Sebastian, she was smart enough to know that the very worst thing a woman could do was invest herself in a man based on the fruitless hope that he would change.

It was crucial that they keep things just as they were.

Light and uncomplicated.

Trina and Jonathan Brookside unknowingly fulfilled Leah's hopes by showing up for church the following morning.

Sebastian sat beside Leah in a pew one section over from the older couple and several rows back. From what Leah had told him, he knew that Sophie, Sophie's husband, and Sophie's younger sister had all attended the service the last time Leah had come here. Today, only Trina and Jonathan were present.

The congregation rose to sing. Instead of focusing on the lyrics, he assessed the couple. Leah had her mother's build and hair color. Trina leaned close to her husband to say something near his ear. Jonathan responded by turning his head to hers. Trina and Leah's profiles were alike, but Leah's cheekbones and chin appeared to have come from her father.

How would Trina and Jonathan react if they knew the daughter that should have been theirs was just yards away? Singing the same praise song?

When the service ended, he caught Leah watching the Brooksides with a combination of interest, pain, and sweetness.

She wore high heels that buckled around her ankles. Her jean dress had a wide skirt and a belt made out of floral fabric that knotted at her waist. The charm dangling from the necklace he'd given her rested just below the hollow at the base of her throat. Her hair shone gold under the lights.

He swallowed against a groundswell of tenderness. The swell was so strong, it was a physical force. So strong, it stole his words.

"Are you going to tell them who you are?" he managed to ask.

"Not today."

"Someday?"

"I don't know. In my mind, I frequently run through the costs and benefits of telling them. I still haven't reached a conclusion." She gathered her purse. "Ready?"

They moved toward the exit.

"Do you have a favorite restaurant around here?" she asked.

"Yeah, but it's casual. It's this little authentic Mexican place."

"Let's go."

"Look at what you're wearing. That dress and you deserve a nicer restaurant."

"And yet, this dress and I want enchiladas."

They ate enchiladas from stools at the restaurant's long bar. Blue paint and framed Latin music records from the '70s and '80s plastered the walls.

They bantered, teased, laughed. Sebastian concentrated on memorizing her characteristics. He wanted to be able to replay them so they could keep him company when she left.

They'd almost finished their meal when his phone pager beeped.

"No," he moaned.

Her face held amused sympathy. "I knew from the start that you were on call this weekend."

He'd planned to take her to the arts district after this. More than anything, he wanted the chance to walk through museums with her.

He read the information on his phone. "They need a consult on an infant who's being airlifted to the hospital."

"Sounds like it's time for you to save small humans." She looked around and signaled their server. "Check, please."

"Will you come with me to the hospital?"

"We took your car this morning. It's only logical for me to go where you go."

I want to go where you go for the rest of my life.

He shoved the thought away before it could put down roots.

For the second time, Leah had been granted exclusive access to Sebastian's office.

She went straight to the long, vertical corkboard full of photos and notes. The day she'd finagled Dylan into touring this place, she hadn't had time to study all the items on the board. Now, very satisfactorily, she did. Once she finished her survey, she made herself comfortable in a leather chair and checked the app on her phone that tracked Dylan's location. He was at home with Tess and Rudy.

Good Dylan. She placed a call to him and proceeded to pry conversation out of him with a chisel. After a few minutes she took pity on the boy and asked him to put Tess on. Not only was Tess much more agreeable to talk to, she could be trusted to give Leah an unvarnished update on Dylan. Dylan had been cranky when Tess had woken him this morning, but after eating half a box of cereal out of a mixing bowl, he'd gotten himself together, and they'd made it to church before returning to Leah's house.

"Rudy!" Tess stopped mid-sentence to call out. "Put that down. That's breakable."

"What does he have?" Leah asked.

"An expensive-looking calculator."

Blimey. She'd continued to carry her old graphing calculator around in her purse. She kept the new one that Sebastian had given her on a shelf at home to use on special occasions.

Tess released a resigned sigh. "I'd best go take it away from him. Enjoy your time in Atlanta."

Leah opened the most challenging math app she'd been able to find and worked problems until the door swung inward, admitting Sebastian. He still wore his church clothes—a beautifully tailored white shirt, gray herringbone patterned tie, navy suit pants.

"Ready?" he asked.

"I am. What's the status of the baby who was airlifted in?"

"Stable." In the hallway, he opened the door to the stairwell for her. "Mind if we stop in the PICU on our way out?"

"Not at all."

She followed him into a room where a toddler boy slept. He had tawny skin and silky black hair. Dressed in Superman pajamas, he clasped a faded stuffed dog.

She watched Sebastian do what she'd seen him do before, assess the monitors and then carefully straighten the tubes running from the child.

A male nurse with a kind face and balding head slipped inside. "Good afternoon, Dr. Grant."

"Good afternoon." Sebastian introduced him to Leah, then asked, "Kidney function?"

"I'm still seeing a negative fluid balance."

"Good. H and H?"

"Steady."

Sebastian and Leah left the room.

"Can we look in on Isabella?" she asked.

"If you'd like."

"I would."

He led her to the room she remembered. Almost everything remained eerily unchanged. Isabella looked the same, with the ventilator sealed to her mouth. Eight weeks had gone by since Leah's last visit, and only a few things had altered: today Isabella's blanket was lavender, and her mom wasn't present. Megan must have just stepped out because her Bible rested open on her chair.

"I thought sepsis might take her down," Sebastian said. "But it didn't."

"Pull through," Leah said to the baby, entreaty in her voice.

"She's a fighter."

"Then fight," she said to Isabella.

Silently, she prayed over the tiny girl.

How would she have dealt with this had it been Dylan lying here with a machine breathing for him? How could she have kept it together if Dylan's life had been the one hanging by the thinnest piece of thread, a thread that God could extend or cut?

All life hung by a thin piece of thread.

Her life included. She knew this.

It's just that inside this room, Isabella's thread seemed excruciatingly fragile.

Leah transferred her focus to Sebastian and found him watching her with a look both soft and somber.

"C'mon." He extended a hand.

She took it.

Sebastian drove Leah to a museum that contained many fine works of art and one particularly private and dim corridor between galleries. When he came to a halt in the corridor, she glanced at him. Immediately, she read what he was thinking in his unrepentant expression.

"*Sebastian*. You're a well-respected surgeon in this city. You cannot be found making out in museum hallways."

"Can't I?"

"No."

He stepped toward her, his hands curving around to support the back of her head. "As far as I know, making out in hallways isn't against museum policy."

"How familiar are you with this museum's policies?"

"As familiar as I want to be."

"How familiar are you with what's in good taste?"

"Leah?"

"Yes?"

"I've never cared about what's in good taste."

She saw so much desire in his eyes that her breath turned shallow.

Heat rose, awareness built. One of his fingertips caressed the tender skin at the back of her neck. She could feel the hammer of her heart, hear the hitch in his inhalations.

"You wouldn't want to 'let a gorgeous guy like me out of your sight,' would you?" he asked.

She *could not* resist a man who quoted Han Solo to her. But in the name of spunkiness, she leaned toward his ear and reciprocated with another quote. "'Don't get cocky.'"

"Kiss me."

"I don't remember a quote about kissing—"

"That last one," he whispered, "wasn't a quote."

Oh, for heaven's sake, who cared about what was or wasn't in good taste? She pulled him to her and they kissed deep and slow.

A sound of approval rumbled in his throat.

Someone might come in.

But the danger of discovery only heightened the thrill.

His fingers speared into her hair.

Sebastian.

CHAPTER NINETEEN

Late the next morning, Leah woke in her hotel room to
a column of sunshine falling across the foot of her bed.
Clean, crisp sheets cocooned her.

A text from Sebastian, who'd be back at work by now on this
Monday morning, awaited her.

Meet me for coffee before you drive home? I
know a place.

Is this my life? she thought, tossing a hand onto the pillow above
her head with a happy sigh.

The enormous gray monolith otherwise known as the Lewis R.
Slaton Courthouse had been constructed more than a hundred years ago. Leah sat in the waiting area of the "closed file
room," smelling the building's age in its dust-scented air and seeing
the building's age in the old-fashioned glass partition separating
her from the room's attendant.

This morning she'd placed a phone call to the courthouse
and learned that criminal records were not available online, but
that both criminal and civil records were available here. So she'd
checked out of her hotel and relocated to the courthouse computer
lab. She'd begun by searching for criminal and civil proceedings

that named her parents, Erica and Todd Montgomery. Her efforts generated no matches. Nor did her efforts generate a match for Trina Brookside.

When she'd moved on to Jonathan Brookside, however, she'd hit pay dirt. So much pay dirt that she'd been momentarily caught by surprise, like a hide-and-seek-player who jumps when they discover their friend blinking at them from underneath a bed.

Seven civil suits had been filed against Jonathan over the years. But only two—one for wrongful termination and one for breach of contract—had been filed recently enough that the associated documents were available digitally.

She'd combed through those two suits and recorded all the pertinent details on her phone. Then she'd jotted down the case numbers for the other five cases.

When none of the nurses' names resulted in a single criminal or civil charge, she'd consulted the staff member in the computer room, who'd informed Leah that she'd need to visit the closed file room to gain access to documents pertaining to the old suits filed against Jonathan.

She'd submitted a records request for the case numbers in question thirty minutes ago. Ever since, she'd been waiting alongside an elderly woman speaking Spanish quietly into her phone and a middle-aged couple. The wife was reading *Better Homes & Gardens* and the husband was dozing while sitting upright.

Seven suits against Jonathan.

Seven! That seemed like an unusually high number, but perhaps it wasn't. Perhaps that was a low number of suits for an individual who owned a company as large as Gridwork Communications Corporation.

"Ms. Montgomery?"

She approached the young blond man stationed behind the glass.

"Here you are." He slid her the stack of pages he'd photocopied from the originals.

She thanked him and returned to her still-warm chair.

Quickly, she skimmed the pages. One suit for breach of contract. One for discrimination. One for intellectual property rights. Two for wrongful termination.

At first glance, it appeared two of the suits had been settled out of court and that he'd been acquitted of the rest. Which, of course, did not necessarily mean Jonathan had been innocent. The acquittals might simply mean that he'd had an excellent defense team.

Leah crossed her legs, collected a pen from her purse, and started wading through the dense legal language of the topmost sheet. Page by page, she circled every key fact—names, dates, the gist of the accusation, the result.

When she reached the intellectual property suit, she circled the plaintiff's name. Ian Monroe O'Reilly.

Instantly, recognition clicked. One of her nurses at Magnolia Avenue Hospital had the same surname.

The mysterious Bonnie O'Reilly.

This particular suit had been filed thirty years ago. Ian O'Reilly (age twenty-seven) had accused Jonathan Brookside (also age twenty-seven) of stealing his idea, his technology, and his research and using it to found Gridwork Communications Corporation.

Leah read through the remainder of the document. The case had been tried. Jonathan had not been found liable.

Think, Leah.

A plaintiff named O'Reilly had sued Jonathan Brookside. Two years later, a nurse named O'Reilly had cared for Jonathan Brookside's daughter on the day of her birth.

O'Reilly was one of the most common American surnames of Irish origin. The fact that Baby Brookside's nurse shared the same name as a plaintiff who'd sued Jonathan Brookside a few years prior could comfortably be attributed to coincidence.

If everything had proceeded normally from there, had she and Sophie gone home with their rightful parents, suspicion would not be justified. But instead, while a nurse named O'Reilly was on duty, Baby Brookside had been switched with Baby Montgomery.

Under those circumstances, suspicion seemed highly justified.

Tilting back her head, she peered at the crown molding dividing wall from ceiling.

Ian and Jonathan had both been twenty-seven. According to Joyce, Bonnie had been fifty or so at the time of Leah's birth. It was feasible to think that Bonnie could have been Ian's mother. Or perhaps his aunt? Cousin?

If Bonnie had been related to the Ian who'd sued Jonathan, then, no doubt, Bonnie was not one of Jonathan's admirers.

So . . . What?

Bonnie had taken it upon herself to punish Jonathan by swapping his child with someone else's?

But why? That seemed far too extreme. It was true that the wheels of justice didn't always turn fairly, yet it looked as if due process had been followed in this case. Ian had had his day in court.

Confounded, Leah Googled Ian O'Reilly on her phone. Several results populated. But just like when she'd hunted for Bonnie, none of these people seemed to be the person she sought. These men weren't the right age or hadn't lived in Georgia.

When she finished reading through the rest of the paperwork, she returned to the attendant, who looked up inquiringly.

"I'm interested in accessing a birth certificate," she told him. "Can you recommend how to go about that?" If she could find Ian O'Reilly's birth certificate, she'd learn his mother's name, his father's name, his place of birth, and more that might help her locate him.

"Are you the person named on the birth certificate?"

"I'm not."

"Are you a primary family member of the person named?"

"I'm not."

"Sorry, but those are the only two categories qualified to request birth certificates."

"Ah. I see."

"You can get a look at some of the information provided on birth certificates through census records."

"How long after a census is taken is it released to the public?"

"Seventy-two years."

"Thank you."

Leah walked toward her parking space. Ian O'Reilly wouldn't have been born seventy-two years ago, so the census would be no help. Bonnie O'Reilly, however, likely would have been born by then if Joyce had estimated her age accurately.

As soon as she settled behind the wheel of her Honda, she logged into YourHeritage.com. She clicked on the tab for census records and began typing in Bonnie's last name—

Stopped.

Joyce had said that Bonnie was a single mother when they worked together. But if Bonnie had been married back when she'd had her child . . . then O'Reilly was likely Bonnie's married name. When the census was taken more than seven decades ago, Bonnie would have been a girl. Her last name would not have been O'Reilly. Her last name would have been her maiden name.

Still, it was worth a shot to search for census records for Bonnie O'Reilly. Maybe Bonnie had never married. Or maybe she had, but had kept her maiden name all her life.

Leah filled in the scant information she knew about Bonnie and ran a search for census records pertaining to her.

No promising matches whatsoever.

She lowered the phone to her lap with a frustrated exhale.

The second Sebastian entered the coffee shop and saw Leah, he knew something was wrong.

His workday had passed incredibly slowly because he'd looked at his watch every few minutes to see how many hours remained until his afternoon break and the chance to see Leah. Now he was finally here. She sat at a small table inside the crowded interior, two cups of coffee before her, talking to someone on her phone. Her eyes blazed accusation at him.

A quicksand sensation overtook his chest. A sinking down, down, down.

"I see," she said to the caller. "Thank you very much for your time." A pause. "All the best." Another pause. "Good-bye."

She pushed her phone into her purse and frowned. Then she carried her cup from the shop. He followed, throwing away his drink when he passed the trash can because, if she was mad at him—which she was—then he definitely couldn't stomach coffee.

She marched into the mouth of a nearby alley, her shoulders stiff beneath the same bright pink sweater she'd worn the day of the farmers market. Brick buildings, dumpsters, and weeds lined the sides of the alley. Above, white clouds that looked like whipped cream blocked the sun.

They faced each other. Her, beautiful. Him, standing very still in his pale blue business shirt and gray suit pants. "What's wrong?" he asked.

Her eyebrows drew together. "While I was waiting for you, I called the dean of the fine arts school at Georgia Southern to thank him for his interest in Dylan. He was very cordial. During our conversation I asked him how Dylan's drawings had come to his attention. He told me that his favorite niece's little boy had been born with a hole in his heart, and that Dr. Grant at the Clinic for Pediatric and Congenital Heart Diseases had performed a fabulously successful surgery. Dylan was brought to the dean's attention by Dr. Grant himself, who called the dean to alert him to Dylan's application. The dean informed me that I'm very fortunate to have the esteemed Dr. Grant in my brother's corner."

He kept his face impassive. His heart thudded in his eardrums, which was stupid. His heart didn't thud like this when he was cutting on a child's aorta.

"I told you about the dean's email concerning Dylan on Saturday," she continued, "and you said . . . What did you say? I think you said, 'Good for him.' You most definitely did not say that you were the one who'd . . . who'd—" she sliced a hand through the air—"manufactured the dean's interest in Dylan!"

"I don't have the power to manufacture anyone's interest. I simply called the dean to tell him about a promising new recruit."

"And, no doubt, to ask him to keep us in mind for scholarships."

"Yes," he admitted.

Color flared on her cheeks. "So. Not only did you go behind my back to pull some strings, but then you didn't come clean about your involvement when you had the chance."

She was blowing this all out of proportion. "I know the college applications have been hard on you and Dylan. When I found out that he'd applied to Georgia Southern and realized I had a contact there, I wanted to do something to help. So I called the dean. But I planned to keep my involvement anonymous—"

"Because you knew I wouldn't like it. But you got caught."

"I got caught doing something *good* for your brother."

She scowled at him. "Dylan and I are not helpless. We are not incapable. We are not incompetent! We don't need a Daddy Warbucks to pull strings for us behind our backs!"

"I know you're not helpless—"

"That's not what your actions say." A strand of hair slipped over one eye. She shoved it back. "Do you, with your degrees and your money, pity Dylan and me?"

"No." But honestly, how could he not pity her? She was supposed to have accepted a full ride to Princeton.

"I think that you *do* pity us," she said, reading his mind. "Which annoys me no end because, in case you'd failed to notice, I'm an exceptionally independent person. My job is important and satisfying. Dylan and I are doing *fine*. We don't need necklaces or graphing calculators or art supplies or hubcaps or phone calls to deans. My affection can't be bought. So, please. No more."

His temper stirred. "I was trying to lend a hand."

"But you didn't ask me first before involving yourself in something that pertains to *my brother*." She drew herself tall. "I've been taking care of him for a long time, and you can trust that I will continue to take care of him. We don't need your intervention."

"Everybody needs the help of others sometimes, Leah."

"I don't need help from you. At all."

Sebastian crossed his arms and said nothing.

"Well?" she said, clearly waiting for him to tell her he was sorry.

For making a phone call for her brother's sake? He wasn't sorry. "If you think I'm going to apologize, I'm not."

Without another word, she stalked from the alley and down the sidewalk.

Seething inside, he watched her go.

Turn around, Leah.

She didn't.

She was leaving. She was going to get in her car and drive back to Misty River. And he was irritated with her, so her departure should be okay with him.

It *should* be. But it wasn't. He set his jaw to keep himself from calling out to her and asking her to stay in Atlanta with him for another few hours, months, centuries.

Leah pointed her car toward home.

As the miles passed, the city dropped away. She drove into the foothills of the Blue Ridge Mountains and then higher as her brain chewed on the events of the weekend the way she'd chew on a piece of taffy that had been mostly delicious but ended with a surprisingly bitter finish.

Fabulous Saturday, with their Halloween dinner at a sky-high restaurant that had as its carpet the lights of Atlanta's buildings. Their servers had been dressed in costume, and she and Sebastian had shared a dessert named Death by Chocolate.

Wonderful Sunday with church and museums, a movie night at Sebastian's apartment, and kisses that incinerated the air.

Rocky Monday, which had started out with promise and finished with the realization that Sebastian had been meddling in her affairs.

In her lifetime she'd received one huge advantage—her years at the Program for the Exceptionally Gifted at Clemmons. She'd had no qualms about accepting that gift. And, had she been able to take Princeton up on their offer, she'd have had no qualms about accepting that gift, either.

Back then, she'd been a teenager. Economically disadvantaged. The daughter of a volatile family. She'd been desperate for education and comfortable with the idea that she'd earned her scholarships through merit.

But ever since she'd turned Princeton down, she'd been a citizen of the real world. She couldn't afford to spend her days in the lofty realms of pure mathematics when she needed to stretch every paycheck in order to keep a boy fed, clothed, sheltered. She taught, graded papers, forced Dylan to eat vegetables, badgered him about turning in his homework. She was the person who haggled with health insurance, called the exterminator, and made mortgage payments.

For ten years, she'd received no advantages. She'd done it the hard way, and she was proud of what she'd accomplished. It humiliated her to think that when Sebastian looked at her, he saw someone in need of assistance.

She was not Sebastian Grant's charity case. And his non-boyfriend status in no way gave him the right to call the dean of the fine arts program on Dylan's behalf.

Sebastian had only met Dylan . . . what? Three times? He hardly knew Dylan.

Sebastian hardly knew her.

She hardly knew him.

Only . . .

That wasn't entirely fair. Or correct. She had a feeling that while it was true that Sebastian hardly knew Dylan, he might know her quite well already. Just like she might know him quite well already.

Bossy. Hard-charging. High maintenance. That's how Markie, his co-worker at the hospital, had described Sebastian the day of Leah and Dylan's tour. All true.

Except Markie had also said, *"A few of the kids he's treated have lived mostly because he was so determined that they wouldn't die."*

Some of the qualities that were trying in a non-boyfriend were to be commended in his exponentially more important role— pediatric heart surgeon.

At every stage of her acquaintance with him, she'd debated whether to move forward. Each time, she'd deemed the next step safe enough to take. Worth taking. And, indeed, her time with Sebastian had been a great deal of fun. So diverting! Through him, she'd learned a lot about herself.

But suddenly—like tree branches coming into view beneath the surface of a lake—she could see the dangers inherent in their relationship that she hadn't been able to see before.

Her mom was similar to Sebastian in several ways. Mom struggled to trust others. She'd constantly sought and never found satisfaction. Because of those weaknesses, Mom's marriage and her relationships with her kids had crumbled in the most miserable way possible.

Leah had no desire to subject herself to the pain of an ill-fated relationship. This was an opportune time to bring her extended flirtation with Sebastian to a close.

Assured of the rightness of that choice, she pulled into her garage. A slice of her reflection in the rearview mirror caught her eye. With dismay, she saw that her lower lashes were wet. So was the skin beneath her eyes.

Without realizing it, she'd been *crying* over the choice she'd just proclaimed to be the right one. For some terrible reason that she didn't want to examine too closely, her heart felt as though it was ripping down the center.

"Leah," she whispered scoldingly, whisking away the moisture with her fingertips. She patted her cheeks a little harder than necessary, then rolled her carry-on indoors.

Tess and Rudy had left for their Monday night Bible study group, so she found Dylan alone on the sofa watching a ghastly show about monster trucks.

"Brother of mine!" She gestured for him to stand, then hugged him. He was much too thin. Mental note: Feed him more protein, dairy, and fruit. "Did you miss me?"

"Sure." Which meant no.

"I brought you a gift." She knelt to her suitcase and came up with a vintage-style T-shirt that read *404*—Atlanta's area code—across the front.

"Thanks."

"You're welcome."

He admired the shirt, then slung it over his shoulder. "Hey, next time you leave . . ."

"Yes?"

"Can I stay by myself?"

She bit her bottom lip to keep herself from exclaiming, *Not in a million years*!

"I don't need babysitters."

"Tess and Rudy aren't your babysitters—"

"They act like it. They were all over me this weekend."

"That's because they care about you."

"I think it's because you gave them a long list of all the things I'm not allowed to do."

"I mean . . . Well. The list wasn't *that* long."

"It's way too long. It's crazy." His curls bounced with agitation. "I'll be eighteen soon."

"Yes."

"Have I done anything to make you think I can't take care of myself? No. I haven't."

He made iffy choices in his social life all the time. He hardly ever studied for tests. He'd eat nothing but Cheez-Its if she let him. "When you were in middle school—"

"That was years ago." His chin set. She could see that he felt passionately about this and yet was making an effort to talk with her about it maturely. "Next year I'm going to go away to school, and then I'll have total freedom."

"Right, and between now and then, my job is to ensure you're ready."

"I am ready."

"You've made huge strides."

"But you don't let me go to parties. You won't let me take weekend trips with my friends' families. You're always tracking the location of my phone and asking me to come straight home after games and practices. All my friends—every single one—has more freedom than I do. It's like you don't trust me."

"I do trust you. It's just that I'm trying to keep you safe."

He studied her, mingled obstinacy and sympathy in his face. "I don't think you do what you do to keep me safe."

"What do you mean?"

He remained quiet for several moments. Her autumn three-wick candle, which smelled of pumpkin pancake, burned sedately on the coffee table.

"I think you put all these rules on me because you want control," he said.

"No. I do what I do because I love you."

"Okay, sure, you love me. But that's not why you're so strict." His Adam's apple bobbed. "You got stuck with a kid when you were around my age."

She blinked at him because, of course, he was correct. Yet the thought of his taking custody of a child at his age was *abhorrent*. He was a kid himself, in no way prepared to take charge of a child. Her eighteen-year-old self and Dylan's seventeen-year-old self had little in common. By that point in her life, she'd lived away from home for four years. She'd come out of the womb a small but old and serious person. Her parents had ensured that she grew up quickly from there.

But Dylan, *and thank God for this*, had been afforded the chance to be young. After Mom had left him in her care, Leah had done her best to give him an elementary school experience free from worries graver than memorizing multiplication tables. As a middle school kid, he'd spent chunks of his weekends immersed in video games. As a high school kid, he had the luxury of playing football and hiding in his room and regarding the adults in his life as hopelessly uncool.

"I did not get stuck with you," she said.

"Yeah you did. You were supposed to go and get your PhD, and it makes me feel like dirt when I think about how you had to take care of me and couldn't go."

She stepped to him and held his face in her hands. The soft little boy face had turned firm and angular. But this was still *her* Dylan. "You're my favorite person. Please believe me when I tell you that having the chance to take care of you has been the greatest joy of my whole life. Would Princeton have been nice?" A rueful chuckle spilled from her. "Yes. But if I had the choice to make all over again, I would choose you *every single time*. There's no contest, Dylan. I got the better bargain."

He stepped back a few feet, looked toward the TV.

Her hands fell to her sides. "Also, just so we're really clear on this, you have nothing to feel like dirt about. You weren't old enough back when Mom left to make a single decision, nor should you have had to. So none of what happened is on you. No one blames you. No one thinks that anything is your fault."

"Yeah." He kept his face pointed to the side.

"Really, though. I mean it. . . . Dylan?"

"Yeah." He sighed. "What I was trying to say is that I think a lot of your freedom got taken away. So even though you talk about trusting God, you're always trying to control me to make up for the stuff you couldn't control before." He met her eyes with a knowing look.

Ouch. He might have hit on a vein of truth there. And it hurt. Over the years, had she started unintentionally yanking away some of the control that rightfully belonged to God and appropriating it for herself?

He ambled toward his cave.

"You don't need to go," she said. "We can talk about this more. Or you can finish your show."

"Nah. I'm done." He turned into his bedroom and shut the door.

She was left with a candle, a clean house, an open suitcase, and Dylan's words, which circled around and around her like a whirlpool.

CHAPTER TWENTY

Isabella Ackerman's medical team gathered in the conference room on Wednesday morning. Sebastian and the other surgeons were present, as was Audrey, the cardiologist in charge of the transplant program. Markie. The fellows and residents.

"These are the best oxygen saturation numbers Isabella's had in weeks," Sebastian's mentor, Dr. Nelson, said. "Is she status seven?"

"Yes, but I think she should be status one," Sebastian answered. Status seven meant that she was on the heart transplant list, but currently ineligible. Status one would designate her as a patient in urgent need of a transplant.

"In my opinion," Audrey said, "she's not an acceptable candidate. Her neural status is unknown."

"Her lungs aren't great," a resident added, "and she's repeatedly struggled with ascites."

"A new heart is unlikely to fix her issues." Audrey tapped her pen against the file before her. "She might die as a result of the transplant surgery."

"But she will certainly die without the transplant surgery." Sebastian's anger, which had been very close to the surface since his fight with Leah, rose like a storm surge. "Our task is to give every child a chance."

"Yes, but if Isabella receives a heart, she deprives another child—a healthier child with a better prognosis—of his or her

271

chance," Audrey replied. "Our task is *actually* to ensure that we're allocating hearts to those most worthy of them."

It might be coldblooded of him, but those other worthy candidates were not his patients. Isabella was his patient, and writing her off was not an option for him. She'd fought her way back from sepsis. "Isabella is worthy of a heart."

"But is she the most worthy?" Audrey challenged.

"Worthy enough for status one," he said.

Tension stretched through the room as they considered Isabella's numbers, her history, her options.

Dr. Nelson resettled his glasses. "I'm inclined to move her to status one. If a heart becomes available and we have any reason to think, at that point in time, that a transplant with Isabella will not be successful, we'll defer the heart to another candidate."

"I worry about the damage we've already done to Isabella's parents over the past three months by giving them false hope," Audrey said. "What will this do?"

"We've given her parents hope," Sebastian said evenly. "But not false hope."

"Can you try to get a heart for her?" Dr. Nelson asked Audrey.

"I have reservations."

"But can you try?"

Everyone in the room zeroed in on Audrey.

"I can try," she eventually said.

Sebastian took the elevator up to his balcony. He stood at the rail and watched the small people and small cars, all of them preoccupied with achieving the next thing on their to-do list. *I've got to visit my brother. I've got to get lunch. I've got to get to my appointment on time.*

He'd gotten what he wanted just now—Isabella upgraded to status one. He wasn't experiencing any happiness over that outcome, however. Partially because that outcome had been, for him, the only and necessary outcome. Partially because Isabella was lying unconscious several floors below with a catastrophically deformed heart, so this wasn't the time to celebrate. Partially because, since his argument with Leah, the space suit had returned that prevented him from feeling much of anything—

No. That wasn't true.

He did feel a few things very sharply and clearly.

He felt miserable. And he felt frustrated.

He'd been waiting for Leah to come to her senses and call him. But she hadn't.

How long was he supposed to wait?

He'd already waited a day and a half, which was a day and a half longer than he'd been willing to wait. He didn't like being far away from her at the best of times. He *hated* being far away from her with angry silence between them.

Old traumas—his mother's death, the earthquake—kept ambushing him in quiet moments.

The day his mom had died, he'd packed his clothing in suitcases while people he didn't know rolled his mother out of the old lady's apartment on a stretcher.

He'd looked at his mom's stuff. Were they going to take everything that belonged to her and roll it away, too? Desperately, he started grabbing items. Her hairbrush, her favorite bracelet, her robe, two picture frames. He hid it all in his suitcase.

Then his social worker drove him across town in a car that smelled so strongly of flowers that he felt like he was choking.

"Sebastian," she said, when they arrived at a brown house, "this is Mr. and Mrs. King. They'll be looking after you for the time being."

"Sebastian! Welcome," Mrs. King said. She and her husband were both round, pink, and smiling.

She looked nothing like his mother.

He didn't speak. He didn't know them, and his mom had taught him not to trust people he didn't know.

"Come inside," Mr. King said.

He was numb. Dead, like his mom.

His mom was gone.

His mom was gone.

She'd been here this morning. And now she wasn't.

The social worker held the door of the house open for him. Mrs. King was saying a lot of things he didn't want to hear. They passed a room where two kids, one older than him and one younger, were finishing dinner. He pretended he hadn't seen them. He followed the adults to a room that had bunk beds with red covers.

He decided he hated red covers.

The social worker was talking to him. The strangers were talking to him.

His mom was gone. *His mom was gone.*

All he'd been able to do in that moment was wrap his hands around his backpack and stare at the strange room where they expected him to live with a kid he'd never met.

A bird's cry fractured the memory like glass. The wind absorbed the shards, and Sebastian came back to the present.

This separation with Leah might be for the best, darkness inside him whispered.

It concerned him, how invested he was in Leah. Yet he wanted to see her again far too much to consider making this separation permanent.

Just like it was not an option to keep Isabella at status seven, it was not an option to leave things the way they were with Leah.

The stalemate between them could not continue.

The following day, Leah sat at her desk in her classroom, prepping for upcoming lessons during her free period. Beyond her windows, the weather was as gloomy as her disposition had been since she'd left Atlanta. The moaning wind whipped trees into unnatural angles.

"I found some blueberry muffins on my desk."

She lifted her face toward the voice, which belonged to Ben. He stood framed by her doorway.

"Are you the anonymous donor?" he asked.

"I am."

"Mystery solved." He took the chair across from her desk, just like old times. "Thank you."

"You're welcome." Did this visit mean—please, Lord—that Ben was willing to get the ball of their friendship rolling again? She leaned back in her chair and focused solely on him. "How are you?"

"My third period class is causing me migraines."

"Sometimes there's not enough patience or Excedrin in the world for this job."

"How are things with you?" he asked.

"Very well." *Not true.* "I've been doing a bit of research into my family history."

"That's cool."

"I think you mentioned to me last year that Genevieve did some research into her family history, too. Is that right?"

"Yeah. I know that she and Sam drove to Clayton at one point to look at records. If you need tips, you should reach out to her."

"Will do." Genevieve had given Leah her number the day Leah had toured Sebastian's house. . . .

Sebastian. For the past three days, every thought of him had affected her like a pin skewering a pincushion. The most painful memories were the tender ones. The way he'd looked at her during their weekend together. The irresistible things he'd said.

This is an opportune time to bring your flirtation with Sebastian to a close!

The sound of footsteps reached her, and she turned to see Claire enter her room for tutoring.

Ben tapped twice on Leah's desk and rose. "I'll see you later."

"Thanks for coming by," she said, meaning it.

"Sure."

Ben greeted the girl, gave Leah a salute, and departed.

Leah waved Claire into the chair he'd vacated.

A few stains smudged the girl's sweater. Her eyes were puffy. She'd bitten her nails to the quick and picked off most of her white polish.

"Everything okay?" Leah asked.

"Mmm-hmm."

"That didn't sound very convincing."

"Everything's mostly okay."

"What's the latest with your mom and dad?"

"My mom, um, moved out last weekend. Which is probably the very best thing." The girl injected a note of levity into the sentence that fell completely flat.

Leah knew what it felt like to be abandoned by your mom, and it didn't feel like the very best thing. "Did you and Becca and Mason and Annie stay at home with your dad?"

"Uh-huh."

Had Claire's mom's departure made things worse for Claire and her siblings? Would they now have to bear the brunt of their dad's anger? "Where has your mom gone?"

"She hasn't let any of us know. Which is also probably for the best. That way Dad doesn't know where to find her. She told us she wants to bring us to live with her as soon as she can."

"Has she given any indication of when that might happen?"

Claire shook her head. "I've been texting her, but she hasn't answered much. She knows Dad checks my text messages."

"Who's been handling your mom's responsibilities for the past few days?"

"Us kids."

"Do you have all that you need? Enough to eat?"

She nodded.

"And has your dad been managing his temper?"

"It's been all right, Ms. Montgomery." But the bleak light in Claire's eyes told a different story.

"If you have any concerns, or simply want someone to talk to, I strongly encourage you to speak with me or Ms. Williams. In fact, I'll send Ms. Williams an email right now." She typed out a brief note, hit send, then faced Claire. "Ready to work on math?"

"Yes, ma'am."

"Outstanding. We can always depend on differential calculus to lift our spirits."

Later that evening, Leah dialed Genevieve from one of her pat-ented out-of-Dylan's-hearing-range spots: inside her turned-off car, inside her garage.

"Anyway," Leah said, wrapping up a very vague description of her attempt to learn more about her genealogy, "I was told that birth certificates are only made available to the person named on the certificate or a primary family member."

"That's true."

"Since I'm neither, I'm not sure what to try next." Yet she was yearning to research Ian and Bonnie O'Reilly further.

"What about death certificates?" Genevieve suggested. "When I was looking into this same sort of thing a year ago, it was actually a death certificate that revealed far more than birth certificates ever did."

"Oh?"

"Unlike birth certificates, death certificates are a matter of pub-lic record. They're available to all."

Leah's hope rose. "How would I go about accessing a death certificate?"

"You can go to the vital records office in the county of death, or you can request a record online for a fee. I can't remember off the top of my head the name of the website that allows you to request death records. But if you Google *death certificates in Georgia*, you should be able to find it."

"I appreciate the help."

"Sure! My sister and I also looked up old newspaper articles and old yearbook photos. I'm not sure if either of those pertain to your search, but they're worth keeping in mind."

Leah thanked her and, after a few minutes of chitchat during which Genevieve talked about how much she adored Ben, they disconnected.

She propped her laptop between the steering wheel and her abdomen, and located one of the record search sites Genevieve had alluded to. VitalCertificates.com.

It could be that Bonnie had died, and Leah simply hadn't

succeeded at locating her obituary online. In fact, if Bonnie had died back when Leah was young, it wasn't surprising that Leah hadn't been able to find her obit on the Internet. The Internet had been in its infancy then. Even after the Internet became more widespread, it may have taken many years for online obituaries to become prevalent.

The website asked her to provide much more information on Bonnie than Leah had to give. Red error messages kept popping up, asking her to fill in more fields. She typed *unknown* into several of the fields, then submitted the request. Perhaps VitalCertificate's search engines would be able to piece together a result from very little.

She had more information on Ian, thanks to the details included in the intellectual property suit. Thus, even though he'd only be in his late fifties now, she completed a second records request for him.

Your request is processing, the site informed her.

Seven days ago Sebastian had gone to church with Leah. Today he was attending a worship service again, sitting alone on a folding chair at the back of a small auditorium.

Then, the church had been formal. Now a smaller, more casual congregation surrounded him.

Then, between holding Leah's hand, breathing in the scent of her body wash, and studying the appearance of the Brooksides, he'd paid almost zero attention to the service. Now he was paying close attention to the pastor.

Then, he'd felt as content as he'd ever felt. Now he was as far from content as it was possible to feel.

He went to church with the Colemans from time to time in Misty River. But he usually spent his Atlanta Sundays reading medical journals, exercising, running errands, or checking on his patients.

He'd come here today because of his itching, scratching discontent. Obviously, he couldn't go on like this. He was sick of the slideshow of scenes—from the ruined building in El Salvador and his foster care years—that kept running through his mind.

He'd hoped for a sermon on a topic like God's grace or love. Instead, the sermon centered on identity. It was as if the pastor, who was wearing a blazer with jeans, had written it just for him.

It wasn't comforting him. It was confronting him.

He'd wanted to slip in and slip out without talking to anyone. But Ellie, the nurse at work who'd told him about this place, had spotted him almost as soon as he'd arrived, and rushed over. She and her friend had taken chairs to his right. Ellie had been shooting glances at him the whole service, which was annoying him almost as much as the sermon.

Ellie had made it clear to everyone they worked with that she was into him. She was a stunning girl—lots of shiny dark brown hair. Green eyes. But she was much too young and much too enthusiastic for him. She made him feel twenty years older than he was, and nothing about her personality or body or bright lipstick attracted him.

Ellie wasn't a math genius. Ellie wasn't too independent for her own good. She didn't make his five senses light up like a pinball machine.

The woman who did make his senses light up still hadn't called him.

If Leah cared about him, she would have called him by now. Right?

Sebastian had been certain that she cared about him, but maybe that had been wishful thinking. At times his ideas and opinions on a subject were so strong that he could project those onto other people.

It could be he was the guy that girls like Ellie had crushes on and that women who hit on him in bars wanted to sleep with. But he was not the guy that women like Leah cared about.

If so, how much of that was his fault? How much of that could be chalked up to the fact that he hadn't let anyone care?

He'd made an error with Leah.

"*My affection can't be bought,*" she'd said to him. It had been clear the day he'd given her the necklace that accepting presents didn't come naturally to her, yet the gifts he'd purchased had served their purpose. They'd convinced her to go out with him.

He should have stopped there, while he was ahead, because he'd clearly crossed an invisible line when he'd made that phone call on Dylan's behalf. In doing so, he'd insulted her.

If he wanted her back, which he did, it looked like he was going to have to make the first move.

What would work with her? How could he win her over in ways that went beyond wrapped packages and expensive dinners?

Long ago, she'd told him she appreciated it when people spoke to her directly. He was a blunt person. Even so, the thought of speaking to Leah about his emotions left him feeling unprotected.

Which was worse . . . losing Leah or feeling unprotected?

He was going to have to get over feeling unprotected, because losing Leah was much worse.

The pastor read from 1 John. "'See what kind of love the Father has given to us, that we should be called children of God.' The most meaningful thing about you," the pastor said, "isn't your job. It's not your status as a father, a mother. A husband, a wife. A son, a daughter. A sister, a brother. A friend. We're all tempted to try to plant our identity in those things. Ultimately, they won't satisfy, because that's not how God created us to find meaning."

Hands down, the most meaningful thing about Sebastian was his profession. He definitely *had* planted most of his identity in it. His degrees and accomplishments had given him his truest sense of pride. Really, his only sense of pride. Yet as much as he loved his work, as committed as he was to it, it hadn't brought him peace or wholeness.

"The most meaningful thing about you is that you are loved by God," the pastor continued. "You're a child of God. That's the only identity that can bring satisfaction."

At the close of the sermon, he prayed along with the pastor, asking God to forgive him, to help him find his identity as a child of God.

It didn't help. His spirit remained distracted and frayed.

When Leah's phone rang the next night, her heart wedged into her throat, just like it had every time her phone had rung for the past seven days. On each occasion, one name had sprung into her head.

Sebastian?

She wanted it to be him.

She didn't want it to be him.

But mostly, as in ninety percent mostly, she did want it to be him, despite her belief that going their separate ways was for the best.

She moved her attention from the paper she was grading to her phone, and for the first time since she'd argued with him in Atlanta, the caller ID displayed the name *Sebastian Grant.*

She covered her mouth with her hand and listened to it ring again. What should she do?

Her body decided for her. Without permission, her fingers shot out and answered. "Hello?"

"I miss you."

"Who did you say was calling?"

"Are you still angry?"

She gathered her thoughts. "No, I'm not still angry. However, I do stand behind the concerns I verbalized."

He made a sound of frustration. "You know what? Talking on the phone with you isn't going to work." She heard rustling. "We need to talk in person."

"Hmm?"

"I'm going to drive there."

"What? It's eight o'clock. On a school night."

"I'm locking my apartment now. I'm already on the way to my car."

She spluttered. "You have work in the morning, don't you?"

"I don't care."

"Round trip, the drive will take you more than three hours."

"I don't care."

"I'm not sure if it makes sense—"

"I'll see you in less than an hour and forty minutes," he informed her.

CHAPTER TWENTY-ONE

Concentration proved impossible after Sebastian's phone call. So impossible that she couldn't finish grading. She ended up funneling her nervous energy and conflicting thoughts into cleaning.

"What're you doing?" Dylan asked during one of his kitchen snack breaks.

"Straightening up."

"When you clean, you make me help. And you never clean at this time of night. Plus, you're moving at, like, twice your usual speed."

"Sebastian is going to stop by."

"Even though he lives in Atlanta?"

"Mmm-hmm."

"And isn't your boyfriend?"

"It's complicated."

He chuckled all the way back to his room.

She was Swiffering the hardwood floor when Sebastian's headlights bounced onto her driveway. She set the broom aside and pushed her arms into a fitted blue sweatshirt. Wearing the yoga pants and tennis shoes she'd donned for her after-work hike earlier, she stepped onto the front porch.

He shut his car door and crossed to her. The serious lines of his features emphasized glowing gray eyes. He'd clothed his tall body in worn jeans and a casual black pullover with a short, open zipper at the neck.

He stopped a yard away and scrutinized her. She scrutinized him right back. She'd had time to prepare for him. Even so, she was *not* prepared for him. Had she really believed just a few short months ago that she was incapable of experiencing physical attraction? Now she was suffused with it to the point that it threatened to decimate clear thought and good intentions.

He'd said on the phone that he missed her. She'd missed him, too. His assurance, humor, self-reliance. And beneath all of that, a very real storehouse of goodness. Her world had been small and dull without him in it.

"Come in." She led him to the now-spotless kitchen, the room farthest from Dylan's room. "Can I get you anything?"

"No." He leaned against the countertop, facing her, his hands curled around its edge on either side of his hips.

She leaned against the opposing counter and crossed her arms. It really was exceptional, the combustion that thickened the air when they were together. Like the Force in Star Wars—invisible and powerful.

"I'm sorry that I didn't ask you first before calling the dean about Dylan," he said. "And I'm also sorry that I didn't say anything about it when you mentioned the dean's email. My motives were good, but my execution sucked. If my execution sucked, then it doesn't matter what my motives were."

"Your motives do matter to me, actually. I know you wanted to help. It's just the—the way you helped happened to poke right at my worst fear, which is my own helplessness. Or, in this case, my concern that you perceived me as helpless."

"I view you as the least helpless woman I've ever met."

"Honestly?"

"Yes."

The admission unwound something tight within her. "I'm sorry, too. I wish I'd reacted with more patience."

Hip-hop music pulsed softly from Dylan's room.

"I can't help but want to do things for you," he said, "to show you how I feel. But there's very little I can do, so when I saw my chance, I took it."

"I don't tend to receive acts of service well, which is a flaw of mine. If you want to express how you feel about me, I recommend that you tell me."

"I care about you." His eyes held hers. "A lot. I'm worried you don't feel the same about me because I haven't heard from you for a week."

"I . . ." She selected her words the way she'd carefully choose shells on a beach. "I care about you, too. I didn't call you because it seems to me that parting ways at this point is the wisest step."

His mouth thinned. "Why?"

"Because our . . . connection was supposed to be carefree and fun."

"It *is* carefree and fun." He spoke in a voice so much the opposite of carefree and fun that she laughed.

"No," she insisted, "it's not."

"Your time with me in Atlanta wasn't fun?"

"It was fun—up until we argued. It hasn't been fun since then. Potentially worse, though . . . my feelings for you are no longer as lighthearted as I'd have them be."

"Explain to me why it's important to you that your feelings for me stay lighthearted."

"So many reasons."

"I'd like to hear them all."

"Well, before I'd feel comfortable allowing my feelings for you to become more . . . entrenched, I'd want to have some assurance that you'll be able to let me in. Otherwise, what are we doing here? We're wasting our time because we're destined for failure."

He seemed to weigh her point of view. "I've been letting you in. As much as I can. This is me, letting you in."

"And what about trust? Do you think you'll be able to bring yourself to trust me?" She hastened to add, "I won't blame you if the answer's no. If the answer's no, I'll understand why."

"Look, I can't stand here with a straight face and tell you that I'm skilled at relationships. I'm not. But I can tell you that I've never felt this way about anyone. I think about you all day. In any given moment, I'm more worried about your happiness than my own. Food tastes terrible to me. I can't concentrate. Markie has accused me of waking up on the wrong side of the bed every day this week." He scratched the back of his neck. "You're worried about taking this to the next level, and I get it—because so am I. I'm worried enough about where this is going that I've been losing sleep over it. But here's what it comes down to for me: I'm willing to lose sleep over it. The thing I am not willing to lose right now . . . is you."

Oh dear. Her inhibitions were swooning like Victorian women.

"I can't guarantee that I can be what you want me to be or anything else about the future," he continued. "We won't know what's going to happen with us until we let it happen."

She appreciated that he'd refrained from spouting lies about his ability to trust. At the same time, uneasiness curved around her lungs, because she truly did see his issues as landmines.

"The timing of our relationship is terrible," she stated.

"How so?"

"At the moment, I'm focused on shepherding Dylan through his senior year."

"Your focus on that shouldn't and doesn't have to change."

"Then next school year, when Dylan goes to college, I'll finally have the opportunity to begin my PhD coursework online. It won't be easy. I'll still be working full time at the high school. Classes, studying, projects, and papers will take almost all the free time I have. It doesn't make sense to sabotage my focus by adding a man to my life who has a very demanding career of his own."

"Leah."

"Yes?"

"If you told me you wanted Saturn on a string, I would do my best to get it for you. I'm a determined person, and I'm determined that you'll get your PhD. If you'll let me, I'll fight beside you to protect your dream."

His words knocked the wind out of her. "I—I don't expect you to protect my dream."

"It's important to you, so it's important to me."

Nothing he could have said would have endeared him to her more.

"What other concerns do you have?" he asked.

"We don't live in the same town. That's a concern."

"I don't like living an hour and forty minutes away from you, but I'm willing to come here for the weekend whenever I'm not on call. I won't pressure you to come to Atlanta."

"You pressured me to go to Atlanta just a few days ago!"

"Okay, fine. I'll do my best not to pressure you in the future. At least—" he looked sheepish—"not often. If there comes a time when someone needs to move, I will."

"You don't mean that."

He looked her right in the eye. "Try me."

"There are no pediatric heart clinics in Misty River."

"If sacrifices or compromises need to be made for our relationship, Leah, I'll be the one to make them."

She'd been to his hospital twice. She'd seen a few of his patients. Extensively, she'd studied his specialty. She'd never condone his leaving Beckett Memorial unless he left to accept a more senior position at an even more influential hospital. So, see? Her vehement reaction to the mere idea of his moving proved her concern valid. Despite his incredibly noble words, if one of them had to make a compromise for their relationship, it *would not be* the pediatric heart surgeon.

She'd watched her mom subjugate her dream of living overseas for her marriage, and look how well that had turned out. Ultimately, Mom's resentment toward her husband had boiled over.

"You're smart," he said. "You rely on your brain to make informed decisions. I respect that. But your decision to take over custody of Dylan wasn't made by your brain because, on paper, it didn't add up." He tipped his head slightly. "Was taking over custody of Dylan the best decision you ever made?"

Confound it! He was good at this. "You know that it was."

"When it comes to me, I'm asking you to draw on whatever

part of you made that decision. Not all good things make sense or can be quantified."

Her years with Dylan had taught her the absolute truth of that.

Sebastian closed the space between them and took her face in his hands. "You've shown how brave you are. Be brave with me."

She might be opening herself up to deep heartache if she let this continue. "Ah . . ." *Lord! What should I do? Show me. Tell me.*

No clear answer came.

Sebastian's talk of protecting her dreams had gone to her head, because it was so astonishingly, shockingly *wonderful* to have someone on her side, supporting what she valued. "The thing is," she whispered, "I don't need a man in my life. I have math." One of her fingertips disobeyed orders and traced the shape of his lower lip.

"I don't want you to need me. I want you to choose me."

"I abhor romance." She slid her fingers into the thick, silky strands of his hair.

"I know."

He took her mouth in a kiss—thorough, urgent, filled with pent-up feelings—and her resistance fell like a building leveled by dynamite.

Drugging minutes passed. He lifted his head a few inches. "Am I your boyfriend now?"

"No."

"Yes I am." He regarded her challengingly. "I am now, Leah."

"We're not together."

"Yes we are. We've had a fight, and I've driven across Georgia to make up with you, and now we're together. Agreed?"

She hesitated. "I'm undecided and in need of convincing." A smile stole across her mouth.

More kisses filled her kitchen with golden heat and wonder.

"Are we together?" His voice had turned raspy.

She answered with "Undecided" the next four times he asked that question, until she was gasping and he was watching her with eyes that made a million promises.

"Yes," she finally said. She defied any woman, given the temptation of Sebastian Grant, to answer differently.

Her misgivings remained.

It's just that, at this awe-laced moment, the joy he offered was greater.

L eah lay wide-awake in bed until well after one that morning. Marveling. Melting. Worrying.

Sebastian had stayed for two hours, which was far longer than was wise, considering the length of his drive home and how early the two of them had to be at work. But a wide strain of rebelliousness ran through Sebastian. He wasn't one to make the sensible choice if the sensible choice wasn't what he wanted.

The text she'd asked him to send when he reached home finally arrived.

I'm at my apartment.

Sweet dreams.

Good night, girlfriend.

I wholeheartedly dislike girlfriend as an endearment.

Fine. Good night, princess.

Princess is worse than girlfriend. I advise you to stick with professor. Professor, I like.

In that case, good night, Professor.

She set her phone to silent, placed it on its dock, and relaxed against her pillows. "What are you up to?" she asked God.

Since Sebastian had asked her out on their first date, she'd been praying for and about him daily.

It comforted her when God provided her with clarity, like He'd done so many times before, regarding the path He wanted her to take.

In this case, He hadn't provided clarity, which left her with circling doubts.

She couldn't fathom why God had brought Sebastian into her life or His objective for the two of them.

"Are you paying attention?" Her words vanished into the darkness. *If I'm veering off track by dating him, please, please let me know and steer me back on course.*

S ebastian's world was right again.

He couldn't have cared less about the sleep he'd sacrificed last night driving to Misty River and back. He didn't even feel tired. He'd succeeded at fixing things with Leah, and today, that was all that mattered.

He'd been granted a week of vacation that would start in two and a half weeks. Soon he'd have uninterrupted days in Misty River with her.

While waiting in line for lunch, a text arrived from Natasha to Genevieve, him, and Ben.

I just found out that Luke has a parole hearing today. I'm praying they let him out.

Sebastian grunted skeptically. Luke had been uncooperative with his attorneys when he'd gone to trial seven years ago, and he hadn't made a good impression the last time he'd come up for parole.

Genevieve immediately responded.

I'll be praying over it, too.

Then from Ben:

Same here.

Sebastian kept his response neutral.

Thanks for letting us know.

His stance on Luke was complex. Sympathy and resentment. Indebtedness and bitterness.

That evening Natasha sent a follow-up text.

Luke has been released, thank the Lord.

God continued to withhold clarity from Leah regarding Sebastian. But what she did receive—every day, day after day—was the heady delight of dating him.

They talked and laughed on the phone each night and texted each other between calls. On Thursday, they reached the one-year anniversary of the day they'd met. They celebrated by simultaneously watching the first *The Fast and the Furious* movie—a film in which cars were wrecked in even more spectacular fashion than Sebastian had wrecked his.

He flew to Misty River the minute he got off work on Friday. Dylan had an away game, so the two of them cooked dinner at her place.

They spent Saturday and Sunday fishing on a remote stretch of river and hiking trails carpeted with crimson and yellow leaves.

He flew back to Atlanta, and their texts and nightly phone calls immediately resumed.

He returned the following weekend, which passed just as gloriously. They drove to the lake and rented a boat for the afternoon. When darkness fell, they moved to a lakeside firepit. Holding hands, they watched orange flames crackle against a backdrop of moon-silver water.

They enjoyed Sunday lunch at Whiskey's restaurant with Dylan

Let It Be Me

and Mr. and Mrs. Coleman. Sebastian's ease with her brother wooed her far better than flowers or chocolates.

When it came time for Sebastian to return to Atlanta, Leah noted that saying good-bye to him was steadily becoming more difficult.

They picked back up where they'd left off with texts and calls.

Am I veering off track by dating him? she continued to ask God. *Please tell me if I am.*

But an answer did not come.

On Thanksgiving morning, the day before Sebastian was due to arrive for his vacation in Misty River, Leah slid a green bean casserole into her oven. She had a blessed gap of time before she'd need to transport her casserole and brother to Tess and Rudy's for the big meal.

She sank onto a kitchen chair and scrolled through new email on her phone. With a jolt, she saw that she'd received two emails in response to her death certificate requests.

She opened the first one. No death certificate for Bonnie O'Reilly had been found.

That might mean that Bonnie O'Reilly was still living, or that might mean that Leah's lack of details regarding Bonnie had ended in a failed search.

She clicked the second email. A death certificate *had* been located for Ian Monroe O'Reilly.

What?

She followed the link provided. A PDF of Ian's death certificate expanded on the screen.

Ian's mother was listed as Bonnie Theresa Byrne O'Reilly. "Blimey," she breathed, astonished. Bonnie's birthplace: Oxford, Alabama. Ian's father: Malcolm Francis O'Reilly. Ian had been born and had died in Atlanta. Cause of death: overdose from heroin and alcohol. Age: twenty-eight . . . the exact same age that Leah was now.

She blinked at the death certificate. Had Ian's overdose been the unintentional outcome of mixing too much heroin with too much alcohol? Or had he purposely taken that cocktail with the intention of committing suicide?

At last, she'd found Bonnie O'Reilly. Unfortunately, though, this information had flowed to her through Bonnie's son's death certificate.

Leah retrieved her computer and brought up YourHeritage .com. This time, she ran a search for census records equipped with Bonnie's full name and place of birth.

The site highlighted the Byrne family in the 1940 census.

Bonnie's parents were named Sean and Ellen. Like Bonnie, Sean and Ellen had been born in Oxford. At the time of this census, Bonnie had been just a few months old. Her elder sister, Orla, had been two. Sean worked construction. Ellen worked as a seamstress.

Additional hunting yielded Bonnie's marriage record. Bonnie married Malcolm O'Reilly in Alpharetta, Georgia, when she was twenty-two.

Adroitly, Leah ran through the now-familiar routine, looking for Bonnie Byrne O'Reilly and Malcolm Francis O'Reilly via Google and social media sites.

Nothing.

She'd found Bonnie in one sense but still had no idea how to parlay that into a meeting with the woman in the here-and-now.

Sebastian made it to Misty River's football stadium by halftime on Friday night. He'd been so eager to see Leah that he'd gone to work at five this morning so he'd be able to wrap things up early and arrive in time to catch part of Dylan's game.

As he maneuvered through the sea of bodies behind the bleachers, he caught sight of blond hair in the crowd.

Leah came into view, walking in his direction, carrying a bag of popcorn in one hand and a disposable cup in the other.

He'd rushed here from Atlanta for her. He'd taken a week of vacation for her. Seeing her proved those decisions right.

When she spotted him, her blue eyes rounded. Smile growing, she neared, then came to a stop before him. "You're early."

"I like to be early."

"I like that you like to be early. I didn't think I was going to get to see you until after the game. Had I known you were on-site, Connor and I wouldn't have spent so long in the concession line."

For the first time, he realized that someone was with her. Connor.

"I just got here," Sebastian said.

"How've you been?" Connor asked.

"Really well."

Ben hadn't listed Connor as one of the school employees who had a crush on Leah. But, in this moment, that didn't put Sebastian's mind at ease. It could be that Leah viewed Connor as a friend but that Connor, like Ben, viewed Leah as more.

"I was just talking with Ben earlier this week," Connor said, "about what you guys went through back in El Salvador."

"He's a good one to talk to about it." *Unlike me.*

"I grew up here, so I have clear memories of watching the news coverage. For days, my mom was either praying about it or sitting in front of the TV set, waiting for updates."

"Thank your mom for me," Sebastian said.

"I'll do that."

Leah gave Sebastian a questioning look. "Are you going to sit with me this time or with the Colemans?"

"With you this time."

"Good. Let's get settled before the second half starts."

They said good-bye to Connor. To lighten her load, Sebastian carried the popcorn as they walked up the ramp.

She had on the same jersey he'd seen her in at the last football game. Because of the colder late-November temperatures, she wore a white shirt beneath. She'd stuck the round pin of Dylan to a jean jacket.

"I'm jealous," he said.

She stopped at the bottom rail of the bleachers. "Why?"

"Connor has something I want. He gets to be around you all week."

"Ah. Well, the answer's simple. Quit your job and become a teacher at Misty River High."

"Don't tempt me."

"Don't tempt *me* with all this—" she waved a hand at his face— "handsomeness. Honestly, Sebastian. It's too much."

"I want to make out with you."

"No. We're surrounded by hundreds of people."

She was right. They were standing in view of the spectators. One of them would be Ben, and Sebastian wouldn't do that to his friend. It's just that it was way harder than expected not to touch her. He hadn't seen her in days.

He followed her up the bleacher stairs.

She pointed to the side. "I'm sitting over here with Tess and Rudy."

"I'll say hi to the Colemans, then I'll join you."

"Excellent."

He passed back her popcorn and made his way to the Coleman family section. They welcomed him with their usual loud enthusiasm.

"You're joining us for church and Sunday dinner at the house, right?" CeCe demanded.

"Yes, ma'am."

"If you stand me up, I'll be after you with a shotgun."

"I'll be there."

Hadley Jane jumped into his arms. "I haven't seen you in so long, Sebastian."

"It's been too long," he agreed. She stayed in his arms while he greeted the rest of the family. Eventually, he reached Ben. They hugged, causing the little girl to giggle when she was sandwiched between them.

"Is it okay with you that I'm here tonight?" Sebastian asked.

Ben gave a good-natured shrug. "You're welcome to cheer for the Mountaineers anytime."

"You know what I mean."

"Yeah. It's okay." Ben's expression looked clearer and less troubled than it had the past few times he'd seen his friend. "What's been going on lately?"

They used to keep in close enough contact that Ben wouldn't have had to ask. "Work's been about the same."

"Any change on the little girl who needs a heart transplant?"

"What little girl?" Hadley Jane asked.

"One of the babies I take care of at the hospital." To Ben, Sebastian said, "We had to take her off the transplant list, but then we put her back on. Now we're just waiting to see if a heart becomes available in time."

"I hope it does. I feel for her and her parents."

Hadley Jane's jaw dropped. "She's getting a new heart?"

"That's the plan."

"I want a new heart!"

"Your heart is already perfect. That's my professional diagnosis as a surgeon."

"But I don't want this old one."

"Newer isn't always better."

"Yeah huh, it is."

"How's your baseball team been doing?" Sebastian asked Ben. Ben had played baseball in college and now competed in a men's league.

"We're still dominating."

"And your strained hamstring?"

"Better."

Ben probably thought he knew how much their friendship meant to Sebastian. After all, Ben had experienced every minute of time they'd spent together. Yet Ben couldn't know what his friendship had meant to a heartbroken, lonely kid. He couldn't know what his dependability had been worth to a boy who'd learned young that the world wasn't a reliable place. "Has anyone seen Luke here in Misty River since he was released?"

"Not that I know of. I'm planning to reach out to his mom soon to see if I can get his number from her."

Sebastian nodded. "See you at church on Sunday?"

"Yes, and also Tuesday night, for dinner with Natasha and Genevieve."

"Right."

"I'm glad you're going to be in town for the whole week."

"Same here."

"Now pass the child." Ben reached for Hadley Jane. "You haven't come over to see me yet, little girl. Which means you haven't discovered the hidden lollipop I brought for you."

She squealed and scrambled into Ben's arms.

Sebastian found Leah and lowered onto the bleacher seat next to her.

Leaning back, she introduced him to the older couple sitting on her far side. They were wearing jerseys and Dylan pins that matched Leah's.

Rudy grinned at him. "Are you two dating?"

"Yes," Sebastian answered before Leah could say no.

"Rudy," Tess said to her husband. "That's not a very polite question."

"I can't help myself!" Rudy replied. "I'm just so happy to see Leah with a young man. It's a pleasure to meet you, sir."

"The pleasure's mine."

"Isn't Leah the best?" Rudy asked.

"The best."

"She's the smartest thing." Rudy's glasses slipped down his nose. "The sweetest."

"I don't consider myself to be sweet," Leah murmured under her breath to Sebastian.

"But smart you'll accept?" he murmured back.

"You better believe I will."

"Push up your glasses, please," Tess instructed Rudy, who hurried to do as she asked.

A whistle sounded, and the teams jogged onto the field for the second half. The Mountaineers were down, seven to seventeen.

"Where's Dylan?" Sebastian asked.

"There. On the sidelines. He played a fair amount in the first half, so I have hope that you'll get to see him in action." She held the popcorn toward him. He took a handful.

It tasted like average quality movie popcorn. But he was starving, so it might as well have been the most delicious thing he'd ever eaten.

"Did you have dinner?" she asked.

"Not yet."

"I'll go down and get you something. Hamburger? Hot dog—"

"You're here to watch your brother. I'm here to watch your brother. I can wait to eat until after the game."

"I really don't mind," she told him.

His chest ached with tenderness. He was a doctor, used to the role of caretaker, less familiar with being cared for. "Thanks, but I can wait."

"Then eat the rest of this." She passed the popcorn over. "I had as much as I wanted when you were talking to the Colemans."

"You sure?"

"Yes." Those thick lashes framed eyes that looked candid. But it might be that he was just a sucker where she was concerned. It might be that she could tell him the sun was made of Play-Doh, and he'd believe her.

"And here." She lifted her cup. "Iced tea. There's at least half left."

He hesitated.

"Good grief. Here." She thrust the tea at him. "For someone who's quick to give gifts, you seem awfully reluctant to take them."

"Oh?" he asked dryly. "How does that feel? To want to give something to someone who's reluctant to take it?"

She laughed. "It's my turn to complain about you! You're not allowed to twist this into an opportunity to complain about me."

On the next play, Dylan jogged onto the field. Leah cupped her hands around her mouth. "Go, Dylan!"

They were too far away for Dylan to hear. She scooted forward on the seat, back straight. The play went off. She shouted encouragement, clapped, winced, then clapped some more as the boys regrouped in a huddle.

Watching her was the best entertainment in Georgia.

"You got this, Mountaineers!" Leah yelled.

A few minutes later, the team failed to convert on third down and had to kick. She shook her head. "When they run the ball, they convert on third down sixty-seven percent of the time. So I'm not sure why they attempt to pass on third downs."

"Can I go get a candy bar?" Rudy asked his wife.

The older woman released a frustrated sigh. "You already had half a Kit Kat, remember?"

"I'm still hungry."

"Here. I have some carrot sticks in my purse." Tess handed Rudy the snack she'd packed in a Baggie.

"Pretty soon," Leah whispered to Sebastian, "Rudy will make a trip to the restroom and, when she's not watching, buy and eat a cupcake."

"I like them."

She surveyed him from the corner of sparkling eyes. "I'm glad you're here."

"There's nowhere I'd rather be."

In a short period of time, she'd become too important to him. Stupidly important to him. His old priorities had crashed like a game of Jenga, and now she sat at the top. Which left him vulnerable. He'd been trying to hold himself and his emotions in check. He was losing the battle, though, and that knowledge planted a seed of dread in him.

If he was smart, he'd live in the moment, enjoy the time he had with her, and accept whatever came.

Instead, he'd begun to long for promises from her she wasn't ready—might never be ready—to give.

He wanted her to promise that she'd love him forever.

That she wouldn't leave him.

That she wouldn't die.

CHAPTER TWENTY-TWO

The following afternoon, Leah waited anxiously at the curb outside her house for Sebastian. She could count on him to be either early or punctual, and he was scheduled to arrive three minutes from now, at 1:45 p.m., to take her to a production of *Fiddler on the Roof* at the historic theater downtown.

Above, charcoal-tipped clouds spat drizzle. She pulled up the hood of her quilted jacket.

Sebastian's Mercedes rounded the corner, and she exhaled with relief. He came to a stop before her, and she slid onto the passenger seat.

"Is something wrong?" he asked immediately.

"Yes, but let's drive while I tell you about it."

The car slid forward, windshield wipers clearing the field of vision. Pinpricks of rain. Cleared again by the wipers. Pinpricks of rain.

"I have a student named Claire," Leah said. "I've told you about her, right?"

"Yes."

"She's this very kind, awkward, uncertain sixteen-year-old who has a dad with an anger management problem. He yells and screams and breaks things, but so far he's stopped short of harming his children. Or so Claire says."

He shot her a grave look.

"I gave her my number in case she ever needed to reach me, and she just texted me. She says things are bad right now and asked if I could give her a ride to a friend's house." Leah consulted the directions her phone had generated. "Stay straight until we get to Lemon Lane, then take a left."

"Doesn't this fall under the purview of child protective services?"

"CPS will get involved if they have reason to believe that a child is suffering emotional neglect. However, that's a difficult accusation to prove in a way that's legally binding."

"Okay. What about referring her to a school counselor?"

"I did, but she hasn't gotten to know our counselor well yet. I had Claire in class last year and again this year. I think she's more comfortable with me."

"Are teachers allowed to pick up students at their homes?"

"In this district, the answer is yes." She twisted to face him. "I realize this is unorthodox and inconvenient. But I'm glad that Claire has asked someone—in this case, me—for help."

"I don't care that this is unorthodox or inconvenient. I do care, a lot, about your safety. I don't like the sound of the dad with the anger management problem."

She didn't like the sound of him, either. She could understand why Sebastian might think it unwise for her to involve herself in Claire's family life. Yet he hadn't looked into Claire's face and experienced a powerful tug of empathy and concern. He didn't have a seventeen-year-old brother, so he couldn't have the same soft spot for teenagers that she had.

Leah texted Claire.

We'll be there in five minutes.

No response.

They pulled into a development of 1980s tract homes aspirationally named Tranquility River. Slivers of space separated structures with tiny fenced backyards. On Serene Court, dehydrated shrubs clung to the planting beds outside Claire's two-story home.

"There's a gun cabinet in the front room," Sebastian said.

She could see it, too. The lights illuminating the downstairs front room provided a clear view of the interior.

Claire did not emerge.

Leah sent Claire another text, alerting her to their arrival.

Still nothing.

"Why isn't she answering my texts?" she wondered out loud. "I'm worried."

"I'm worried, too."

"Should I go knock on the door?"

"No. If someone needs to, I'll go. But I don't think it'll help. I can't imagine a parent sending their daughter off with a man they've never met."

"I think I'll try to call—"

"Is this her?"

Leah's vision swung up. Claire hurried down the front walkway. Sebastian walked around the car to open the back door for her. Leah punched the button to lower her window. "Hi."

"Hi," Claire said in a small voice.

Leah introduced Sebastian as Claire got settled in the back seat.

"You okay?" Leah asked while Sebastian returned to the driver's side.

"Mmm-hmm." Converse and jeggings poked out from today's huge black sweater. Her skin looked pale; her reddish ringlets weary.

"Are your sisters and brother all right? We can give them a ride somewhere, too, if needed."

"They're all right. It's me he got mad at."

"Where to?" Sebastian asked.

"My friend's house. Um, do you know Abby Michaelson, Ms. Montgomery?"

"I know who she is, yes."

"She lives on the west side of town. So if you just drive toward Azalea Avenue, that'll be good."

The car swung into motion.

"Sorry to interrupt your day," Claire said. "I don't have my license, and neither does Abby. Abby's mom usually comes by for me, but she's shopping with friends right now, and I couldn't think of who else to call."

"It's not a problem," Leah assured her.

Leah and Claire made small talk until they arrived at Abby's house.

"Should we come back by for you later?" Leah asked.

"No, Abby's mom can drive me home."

"Then I'll see you at school Monday."

"Yep. Thanks again."

Wordlessly, Leah and Sebastian watched Claire approach the front door. Abby answered, and Claire disappeared inside.

They headed toward town through a natural tunnel of autumn trees.

Leah contemplated Sebastian's chiseled profile and strong throat. Dr. Grant. Purveyor of disco ball slow dances to '80s songs. Surgeon. Orphan. Friend of Ben. The most phenomenal kisser in the universe. Today, he wore a North Face jacket over a collared white shirt and black pants.

"Do we still have time to make the show?" she asked.

"I think so. We might be a few minutes late, but I'm guessing they won't turn us away."

Last night—at the football game and afterward at his house—had been something for the memory books. As delicious as a cookie warm out of the oven.

He'd been on her mind every waking minute since. And many of her non-waking minutes, too. After their first date, both her old anxiety dreams and her wonderful Sebastian dreams had given way to silky, dreamless sleep. But last night he'd finally visited her in her dreams again. They'd been caught in a sandstorm in the desert, but when he'd taken her into his arms, a globe of safety had formed around them that the sand hadn't been able to penetrate.

"Thank you for helping me with Claire," she said.

"You're welcome." His hard jawline didn't soften. "If she calls you again and asks you to come to her house, will you promise me that you won't go over there alone?"

She couldn't remember the last time someone had asked her to promise to behave in a certain way. Which might speak to her independence. Or to her good choices. Or to the fact that not many people were close enough to her to care about her safety.

Before she could formulate an answer, they reached a stoplight. He gazed at her. "If something violent is happening with Claire, do you agree that you should call the police and let them handle it?"

"I do."

"And if the situation's troubling but not violent, like today, and you decide to pick her up, I still think you should bring someone. Me, if I'm in town. But since I'm usually not, maybe Ben. Or Ben's dad, Hersh."

"I waited for you today because I agree that it's important to have someone with me if I'm going to drive a student. For many reasons. One being that I'll have a corroborating witness should a student try to accuse me of doing something I didn't do."

"Right. The bottom line here, though, is that Claire's dad has a temper and a gun. Please promise me that you won't go to Claire's house alone."

"I promise."

They were five minutes late to the show. An usher had to scurry them to their seats with a penlight. The predicament with Claire had disturbed Sebastian. But as the musical progressed, she sensed his stress level lowering.

By the time they exited the theater, the storm front had tugged away the rain. They strolled Misty River's quaint downtown on sidewalks glimmering with puddles. They passed the central park, numerous shops, a smattering of office spaces, The Grind coffee shop, the Doughnut Hut. Sitting together at a table with a view of the steel blue river below, they ate an early dinner at Cork and Knife.

She liked him *so foolishly much* that she experienced a twist of delight each time she remembered that he'd be in town all week, and she'd get to see him every day.

Leah! she said to herself when he gave her a heated look that sent a warm pulse to the backs of her knees. *It's nice to hang out with him, but it's fine to be apart, too. It's not like he's the most important person in your life. It's not as if you suddenly have to see him every day or die.*

Only the words fell like stones plunking into a hollow barrel. While they might have merit, they possessed no power.

I've been thinking about what you said to me," Leah told Dylan the following day. "About how I'm too strict because I'm trying to control you."

"Yeah?"

They traveled to church in her car every Sunday, so her brother was, effectively, her hostage until she returned him home and he had access to his bedroom or car keys. After the worship service, she'd brought him here, to a dive called The Junction, in hopes that his desire to fill his belly with fried chicken would make him more amenable to talking with her.

"You made some good points," she continued. "Perhaps I have been trying to control you in an effort to gain control over my life in general."

He watched her as he chewed.

She stacked her hands on the booth's laminate tabletop. "When Doves Cry" played on the jukebox. "I know that God's the one in control and not me. But it really is easy to labor under the misapprehension—"

"Huh?"

"It really is easy to think that I have some control over what happens to you. The more control I imagine myself to have, the safer I feel."

She'd done some soul-searching and realized that she'd gotten in the bad habit of relying on herself for the majority of Dylan's welfare and letting God "assist" with the rest. She wanted to trust

God with all of it, as she had when she'd first taken over custody of her brother. And yet . . .

All of it? He was a teenager now, capable of making life-threatening mistakes.

"I don't want to be a controlling person," she said. "I want to be a person who trusts God."

Grease shined on Dylan's fingertips, which still gripped the chicken. "Does this mean you're going to let me do more stuff?"

"Potentially, yes. We'll talk about the things you want to do and decide on a case-by-case basis. I'll do my best to keep an open mind and view you as what you are now: a high school senior."

"Almost old enough to vote."

Lord, help us all.

"This is great timing," he said. "Braxton's family is going skiing over Christmas break, and he wants me to come along."

Lord! Help us all! "Mmm."

"Also, it would be really cool if you could stop warning me about teenage suicide, drinking, drugs, and everything else."

"Don't push your luck, Dylan."

Dylan took another bite. The crispy skin of his chicken leg crackled. "If you stop all the warnings, I'll watch *Return of the Jedi* with you after this."

"You will?"

"Yep."

"I'll take you up on that, darling boy of my heart."

On Tuesday morning, Sebastian came face to face with a ghost from his past.

He was passing the gas station on the way to Ingles to get groceries when he recognized a blue 1974 Chevy C-10 truck at one of the pumps.

Sebastian U-turned. The C-10 was a beast. A tough-guy's truck. He parked, walked up to the vehicle, and found it empty. Bracing himself, he pushed his hands into his jeans and waited beneath the cold gray sky.

As expected, Luke Dempsey exited the station's door. When he saw Sebastian, his expression tightened. Luke came to a halt, facing Sebastian across two yards of space and two miles of memories.

A powerful sense of déjà vu jerked Sebastian back in time to the earthquake. It had been dim then, too.

The collapsing corridors in that basement hadn't stopped Luke from trying to run back in the direction they'd come.

Sebastian had lunged forward and grabbed his arm.

"Let me go!" Luke yelled at him. "I have to get my brother."

"You'll be crushed." Luke was one year older, but Sebastian was equally as tall and strong.

Luke wrenched free. But just as he tried to enter the hallway, concrete filled it, blocking it completely.

"No!" Luke had screamed.

All these years later, Luke wore a black motorcycle jacket over a black hoodie and battered jeans. His brown hair was longer than Sebastian had ever seen it—as if he'd had a short haircut nine months ago and hadn't bothered to trim it since. His five-o'clock shadow was so thick, it had turned into a short beard.

He looked like what he'd become: a man you wouldn't want to cross. Dangerous.

Even so, Sebastian could see the boy he'd been in the long, aristocratic nose. The sharp, deep-set hazel eyes. The inflexible chin.

They were the same height, though Luke was leaner.

The summer they'd gone on that doomed mission trip, Luke had been the most well-liked, athletic kid in the eighth grade. He'd had every advantage Sebastian had not. A family, a home, upper middle-class money.

Luke's life had been heading in an upward direction, and Sebastian's life had been headed down. By the time they left that wrecked building after eight days buried alive together, their trains had jumped tracks. Sebastian's track had gone up. Luke's had gone down.

Luke should've been a doctor. Sebastian should've been a felon.

He couldn't call Luke a friend, and yet he was more bonded to this man than he was to any of his colleagues or acquaintances.

"How long have you been back?" Sebastian asked.

"A day."

"Why'd you return?"

"None of your business."

"I'd like to know."

Luke regarded Sebastian with impatience. "I have a job lined up in January."

"What job?"

"A job with an animal rescue charity."

An animal charity? Sebastian had expected him to say he was going to be working on restoring cars, something he'd been good at once. "Ben, Natasha, Genevieve, and I are meeting for dinner tonight. We'd like for you to join us."

"No thanks." He moved to pass.

Sebastian stepped in front of him. "It's just dinner." He knew how much it would mean to Natasha and Genevieve, in particular, if Luke would show.

"No." Luke climbed into his truck and drove off without another word.

After their rescue, when the four of them had repeatedly tried to include him in the things they were doing—traveling to speak to churches, interviews with the media, conversations with the writers who'd handled the book and the screenplay—Luke had refused involvement. Ever since, he'd been stubborn and uncommunicative.

Luke was a pain. And yet there was no way of getting around one fact. Sebastian owed Luke for saving his life.

I'm so bummed that Luke's not willing to get together with us," Genevieve said that evening.

Sebastian, Ben, Natasha, and Genevieve were sitting around the table at Natasha's house, open containers of Thai food standing between their plates. Pad Thai noodles. Rice. Curry shrimp. Beef and basil.

Sebastian had just finished telling them about his interaction with Luke.

"It's like he's determined not to acknowledge that we're awesome," Ben said.

"When we clearly are," Genevieve said, "very awesome."

"'True humility is not thinking less of yourself; it is thinking of yourself less.'" Natasha winked. "C. S. Lewis quote. It seemed apropos."

"He hasn't been open to getting together with us or acknowledging how awesome we are for almost two decades," Sebastian pointed out. "I think it's time we accept that's not going to change."

Natasha's fork stopped swirling noodles. "I can't."

"Me neither," Genevieve said. "There's something within me that simply *won't* give up hope of reconnecting with him. He was down there with us. He survived it with us. Only we know what he endured. The fact that he hasn't been a part of our group since then has been a sore spot in my heart all this time."

"He told you he was going to work at an animal rescue charity?" Natasha asked Sebastian.

"Right."

"That seems like a bizarre choice," Ben said.

"He probably didn't have many options." Natasha gave up on the noodles. "Employers aren't exactly lining up to hire parolees."

"The only animal rescue charity in town that I know of is Furry Tails," Ben said.

"Oh!" Genevieve brightened. "Furry Tails is owned by Finley Sutherland. She's great. She comes out to the farm stand to buy fruit and vegetables almost every weekend. Do any of you know her?"

"I think I've met her," Ben said. "Does she have dark hair?"

"Yes, she looks like a modern-day Snow White. Long black hair. Blue eyes. I love how she dresses . . . very boho chic. She's definitely a champion of lost causes."

Sebastian snorted. "Then she's Luke's perfect employer." He checked his watch. He was due at Leah's soon to watch a movie, and he planned to arrive early.

"Wyatt keeps trying to talk me into visiting Furry Tails and adopting a dog," Natasha said. "I've resisted because if I go, I'll probably bring home several aging animals. No thank you. My hands are full. I have children."

"Doesn't Furry Tails specialize in pug rescue?" Ben asked.

"That's what I've heard," Natasha said.

"Aww," Genevieve said. "How come you haven't adopted a pug, Ben? You'd be a great dog owner."

"You want me to adopt an aging animal?"

"Yes," the sisters said in unison.

"I wouldn't want to leave a dog at home all day while I'm working."

"If it's aging," Sebastian pointed out, "it might not mind."

Genevieve laughed. "Well, in order to see and speak with Luke, a few of us might need to start making regular visits to Furry Tails come January."

"I'm game," said Ben, always a team player.

"Not me," Natasha stated, "for the reasons previously mentioned. But once we figure out where Luke's living, I'm not above ambushing him there and forcing him into a conversation."

"If he doesn't want my friendship," Sebastian said, "I'm not going to shove it at him."

Genevieve sliced a shrimp in half. "Speaking of shoving things at people, Leah called me a few weeks ago, Ben. And so, of course, I shoved all your best attributes at her."

"Anything happening on that front?" Natasha asked.

Ben choked on his water. Sebastian could feel heartburn coming on.

"Can I tell them?" Ben asked Sebastian.

Sebastian nodded.

"So, ladies." Ben's face looked like it belonged to a dad who'd been forced to tell his kids about puberty. "Sebastian is dating Leah."

Genevieve set down her glass and braced her hands on her thighs. *"What?"*

"Explain *everything*," Natasha demanded.

They were going to be here awhile.

A mazing how the chance to see someone for several days in a row could feel like a luxury. But that's exactly what his days in Misty River had felt like to Sebastian.

His running shoes hit the pavement as he jogged his neighborhood.

He'd arrived here Friday. It was now Wednesday. Six days in a row so far.

Six of his best days.

Because of her.

He could have spent his vacation in Bora Bora or Cairo or London. But there was no place he'd rather be than here. During Leah's work hours, he slept late, then thought about her while he mowed his lawn or watched soccer or ran errands or did projects around the house. Then, every evening, he got to spend time with her.

Gradually, the pressures of his job had slid off of him. The world had gained color and detail. His lungs could breathe deep. The space suit had gone, and when he was with Leah he was alert, healthy, whole.

Tomorrow after school let out, they planned to go kayaking.

He was already smiling, anticipating it.

As it turned out, kayaking was not to be because, in the early hours of the following morning, Sebastian's pager yanked him from sleep.

CHAPTER TWENTY-THREE

Sebastian slit his eyes until the red numbers on his bedside clock came into focus.

3:46 a.m.

With a groan, he pressed himself into a seated position in bed. He was supposed to be on vacation.

He scrubbed his hands over his face, then called in.

"Sorry to disturb you, Dr. Grant." It was Judy, one of the senior cardiac nurses. "Audrey thinks they may have a heart for Isabella Ackerman."

Her words swept the cobwebs from his head. "Age of donor?"

"Thirty-three days old."

"Blood type? Weight? Existing defects?"

She listed the donor's information. All of it indicated a good fit.

"Cause of death?"

"SIDS. First responders were able to resuscitate. Unfortunately, the infant progressed to brain death."

"Let's move forward." In the past, some of the people in the heart transplant community had been unsure of the efficacy of donor hearts from babies who'd died of sudden infant death syndrome because the mechanism of death in SIDS was unclear. However, recent studies had shown that the prognosis for children who received hearts from SIDS babies was the same as that of other patients.

"Where's the heart?" he asked.

"Virginia."

"Who's the fellow on call?"

"Holmes."

He knew the drill. Holmes, a PA, a nurse, and a perfusionist would make the trip to retrieve the heart. The police would escort the team to the airport. They'd take a private jet to Virginia and an ambulance to and from the waiting hospital.

"When will they be back?" he asked.

"I'm not sure. Ten a.m. at the earliest?"

"I'll arrive at the hospital long before that."

Shortly after waking, Leah had discovered a text from Sebastian asking her to give him a call. She'd dialed him, and he'd just finished updating her on Isabella.

So far this morning, she hadn't even eaten a bowl of cereal. He'd soon reach Beckett Memorial to begin preparations for heart transplant surgery.

"I'm thrilled to hear that Isabella will be receiving a heart," she said. "At the same time, I can't imagine the heartbreak the donor baby's parents are experiencing. They must be devastated."

"Devastated," he agreed. "This field is often like that. On one hand, terrible grief. On the other, hope."

"Isabella has been seriously ill since the day she was born. The donor baby was born perfectly healthy, right?"

"Right."

"And now the sick one, Isabella, is going to live. And the healthy one is gone."

"The sick one is going to live *because* the healthy one is gone and because his parents chose to donate his organs."

"How many transplants has the clinic performed this year?"

"This will be our tenth."

Sunlight filtered through leaves to splash shades of orange against her bedroom's white window shade. Another new day had come for her, but not for the donor baby. The back of her eyes pricked as she thought about what it must have been like for his parents to give permission for doctors to cut open the chest of their beautiful, unscathed infant so that a little girl they did not know could have a second chance at life. The excruciating pain of that. The unselfishness. "I'll pray that everything goes smoothly."

"Thank you," he said. "I'll be back in Misty River in time for dinner. See you then?"

"See you then."

Sebastian spent forty-five minutes with Megan and Timothy, explaining the surgery. Then he walked them to the family lounge.

"I've been waiting and waiting for this day," Timothy told him. "I thought I'd feel nothing but relief and excitement. And I do . . . feel that way. But I'm also frightened."

"Me too." Megan secured her grip on her husband's elbow.

"That's normal," Sebastian said. "You became familiar with the holding pattern Isabella has been in. Today that changes." Holmes had called him after removing the heart to say that the organ showed a little bruising from CPR, but overall looked to be in great condition.

"The next several hours are going to be long ones for us," Timothy said.

"We'll keep you updated throughout," Sebastian said.

They stopped at the entrance of the lounge. A large number of Ackerman family members of all different ages had already gathered. Their faces communicated eagerness, worry.

"This is Isabella's doctor," Timothy announced to them. "Dr. Grant. He'll be performing the surgery."

A wave of comments washed over him. Mostly greetings, thanks, and assurances that they'd be praying.

He was praised more than he deserved when a patient's outcome was good. He disappointed people more than he deserved when a patient's outcome wasn't good. Either way, in this line of work, there was never any place to hide.

He excused himself. Keeping a close eye on the clock, he stopped by the break room for a snack and a drink, then did some stretches in his office.

The timing of a heart transplant required more precision than the gears of a Swiss watch. After scrubbing in, he entered the OR when the senior fellow was opening Isabella's chest. The perfusionist stood ready with the heart and lung bypass machine. An anesthesiologist, two nurses, and Markie rounded out the group.

"Good morning," Sebastian said.

"Morning," they responded.

"Let's get to work, people."

"Some of us are already working," Markie replied.

Sebastian watched Isabella's numbers and answered friendly questions about his vacation days in Misty River until the new heart arrived. It floated inside sterile solution within a plastic bag, surrounded by a Playmate cooler's icy water.

Sebastian set about removing Isabella's defective heart. It was swollen, dark red in color, too deformed to be functional. Once he'd freed it, he handed it to the scrub nurse, who placed it on a towel on the set-up table. Immediately, it became an inanimate lump of ruined muscle. Useless.

Meticulously, Sebastian worked to secure the new heart—light pink, shiny, smooth—inside Isabella's small chest.

After thirty minutes of stitching, he asked the perfusionist to begin warming the blood. Soon he'd be able to remove the cross clamp and allow her blood to flow.

Sebastian found Megan and Timothy waiting for him in the hallway outside the restricted area of the operating wing. The staff had sent them frequent messages regarding the stages of the surgery and their daughter's stability. Even so, they both looked wrung out.

"Everything went as smoothly as it could possibly have gone," Sebastian said.

Some of Megan's tension appeared to ease. "Praise the Lord."

"As you know, she has a long road ahead of her." The first of many obstacles—the possibility that Isabella's body would reject the heart. "But for now, she's doing very well."

"And the new heart," Timothy said. "It just . . . started beating?"

"The new heart is flawless and strong. Sometimes, when we start blood flow, hearts are reluctant to start up again. But not this time. The second we started blood flow, the new heart began to beat in perfect sinus rhythm."

Sebastian understood the science and medicine behind heart transplant. Even so, he regarded the fact that a donor's heart could beat in a recipient's body as a miracle. Every time he'd witnessed a heart transplant, he'd watched a miracle just as legitimate as the one God had performed when He'd defended Sebastian from death in El Salvador.

Megan started to cry.

In the past he'd removed his emotions as much as he could from his patients and their parents. But now, because of Leah, his own feelings were much closer to the surface.

Timothy turned Megan to him and hugged her.

"It's a good day," Sebastian assured them. "Your daughter has received a brand-new start."

Leah treated herself to a dessert break at Polka Dot Apron Pies that afternoon. She'd stopped at the post office, and the pie truck was too conveniently close to pass up.

She sat at one of the round tables on the sidewalk near the food trucks delighting in a slice of pumpkin pie and contemplating how to further her investigation into Bonnie and Ian O'Reilly.

It wouldn't hurt to reach out to Joyce Caffarella, Bonnie's fellow nurse, one more time. Joyce remembered Bonnie. And Leah was fairly certain that Joyce had invited Leah to contact her again, if needed.

She consulted her text message conversation with Joyce. Sure enough, the older woman had said, *Let me know if there's anything else I can do.*

Leah crafted a text.

> Hi! This is Leah Montgomery. Thanks again for talking with me and sending me Bonnie and Tracy's contact information. I've made some headway in my search for information on Bonnie O'Reilly, but now I'm stuck again. If, by chance, you remember anything else, please let me know.

Leah sectioned off another bite of pie. Crisp, buttery pastry crust supported rich filling and a dollop of whipped cream.

In addition to researching death certificates, Genevieve had mentioned that yearbooks and newspapers had proven helpful. Leah didn't see how yearbooks could be relevant to her search, but a newspaper article might divulge facts she could use as a springboard to get in touch with friends, relatives, and employers of Bonnie's—any of whom may have a phone number for her.

A return text from Joyce arrived.

> I'll think on it, hon! If anything occurs to me, or if I can find any Bonnie memorabilia in one of my closets, you'll be the first to know.

> I appreciate your help.

Bonnie had been living in Atlanta by the time Ian had been born. Atlanta was a city of half a million people. Trying to find Bonnie in an Atlanta newspaper brought to mind the proverbial needle in the haystack. She'd likely have better results searching for Bonnie in her hometown paper.

On her phone, Leah pulled up information about the town that had been listed as Bonnie's birthplace on Ian's death record. Oxford, Alabama. Its population had enjoyed a forty-six percent increase in the past twenty years and now boasted twenty-one thousand residents. It made sense that Bonnie might have migrated to Atlanta from Oxford, because even though the Alabama/Georgia line separated the two cities, they were located only eighty-eight miles apart.

She typed *Newspaper for Oxford, AL* into her Google app, then dialed the number provided.

"Calhoun County Post," a young, sweet-voiced woman answered.

Leah explained that she was looking for newspaper mentions of a woman who'd been born in Oxford named Bonnie Byrne or Bonnie O'Reilly.

"I'd be glad to help," the woman said. "But, just so you know, this isn't something I can pull up quickly. I'll have to work on it in my downtime. It might take me a bit."

"No problem at all." A thought occurred. "Would it be too much trouble to also keep an eye out for mentions of Ian O'Reilly?"

"That's absolutely fine. I'll add him to the list."

Almost as soon as Leah ended the call, her phone dinged. She checked her texts, anticipating another follow-up from Joyce. It wasn't from Joyce. It was from Claire.

> My dad's really, really angry. Can you come get my sisters and brother and me?

Panic flashed in Leah's chest. She placed a call to Claire. No answer. Leah texted instead.

> Claire, call the police. If you can get out of the house, do. If you can't, try to lock yourself into a room.

No answer. No scrolling dots to indicate Claire had seen the message.

Tossing what was left of her pie in the trash, she rushed to her car. Once she'd shut herself inside, she dialed Misty River's police headquarters.

A female voice answered.

Leah identified herself and rapidly relayed the text she'd received from Claire.

"Leah, this is Marilyn." They knew each other slightly from church. "I'm so sorry to hear about your student."

"I'm concerned."

"I understand. Listen, the officers we have on duty are currently at the scene of a collision on Summit Road. I'll ask if one of them can drive over to Claire's residence as soon as possible."

Leah supplied Claire's address, thanked Marilyn, and disconnected.

Summit Road was on the outskirts of town. Depending on how severe the crash was, that emergency might take precedence over Claire's emergency.

She dialed Sebastian. It was 4:40. He was likely on the road back to Misty River since he'd anticipated that he'd be home for dinner.

He didn't pick up. She tried again.

No answer.

She called Ben. His line rang and rang. She left a brief message, but halfway through remembered his baseball team practiced on Thursday afternoons.

Anxiety scratched the inside of her lungs. She was burning time sitting here, time that might be precious to Claire. She should have done more for Claire before now. Why hadn't she done more?

She called Connor. No answer.

Sebastian had suggested she reach out to Ben's dad if she needed reinforcements for a visit to Claire's house. But she'd only met Hersh on a handful of occasions. She didn't have his number in her phone.

She started her car. Read Claire's message again. Tried calling the girl. Sent another text.

Are you all right?

319

No scrolling dots.

She'd told Sebastian she would not go alone to Claire's house. But what choice did she have?

Worry fused with the responsibility of this, sickening her. How was she supposed to justify doing nothing when she might be the only one Claire had contacted? The only one who knew Claire and her siblings were in trouble?

She drove toward Claire's, arguing with herself, trying to formulate a strategy.

When she came to a stop in front of Claire's house, the structure looked cold and still. It could be that fury was snarling off its leash indoors, scaring children, hurting children. But from her vantage point, there was no sign of that. The last time she'd come here, she'd glimpsed the interior of the house through the downstairs windows. This time, drawn curtains guarded the family's secrets.

A potentially expired canister of pepper spray languished in the bottom of her purse. She dug it out, stuck it in her back pocket, and let herself from her car. Her outfit—skinny jeans, white top, emerald cardigan—had felt entirely right this morning but felt entirely wrong now. Too frivolous. The soles of her ballet flats slipped against slick concrete as she made her way to the front door.

Sebastian had spent most of the drive back to Misty River on the phone. First, he'd spoken to the intensivist on shift about Isabella's care. Then Dr. Nelson, who'd oversee her progress. Then Megan and Timothy, who'd contacted him with questions.

It wasn't until he stopped at a light several miles outside of town that he realized he'd missed two calls from Leah. He dialed her. No response, so he texted her.

She didn't text back, even though the school day had ended a while ago.

He turned on the Siriously Sinatra station and listened to a few songs, but his brain refused to focus on the music.

He called Leah again. No answer. Obviously, she was busy. She'd call back when she was free. No reason to overreact.

Except terrible images started to filter into his head, images that explained why she couldn't answer her phone. Car accident. Injury.

That's ridiculous, Sebastian. She's fine.

His instincts, though, were telling him otherwise.

It wouldn't hurt to check with Dylan. He could do so without sounding like a nervous psycho.

He silenced the music and woke his phone using voice controls. "Call Dylan Montgomery."

The call connected through Bluetooth, his car's speakers amplifying the sound of the ringing phone.

"Hey, Dr. Grant," Dylan said.

"Hey, I'm having a little trouble reaching your sister. Do you know what she's up to this afternoon?"

"Nope."

"Any guesses?"

"No, but I can check the app that shows me where she is, if you want."

"That would be great, thanks."

"'Kay, hang on."

Sebastian dug the tip of his thumb into his steering wheel.

"It looks like she's on the north side of town. Um. On . . . Serene Court. I don't know what's over there."

Fear—cold and raw—pierced Sebastian. He knew exactly what was over there. He'd driven Leah to that street on Saturday to pick up Claire.

It felt as if his lungs were folding in on themselves as he ordered his phone to supply directions to Serene Court.

CHAPTER TWENTY-FOUR

Leah pressed Claire's doorbell and listened to its chimes reverberate within. Anxiously, she waited next to the two metal lawn chairs standing guard on the front landing.

No one answered, so she tried the doorbell a second time. After a minute or so, she heard movement on the other side.

She took several steps back.

A forty-something man, big and broad with dark red hair, answered the door. Color flushed his pale skin, and his eyes glittered with adrenaline.

Alarm bolted down her spine. "I'm Leah Montgomery, Claire's math teacher. I don't believe we've had the opportunity to meet."

"Wes Dobney."

"Nice to meet you. I'm here to pick up Claire and her siblings for the outing to the library."

"What outing to the library?"

"Oh! Well . . . the library recently completed an excellent math exhibit." Not true. She'd invented this scenario on the drive over. "Very interactive. I told Claire about it, and she seemed interested, so I volunteered to take her and her sisters and brother through the exhibit this evening."

"I don't know anything about that."

She feigned surprise and contrition. "My apologies. I set this up with your wife, but I should have emailed you both to confirm. Are . . . the kids available for an hour?"

"Just a minute." The door shut.

Leah wrapped her arms around herself. Painful seconds dragged by, then the door slid open again, this time revealing a girl no older than five or six, with a round face and orange curls.

"I'm Ms. Montgomery," Leah told her.

"I'm Annie. Are you . . . here for us?"

Leah nodded.

"Daddy locked Mason in his room. We need to get him out so he can go, too."

"I don't have a key to Mason's room."

Annie glanced over her shoulder, then focused on Leah. "You don't need one. The lock's on the outside but it's too high for me to reach."

"I don't think I should come in."

"Please? Just real quick?" she begged. "His room's right there." Low-pitched angry tones were coming from the left. She pointed to the right.

Protect us, Leah prayed. Easing inside, she followed Annie as silently as possible. The smell of burned toast clogged the air.

Annie stopped at the first door they came to and gestured to the lock she'd mentioned earlier. A slide lock.

Breath shallow, Leah's mind screamed, *Get out! Get out!* as she freed it.

Within the room, Mason, his face splotchy from crying, pushed to his feet. He looked a few years older than Annie.

"Get on some shoes," Leah whispered to them, "and meet me in the front yard."

They scrambled to do as she'd asked.

Leah rushed outside. In less than a minute, Mason and Annie exited. A minute after that, a middle-school-aged version of Claire slipped from the house. Her skin was ashen, her mouth set. This must be Becca.

"He's not going to let Claire leave," Becca told Leah flatly.

"No?"

The girl gave an abrupt shake of her head—

Wes jerked open the door. His attention swept to the three children in the yard. His brow crimped. "You can take them, but not Claire. She's grounded."

"I'm so sorry to hear that. She's been struggling slightly with the concept of integrals, and the display does a great job of illustrating that in a way I think will help her understand."

"She's not going," he said.

Claire would want her to take Becca, Mason, and Annie away. Yet everything in her was rebelling at the prospect of leaving Claire behind. Should she brave further entreaties?

No. Wes's expression left no room for that.

"All right," she said. "I'll be back with these three shortly." Or not. How was she going to handle this? She didn't have the right to kidnap this man's children.

The kids bundled inside her car. Three was better than none. She'd get them somewhere safe, discuss the situation with the police, then decide what to do about Claire. She executed a U-turn in order to leave the neighborhood.

"Wait," Becca said as they drove back past the house. "There's Claire."

Motion caught Leah's eye. Claire, climbing out one of the downstairs windows. Leah's heart wadded in her throat. The girl's head and shoulders were out, but when she tried to step through, something held her in place. She tugged but could go no farther.

"We have to help her!" Annie cried.

"I will. Just let me . . . let me park out of sight."

Two houses down, she came to a halt. "Wait here." She dashed toward Claire.

Claire was weeping silently when Leah reached her. The teenager strained forward. "My sweater's caught."

"I'll help you."

"No, you'd better go, Ms. Montgomery." Making a ragged sound, she heaved forward again. It was like watching an animal trying to escape from a trap. Behind Claire lay a messy bedroom and a discarded window screen, but Wes wasn't in sight.

"I'll help you," Leah repeated forcefully. The knit of Claire's sweater had snarled in the crank handle. Leah wrapped her fingers around the threads and pulled. They began to give way. "Move to the side, Claire."

The girl did so. Leah got a better grip and yanked with all her might. This time, they ripped. She supported Claire as the girl jumped down. They jogged, holding hands, toward the car.

They'd only gone a few yards when Claire's dad stormed from the house, swearing. "Stop!" he yelled.

Claire wrenched to a halt, separating herself from Leah.

"What is this?" Wes glared at Leah's car, then at Leah. "Are you stealing my children from me?"

"No, sir." Her voice sounded thin. "As we were pulling away, we saw Claire trying to get through her window. I stopped to help her."

"I told you that she's grounded." Another expletive hissed from him. "You didn't think you were in enough trouble already?" he demanded of Claire. "So you decided to sneak out?"

Claire stared at the grass.

He turned away. Took a few paces toward the door. Rounded on them again. Sweat beaded his forehead. "Claire is not leaving," he spat. "*None of them are leaving.*" He threw one of the metal chairs in their direction. They darted apart. The chair clattered between them, narrowly missing them both.

Wes charged to Claire, grabbed her forearm, and marched her toward the house.

"No!" Leah extended a hand. "I'm very sorry. I don't want Claire to get in trouble—"

A blur shot past Leah. Then another. Becca and Mason launched themselves at their dad, trying to free Claire. He shoved them away.

"That's enough!" Leah yelled. "Stop—"

Pattering footsteps neared. Leah turned to see Annie hurtling toward the mob. Leah intercepted her, wrapping her arms around the girl's waist. Screeching in outrage, Annie flailed.

"You can help them best by going to get a neighbor," Leah told her. "Any neighbor you trust who you think might be home." She set the girl down.

Annie froze.

"Go!" Leah ordered. Annie sprinted away.

Leah moved toward Wes, who continued to grapple with his children. Hateful words roared from him as he thrust Mason to the ground and tossed Becca aside. Mason sprang back at his father. While Wes's attention was on his son, Leah drew Becca away, then attempted to pry Claire from his grip. Just when she thought she might succeed, Wes's elbow collided with her cheekbone.

The impact filled Leah's vision with stars. She stumbled back. Her equilibrium tilted . . . the world dimmed . . . then slowly righted itself.

Wes was far stronger than any of them individually and maybe all of them collectively. Claire and her siblings were already hurt, and he'd hurt them more severely—

A figure barreled forward and entered the fray with the force of a silent and deadly wind.

Sebastian, she realized.

Sebastian.

He threw a punch at Wes that connected with the older man's jaw. Wes's head snapped to the side, and his hold on Claire released.

With quicksilver speed, Sebastian positioned the kids and Leah behind himself. "Get back," he gritted out.

Leah steered the kids a safe distance away.

Wes stormed at Sebastian, his shoulders lowered so that he caught Sebastian in the stomach and drove him into the ground. They rolled, struggling. Wes rose on top, clobbering Sebastian with a fist to the temple. He pulled his arm back again—

Leah shoved Wes to the side. He fell and the two men wrestled, each landing blows to the other's ribs.

A stranger—a muscular man in his fifties—entered the scene. He hauled Wes off Sebastian. Wes retaliated by swinging at the stranger, barely missing him.

Sebastian gained his feet. Together, he and the stranger worked to subdue Wes. It was like bringing down a thrashing bull, but they finally pushed him facedown on the grass and held him there.

Wes continued to swear and strain.

Leah's pulse jangled. Her breath came hard. The children were breathing hard, too—all of them blinking and shell-shocked. "Is everyone all right?" Leah asked.

They nodded, though they didn't look all right. Mason had a split lip. A red ring marked the skin of Claire's forearm where her father had gripped her.

Annie hugged Claire. "I went and got our neighbor, Mr. Hawthorne," the little girl whispered to Leah.

"You did very well."

A police car arrived at the curb. A stout officer with a graying crew cut crossed to them. His name tag read *Wagner*. "What happened here?"

"He assaulted his children," Leah said, "as well as these two men."

"The children attacked *me*," Wes sneered.

"The kids were trying to protect one another from him," Leah said.

Officer Wagner freed the handcuffs from his belt. "You have the right to remain silent. Anything you say can and will be used against you in a court of law."

Sebastian and Mr. Hawthorne helped move Wes into the back of the squad car.

Leah's knees felt liquid. "Let's all sit down for a minute," she said to the kids, "and catch our breath until the police officer is ready to speak with us." She sat heavily on the grass.

The kids plopped around her.

It didn't take long before the officer began asking them questions. While they answered, Sebastian stood several yards to the side, alone. The long-sleeved work-out shirt he wore with scrub pants emphasized his muscled shoulders. Arms crossed, features granite-hard, he peered at the street . . . though he didn't appear to be registering anything at all.

"Can you please contact your mom for me and explain to her what's happened?" Officer Wagner asked Claire.

The teen nodded and brought her mom up to speed with a quick and hushed conversation. "She'll be here in about thirty minutes to pick us up," Claire told the officer.

"Good. I'll take Mr. Dobney to the station." He looked between Leah and Mr. Hawthorne. "Can one of you stay with the children until their mother arrives?"

"I'd be happy to," Mr. Hawthorne said. "I know the kids well. My wife and I have lived next door for ten years."

"Is that okay with all of you?" the officer asked the four children.

"Definitely," Claire told him.

"Then that's what we'll do. Let your mother know that she can reach me by calling the station." He drove off, Wes a hulking figure in his back seat.

One by one, they stood. When Mr. Hawthorne approached Mason to have a look at his injury, Claire drew near Leah. "Thank you." Her mouth trembled. "Thank you for coming to help us."

"You're welcome. How your father treated you just now . . . it's not acceptable or right. That's not what love looks like."

Claire nodded.

"Those of us at school," Leah continued, "will team up with your mom to make sure you're all safe and protected and cared for."

"We'll be good with my mom."

"I'll call and check on you tomorrow. If you need anything between now and then, let me know."

"I will. Ms. Montgomery . . . I'm so, so sorry about this."

"It's not your fault. I'm glad that you texted me."

"I'm really sorry, though."

Mr. Hawthorne led Claire and her siblings inside, and Leah was left in the suddenly empty, silent front yard with Sebastian.

She'd seen a side of him just now that she'd known existed but hadn't witnessed. Today, she'd glimpsed the tough foster kid who didn't back down and wasn't afraid to use his fists.

She placed herself directly in front of him and saw that a pink-

and-red bruise stretched from near the corner of his eye across his temple. His pale gray irises glistened like jewels.

A wave of love rolled from her heart to the tips of her fingertips. She had no familiarity with falling in love. But because of her love for Dylan, Tess and Rudy, and others, she definitely *did* know what love was. She recognized the staunch commitment at its core. The fierce protectiveness. The willingness to sacrifice for the other. The determination to hold on.

Do the math, you ninny. You love him.

A tornado had formed within Sebastian back when Dylan had told him Leah's location.

It was still spinning.

Still stirring up old terror and pain.

He studied Leah's face. "Your cheek," he said.

"Oh." Her hand lifted to her swollen cheekbone. "Do I have a bruise?"

He dipped his chin, wanting to *kill* Claire's dad. He'd arrived just in time to see the man clock Leah with his elbow. The sight had affected him like a body blow, and after that, he didn't remember exiting his car or running forward.

She reached out and skated a fingertip across the throbbing skin next to his eye, leaving sparks. He inhaled raggedly.

"Are you okay?" she asked.

"Are you?"

"Yes."

"Then so am I."

"Thank you. For defending us."

He didn't reply.

She tucked her hands into the front pockets of her jeans. "How did you know where to find me?"

"Dylan. He checked his app and told me where you were." Inside himself, he was fighting his temper with just as much strength as he'd used earlier with Claire's dad. "Why did you come here?"

"Claire texted me and said that her dad was on a rampage. I called the police, but they were at the scene of an accident. I drove here and told Claire's dad that I was scheduled to take the kids to the library."

Nearby, a metal lawn chair lay on its side. It, and the situation he'd found when he'd arrived, gave evidence to the chaos that had resulted from her attempt to help.

"Claire's dad wouldn't allow Claire to leave with me," she went on, "so Claire climbed out her window. Her dad caught us and dragged Claire toward the house."

"At which time you confronted an abusive man who owns guns?"

"His other kids confronted him. I was just trying to keep everyone safe."

"You could have been hurt badly."

"And yet, look." She spread her hands. "I'm fine."

"You could have been hurt badly," he repeated.

"But I wasn't."

"But you could have been."

A short pause. "You . . . might be reacting slightly overprotectively." Her tone was mild.

She was accusing him of being overprotective? That was rich. She wouldn't allow her brother two seconds of freedom. Yet he was supposed to be fine with watching her get whacked in the face by an enraged man?

"In the end, things worked out well," she said. "You told me that you're okay. The kids are okay. I'm okay. I stand behind my decision to intervene."

"Even though you promised me that you wouldn't come here alone?"

"I take promises seriously, and I'm sorry that I broke my promise to you. But I *couldn't* leave the kids to fend for themselves."

He had zero tolerance for broken promises. "You promised me, Leah."

"Today's situation forced me to go back on that promise for the greater good."

"That's a cop-out." Frustration tightened his words. It was hard to think straight, to speak. *This* is why he didn't trust people. This is why he shouldn't have trusted her.

His mom had failed to keep her promise when she'd told him she'd recover. Her death had stripped him of family and security. It had wrecked his life and his faith in people. It had taught him that the safest course was to depend on himself. So why had he strayed from that?

He'd strayed from that because he'd been unable to resist Leah. "I have to step back from this relationship," he stated.

She flinched. Wind stirred through the strands of her hair. "Why?"

"I can't get any more involved."

"You're upset, and I want to understand why."

He backed away from her.

"Stay," she said. "Let's talk this through—"

"I can't."

His self-control was cracking like plaster. He couldn't let that happen in front of her.

"Sebastian," she said.

He climbed into his car and drove away.

As he took one unthinking turn after another, the sensation that he couldn't get enough air into his lungs grew more and more urgent. Finally, he pulled onto a half circle of dirt that formed an overlook and exited his car.

The land fell away, providing a view of mountains retreating into the distance. No houses or people nearby. Just nature.

He wrapped his palms around the metal railing at the curve's edge and concentrated on breathing. Anger flew around inside him like a black crow.

"I'll be fine," his mom had told him, when she'd spent all day one Saturday in bed.

"What's the matter?" He handed her the Pop-Tart and glass of milk he'd made her for dinner.

"I'm just a little under the weather." She sat up in bed, her back supported by pillows. "All of us get sick sometimes. Remember when you had strep throat a few months ago? Now you're as healthy as can be."

"Yeah, but . . ." She didn't look good. Why was she so thin? Her face was too white. He swallowed down worry. "I went to the doctor for medicine. You need to go to the doctor, too."

"I'll go on Monday, 'kay? Will that satisfy you?"

She was teasing him, but it wasn't funny. It was dark and scary in here with the blinds closed.

"Will that satisfy you?" she repeated.

"Mmm-hmm."

"Hey. I've taught you to say what you mean. So don't say 'mmm-hmm' if it isn't what you mean. What're you afraid of? You can tell me." She looked right at him, challenging.

"That you'll die."

She smoothed his hair, then took hold of his shoulder. "I promise you that I won't die."

She was his mom. He believed her. He *needed* to believe her.

"I'll go to the doctor and get medicine," she said, "and they'll fix me up. I've never let my health beat me once. I'm a fighter. You know that about me, right?"

"Right."

"I'm raising you to be a fighter, too." She squeezed his shoulder. "You can't let fear have control. We're Grants, and Grants are strong. We can do whatever we put our minds to." She shooed him. "Now go make me another Pop-Tart. I don't think one will be enough."

He'd made her another Pop-Tart, but it had gone to waste. She'd only eaten half of the first one.

When she'd died, and for a long, long time after, his feelings had been on one side of a glass pane while his body had existed on the other side. No longer. Leah had broken the glass, and now he was experiencing the weight of every emotion he'd never wanted to feel.

"You can't let fear have control," his mother had said.

Too late.

He did *not* want to be parted from Leah. Just the idea of that turned his stomach. Yet to love her then lose her would cost more than he could afford. His mom's death had sent him down a destructive path that had lasted for years. What would the loss of Leah do to him?

He turned away from the rail and interlaced his hands behind his skull.

Already, he'd put himself at risk by allowing Leah to become one of the most important things in his world.

He'd made a mistake—a mistake he'd just tried to fix by breaking up with her.

A deep, black hole opened in his soul.

Upon arriving at home, Leah immediately shut herself in her room. She sat on the floor, leaned against the foot of her bed, and pressed the heels of her hands into her eyes.

She would not behave like a lovelorn girl and cry!

A soft knock. "Leah?" Dylan asked.

"Hmm?"

"Everything cool?"

Their roles had reversed. She was the one hiding in her room and he was the one checking on her. Affection lumped in her throat. "Yes. Everything's cool."

"Sebastian called earlier, wondering where you were."

"I saw him. It's all good."

"Sure?"

"I'm sure."

"'Kay." His footsteps retreated.

Internally, she shook her fist at romance and called it a string of bad names, because it turned out that she *was* going to cry like a lovelorn girl. Her immunity to men had been disproven. Her feelings of superiority regarding her singleness had been humbled.

When you met a man you couldn't help but love . . . it changed everything.

She'd kept it together while talking with Sebastian. But just now, while driving home, the spent drama had heavied her body. Subtle shaking had overtaken her limbs. The reality of Sebastian's words had crushed down.

"I can't get any more involved."

Every step of the way, she'd been very cautious about dating him.

He'd overcome her barriers by treating her beautifully, respectfully, devotedly. By speaking vows with his kisses.

Was it possible that she'd misinterpreted the depth of his feelings? She was not gifted at reading people. Maybe she'd ascribed meaning to his words and actions that wasn't there—

No.

She'd asked him to be direct with her and he'd honored that request. She'd stake money on the fact that he cared about her a great deal. If she had to guess what had happened between them this afternoon, she'd guess that he'd been propelled over the dividing line between his affection for her and his wounds.

She'd given him a reason not to trust her. And he'd pulled away. She'd been clear-eyed about his issues and limits from the start. Which is why she'd prayed again and again, asking for God's guidance concerning Sebastian. God had remained stubbornly silent.

"Why did you put me through this?" she asked Him softly. "This is exactly what I was afraid would happen."

God had stood back and allowed her to follow Sebastian into a trap. He'd let her feelings for Sebastian break free of the box where she'd wisely been trying to keep them.

In the past, God had always steered her. Always defended her.

Why not this time? *I don't understand why you didn't answer when I repeatedly asked you to show me your will.* She'd been poised to obey Him, willing. But He had not spoken.

For the first time since she'd believed in Him, He'd let her down, and now she'd landed herself in a wretched predicament. She'd fallen in love with a man who'd promptly broken up with her. She was experiencing the pain she'd seen other women endure when their relationships ended, a pain she'd planned to sidestep.

She truly couldn't stand to think about facing the lack of Sebastian's phone calls, smile, presence, conversations. He was loneliness and staggering success and childhood sorrow. He was a brilliant brain in a rugby player's body. Inky hair and uncompromising features.

She'd done what she had to do for Claire today. Yet it devastated her to think that her actions had cost her Sebastian.

CHAPTER TWENTY-FIVE

Never. That's when Luke Dempsey had planned to return to his hometown of Misty River.

But here he was.

On Friday morning, an elderly woman unlocked the door to the apartment she'd listed for rent. She went in ahead of him, eying him suspiciously.

She was right to be suspicious. He could snap her in half.

He'd found this place the old-fashioned way, by buying a newspaper out of one of the few machines left in town and scanning the For Rent section. This landlady was old-fashioned, wearing tight gray curls and an apron over a faded dress. The apartment was old-fashioned, too.

Green carpet that stank of dust stretched from wall to wall. The kitchen had yellow Formica countertops and wooden cabinets with brass handles. He entered the one bedroom. More green carpet. The bathroom hadn't been updated since the fifties.

He returned to the living area, which felt big to him after the jail cell that had been his home for the past seven years. The ceilings were at least twelve feet high. Square panes of glass divided the tall rectangular windows that let in views of the town and mountains.

Having grown up in Misty River, he was familiar with this building. It had been constructed for commercial use more than a century ago on the edge of the historic downtown. A warehouse currently occupied by a lumber company took up the bottom floor. The next floor, offices. The top floor, this floor, contained a few apartments that had probably once housed either the original owner's family or supervisors.

"Are there hardwood floors under the carpet?" he asked.

"Yes."

"If I rent this place, can I pull up the carpet and refinish the floors?"

"Yes."

"Can I renovate the kitchen and paint all the walls?"

A frown wrinkled her forehead. "I'm not paying for that."

"Can I do it if I pay for it?"

"Yes."

"I'll take it."

Despite his many sins and failures, Luke was a man of his word. He'd returned to his hometown to fulfill the promise he'd made to his friend and fellow inmate, Ed Sutherland.

When Ed was dying, he'd begged Luke to protect his only child, Finley—who wasn't even aware of the danger her father's actions had brought to her door.

Luke had told Ed that he'd keep her safe.

He hadn't yet met Finley. He didn't care about her. And he didn't care about working for her animal shelter. He only cared about one thing.

Doing what he'd said he'd do so he could finally be free.

After a night of shredded sleep, Sebastian woke to overcast weather and a black mood.

He spent hours in his media room watching violent movies. Finally, unable to take another movie, unable to take the thoughts in his head, he hauled himself to his feet and made his way to his bedroom for shoes.

The clock told him it was late afternoon. He still wore the track pants and long-sleeved athletic shirt he'd pulled on this morning. His face was unshaven, his hair a mess.

His phone rang.

He checked it. Ben.

Since it wasn't Leah, he didn't answer.

Almost as soon as it stopped ringing, it started ringing again. Ben.

"Yeah?" He wedged the phone against his shoulder while he laced his Adidas.

"You didn't respond to my morning or my lunchtime text, which isn't like you. What's wrong?"

"Everything."

Ben hesitated, then said, "Good grief, Sebastian."

Sebastian could tell that his friend had already diagnosed his mental state.

"Where are you?" Ben asked.

"On my way to the cemetery."

W hen miserable, Leah became maniacally industrious.

Last night she'd reorganized every closet in her house, including Dylan's (which he had not appreciated). She'd gone on a late-night run to the grocery store and prepped her pantry for doomsday. Then she'd stayed up until 2:30 a.m., making so much chicken noodle soup that she'd frozen three-fourths of it for future dinners.

The frenzied activity had kept her body busy but, to her dismay, it hadn't mitigated her heartache, confusion, or disillusionment.

As soon as school let out this afternoon, she'd changed into yoga pants and a hoodie, then driven to the heart of town to power walk the concrete footpath that followed the curving course of the river.

Her breath came in huffs. With an edge of desperation, she increased her speed, wanting . . . What? To outrun her sorrow?

Burn off her churning feelings? Punish herself for loving someone who didn't let people in?

She had no track record with boyfriends and didn't understand how to handle something as crucial and devastating as their current impasse. Should she leave Sebastian alone? If so, for how long? Forever? Should she go to him and insist they work through this?

Arms pumping, she stormed forward—

Her phone rang.

She freed it from her arm strap. The caller's number originated in Oxford, Alabama.

She stopped, moving off the path onto nearby grass as a middle-aged man jogged past.

"Hello?" Her breath jerked in and out.

"Hi, I'm calling from the *Calhoun County Post*. We spoke yesterday?"

Leah recognized the woman's friendly voice. "Yes. Thanks for following up."

"My pleasure. I wanted to let you know that I was only able to find one mention of Bonnie Byrne in the back issues of our paper. Her birth announcement."

"I see," Leah said, trying to hide her disappointment.

"I was also able to find just one mention of Ian O'Reilly."

"Oh?"

"It's from thirty-some years ago. It ran on the Gallivanting About page we had back then, where we'd publish pictures of people and events from around the county. All I have is a photo and a caption."

"I'd love to see both the birth announcement and photo, if possible."

"I have pictures of them loaded into an email, ready to go. If you'll provide your email address, I'll shoot them straight over."

Leah supplied her email address and profuse thanks.

She opened her email app and waited for it to download new email. Several things populated, but nothing from the *Calhoun County Post*.

Chewing the edge of her lip, she tried again.

Still no.

And again.

This time, an email from the newspaper appeared. It took a few seconds for the birth announcement to load.

Sean and Ellen Byrne announce the birth of their second daughter, Bonnie Theresa Byrne. She was born on January 20th and weighed seven pounds, eight ounces.

The only new piece of information provided: Bonnie's birth weight.

The second attachment, a photograph, showed a group of at least twenty people of various ages.

Sean and Ellen Byrne hosted a family reunion this past weekend to celebrate the graduation from college of their grandson, Ian O'Reilly (center in the above photo).

Leah turned her phone horizontal so the image filled the entire screen. The man in the center, Ian, smiled out from the picture with gentle eyes, handsome young features, a lean build. He appeared full of life. Hopeful.

A few of Ian's elderly relatives sat on folding chairs in front. The rest stood. Surely Bonnie had been present for a reunion held in her son's honor. Carefully, Leah assessed the faces of the women in the photo who were the right age to have been Ian's mother. Several fit the bill. Unfortunately, even if one of them was Bonnie, she had no way of knowing which one—

Except no. That wasn't right.

Because . . . she did. She did know which one was Bonnie.

Surprise rolled into Leah like a heavy boulder.

One of the middle-aged women pictured here had blond-gray hair cut into severe horizontal bangs with straight sides. An assertive nose and eyes that tipped downward at the outer edges.

The woman in this picture was younger than the woman Leah knew, but unmistakably recognizable, nonetheless. The woman in this picture, the one whose hand rested on the shoulder of her son, Ian O'Reilly, was the woman Leah had long known as Tess Coventry.

Sebastian came to a stop next to his mother's grave.

Her small rectangular marker lay flat against the earth. *Denise Marie Grant* and the dates of her birth and death had been engraved into dull black stone.

He'd stood here just three times before.

The first time, the day they'd buried her. Vaguely, as if the scene had come from a movie he'd watched decades ago, he recalled her coffin lowering into the ground. Then someone tossing dirt on top of her.

He knew he'd worn a plaid suit Mrs. King had given him that had been too small and itchy. He knew their old lady neighbor and his social worker and his teacher and several strangers had been there.

However, he didn't know who'd paid for her funeral, burial, plot, and marker. As a kid, the expenses hadn't crossed his mind. Now that he lived in an adult world full of price tags, it shamed him that he had no idea whom to reimburse.

The second time he'd come here, he'd come because of CeCe. Every Memorial Day, the Colemans left flowers on the graves of their relatives. On the first Memorial Day after the earthquake, she'd insisted that they bring flowers to Sebastian's mother's grave, too. When she'd asked him where his mother was buried, he'd had no answer, so she'd made phone calls until she'd learned the whereabouts.

They'd gone first to the Coleman family cemetery, which had rolling hills and big trees. The contrast between that and the flat plainness of this parcel of grass by the freeway hadn't escaped him.

CeCe had invited him to say a few words. He'd been rigid inside and out, unable to speak, haunted by thoughts of his mom's decomposing body below the earth. CeCe and Hersh had taken turns praying. When Sebastian looked up, he'd seen Ben watching him with kindness. He'd quickly glanced away and wondered if a good son would have . . . should have . . . died right along with his mother.

He'd come here for the third time after graduating from medical school. That milestone had been a point of sentimental pride for CeCe, which, in turn, had made her think of Sebastian's mother. The day after the Colemans had celebrated his accomplishment beneath the black-and-gold congratulations banner, CeCe had brought him here again.

That time guilt had made him as uncomfortable as the itchy plaid suit. Guilt because he avoided visiting her grave to pay his respects. Because he'd moved on with his life. Because he wanted comfort to come from his memories of her—but they still brought only hurt. Because he'd found a new family.

Now, on his fourth visit, he stared at his mom's name for so long that it blurred.

He struggled with abandonment, with loving people, with broken promises. And all of that had started here . . . with Denise Marie Grant.

It would have been nice if his miraculous rescue from the earthquake had fixed what his mom's death had broken. But reality was more complicated.

His rescue had shown him that God existed and was capable of mighty things. On one hand, he was grateful that God had brought him out of that basement alive. On the other hand, his rescue forced him to acknowledge that God hadn't chosen to save his mother from her illness.

God had protected Sebastian's life, so it seemed that God loved him.

God had taken his mother away, so it seemed that God didn't love him.

In the face of those mixed messages, he'd concluded that he couldn't count on God. So he'd done everything possible to insulate himself from the kind of vulnerability he'd endured when his mom died.

He'd been certain that his job would give him both security and the ability to right the wrong of his mom's death with every child he saved.

It hadn't worked that way.

Isabella Ackerman and his other patients were not his mother. It turned out that what his mother had been to him was irreplaceable. His career and his money couldn't give him his mother or his childhood back. Nor could they give him safety. Or worth. Or identity. Enough had never been enough.

At this rock-bottom place without Leah, he needed to be honest with himself. The truth? Resentment toward God had been burning inside him like a pilot light for decades. Nothing had extinguished it. Not his gratitude over God's rescue of him after the earthquake. Not the Coleman family's support. Not his achievements.

Before he could move forward . . . before he could remember his mother without feeling like a thirty-pound barbell had been placed on his ribs . . . he needed to find a way to forgive God. For stealing his mother from him and, in so doing, teaching him that loving someone was the worst thing he could do to himself.

In his mind, he tested the words *I. Forgive. You.*

But he didn't. Forgive God. His emotions remained jagged. The sentences that formed in his head were the opposite of forgiving. *How could you? I was just a kid. Not the best kid, but not the worst. I didn't deserve what you did to me. You ruined me when you took away all the family I had.*

He heard a noise and looked over to see Ben approaching. His friend stopped on the other side of his mom's grave and observed him levelly, waiting for Sebastian to speak.

"I don't think I can forgive God," Sebastian said, his voice hoarse.

"For?"

"For taking my mom's life and leaving me alone."

Several seconds ticked by as Ben appeared to process his statement. "God never left you alone." Ben spoke with calm certainty. "I understand why you felt that way, but sometimes our feelings are liars. Think about everything you've been through since your mom's death, but try to think about it differently. Instead of remembering how alone you were, try to remember how alone you weren't."

"Like when?"

"Did God give you a good social worker? Did He provide foster parents who tried their best to be there for you?"

Sebastian grimaced.

"Was God with you in that basement in El Salvador? Did He hold up a wall in order to defend you?"

"Yes, but—"

"Did He open every single door for you so that you could attend college and medical school free of charge?"

"That's enough. I get the point."

"Then try it," Ben said. "Try remembering through that lens."

Frustrated, Sebastian rubbed his forehead.

"I can't count the number of people who've tried to convince you to let them in," Ben said. "You pushed them all away. Then you turned around and blamed God for your aloneness."

Ben's words cut through to the center of him with such accuracy that he couldn't move.

The cars dashing past on the freeway became moving smudges of color as he forced himself to do what Ben had challenged him to do. To confront his history.

After the earthquake, God had given him the best gift Sebastian had ever received—the Colemans. A thousand times, God had shown Himself to Sebastian through their commitment, words, and love.

The day Sebastian wrecked his car, God had brought Leah into his life.

God had been there during every surgery Sebastian performed, faithfully healing the sickest children again and again and again.

344

In case he needed additional proof of God's nearness, here was Ben, beside him today in this cemetery. Inarguable proof that even now, God hadn't deserted him.

Sebastian could powerfully sense God in this moment. But it could be that God had been with him in *all* the moments.

Some of the events of his life had been bad. But some had been amazingly good. If he could roll with the blessings God had extended to him, why had it been so impossible for him to roll with the hard?

Because he'd taken his mother's death as evidence that God either wasn't sovereign, wasn't good, wasn't powerful, or wasn't involved.

Could he accept a more complex truth? That the God who'd let his mother die was *still* sovereign, good, powerful, and involved?

If he could accept that, then he could quit trying so incredibly hard to protect himself all the time.

He was tired. . . .

He was so very tired of protecting himself.

Ben knelt and placed his palm on the gravestone. He bent his head to pray.

Sebastian followed his lead. He went to one knee, which caused dizziness to scramble his senses. He hadn't had enough sleep or food. Cold radiated from her marker into his hand.

He prayed for long minutes, doing his best to forgive God.

I forgive you, he repeated numerous times.

At some point, he finally started to mean it.

You could have saved my mom, but I forgive you for taking her.

He pushed the knuckle of his free hand across his eyes because he was crying.

Can you forgive me? he asked God.

Yes, came the immediate answer.

When he finally stood, his chest felt hollowed out, his body shaky. Yet something stable had taken root within him in the place where his anger and insecurity had been living.

Ben pressed to his feet. "What motivated you to come here today?"

"Leah and I broke up."

"I figured," Ben said. "Who broke up with whom?"

"I broke up with her."

"Because?"

"Because I couldn't . . . handle it."

Ben took his measure, his face grim. "Remember when I gave you the go-ahead to date Leah, and I told you not to insult her or me by keeping her at arm's length?"

"Yes."

"So?"

"She broke a promise to me."

"You're going to have to accept that no human being is going to be perfect enough to heal your scars."

Sebastian set his teeth together.

"How much do you want Leah in your life?" Ben asked.

"More than I've wanted anything."

"Then open yourself up to her."

Sebastian didn't answer.

"We *all* have to risk ourselves if we're going to earn the reward of a genuine relationship," Ben said. "You're not the only one."

"If I love her and lose her, it will gut me."

"*If* you love her? *If?*" Ben asked, incredulous. "You already love her, you idiot."

Ben's words hit him twice as hard as Claire's dad had yesterday. Because *of course* he did.

He loved her.

And had for a long time.

"Since the ship that would enable you not to love her has already sailed," Ben continued, "all you can do now to save yourself from being gutted is convince her to give you a second chance. Then channel all that famous determination of yours into putting her interests and her well-being ahead of your own."

Sebastian's brain spun.

"Show her how you feel and tell her how you feel every day," Ben said. "For the rest of your life."

CHAPTER TWENTY-SIX

An hour later, Leah arrived at Tess and Rudy's cabin.

Tess greeted her warmly, and Leah entered an interior she knew well. Walls of honey-colored wood complemented Southwest-style area rugs inspired by the Native American history of the region.

Today, neither the familiar environment nor the familiar woman soothed her. When she'd called Tess to ask if she could swing by, Leah had hoped she'd be able to conduct herself normally during this confrontation. Now she doubted that possibility. Tension had turned her stomach to stone. Moving oxygen into her lungs required effort.

"I made cookies." Tess moved toward the breakfast nook, where they'd shared many, many cookies and conversations.

Leah remained still. "This isn't a social call."

"Oh?" Tess halted.

"I know that you switched me with another baby the day of my birth."

Sadness lit inside Tess's eyes. Otherwise, she remained dignified and still. "I see."

Rustling sounded from the hallway just before Rudy appeared, beaming. "Leah!"

"Leah and I need to speak about something privately," Tess said to her husband. "I'll let you know when we're done."

"That'll be fine, but . . . are those oatmeal chocolate chip cook-ies I smell?"

Tess fetched two cookies and handed them to him.

"How 'bout one more?" he asked.

"No," Tess answered crisply. "I wouldn't want to spoil your appetite for dinner. Now head back and watch TV for a bit."

He winked at Leah. "Good to see you, hon."

"Good to see you, too."

He trundled down the hallway.

Tess motioned to the breakfast nook. "Shall we?"

Leah hesitated. Cookies were cozy, and she wasn't feeling cozy.

"I expect that you have questions for me," Tess said. "We'll be more comfortable sitting down. Shall we?"

Stiffly, Leah took her usual seat at the round table.

Tess poured milk into two glasses. A dusky blue plate supported the cookies . . . a testament to the dozens of batches of oatmeal chocolate chip cookies that Tess had made for Leah and Dylan through the years.

Tess sat, then took a slow sip of milk.

Leah didn't reach for either the milk or the cookies.

Tess was a controlled person, not given to fissures of emotion. Even so, given the magnitude of Leah's bombshell, Tess's response seemed tremendously understated.

The older woman carefully positioned her glass on the table, her knobby fingers loosely encircling its base. "I've thought for some time that you might find out."

"Why did you do it?"

"If you know what I did, then I'm guessing you know something of my motive."

"I think it has to do with your son Ian."

"Yes. My son Ian." Her sigh spoke of pain. "I wish I could ex-plain to you what a joy he was to me. He had such a sweet nature. Quiet and kind. Full of fairness. Every year his teachers would give him citizenship awards. Best Listener. Best Helper and the like."

Tess's focus drifted toward the living room, but Leah guessed that it had actually drifted back decades. "He grew and became a little more serious, a little more subdued. But he was still *good*, through and through. There wasn't a mean or malicious bone in his body. He cooked dinner for the family when I wasn't up to it. If I asked him to take out the trash, he'd do so immediately. If I told him to come home at ten, he'd come home at nine fifty."

Leah waited.

"He went off to college and earned a degree in business, then started work for an electronics company. It was during those years that he had an idea for a web browser that could display images. He did all the research, worked out all the logistics. He told a few of his closest friends about his idea."

"Was one of those friends Jonathan Brookside?"

Her lips thinned. "Yes. They were the same age and had started at the company the very same day. Jonathan stole Ian's idea. He went behind Ian's back and assembled a team. He was from a wealthy family, and his father lent him the capital to start a company of his own."

"Gridwork Communications Corporation?"

"Exactly. Jonathan was able to get the web browser off the ground long before Ian could raise the funds."

"And Jonathan's company went on to become a huge success."

"It did. Ian was devastated. He'd been betrayed by someone he trusted. He slipped into depression."

Tess's heartache was a palpable thing. Leah could feel it against her skin. "His father and I persuaded him to sue Jonathan," Tess continued, "and he improved somewhat during that process. He had hope that right would prevail . . . that justice would win."

"I know that the suit didn't go his way."

"I wish, very dearly, that it had. Jonathan was able to afford excellent lawyers. So, no. The case didn't go Ian's way. Afterward, we tried and tried to reach him, to help him. But we couldn't get through. He committed suicide a year later."

"I'm very sorry."

Tess's gaze met hers. "Unless you've lost a child, you can't imagine the grief. I loved Ian with every fiber of my being. His death is not something I've ever recovered from, nor ever will. I went on because I had another child, family members, work responsibilities. But I *did not* get over it. Half my heart belonged to Ian. And still does."

"I understand."

"My marriage to Malcolm fell apart. We divorced. Suddenly I was without one of my sons, without my husband. I was struggling with depression myself when one day, at work, I learned that Jonathan Brookside's wife was giving birth at my hospital. Magnolia Avenue was located near Atlanta's best neighborhoods, of course. Some of the most well-respected obstetricians in the city delivered babies there."

"Did you see Jonathan that day?"

She shook her head. "I was working in the nursery when both you and the Montgomery baby arrived for treatment and observation. After the pediatrician finished and said that you were both well enough to be returned to your mothers, I found myself alone with the two of you."

"Jonathan had taken your baby. And now you had the chance to take his."

"Yes. That was the precise thought that entered my head."

"You wanted to punish Jonathan."

"It's true. I wanted retribution for what he'd done to Ian. He'd gotten off scot-free, you see. He'd never paid any price at all for ruining my son's life . . . and mine." She turned her glass in a circle, then set her hands in her lap. "The things I felt and did in that moment are difficult, even for me, to comprehend. I'd never broken a rule in my life. But neither had Ian, and look where that got him."

Quiet wafted between them, and Leah registered the distant sound of Rudy's TV show, of a bird's song.

"I switched you with the Montgomery baby, which took some doing, as far as your ID bands and records went. When Tracy entered the nursery, I asked her to take you back to your mothers. And off you went."

"And that was that."

"I was certain I'd get caught. For days. Weeks. But no one was the wiser."

"How did the Bonnie O'Reilly who worked at Magnolia Avenue become Tess Coventry?"

"I was born Bonnie Theresa Byrne. My mother gave me the middle name Theresa in honor of her sister, then called me what she'd always called her sister: Tess . . . which is short for Theresa. Everyone in my family called me Tess, but at school and around town, I went by Bonnie. When I married Malcolm, I became Bonnie O'Reilly. Then, years afer my divorce, I met Rudy. When he found out that my family called me Tess, he started calling me Tess, too. Then I married him and my last name changed to Coventry."

"But even if you were Tess to Rudy and your family, shouldn't you have been Bonnie Coventry to everyone else?"

"Had I not switched two babies, I would have been. In an effort to at least partially cover my tracks, ease my paranoia, and make things difficult for anyone searching for Bonnie O'Reilly, I convinced Rudy to move outside of Atlanta. I took a job at a new hospital and introduced myself to everyone there as Tess. Over time, I became Tess to all." Politely, she moved a cookie onto her napkin. "May I ask how you found me?"

Leah gave Tess the SparkNotes version of her search.

"Ah."

"Who else knows that you switched Sophie and me?" Leah asked.

"Just you, me, and God. The secret of what I did has been a companion invisible to everyone except me. Until now."

"I'm inferring that our meeting at the middle school in Gainesville was not a coincidence."

"No, it wasn't. I often worried that what I'd done had impacted you and Sophie negatively. I looked for information on the two of you but never could find anything until I came upon an article featuring you as the brightest of the students who were attending

Clemmons. I was delighted, truly, to discover that you were a math prodigy, to know that you'd flourished."

Tess picked up invisible cookie crumbs with her fingertip. "But then, a few years later, around the time I learned that Sophie had gone to Vanderbilt and appeared to be doing very well for herself, I found you on the Internet as a high school teacher. In your biography, you said that you were caring for your brother, Dylan. That concerned me. I wondered why an eighteen-year-old girl was working full time and caring for her brother. I couldn't let it go. I was retired by then, and Gainesville was just twenty miles from where Rudy and I were living at the time, so I took it upon myself to contact the PTA and volunteer in hopes that doing so would provide me an opportunity to meet you."

"Which it did."

"I struck up a friendship with you. When you told me about your parents and your brother, I felt responsible."

"You *were* responsible for placing me with that family."

"And I knew that I was. I liked you at once. And, of course, I liked Dylan at once, too. He reminds me of Ian. Pale skin, brown hair, brown eyes."

Fresh understanding filtered in. Tess had always doted on Dylan.

"I wanted to help you, as a way to make amends for what I'd done and for your parents' deficiencies. I also wanted to build a relationship with the two of you. Rudy and I have five granddaughters and we now have three great-granddaughters. Here was a boy. Here was another chance to know and care for a little boy. You and Dylan have made our lives, Rudy's and mine, so much richer these last ten years."

"When I wanted to leave Gainesville for Dylan's sake, you encouraged me to apply for a position in Misty River."

"Yes, because our cabin was here. I love this place, and I had reason to believe you'd love it, too."

The villain who'd switched her at birth was the same woman who'd functioned as a grandmother to her and Dylan. Tess had taken care of them more dependably than any of Leah's actual relatives ever had. Tess had picked up Dylan from school for *years*. Tess had brought Leah food when she was sick, given her gifts every birthday and Christmas. Tess and Rudy had functioned as her trustworthy babysitters.

What was it that she needed to communicate to Tess?

"It was wrong of you to switch Sophie and me." She definitely *did* need to say that.

"Yes," Tess acknowledged. "It was. Unequivocally."

"You played God when you did that, and no one has the right to play God. Not for any reason. Regardless of what Jonathan did to Ian, Jonathan was the father I should have had."

"I'm very sorry, Leah."

"He and his wife could have given me . . ." Her voice broke. The depth of her emotion took her by surprise. "Stability and the chance to pursue my education, which I would have cherished." Yet it sounded like Jonathan was a snake. So while growing up as his daughter would have granted her some advantages, there was no telling what hardships it might also have served her.

"Are you going to tell Sophie and her family what I did?"

"I haven't decided. Imagine how they'll feel if I do tell them. As terribly as I felt when I learned I wasn't biologically related to Dylan." Tears piled on Leah's lashes. "Your actions will decimate them."

"Are you going to turn me in to the police?" Tess asked after a time. "Or to a reporter?"

"No."

Tess handed her a napkin. "I won't blame you if you do."

Leah blotted her eyes. "If I tell Sophie and her family the truth, I can't say how they'll respond to you. But I'm not interested in bringing you down. You took your revenge, but I won't be taking mine."

Tess's composure finally slipped, revealing regret. "I truly am sorry."

Leah couldn't bring herself to tell Tess she was forgiven.

"Do you think, given time, we can continue as we have been?" Tess asked. "You, me, Dylan, and Rudy?"

"I don't know." Leah stood. "I honestly don't know."

They looked at each other for an agonizing stretch of time.

Then Leah walked from the cabin.

As she drove home, she wished with a yearning that stole her breath that she could go to Sebastian's house, pour out her story, and find comfort in his arms.

God, her spirit howled, *where are you?*

CHAPTER TWENTY-SEVEN

The next morning, Saturday, Leah attempted to sleep off her misery hangover. The thought of Sebastian, Tess, and Rudy being deleted from her life all at the same time? Unconscionable.

Sadly, life dictated that when you wanted to sleep to avoid reality, you could not. She woke at 6:02 and couldn't fall back to sleep.

Burrowing under her covers, she tried to escape into Han Solo's world by watching movies on her laptop.

It didn't work.

Eventually she talked herself into making breakfast, though she wasn't hungry. Then she talked herself into showering and dressing to go hiking, though hiking didn't appeal, either.

Around eleven, she finished blow-drying her hair and padded to Dylan's bedroom door. "You awake?"

He answered with a grunt.

"Blueberry muffins are on the counter," she told him. "But if your tastes tend more toward the savory on this fine morning, we also have enough chicken noodle soup to soothe a thousand head colds."

"I'll eat the muffins."

"Okay. Fair warning—we're out of orange juice."

As she was crossing the living room, her peripheral vision registered movement through her front window. She glanced toward it just in time to see Sebastian come to a solemn stop on her walkway.

Their eyes met and a crescendo of need, love, caution, joy, and pain exploded inside. Why had he come? To make amends? To say good-bye?

She loved him. However, her elation warred with practicality. *Don't get your hopes up*, she told herself. *You are a woman of logic and reason. Stay logical. Stay reasonable.*

She pulled on a pink athletic jacket, stepped outside, and gestured for Sebastian to follow her. They came to a stop on the patch of driveway in front of the closed mouth of the garage. This position would give them at least partial privacy from Dylan, should he rouse himself from his room.

Sebastian wore a severe black wool coat over an untucked white business shirt and dark jeans. The hue of the coat matched the hue of his hair. His bruise had turned purple.

Behind him, the sky widened, hazy and pewter. The ice-tipped breeze paled his unsmiling face. "Are you all right?" he asked.

Obviously, the observant doctor could tell that she was off her game. "Physically, I'm fine. My bruise was less severe than yours, because it's almost gone. Emotionally, though, I'm as unhappy as I've ever been. I've hardly slept the last two nights."

"Why?"

"The state of our relationship. But also because I discovered the identity of Bonnie O'Reilly."

"And?"

"She's my friend Tess. They're . . . one and the same."

"What?"

She described how she'd come to realize Bonnie was Tess. "A woman I've trusted for years switched me at birth. She took Jonathan Brookside's baby—me—and gave me to Erica and Todd Montgomery. Which was a terrible thing to do. Yet, she did it for reasons I can somewhat understand. In summation, I don't know what to think—"

"Leah." Sebastian nodded toward the corner of the garage.

She swung in the direction he'd indicated and saw Dylan standing there.

Dylan. Had heard her.

Undiluted horror washed through her.

Dylan's face leached white. His car keys dangled from his hand. "I was going to get orange juice."

Because he threw his stuff down in the mudroom, he always exited through the back door and walked around the garage to his parking spot on the street. She'd been so fixated on Sebastian that she hadn't heard him.

"You were switched at birth?" Dylan asked.

No. She didn't want him to know! Until now, she'd been so careful to shield him.

"Dylan," she began. Her voice sounded unnatural, rattled. "Let's go inside and talk about this—"

"Were you switched at birth?" he asked, angry now.

She pursed her lips and sought for an escape route that would enable her to give anything other than a direct answer. "Let's go inside."

"I don't want to go inside!" He gestured sharply. The keys made a jangling sound. "It's a simple question."

"Watch it," Sebastian warned Dylan in a low tone.

"Were . . . you . . . switched . . . at . . . birth?" Dylan asked her, as if she were hard of hearing.

She looked at him pleadingly. "Yes."

"I'm not your brother?"

"You most definitely are my broth—"

"But I'm not, by blood?"

"There are more important things than blood—"

With a guttural sound of frustration, he stormed down the driveway toward his truck.

"Come back!" she ordered.

He didn't slow.

"Dylan," Sebastian called.

He didn't slow.

She jogged downhill, but her brother was pulling away when she reached the road. He peeled out and sped away.

Anguish slid down the back of her legs, weakening them. "Slow down!" He was upset and driving much too fast. *"Slow down!"* she yelled.

His truck disappeared around the bend.

"Dylan!" she couldn't stop herself from screaming, even though she knew he couldn't hear.

His engine growled. A horn blared. Brakes screeched. Then she heard the sickening noise of crunching metal.

Quiet.

She opened her mouth, but no voice or breath emerged. To the bottom of her soul there was nothing, *nothing* but immobilizing fear.

Sebastian was beside her, hurrying her to his car. She was in the passenger seat. He was driving them around the curve. Dylan's blue truck had rammed into a tree. Another car, a sedan, had pulled onto the opposite side of the road.

Leah was out of Sebastian's Mercedes before it had come to a stop and running the way she always did in her anxiety dreams many times before. Leaden legs. Too slow.

The grandfatherly driver of the sedan was also rushing toward Dylan, but Leah dashed past the older man and got there first. Dylan's window was down.

He looked fine. No blood. Unharmed.

Relief hit her like a visceral thing.

But then Dylan, who was leaning back against his headrest, rolled his face toward her, and she saw panic in his dark eyes. He made a high-pitched rasping sound that told her he was fighting to get air. "Can't . . . breathe." The words were barely audible.

She tried to jerk open his door, but the impact had warped it. "Sebastian!"

"I'm here."

"He can't breathe."

Sebastian leaned inside the truck. "Can you move your hands and feet?"

Dylan gave a desperate nod.

Sebastian reached in, hooked his arms around Dylan's upper

body, and pulled him through the opening. Leah caught his legs. They lay Dylan on a flat stretch of earth and dropped to their knees beside him.

"Leah," Dylan wheezed, looking at her the way he had when he was little and scared.

"It's okay," she told him, though she was dying inside. She wrapped her hand around his. "You're going to be fine."

Sebastian rested his ear on Dylan's chest. Then, gently, he probed Dylan's throat. "Injury to the larynx. It's preventing airflow down the trachea."

"I didn't do anything wrong," the driver of the sedan said. "He was in my lane. I honked and he swerved—"

"Call 9-1-1," Sebastian told him.

The man blanched. He fumbled for his phone.

"I need a straw," Sebastian said.

"There's one, ah . . ." The man pushed a shaking hand to his temple. "In my car. I stopped at 7-Eleven earlier."

Sebastian sprinted to the man's car.

Dylan was trying to say her name, she could tell by reading his lips. But no sound was coming out now. She squeezed his hand. He was struggling for air, like a fish in the bottom of a boat, and the sight of it was the very worst thing she'd ever seen. She wrestled down the sob that wanted to rise.

"I love you," she told him. "So much. Everything's going to be all right."

Dylan's lips were beginning to turn blue.

Frantic, she looked up for Sebastian. He was reaching into the trunk of his Mercedes. The stranger was talking to 9-1-1 dispatch.

God! she begged silently. *God, please. Please!*

Sebastian ran to them, knelt on Dylan's other side. With one hand, he flicked open a Swiss Army knife. With his other, he felt the area just below Dylan's Adam's apple. "Dylan, I'm going to open an airway into your lungs." Then with full assurance and zero hesitation, he slid the knife through the skin of Dylan's throat. Instantly, blood rose to meet the blade. He twisted the knife just enough to open the incision he'd made, pulled a wide red straw from his jacket pocket, and inserted it into the hole.

She heard air pulling through the straw, urgent and deep. Dylan relaxed slightly.

"That's it." Sebastian used his fingers to close the hole around the straw. "Take it easy and breathe."

The whistling, beautiful sound of an exhale. Inhale. Exhale.

"Good job." Sebastian looked straight into Dylan's eyes. "Did your throat ram into the steering wheel when your truck hit the tree?"

Dylan gave a slight nod.

"Your lungs are getting the air they need," Sebastian said. "You're going to be okay. Do you hear me, Dylan?"

Another nod.

Leah was too terrified to believe what Sebastian had just said, that Dylan was going to be okay. And much too terrified to believe that he wasn't.

Dylan's focus flicked to her. Brown curls fell against the bright autumn leaves blanketing the ground.

"I'm here," Leah said to the boy she'd loved since the day he was born. The one who was more important to her than her own wants, her own desires, her own life. "I'm here, sweetheart."

Sebastian tightened his hold on the skin around the straw, doing his best to create a seal.

He loved Leah. And Leah loved Dylan. He'd once lost what he'd loved, so he would move mountains and oceans with his bare hands to ensure that she did not endure the same pain.

He'd perforated the cartilaginous rings of the trachea. The pressure he was exerting on the wound would mitigate the loss of blood. Even so, he could feel it running down the sides of Dylan's neck.

"I performed a tracheotomy," he explained to Dylan, "which means that the straw is functioning as your windpipe, allowing oxygen in and out. The straw will tide us over until we get you to the hospital. There's a trip in an ambulance in your near future. And a hospital stay. I'm sorry to tell you that hospital food is just as bad as its reputation would lead you to believe."

This situation had stripped years off Dylan. Though he was trying to appear brave, he looked young and defenseless.

Leah's concentration remained trained on her brother. She probably wasn't aware that tears were wetting her face and turning her lashes spiky.

It was too late, much too late, to protect himself from her. From now on, for the rest of his life, there would be no hiding from the things she made him feel.

A siren's blare started small and grew in volume.

"You can look forward to a few days off of school for this," Sebastian told Dylan. "This is a tough way to cut class. But congratulations. You managed it."

Dylan tried to smile. The straw made a gurgle and Sebastian adjusted the angle of it so Dylan would continue to receive plenty of clean air.

The paramedics arrived. Sebastian gave swift instructions. They brought over tape and Sebastian used it to secure the straw so that there was no leakage around it and no possibility of dislodging it.

He helped the paramedics move Dylan onto the stretcher. Blood smeared bright against the boy's sweatshirt.

Once they'd secured Dylan inside the ambulance, he helped Leah into the back of the vehicle.

"Thank you," she said.

"I'll follow behind."

But she was already looking back at her brother.

Leah had spent the last ten years worrying about the dangers that might devour Dylan. Today, one of them had devoured him, in part, because of *her* and the things Dylan had overheard her saying to Sebastian.

The ambulance ride ended at their local hospital's emergency room. Doctors, nurses, white walls. Dylan, at the center of it all, the only entity she could see in sharp focus.

They replaced the temporary straw with a much more sophisticated tracheostomy tube. Dylan's vital signs stabilized. The staff informed Leah that they'd treat Dylan here until surgery could be arranged—which would likely take a day or two.

No doubt the surgery and recovery would be difficult, and Dylan might face a degree of lasting damage to his vocal cords. But all Leah could think, sitting beside his bed in the room they'd been assigned, was that the consequence of his injury could have been much, much worse.

Without a doubt, he would have suffocated, if not for Sebastian.

Sebastian hadn't sought out her attention once. However, she'd been aware of his presence ever since the accident. Two different times, when she'd looked up to find him so that he could answer a medical question, he'd been there. Because of him, she knew not to allow Dylan to be passed off to the nearest surgeon but to insist instead that only the best larynx surgeon in Georgia would do. She'd heard him sharing his opinions with the people who worked here—also known as bossing people around. At one point, she'd discovered a bottled water in her hand. At another point, a cup of tea. She didn't know how they'd gotten there, only that Sebastian had provided them.

Even now a container that smelled of bacon potato soup and warm bread waited for her on Dylan's bedside table. Sebastian had left a while ago, saying he wanted to give them time alone. But before he'd gone, he'd brought her food.

She'd eat it. Soon. She just couldn't bring herself to do so quite yet.

She'd just finished texting people to tell them what had happened. Their mom, who'd yet to respond because it was probably the wee hours of the morning in Guinea. Dylan's friends. Ben. And, after a moment's debate, Tess and Rudy. She'd supplied their room number and details about hospital visiting hours.

Dylan was staring listlessly at ESPN on the TV mounted on the wall. Since air was no longer passing over his vocal cords, Dylan's doctor had said it would be best for him to communicate through texts or notes until speech therapists could begin work with him post-surgery. He'd said that for now, Dylan would have his hands full simply adapting to breathing through a tube.

Indeed, Dylan appeared to be concentrating on his breaths as if in a yoga class. His inhales and exhales sounded normal, just much more audible now that they were transitioning through the tube rather than his nose.

She'd never wanted her switched-at-birth calamity to rock Dylan's world. She still didn't. But at this point, her preferences on that had been rendered moot. His world had been rocked. And now was the time to say what needed to be said.

She reached over and silenced the television, then waited for him to look at her.

Now's the time. "Seven months ago, I learned from a DNA test that I'm not biologically related to Mom and Dad. I began searching to find out who my biological parents were and what happened at the hospital the day I was born. I discovered the truth. So, when you're ready, I'll answer every question you have. I won't keep any of it from you." When he didn't reply, she said, "Text me your responses, please." Like all teenagers, he could text at the speed of light.

His thumbs went to work on his phone. She received his effusive answer on her own phone.

Okay.

"I want you to know," she said, "that the things I discovered didn't change—not even slightly—how I view you in my mind or in my heart. You're my brother. You will always be my brother. I very much hope that my DNA won't change how you view me, either."

It won't.

363

She believed him because when he'd been stretched out beside his wrecked truck, it hadn't mattered that they weren't born of the same two parents. He'd looked to her for reassurance because only one thing had mattered—the fact that she was the sister he'd known all his life.

Are your mom and dad still alive?

She nodded.

Do they know their kid got switched?

"I don't think so."

Are you going to tell them?

"I've been debating that question for months." Today's events had clarified her decision. "The answer is no."

Why?

"I don't want to disrupt their lives. But also, I'm content with the way things are." She shrugged. "I have a family. I have you."

What happened to my biological sister?

"As far as I can tell, she's had a wonderful life. Her name is Sophie. She's married and lives in Atlanta. I've chosen not to reach out to her and her parents. But if you want the opportunity to know Sophie, then I'll support that. I'll help you contact her."

He took a moment to think.

I don't want to contact her. Like you said, I have a family.

"All right." She did her best to hide her relief. "I love you."

I love you, too.

The connection that had always existed between them was still there—tenacious and strong.

I'm afraid that you're never going to let me
leave the house again.

It felt good to smile. "I'll confess that I wish I'd had a *wee bit* more control over you today than I ended up having. If I had, I could have kept you safe." She clasped her phone tightly in her lap. "Back in the emergency room, I was contemplating how hard it must be for God to give people their freedom and then watch them crash their metaphorical cars into metaphorical trees. Yet He gives us our freedom anyway. Because that's how we grow and make mistakes and fail and learn. You made a mistake today, but there's no doubt in my mind that you'll grow and learn from it."

Are you gonna ground me?

"I won't have to. Your surgery's going to ground you."

But when I'm better? Can I go back to normal?

"Yes, with a few small additions. You'll need to watch numerous instructive videos on the dangers of angry driving. And you'll have to allow me to cover you in bubble wrap every time you leave my sight."

He rolled his eyes.

"In all seriousness, once you're better, we can go back to where we were in our efforts to negotiate a middle ground between my oversight and your autonomy."

What's autonomy?

"The ability to make your own choices." Then she added, "Darling boy of my heart." Surely the time had finally come when he'd respond with an equally flowery endearment. Right? She waited expectantly as he typed.

Can you turn the TV back up?

Laughing, she did so.

Fifteen minutes later, Tess and Rudy appeared at the door.

Leah beckoned them forward and they bustled inside, full of concerned questions and sympathy. The older couple had made it here even before Dylan's friends, who had phones permanently grafted to their hands.

"Buddy!" Rudy gripped Dylan's shoulder. His glasses were askew. His chin quivered. "We were so frightened when we heard. Are you all right?"

Dylan nodded.

Rudy carefully hugged him.

Tess straightened Dylan's blankets and hair, her lips tight. That subtle sign was a giveaway. It informed Leah that seeing Dylan, injured and lying in a hospital bed, was supremely difficult for Tess.

"What do you need?" Rudy asked. "I'll go get it for you. Pizza? Cheez-Its? Gatorade? One of those really big cups of Coke?" He held his hands about a yard apart to indicate the Coke's size. "You name it."

"Rudy." Tess heaved an exasperated sigh. "We don't yet know how Dylan is receiving his nutrition, since he has a tube in his throat. Nor can we offer food and drinks his doctors might have forbidden him to have."

Rudy winked at Dylan. "If you want a giant Coke, I'll get you one."

"Rudy!"

A nurse had left paper and a pen on Dylan's bed tray. He pulled the tray closer and wrote, *Thanks, but I'm good right now. I'm glad you're here.*

"Leah?" Tess asked. "May I have a word?"

Leah followed her into the sterile-smelling hallway.

"Thank you for contacting us," Tess said.

"You're welcome."

"Rudy and I will stay here with him if you need to take a break. Or go home and get some of his things."

"I don't plan to go anywhere for the rest of the day. In fact, I'm wearing work-out clothes, so I'll just sleep here on the futon."

"When will you be making a trip home?"

"In the morning?"

"We'll come back then to relieve you." Tess captured a renegade strand of gray hair and forced it behind her ear. "Today must have been awful for you."

"It was. I watched him struggle to breathe. I . . . thought he might die."

Today, Leah had glimpsed what the world might have been like if death had stolen her brother. Now she could understand a glimmer of what Tess must have felt when death had stolen her son and what Sebastian must have felt when death had stolen his mother.

Tess took hold of Leah's hand, and the comfort only grandmothers can provide flowed from Tess to Leah.

Because of what Leah had been through with her parents, the brand of love she valued most was the brand of love that *stayed*. That showed up over and over, year after year.

That was the kind of love Tess and Rudy had given to her and her brother.

It was no longer possible for Leah to view Tess with the same wholehearted trust that she had before. But even if she could not forget what Tess had done, she *could* forgive.

CHAPTER TWENTY-EIGHT

I t was Dylan's closet that precipitated Leah's breakdown.

The morning after his accident, Tess and Rudy arrived at the hospital just as they'd said they would. Leah returned home to shower, change, and gather the items Dylan had requested.

To her astonishment, she'd slept well last night on the hard futon. She and Dylan had shared a room when he'd been small, so sharing a room with him last night had wrapped her in a blanket of nostalgia. Even the middle-of-the-night visits from the nurses had soothed her because it had been reassuring to know she wasn't the only one in charge of Dylan's well-being. Trained professionals were watching over him!

It wasn't until she opened his closet in order to pack some of his clothes and smelled the familiar scent of his soap that a wave of emotion swelled up and enveloped her.

Every article was so *him*. So familiar.

Her brother was going to live.

Thank God, her brother was going to live. Her gratitude was too enormous to contain.

Knowing everything she knew now . . . if she could go back to the hospital nursery on the day of her birth and change the course of events . . . would she choose life with the Brooksides over life with Dylan?

She would not.

It wasn't even a close call. No set of circumstances could tempt her to give her brother up.

Tears slid down her cheeks.

Tess's action had impacted Leah's life in drastic ways. It was easy to think that Tess had entered in and mucked up what God had ordained. But could Tess's error in judgment actually have been used by God?

Could something happen in a way that was so strange and amazing that it could *only* have been Him?

In recent days, she'd been disappointed by what she'd perceived as God's inattention. Dylan's accident revealed that God had not been inattentive. He'd simply been working in ways she hadn't understood.

Yesterday, when Dylan raced off in his truck, her false sense of control had been stripped from her. She'd been powerless.

Yet God had not been.

He'd brought Sebastian to her months ago. When Dylan overheard her switched-at-birth secret, God had placed Sebastian there. When Dylan collided with that tree, God ensured that Sebastian possessed the skills needed to preserve her brother's life.

Despite her quibbles over some of the twists and turns her life had taken, everything was, ultimately, exactly as it should be.

Praise you, God. Thank you.

She cried and praised Him, praised Him and cried.

The woman who delighted in tidy math quotients enjoyed feeling as though she understood God's plan. She liked clear guidance and guarantees. It made her comfortable to believe she had a degree of power over her brother and her relationship with Sebastian.

But God was bigger than her wishes. His methods didn't always suit her. Often, He didn't make her privy to His ways. Sometimes, she couldn't fathom His plan. And in the end, she had no power to wield.

He was the only guarantee she was going to receive.

Fortunately, He was the only guarantee she needed.

Her task: to surrender.

If God could accomplish His will for Dylan so beautifully, then He could accomplish His will for her and Sebastian, too.

Still sniffling, she texted Sebastian.

> Meet me at the garden next to the hospital in an hour?

Years ago, the industrial building adjacent to the hospital had been demolished. A husband had purchased the lot in order to show his appreciation to the doctors and nurses who'd saved his wife's life. He'd turned the rubble into a lavish garden for hospital staff, patients, and community members.

Sebastian responded immediately.

> See you then.

Sebastian had been trying not to sink into depression over Leah. Her brother was recovering, and so, of course, Dylan was her priority. The fact that she hadn't asked to speak with him until now didn't necessarily mean that she was fine with their breakup. He'd been telling himself that she might still be willing to take him back.

He hadn't convinced himself.

Fighting down stress, he sat on a wooden bench in the garden, elbows planted on his knees.

It scared him to want something as much as he wanted Leah. Especially because he wasn't sure what to do to convince her to give him another chance.

If you want to express how you feel about me, I recommend that you tell me, she'd said to him once.

So he'd decided to do just that. To tell her. That's what he'd shown up at her house the other morning to do. But then Dylan had injured himself, and the time hadn't been right since for an honest conversation between them.

370

Was the time right now?

Had he chosen the right approach? Not only did simply telling her that he loved her—putting himself out there like that—terrify him, it also seemed too simple.

He'd reached one of the most important moments in his life, a moment that would affect everything that came after. . . . And the man who'd always set clear goals, then taken steps toward those goals, had no confidence in the step he planned to take with Leah.

He'd have felt better if he'd booked them a trip or bought her a diamond bracelet or . . . anything else. Instead, he was here alone. Just him. And the words he needed to say to her.

He was trying to put her first. She'd communicated that she didn't want gifts or grand gestures.

Even so, this setting and strategy didn't feel like enough.

He didn't feel like enough.

A sinking sensation moved through his torso. This was going to fail.

Leafless trees sent strips of shade across the dirt path at his feet. The plants across from him bloomed with white flowers. He picked a piece of fluff off his navy sweater and wondered if he should have chosen something nicer than jeans—

"Sebastian."

He turned toward the sound of Leah's voice. Sunlight highlighted the slopes of her face and the shiny lemon-colored strands in her hair. She wore the outfit with the polka dot shirt she'd worn in Atlanta.

The day they'd met, he'd thought she had the face of a world-weary angel, but he hadn't known the half of it. He'd had no idea then of her quickness, feistiness, fairness. He hadn't known what it felt like to kiss her. Or how one look from her blue eyes could set his world on fire.

Sick with worry that she'd reject him, he straightened to his full height.

She stilled. "You saved Dylan's life, and I'll never forget it for as long as I live. How can I thank you?"

He didn't want her gratitude if he couldn't have her. "A better man would say that you don't have to thank me. But I'm going to press my advantage."

"I expected nothing less."

"As you know, I never let indebtedness go to waste."

"I'm very aware of this truth."

"You can thank me by taking me back."

She angled her head a few degrees. Not shooting him down, but not saying anything, either.

Dread constricted his ribs. "Since the day we met," he told her, "all I've wanted is to be with you."

"At Claire's house, you told me you couldn't get any more involved with me."

"That was stupid," he said bluntly. "When I watched Claire's dad hit you and realized that you'd broken your promise, it rattled me." He struggled to find the right words. "You know when you fall, and you see the ground rushing up at you?"

"Yes."

"The things that happened at Claire's made my fears rush up at me. I'm sorry about how I reacted."

"Okay," she said simply.

"I definitely *do* want to get more involved with you." It felt as though a splinter had lodged in his throat. He looked right at her, bulldozed past all his doubts, and forced himself to speak the words he hadn't said out loud in twenty-four years. "I love you."

She blinked. "Sebastian, I—"

"Almost all my life, I've felt like an outsider." He couldn't let her tell him they were over until he'd said what he had to say. "But I don't feel that way with you. With you, I belong. That might not sound like much. But to me, it's everything."

She stepped to him, set her palms on his chest, and kissed him. The contact was feather-light, brief, tender. Even so, it had the power to flatten forests.

Did this mean she'd forgiven him?

Pulling back a few inches, she smiled in a way that gave him hope.

His hands cradled her jaw. "You are galaxies of stars to me, Leah. The most beautiful woman I've ever seen. I can see my whole future in your face. And I desperately want the chance to love you."

"Sebastian."

"Yes?"

"Are you ready for me to complete the sentence I began earlier?"

"The one that started with 'Sebastian, I'?"

"That's the one."

"Feel free, so long as your sentence isn't 'Sebastian, I never want to see you again.'"

"It isn't."

"I also hope it isn't 'Sebastian, I just want to be friends.'"

"It isn't."

"Then go ahead, Professor."

Her body was warm against his. Her fingers interlocked behind his neck. "I was about to say . . ." She cleared her throat. "Sebastian, I love you."

His heart stopped for a split second, then thundered. He scoured her face, hunting for proof that she meant what she'd just said.

"When I say that I love you," she continued, "you can take that to the bank. I'm a mathematician and certainty is my currency."

Joy overwhelmed him. He wasn't experienced with this kind of joy, and now so much of it filled him that he couldn't speak.

"You're a hero," she said.

"No."

"You're not going to be able to convince me otherwise," she insisted. "You're a hero—to me, and to a lot of other people, too."

"I'm messed up in a lot of ways."

"You're not perfect," she acknowledged. "But—"

"You are. You're perfect."

She laughed under her breath. "No I'm not!"

Yes. She was. He kissed her and his worries disintegrated at the feel of her lips and the scent of her lavender soap. His devotion to her was a storm within. Life-changing. Steadfast. Stronger than hardships or time.

She set her forehead against his. They were both short of breath. "Do you know what you are, Sebastian?"

"Difficult?" he asked wryly.

"You're perfect *for me*. And that's enough."

"The Lord has established his throne in the heavens, and his kingdom rules over all."

—*Psalm 103:19*

DISCUSSION QUESTIONS

1. The plot of *Let It Be Me* revolves around Leah's discovery that she was switched at birth. Were you surprised when the culprit behind the switch was revealed?

2. Were you satisfied with Leah's decision not to contact her biological parents? Why or why not?

3. Becky was fascinated by her research into the field of pediatric cardiac surgery! Did you learn anything new about that profession while reading *Let It Be Me*?

4. Becky has a teenage son and so she had a wonderful time writing about a sister serving as the caregiver for her teen brother. What qualities of Leah's did Becky reveal via Leah's relationship with Dylan?

5. Raise your hand if you've ever thought or said, "I'm bad at math," like Dylan does in the novel. Becky spent most of her life believing herself to be bad at math. However, while researching this book, she watched numerous lectures given by women with PhDs in math. The following thought of Leah's was inspired by those lectures: "*No one* was bad at math. Many people didn't respond well to the way math was taught in school. But that did not mean they were bad at it." Do you agree? Disagree?

6. What characteristics of Sebastian's and Leah's made them a great match for one another? Can you name a celebrity who resembles the Sebastian or the Leah of your imagination?

7. For Becky, one of the joys of writing this novel was the opportunity to explore the friendship between Sebastian and Ben. Was there a specific aspect of their behavior toward each other that you appreciated?

8. Which characters or scenes in *Let It Be Me* made you smile or laugh?

9. At one point in the novel, Leah thinks that Sebastian is "a heart surgeon who did not understand the inner workings of his own heart." Becky used baby Isabella's journey to a new heart as a metaphor for Sebastian's emotional/spiritual journey over the course of the novel. What scene in Sebastian's evolution was the most meaningful for you?

10. The hero of the next MISTY RIVER ROMANCE novel, Luke, was introduced within the pages of *Let It Be Me*. What do you expect to happen characterization-wise or romance-wise in his book?

In 2022,
look for Luke Dempsey's story in

Turn to Me

Book Three of the
Misty River Romance
series

By

BECKY WADE

Becky Wade is the 2018 Christy Award Book of the Year winner for *True to You*. She is a native of California who attended Baylor University, met and married a Texan, and moved to Dallas. She published historical romances for the general market, then put her career on hold for several years to care for her three children. When God called her back to writing, Becky knew He meant for her to turn her attention to Christian fiction. Her humorous, heart-pounding contemporary romance novels have won three Christy Awards, the Carol Award, the INSPY Award, and the Inspirational Reader's Choice Award for Romance. To find out more about Becky and her books, visit www.beckywade.com.

Sign Up for Becky's Newsletter

Keep up to date with Becky's news on book releases and events by signing up for her email list at beckywade.com.

More from Becky Wade

Led to her hometown by a mysterious letter, Genevieve Woodward wakes in an unfamiliar cottage with the confused owner staring down at her. The last thing Sam Turner wants is to help a woman as troubled as she is talkative, but he can't turn her away when she needs him most. Will they be able to let go of the façades and loneliness they've always clung to?

Stay with Me
A MISTY RIVER ROMANCE

You May Also Like . . .

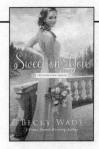

Britt and Zander have been best friends since they met thirteen years ago—but unbeknownst to Britt, Zander has been in love with her for just as long. When Zander's uncle dies of mysterious causes, he returns to Washington to investigate. As they work together to uncover his uncle's tangled past, will the truth of what lies between them also come to light?

Sweet on You by Becky Wade • A BRADFORD SISTERS ROMANCE
beckywade.com

Willow Bradford is content taking a break from modeling to run her family's inn until she comes face-to-face with NFL quarterback Corbin Stewart, the man who broke her heart—and wants to win her back. When a decades-old family mystery brings them together, they're forced to decide whether they can risk falling for one another all over again.

Falling for You by Becky Wade • A BRADFORD SISTERS ROMANCE
beckywade.com

After a broken engagement, genealogist Nora Bradford decides focusing on her work and her novels is safer than romance. But when John, a former Navy SEAL, hires her to help find his birth mother, the spark between them is undeniable. However, he's dating someone else, and Nora is hesitant. Is she ready to abandon her fictional heroes and risk her heart for real?

True to You by Becky Wade • A BRADFORD SISTERS ROMANCE
beckywade.com

◊ BETHANYHOUSE

More from Bethany House

After her dreams of mission work are dashed, Darcy has no choice but to move in with the little sister of a man who she's distrusted for years. Searching for purpose, she jumps at the chance to rescue a group of dogs. But it's Darcy herself who'll encounter a surprising rescue in the form of unexpected love, forgiveness, and the power of letting go.

Love and the Silver Lining by Tammy L. Gray • STATE OF GRACE
tammylgray.com

Molly McKenzie has made social media influencing a lucrative career, but nailing a TV show means proving she's as good in real life as she is online. So she volunteers with a youth program. Challenged at every turn by the program director, Silas, and the kids' struggles, she's surprised by her growing attachment. Has her perfect life been imperfectly built?

All That Really Matters by Nicole Deese
nicoledeese.com

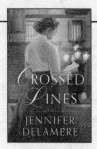

Mitchell Harris is captivated by Emma Sutton, but when his best friend also falls in love with her and asks for help writing her letters, he's torn between desire and loyalty. Longing for a family, Emma is elated when she receives a love note from a handsome engineer, but she must decide between the writer of the letters and her growing affection for Mitchell.

Crossed Lines by Jennifer Delamere • LOVE ALONG THE WIRES #2
jenniferdelamere.com

⬥ BETHANYHOUSE